Praise for novels by Tracy Groot

"[*The Brother's Keeper* is a] lyrical and affecting first novel."
BOOKLIST, STARRED REVIEW

"Groot vividly portrays both the heroism and the horrors of World War II. With the July release of Christopher Nolan's film *Dunkirk*, there is bound to be interest."
LIBRARY JOURNAL ON *THE MAGGIE BRIGHT*

"Groot's well-researched, inspirational historical tale . . . will be compelling and memorable for a diverse audience."
BOOKLIST ON *THE SENTINELS OF ANDERSONVILLE*

"Groot has done good historical homework. . . . The pacing is page-turning. . . . This Civil War–era story grapples with fundamental moral questions about decency and conscience—questions that can be asked about all wars."
PUBLISHERS WEEKLY, STARRED REVIEW OF *THE SENTINELS OF ANDERSONVILLE*

"Richly detailed, engrossing historical fiction."
KIRKUS REVIEWS

"If the truth hurts, [*The Sentinels of Andersonville*] is like a knife to the heart. . . . This story of a Good Samaritan shines brightly as the characters place themselves in danger
ROMANTIC TIMES, TOP PICK REVIEW

"Groot . . . does good historical work with details and subtle psychological work with her characters. WWII-era novels are popular; this is a superior, page-turning entry in that niche."

PUBLISHERS WEEKLY

"Scrupulously researched and lovingly written, *Flame of Resistance* plunges the reader into an exhilarating story of courage, grace, and one endearing woman's leap of faith."

THE BANNER

"[A] well-paced, beautifully written historical novel. . . . Entertaining and compelling."

PUBLISHERS WEEKLY, STARRED REVIEW OF *MADMAN*

"Groot cleverly combines historical research, Scripture, and thrilling imagination to create an ingenious story built around the Gerasene demoniac described in Mark's and Luke's Gospels. It's one of the best fictional adaptations of a biblical event I've had the pleasure to read."

ASPIRING RETAIL MAGAZINE

The Brother's Keeper

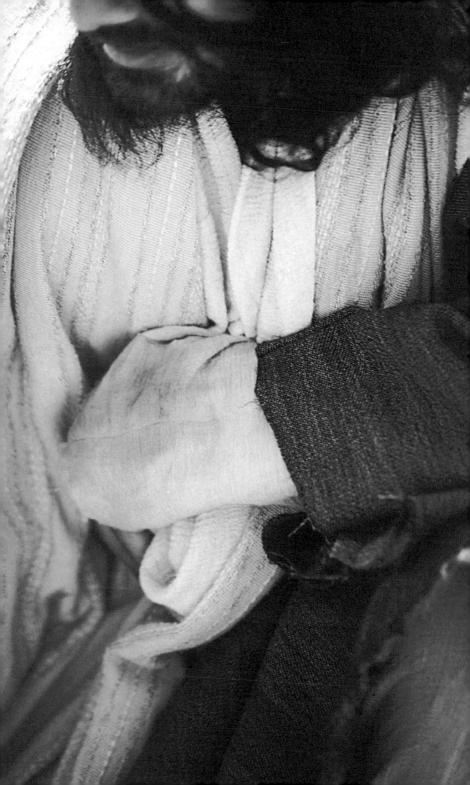

Tracy Groot

The Brother's Keeper

Tyndale House Publishers, Inc.
Carol Stream, Illinois

Visit Tyndale online at www.tyndale.com.

Visit Tracy Groot online at www.tracygroot.com.

TYNDALE and Tyndale's quill logo are registered trademarks of Tyndale House
Publishers, Inc.

The Brother's Keeper

Previously published in 2003 by Moody Publishers under ISBN 0-8024-3105-4. First
printing by Tyndale House Publishers, Inc., in 2018.

Designed by Mark Anthony Lane II

Published in association with Creative Trust Literary Group, 210 Jamestown Park Drive,
Suite 200, Brentwood, TN 37027. www.creativetrust.com.

Some Scripture quotations are taken from *The Holy Bible*, English Standard
Version® (ESV®), copyright © 2001 by Crossway, a publishing ministry of Good News
Publishers. Used by permission. All rights reserved.

Some Scripture quotations are taken from the New American Standard Bible,® copyright
© 1960, 1962, 1963, 1968, 1971, 1972, 1973, 1975, 1977, 1995 by The Lockman
Foundation. Used by permission.

For information about special discounts for bulk purchases, please contact Tyndale
House Publishers at csresponse@tyndale.com or call 1-800-323-9400.

Library of Congress Cataloging-in-Publication Data

Names: Groot, Tracy, date- author.
Title: The brother's keeper / Tracy Groot.
Description: Carol Stream, Illinois : Tyndale House Publishers, Inc., [2018]
Identifiers: LCCN 2017039696 | ISBN 9781496422224 (softcover)
Subjects: LCSH: Jesus Christ—Fiction. | Jesus Christ—Family—Fiction. | Bible. New
Testament—History of Biblical events—Fiction. | GSAFD: Christian fiction. | Bible
fiction.
Classification: LCC PS3557.R5655 B76 2018 | DDC 813/.54—dc23 LC record
available at https://lccn.loc.gov/2017039696

Printed in the United States of America

24   23   22   21   20   19   18
7   6   5   4   3   2   1

For the One True God

Your wind breathes where it wishes,
moves where it wills, sometimes
severs my safe moorings. Sovereign gusts—
buffet my winds with your blowing,
loosen me, lift me to go
wherever you're going.
                    —Luci Shaw

and

For my brother and sister,
Rick Harmon and Darla Fitzpatrick

(Not bad, sharing a dedication with the Ruler
of the Universe. Don't let it go to your heads.)

Acknowledgments

To each of the following, I am in debt.

Kathy Helmers, Moody Publishers, and LB Norton; Bernie Groendyke and Ron McClain; D. Michael Hostetler and staff at Nazareth Village, Nazareth, Israel; Amy Sample PA-C and Jill Smidstra; Rich DeVos, Lisa Groot, Karla Huitsing, Anne-Marie Jacobson and Bob "The Forgotten Disciple" Jacobson; Riva Cohen; John and Tami; Ed and Karla; Joel and Bonnie; and most of all, Jack.

Prologue

JAMES. Seek James.

The madness was upon him once again. It prodded when his steps lagged; it prickled when he stopped. It drove him as it had the first time, a time when Balthazar's companions knew its pursuit and had none but to heed as well. No glowing orb in the sky accompanied the madness this time. His eyes drifted to the place it had once hung.

Alone now. Riven from all familiar, thrust into mile after mile of barren strangeness. Alone, save the madness.

"I am too old for this," Balthazar muttered to the purpling heavens. He gained the top of the knoll and paused, as much for breath as to survey the patterns of the sky. He rubbed the back of his hand over a crusty mouth.

"I could do with some water, let alone a lamp in the sky."

It was easier then. *Follow the star,* the madness had told him. Where the simple injunction had lacked ceremony, he himself made up for it: The drivemasters wanted to know where their journey lay, so he threw grass to the wind. He listened to crickets. He turned in a circle three times while chanting some nonsense, then consulted the charts and pointed imperiously: west. Much more credible than pointing to a lamp in the nighttime sky.

Now he had no star. No charts. All of his companions were gone, presumably. Gasparian for certain. Probably Melkor. Alazar had not returned with them from the first journey. And a fourth, Baran, had never arrived.

The old man sank to the earth and from his shoulder bag pulled out a waterskin. He loosed the fitting and rubbed a few drops of water over his ridged lips. Very different, this journey. Very different from that of long ago.

They had found Baran a day outside of Susa. He was nearly dead when a scout came back with the news that a traveler lay on the roadside, part of his leg eaten by wolves. Melkor was not for stopping; the poor wretch would be dead within the hour, he said. It was not the first time Melkor had been wrong.

Balthazar had cursed six different gods and their uncles when he saw Baran's wound and realized he had left the medicaments at home. The young man was well into the bone fever, past fetching back, by the time the entourage reached him. The scout had sharp eyes; only a scrap of wool alerted him to the man wedged in the rock and debris. How the poor, miserable creature had come to these straits, they never learned. He spoke few words before he died, and nothing of his circumstances. No explanation save "wolf," no travel gear or possessions save a box wrapped in cloth, protected by his ravaged body. Extracting the wretch from the rocks was less painful to watch than his pathetic attempts to keep the box at his side.

"Balthazar, have you your herbs?" Gasparian asked in a low tone as Alazar and Melkor tended the man. "Alazar left his, and I would not give a shining beryl for what Melkor has in his bag."

"Nor I," Balthazar agreed, though he had to add, "Mine are home as well."

If Gasparian's raised brows had annoyed him, more so the bag he'd left behind. It was new, recently made for him by his mother, a length of cloth with several little pockets sewn in three rows. Ties were sewn at the ends; he could neatly roll his powders and herbs and secure the bundle with the ties. He had filled it with all he could gather and dry and grind and prepare in the little time he had to do it—and then forgotten it.

Forget a blanket; forget a packet of bread. To forget his medicaments vexed him to the roots of his teeth. Eight weeks out of Zabol, and still it vexed him. But the herbs left his mind as he grew aware of Melkor.

Melkor stood unwrapping the square bundle, taken from the dying man. Balthazar heard the whisper of a groan and watched the young man feebly reach toward his possession.

"What have we here?" Melkor mused as the cloth fell away. Balthazar blinked as the sinking sun caught the box in a silver gleam. Curious, the box, but he did not look long. His eyes went from the wasted form on the ground to Melkor, who did not seem to notice the feeble, reaching arm.

"Melkor . . ."

"This looks like lapis lazuli." He brought the box closer to his eyes. "It *is* lapis. Some of the finest I have seen."

"Melkor, give him back his box," Balthazar said.

Melkor regarded the man at his feet. "Maybe he stole it from somebody."

In two quick strides, Balthazar reached Melkor and snatched the box from his hands. He paused long enough to make sure Melkor saw his glare, then knelt and placed the box on the man's chest. He took the man's arm and circled it about the box, and saw gratefulness deep in the tortured eyes. He smiled back, then looked down to the leg, where Alazar was gingerly pulling away cloth. Alazar hissed softly and sat back on his heels.

It was likely the stench of rotting flesh as much as the sight of the grievous wound that set Alazar back. Balthazar winced at it, then met Alazar's eyes. Alazar sighed grimly and rose to consult with the others.

One of the drivemasters arrived with water and dribbled some into the man's grime-coated mouth. His face was waxen white, like a dirty candle. Balthazar brushed grit from the man's chin, then realized he was trying to speak. He leaned closely.

"Wolf," the man whispered.

Balthazar nodded and patted his shoulder. "Do not speak, my friend. Save it for getting better." This brought a stare from the drivemaster, which he ignored. "Perhaps you are far from home, as am I. A nasty business, traveling on these strange roads."

"Baran," he whispered.

"Your name is Baran?" He touched his fingertips to his forehead. "I am Balthazar, in the company of the strangest lot of miscreants ever assembled under the heavens. I would tell you of our business, but you and I both would not believe me."

"Balthazar," Gasparian called behind him.

He gave Baran's shoulder a gentle squeeze. "I will be back." The drivemaster trickled more water into his mouth.

Alazar, Melkor, Gasparian, and one of the drivers stood apart in consultation. Balthazar knew the outcome from five paces away. By Gasparian's dark look and Alazar's sad one, and by Melkor's folded arms, he knew they meant to leave him.

Balthazar stopped short and lifted his chin. "His name is Baran," he said, feet planted apart.

"An unfortunate wretch," Melkor murmured. His eyes drifted to Baran's wound.

"The wretch has a name," Balthazar said evenly.

"We cannot stop," Melkor replied.

Balthazar could feel his teeth clench. What was it about Melkor that set his molars to grinding? His teeth would be powder at the journey's end. He looked at the others. Only Gasparian met his eyes.

"I think Melkor is right," Gasparian said, doing little to conceal his reluctance for the decision. "We all feel the urgency to move on. You know of what I speak."

"But the light in the sky—"

"It is more than that," Melkor cut in.

"That is not what I mean!" Balthazar hissed. Yes, the urgency . . . the unseen prodding to move on . . . yes, it was there. They all felt it. "What I am *saying* is, do you suppose the one who put that light in the sky would mean for us to leave this man at the side of the road?" He shook his head. "I will not believe that."

They all began to talk at once.

"Our commission," Alazar began pleadingly.

"We have a responsibility as emissaries of our people," Gasparian started.

"We cannot fail." Melkor pulled himself up.

Balthazar put himself under Melkor's nose and glared contempt into his cool, dark eyes. "We have failed already if we leave this man to die alone."

Why couldn't the universe have left him to his herbs? He was not made for this, this *madness*. He turned away from the others, unsure where to go, then simply began to walk and walk fast.

They would send Gasparian, he knew, because Gasparian was the only one he trusted.

And indeed, presently Gasparian puffed alongside him. "How about slowing down for an old man?"

"Not until I do not want to kill Melkor."

"Ah, you will keep this pace until Judea?"

Balthazar couldn't stop the smile. "Perhaps there and back again. All the way back to my village." The thought of his village brought a pang of homesickness, and his steps slowed.

He looked at the hills surrounding them, shaking his head. Every day he saw something new. Every day he hoped Reuel lived long enough to hear of the wonders beyond their village border. The mighty fire altars at Nakshi-Rustem; a giant-sized statue of Cyrus the Great.

"Do you wonder what we are doing out here, Gaspar? In my village, I was an herbalist and a second-rate priest. The gods strike me, I had no desire to guard the holy fire of Ahura

Mazdah." He looked sideways at Gasparian. "You did not hear that from me, understand?"

When Gasparian nodded, he continued.

"Our high priest was too old for the journey. It was heartbreaking. I never saw such longing. Reuel had the gift, as no one in our village has ever had before. He spoke often of a coming omen, a great portent from the west. No one really listened—until the star appeared and the council came to our village. Then suddenly, a humble old man no one gave a wormroot for is a hero. He was selected for the journey, but everyone knew he would never make it a week outside the village." Balthazar's steps stopped altogether. "Reuel thought he was doing me a favor."

Gasparian looked over his shoulder, down the road to the waiting entourage. "Balthazar . . . ," he began gently.

"I do not know if I believe, Gaspar. Worse, I do not know if I care. What do you think about that?"

"I think we have to be going," the older man said. "Baran will die. Melkor thinks he will not last an hour. We can make him comfortable." Doubtfully, he added, "Melkor has a few powders with him that can ease the poor man's pain."

"I would not give his powders to a murdering zealot. Melkor may be a first-rate priest, but he is no herbalist."

"Come, young friend. You may not believe, but I do."

Balthazar cocked his head. "Enough to leave a man to die alone?"

Gasparian's gaze did not flinch. "Yes."

Balthazar looked away and said, "Now, that is passion. Reuel would be proud."

"Balthazar."

But he was not listening anymore. He looked down the road at the stopped entourage. The drivemasters were checking supplies, adjusting cinches, and inspecting ropes and stays. Alazar was kneeling next to Baran. Melkor was rummaging in one of his packs. Shortly they would be on the move again. Two months of this, from sunup to well into the night, with nothing but the star and the madness. Two months and many more ahead.

Ahriman take him; he was done with it.

He started for them, aware of his grinding molars, aware of the long journey back home. A solitary journey and unsafe—he might end up like Baran—but he would be free. Back to his herbs, back to everything normal, back to where things made sense. To a place where a man with a name would not die alone.

"I know that look," Gasparian said, hurrying to his side.

"You have never seen this look."

"I know it well. Do not make a hasty decision, my friend."

He stopped short to scowl in Gasparian's face. "You do not seem to realize there has been a mistake. This was Reuel's mission, not my own."

Gasparian returned the look thoughtfully, shaking his head. "There has been no mistake. You have been chosen for this. As was I. As was Alazar. *And* Melkor. We must press on."

Balthazar felt the anger recede, replaced by something worse. He had thought Gasparian was different from the rest. *Ahriman take him,* he thought.

"I want no more of this," Balthazar said hoarsely and turned away.

Melkor was tapping a fine, sage-colored powder into a cup.

He swirled the cup and watched the powder dissipate. He looked about for a twig and stirred the mixture thoroughly. Balthazar watched, keeping his disdain hidden.

"Coralwort?" he asked, almost pleasantly.

"Mancow," Melkor replied, in a tone that said it shouldn't be anything but. "Mancow, with bitters. A pinch of fiddleleaf."

Balthazar nodded. Fiddleleaf. The idiot.

Melkor rose, but Balthazar placed a hand on his shoulder. "Do not trouble yourself further. I will give it to him." He held out his hand.

Melkor looked at the hand, a trace of suspicion crossing his face, but he gave him the cup. He shook his cloak free of dust and said, "We ride shortly. Make haste."

Balthazar gave a tight smile, which vanished when Melkor turned away.

Alazar was wiping Baran's face with a damp cloth when Balthazar knelt beside him. He glanced at the cup in Balthazar's hand.

"I will tend him now. Melkor says we ride. Perhaps you should make ready."

Alazar nodded. He clapped his hand on Balthazar's shoulder, then used it as leverage to rise. Balthazar watched him head for his mount. He glanced quickly at every member of the party, making sure each was occupied, then dumped the contents of the cup behind a rock.

"Mancow, with bitters," he mocked under his breath. "A pinch of fiddleleaf." Well and good—if one wanted to hasten the delivery of a woman's first child. Not many days ago Melkor had given a paste of crushed limestone and olive oil to one of the drivers for a rash on his shins. Better to mix it with the flour for bread. The man claimed it worked, but he feared Melkor. Probably feared he would get a nasty tonic if it did not work.

Balthazar settled himself on the ground next to Baran. The young man was muttering, weakly moving his head back and forth. Balthazar placed his hand on Baran's shoulder to let the man know he was not alone. From habit he began the death prayer, consecrating Baran's soul to the next life. From habit only. His belief in Ahura Mazdah had dwindled long before this journey. He decided to direct the death prayer to the one who fired the star in the sky. Reuel believed in this god. Balthazar believed in Reuel.

A shadow fell across Baran. Melkor stood beside him and, after listening to Balthazar's soft murmur, took up the chant with him. It contented Balthazar deeply to know their prayers ascended to different gods. They intoned through the first set, the second, and the fourth, seamlessly omitting the third. The third set in the dirge was for kinsmen only. Balthazar would offer the third later, when the entourage had left, in the stead of the relatives this man would never see again.

The fourth set ended, and Melkor reached for the box on Baran's chest.

"Leave it," Balthazar growled between clenched and aching teeth.

"We may encounter someone who knows of him," Melkor protested, though he drew his hands back. "We cannot leave this to thieves."

"He is not dead yet. It is sacred to him."

"Not de—? How much of the cup did he drink?"

Slowly, Balthazar rose. He deliberately took two fistfuls of

Melkor's tunic and yanked him down, eye level to himself. "What else did you put in that cup?"

"Bristlebane."

Balthazar released him with a shove. Melkor staggered back, gained his balance, and smoothed his garments indignantly. Gasparian came to stand warily apart from them, looking from one to the other. Alazar appeared at his side.

"Brothers . . . ," Alazar began uncertainly.

"Bristlebane," Balthazar mused, nodding. It would have killed Baran in moments. Then Melkor would have taken the box from a dead man, not a dying one.

He nodded again and shifted his jaw, then looked away to the sky. He stared at it a moment before he realized his eyes sought the place where he had last seen the star. It was habit, for all of them. When stopping for meals in the broad of day, when gazing at strange rock formations and new landscapes, it was not long before a look flickered to the sky, to the place of the star.

One evening he had lost himself in the daze of the glittering nighttime sky, muttering an absent prayer of thanks to Tishtrya for the glory of the night; then he looked for the star and did not immediately see it. Disoriented, alarmed, then panicked, he leapt up and whirled about, searching, frantic, until he saw it again and allowed its soft glow to soothe him.

It was the first star to illumine the seeping twilight, the last to fade at dawn. He would try to guess where it would appear and learned the guess grew more accurate if he tried to sense the location first. Once on a visit to the brush, he made sure no one was looking, then closed his eyes and turned in a circle until insensible of direction. Eyes tightly shut, he drew a slow breath, held it, quieted his heart, smoothed his mind, and spread his arms wide . . . then slowly raised an arm and pointed. He opened his eyes, gazed straight down the length of his arm and pointing finger, and there, balanced on his fingernail, was the cool white glow of Reuel's star of portent.

Follow the star. The injunction had become a part of him. It pulsed along with the beat of his heart, as if he had been born with its mystic force. He sought the star for solace, as his tiny nephew sought his thumb. He sought the star for reason, for times like this when the only thing on earth that made sense was not on earth at all.

He found the place where it would soon appear and knew he gazed at it dead-on.

"Brothers?" Alazar said again.

"I am staying with Baran," Balthazar said softly. "And then I am going home." He and the unseen star regarded each other while the others regarded themselves.

Melkor stalked past him without a word. Gasparian looked as if he would speak but held his counsel and turned away. Only Alazar tried to dissuade him, and that not for long. Balthazar shut out his words, and Alazar finally gave up.

He settled down next to Baran and watched the party prepare for departure. Though his eyes were mostly shut, Baran seemed to watch too. The drivemasters did not appear to notice the tension in the camp as they readied themselves to depart, though one of them looped an extra waterskin to the cantle of his mount. Melkor threw Balthazar an occasional disgusted look, probably for the loss of the silver box. Alazar was clearly distressed, and Gasparian he could not figure out.

Balthazar slowly reclined against a rock, hands clasped

behind his head. "The sad fellow there, that is Alazar," he told Baran cheerfully. "He is decent enough; I think you would like him. I will miss beating him at knucklebones. I will not miss his snoring. The one over there in the orange-and-purple-striped robe, the one who fancies your box, that would be Melkor. First-rate priest, Melkor is, straight as an arrow. Strange, though—I do not think Reuel would like him." When he came to Gasparian, his cheerful tone softened. "The one slipping the extra loaves of bread into my day pack would be Gaspar."

The silent party mounted and left, with only Gasparian looking long over his shoulder in good-bye. Balthazar watched them until they disappeared, swallowed up by the road that reached for Judea.

By habit he looked for the place of the star. Soon it would appear. It would be his only comfort in the lonely, anxious journey back to his village. Oddly, though his direction would be opposite, he knew Reuel's star would shepherd him home.

"I enjoy a good riddle, Baran. Gaspar and I have discussed long into the night one peculiar and engaging puzzle: How is it, during the times of cruel doubt in the madness of this venture, we seek the star for solace, when the star is the very reason for the journey?" Balthazar chuckled softly; then his smile slipped away as he gazed down the empty road. *I will miss you, Gaspar.*

Baran moaned, and Balthazar moved to tend him. Alazar had draped a length of cloth over the wound, as much to hide its distressing visage as to reduce the repulsive smell. Balthazar peeked under the cloth and tried to think of a few more gods to curse. If they had found Baran a few days earlier, if Balthazar had his medicaments . . .

Baran was trying to speak. Balthazar leaned close, patting his shoulder. "I am here, my friend. Baran. I am here."

"Gift . . ." The word came in a long whisper from the dried-up mouth.

"Gift?" Balthazar asked.

"Gift."

A motion caught Balthazar's eye, and he looked down to see Baran erratically patting the box on his chest.

Balthazar sighed. "I think Melkor would have liked your gift, Baran. Me, I am not worthy to accept the gift of a—" He caught himself in time. He had nearly said *dying*. He swallowed and tried again. "Of a, a man of such obvious, ah, *dignity* as yourself."

But Baran was shaking his head no.

Balthazar said gently, "Then I am afraid I do not understand. The box is not a gift for me, but it *is* a gift?"

Baran moved his head fractionally in a yes.

"It is a gift for someone special?"

Fractionally, yes.

"For your wife, perhaps? For your betrothed?"

Fractionally, no. The dying man moaned again, distress now visible in his pallor.

Balthazar wet his lips. Baran would soon sleep with his fathers. He leaned closer and tried again. "Baran, do you wish for me to deliver the box to someone in your stead?"

Tears began to seep from the nearly closed eyes.

"Ah. We understand one another. Consider me hired, and you are in luck, my friend—my services are free to all who wear indigo. It's my favorite color." He patted Baran's arm and added gently, "Rest a minute, Baran; then you can tell me who it is for." He sat back from him, momentarily relieved.

But Baran was not for resting. His hands twitched restlessly. His breath came harder. It seemed as though he were summoning strength. He raised a thin, shaking arm and pointed.

Immediately Balthazar was at his side, looking with him down the length of his arm. "That hillside over there? A village is beyond it?"

Baran weakly shook his head. The arm trembled and stayed where it was.

Balthazar swallowed. Ahriman take him, he did not understand. "Uh, the hillside . . . the box goes to someone past the hill. A name, Baran. I need a name."

But Baran's arm still pointed, trembling harder.

"Save your strength," Balthazar pleaded. "I need a name."

Still Baran pointed. Balthazar felt the bloom of despair at the root of his stomach.

"Please, Baran, *please* save your strength! You need it to tell me the name."

Waxen pallor gave way to scarlet in Baran's strained face. His eyes were tightly closed, teeth bared in furious effort. A low growl began in his throat. His arm shook violently, and Balthazar's despair agitated to a groan.

"I do not understand! Ahriman take me, I do not—"

From habit, for comfort, he sought the place of the star . . .

. . . and saw . . .

. . . Baran's outstretched arm.

He dropped cheek to cheek with Baran and stretched forth

his own arm. He squeezed his eyes shut, held his breath, quieted his heart, and opened his eyes.

In the newly twilight horizon, balanced on the tip of his fingernail and Baran's, was the soft cool glow of . . .

"The star," Balthazar breathed.

Baran's face cleared. His arm dropped.

And now Balthazar began to tremble.

❧

The old man replaced the fitting in the waterskin and wiped his lips with the back of his hand. He studied the sky and chose a star low on the horizon to be his old companion Gasparian.

"You were not surprised to see me, old friend, when I caught up with you the next day."

Reuel's star was now gone, but the comforting madness that had accompanied the star had never left him. That same comforting madness had him here again to trek the journey of old. There was no star to follow this time—only the memory of a silver box inlaid with lapis lazuli . . . and a name.

"The name guides me as the star did, Gaspar."

He pointed west to show Gasparian. It was as if the name hung in the sky, above the place of his destination.

"I am not sure what I am to do with the box once I find it again," he admitted to Gasparian's star. "Surely the frankincense is gone by now."

He rummaged in his pack for bread, tore off a piece, and began to eat.

"You know," he said with his mouth full, eyebrows quirked, "it was a fine-quality frankincense. Melkor would not have known that. But I knew. You see, Gaspar, old friend, in my village some came to offer frankincense to Ahura Mazdah's flame. The greater the adoration—" he shrugged—"or the richer the adorer, the greater quality the frankincense. Baran's frankincense was fine indeed, first harvest. He paid a small fortune to fill that box." He smiled, pausing mid-chew. "Maybe it took a first-rate herbalist and a second-rate priest to know." He glanced about the sky and chose another star to be Baran.

"I wish I knew if you had made the box yourself. Such exquisite beauty. Such workmanship. The young woman, she was amazed. A gracious thing she was; you would have liked her, Baran. And the child . . . I think he liked your gift too."

He finished his meal and brushed away the crumbs, then stood and shrugged on his shoulder bag and took up the waterskin. He bent to pick up his walking stick and leaned upon it to gaze at Gasparian's star.

"The other riddle we puzzled over as well, did we not, Gaspar: how the star for which men left another to die . . . is the star the same man died for."

His eyes flickered to Baran's star, and slowly Balthazar smiled.

"A great company I am in on this grand and splendid evening," he declared as he started down the knoll. "A great company indeed."

His journey lay west and north, to Galilee this time, to find the silver box inlaid with lapis lazuli and the one the comforting madness called . . . James.

Not even his brothers believed in him.

THE GOSPEL OF JOHN 7:5, ESV

1

He did not know what to call them. They were not Essenes, nor were they Zealots. Some were not even Jewish. He watched the latest two retreat down the slope that led to his home. The tall one, the ruder of the two, looked over his shoulder to stare boldly at James. The fact that these pilgrims never got what they came for pleased him greatly. To be sure, the shorter one carried away a pocketful of sawdust, scooped from the floor when he thought James was not looking; no matter. The fool had more sawdust in his head than in his pocket.

They were heading for the village. And how would these visitors find Nazareth? Would they be disappointed to see that it was no different than their own hometown? They would see the same filthy beggars and the same people who did not notice them. The same smelly streets, the same noisy market-place. They would hear women arguing prices with the merchants. They would see the usual mix of people in typical Galilean villages: Jews, Gentiles, a few strutting Romans, traveling foreigners. They would see people who lived the hard facts of life, people who sweated and smelled like them.

Would they be as disappointed with Nazareth as they always were with James and his family?

James leaned against the workroom doorway and watched until the two disappeared down the hill. When the first of these strangers had come to visit, James and his brothers had treated them politely. Answered questions, showed them around. Pointed out the corner workbench; they always liked to see that. In the beginning the attention was entertaining. It amused them; truth to tell, it even flattered. Nearly three years later, James was no longer amused.

Many carried away tokens of their visit: a curled shaving from the workroom floor, a pebble from the path, a handful of stone chips from a roof roller James was chiseling. Once he caught Jorah giving tours of the home for two copper prutas per person. Though Mother put an end to that, James thought it time for recompense. At least someone had the sense to make these strangers pay for their intrusions.

What did they expect the home to be like? James saw it all the time, the looks that said their Teacher's home fell short of their expectations.

Those who made it past the workroom, and precious few did, came to the smallyard, an area where the sleeping rooms, the main courtyard, and the workroom converged. In the smallyard was the cistern. If there the stranger turned right, he would walk a few steps through a cool stone passage that opened left into the foreroom where the brothers slept, then the aftroom where Mother and Jorah slept. If instead the stranger went past the smallyard, he would find himself in the courtyard. There he would see Mother's oven in one corner, those corner walls blackened from smoke. He would see pots to dye wool, pans for cooking, a grindstone for wheat and barley, a small loom for cloth. He would see a shelter of coarse cloth covering half the courtyard, under which Mother and Jorah made food, cleaned and carded wool, and mended baskets, tunics, and sandals.

The strangers would see a home much like their own, if they were neither poor nor rich. They would see nothing remarkable. Nothing to account for an unordinary man in an ordinary world.

But they needed a name. James had a few he called them privately, names of which Mother would not approve. He rubbed his lower lip, looking at the place where the last two had disappeared. The tall one had looked long at James and the home . . . perhaps to put them in his memory to tell his grandchildren.

What would James tell his own?

He shoved off from the doorway to turn into the workroom and noticed the gouge in a ridge of sawdust on the floor. He bent and picked up a handful himself, rubbing the coarse wooden filings between his fingers. What did they do with it? Sprinkle it on sick relatives? He shook it away and went to his bench.

Jesus-ites. Nazarites would work, except it was taken. *Nazarenes* would fit, but were not all the occupants of

Nazareth called Nazarenes? He could just imagine how the villagers would take it, mistaken for followers of Joseph's son.

He picked up a hunk of cypress, hefted it in his hand, looked down the length of it. Five palms long, four fingers wide. He picked up his measuring stick, ever hearing his father's voice when he did so—*"Twice measured is once cut—"* and rechecked the measure. He would soon fashion the length into a replacement support for a threshing sledge. He ran his thumb over a knot, traced calloused fingertips along the grain, then tossed the chunk of wood onto the ground next to the thresher and wearily rubbed his eyebrows.

They came more frequently now—two, three times a week. Some were shy, some as rude as this last visitor. Some came to argue the Torah and the Prophets, some to rouse support for another go at an uprising. Some treated James and his family with a sickening awe, others with pity, as from a strange self-righteousness. He was not sure which he hated more.

Those in the village were too eager to give directions to the seekers. James did not blame them, after all. Fair trade for the notoriety inflicted upon Nazareth. Last week he overheard a merchant giving cheerful directions: "Straight up the main road, past the well; you will come to a home on the left; that would be Eli's place. The home past that one, up the hill, is Joseph's place." The seeker had turned away, with the trader calling after him, "Be sure to ask for a relic! They love to give away relics!" Then he laughed with the customers at his stall.

James knelt and looked under his workbench. In the corner against the wall was a box full of seasoned pieces of wood for carving. He dragged the box to himself and brought it to the top of the bench, where he rummaged through it, holding certain pieces out from under the awning to see them in the sun. He remembered this one with the crook at the end. A remnant of the olive tree he had sectioned off last summer. He had thought to fashion a water dipper out of that crook. He laid it on the table and rummaged some more.

Time was when he was James ben Joseph. Time was when James, Joses, Simon, Judas, Devorah, and Jorah were all children ben Joseph, the carpenter. Now he was James, brother of the scourge of Nazareth.

Here was an oblong chunk of sycamore. Maybe Jude had put it into the box; he didn't remember it. Perhaps left over from the synagogue project. He turned it over. Make a nice platter, maybe a good oblong bowl. When was the last time he had carved? With jobs and projects and the time-wasting seekers to fill their days, he didn't often have the leisure for this pastime.

"This is the carpenter's home?"

He slowly put the piece of sycamore back into the box, resting his hands on the edge.

He looked over his shoulder and squinted at the young man who stood in the doorway, gazing at the workroom. He was younger than James by at least ten years—maybe eighteen or nineteen. He had wild reddish-brown hair barely kept in place with a thin leather tie circling his head. A vain attempt at a beard gave him a dusky jawline. When James did not answer, the lad's wandering gaze came back, showing his brightly colored eyes.

"Is this the carpenter's—"

"We are bread makers," James cut him off, with a gesture at the workroom. "What do you think the wood and stone is for?"

On the heel of the young man's startled look came a grin. "You must be James. Annika said I remind her of you."

For the first time since the seekers left, the knot inside began to loosen. "You are Nathanael?"

The young man nodded and stepped inside, inhaling deeply. "Smells wonderful in here." He picked up a handful of stripped cypress bark and held it to his nose, closing his eyes as he breathed deeply. "I love cypress. I've missed it."

James noticed that Nathanael did not kiss the mezuzah fixed to the doorjamb, but he did not care. Religious Jew or nonreligious Jew, as long as he was not one of the seekers. Annika hadn't said much about Nathanael, only that he was new to Nazareth and in need of work.

"Have you worked with wood before?"

"I apprenticed with my uncle. Once in a while."

Hands clasped behind his back, Nathanael gave himself a tour. He strolled under the shade of the awnings, erected at the top of the walls to shelter the workbenches from the late-winter rains. He came first to Judas' bench, appraising every detail. Most of Jude's tools were hung neatly on a rack above the bench; some were jumbled less neatly on the table. He passed James' bench; James watched his amber-hued eyes, a different color for these parts, whisk eagerly over everything. He stopped at Father's bench near the passage to the small-yard. Father's bench looked more like what it had become, the catchall spot for odds and ends. Opposite Father's bench was the fire pit. He crossed the room to the pit, looked it over, then walked past Joses' bench and Simon's bench and came to stand at the bench in the corner.

The corner workbench was the only one without wood chips near it. It was as neat and tidy as the day it was left. The tiny wooden boat James had carved when he was seven still lay where it always had, on the shelf above the bench in the corner, tilted on its side. A little vase Jorah had made was on the other side of the shelf. Jesus would put a sprig of fresh herbs or a posy of wildflowers in it.

Nathanael reached for one of the tools. James gave an involuntary start but held fast. It was the first time in three years . . .

Nathanael did not see his reaction. He turned the heavy gouge adze over in his hands, thumbed the curved blade. "It's a little rusty. Needs a fresh edge. Where is your grinding stone?"

"Outside, by the steps to the roof." Nathanael started for the door, but James said, "We need to talk first."

Nathanael stiffened. Studying the adze edge, he said flatly, "You hired someone else."

James regarded the young man, who now had a defiant set to his jaw. Annika, the woman who could not spare her tongue to save her life, had not offered much information about this lad.

James took a stool and gestured to another by Joses' bench—away from the corner. "Please, sit. Rest yourself. Don't I get a full ear of how far our place is every time Annika brings the eggs?"

"What is far?" Nathanael muttered. "She is an old woman."

On the way to the stool he studied the adze as though he would rather be sharpening it. He took the stool, then looked straight at James with those strange-hued eyes. "If you do not want me, just say it."

James pulled back. "If we do not want you . . . ? That is not the question. The question is if you want us. Our apprentices come and go. Nobody wants to stay."

"Why not?"

James cocked his head, squinting at him. "What did Annika tell you about us?"

The lad shrugged. "That you needed an apprentice. And that you have a pretty sister."

Annika the matchmaker. Annika the meddler. "She did not say anything else?"

"What's there to say? You need help; I need work."

A movement at the doorway caught James' eye. "It isn't that simple," he muttered as he took in the group of three now standing at the door.

The familiar knot returned to his stomach, hardening to a fist of iron.

The girl in the middle chittered to the boys next to her in a lordly way, gesturing toward the workroom. Keturah. She used to come for carving lessons, trading cucumbers for instruction. But the young men with her, near Nathanael's age, he had never seen before. James rose from his stool.

"Hello, James," the girl said airily, as if she spoke to him in the market all the time. To the boys she said, "That is his brother, the next oldest. His other brothers, Joses and Simon, are still away on a trading trip. Aren't they, James?" When James did not answer, she chattered on. "Judas just left for Capernaum; he should be back in a week or so."

She pointed to the corner workbench. "Over there. That is where he worked. He was the one who taught me to carve. He was the best wood-carver in Galilee."

"Simon is the best," James stated.

She only glanced at him. "He carved a bowl for my grandmother," she told the boys. "Finest bowl I have ever seen. It's her favorite."

The girl would not be able to tell apart a bowl carved by Simon or—

"Do you have business here, Keturah?" James asked, and reached for his mallet.

Her brown-eyed look flickered over him. "So, you remember my name." Some of her lordliness softened.

"I remember," James said quietly.

He used to feel like a lumbering fool around her. Every time she came to the shop, every time he saw her in the marketplace . . . instant idiot is what he would become. But after her favorite wood-carver left, she stopped coming around. And James' trips to the market became fewer. He glanced at her tunic. She was wearing lavender again.

He realized he did not feel stupid around her anymore, and strangely, the thought brought a flicker of sadness.

She was already pointing out another attraction to the boys.

"Do you have a loom that needs mending?" he said, his voice tight. "Stones to be cut, a tool to be sharpened? Do you have *business* here, Keturah, or are you here to waste my time?"

He had learned something about the seekers: the ruder he was, the quicker they left. He had never been so rude when his father was alive. He never imagined he could be so rude.

She broke off midsentence to stare at him. "I—no. I was only—"

"I have work to do," James snapped. He pointed with the mallet to the outdoors beyond them. He did not miss the darkening of her cheeks.

"This is his brother?" one of the lads muttered, looking James up and down as he crossed the threshold and sauntered into the workroom.

"Not much like him, is he, Avi," the other commented, upper lip pulled to sneer.

The iron fist lurched painfully in James' stomach, and he gripped the mallet handle convulsively as the hatred flared. They did this. They touched off something inside him that ought never have been touched.

God of Israel, help me now, because I surely want to kill them.

The one called Avi pulled himself tall. "How is it you are not out there with him? Why does not a single brother of his help him?" He snorted. "I would give anything to be one of his twelve. Anything! You are his own brother, and you cannot find the time of day even to listen to him."

"The Teacher said it himself, Avi." The other lad shrugged and stepped into the workroom after his friend. "'A prophet will have honor, but not from those of his own household.'"

God of Israel . . .

Any words but those . . . any words that filtered back to the workroom but those words. The images of the one day Jesus had come back to Nazareth, and what happened in the synagogue . . . the memory rioted his senses, flooding his gut with torment.

"You do not even care." Avi's voice dripped scorn, and he shook his head. "This whole village is crazy."

Keturah's fists went to her hips. "I did not bring you here to flail your tongue. Come. It is time for us to leave."

"The greatest leader our people has seen since Judah the Maccabee, and we sit around sawing wood," Avi scoffed. He brushed past Keturah as he strolled to the bench in the corner.

"*Now* is the time to throw off the Roman yoke! We did it to the cursed Syrian Greeks; we can do it to the cursed Romans.

And throw out all the rest of the Gentiles as well. This is *our* land. God has seen and heard, and the time of the Jew has come once more."

His dark eyes glittered as he placed both palms lightly on the surface of the workbench, either in wonder or perhaps to infuse himself with residual power.

"The time is coming soon, I can feel it," he whispered. "He will declare soon, and I will be there when he does."

Oddly, the rage in James' stomach diffused and died away.

"Just leave," James whispered. The crooked piece of olivewood, his whittling knife . . .

Day after day, for nearly three years, he had heard it all. From the passioned Zealots like this one, from the gentler and much more polite Essenes. From the Pharisees, the Sadducees. From other sectarians whose tenets blurred into the rest. From synagogue leaders, and once a Temple leader. Even from Annika the meddler. Everybody had an opinion about Joseph's son.

Interesting, the effect these people had on his family. They set Simon to studying with fury, draping himself over the family's two scrolls any chance he could get. They caused gentle Joses to plead and argue. They made Judas hide. And all James wanted to do was carve.

"Five hundred years of foreign domination! Persia, Greece, Egypt . . ."

If it were not for the fact there wasn't any money in it, not real money, he would carve all day and fashion beauty out of jagged castoffs of sycamore, cedar, and oak. He would save for some fancy imported pieces, get them from Amos in Gaza.

". . . has heard and he will give us back our land. Jesus is our prophet to speak the word of God and *unite* us! That's the key! Unity!"

Satinwood from the East, that sparkled in the sun. Purpleheart from Africa, with a hue so deeply rich and luxuriant no stain could ever match it. Rub it with olive oil is all.

"Somebody needs to talk to him! I have tried, but those fool fishermen will not let me near him. He needs to know the plan! Raziel from Kerioth—"

James looked at Avi sharply. "Do not say that name here."

"What? You do not wish to have your brother's name associated with a man of real courage and honor?"

"My brother is not an insurrectionist," James said between his teeth. He flicked a glance out the workroom door. All it would take was one passing Roman . . .

"None of his brothers believe in him. They are all cowards," Avi's friend said scornfully.

"You are right, Joab." Avi's tone oozed disdain. "The only one with courage is the Teacher himself. Out there daily with the *people*."

On her way to escort out her overly zealous guest, Keturah leaned toward James and whispered, "I am sorry."

She took Avi's arm and said, "We must go." He angrily shook her off.

"Are you all blind? The time is now! We have to be united! All he has to do is say the word, and thousands will be at his side! The cause is everything. Everything! Anyone who does not agree is not Jewish."

To his left, James caught movement. Jorah stood in the passageway to the smallyard with the sackcloth flap pulled to the side. "What is all the shouting in here?" she demanded, brushing aside a curled wisp of hair with floury fingers.

"With his powers and our swords, we could gouge the side of Rome and bring Caesar's empire crashing down!"

Jorah rolled her eyes. "Not again," she groaned, and let the flap fall back into place.

"Never before has Israel seen these miracles! I myself tasted of the bread he brought down from heaven. I have never tasted anything more delicious. Surely a thousand times better than manna."

James had heard others claim the same, yet Joses had been there that day. He reported that it tasted no different than Mother's loaves. It was probably where Jesus got the recipe.

". . . realize what can be done? No need to pack supplies! Do you realize what kind of strategic military advantage that would have? Raziel says all we have to do is—"

"Don't say that name!" James thundered at him.

"I have to get to Jesus!" Avi thundered back.

"How would you like a personal audience with him?" Nathanael drawled.

The Zealot snapped his mouth shut, blinking in surprise. James slowly turned to stare at the lad on the stool who toyed with the gouge adze.

"You—you could do this?" Avi stammered, with a fast exchange of glances with his friend. "You could get me a personal audience?"

"Of course." Nathanael shrugged, as if it were a petty thing. He rose from the stool and strolled to Avi at the corner bench, all the while inspecting the curved blade of the heavy adze. He lounged conversationally against the bench, thumbing the adze blade. He lifted the blade even with his eyes, then looked at Avi beyond it and with a wicked smile softly said, "I will give you a chance to experience his healing powers firsthand."

It had been so long since James had laughed, his own outburst startled him.

The greedy excitement in Avi's face shriveled to contempt. Nathanael spread his arms wide, carelessly swinging the adze so that Avi jumped aside. "What?" Nathanael asked innocently. "It's perfect! What better way to get his attention? He heals you; you tell him the plan . . . brilliant." He suddenly frowned and puffed out his cheeks. "Of course you might bleed to death before you get to him, and that would not be good. But the cause is everything, right? We have to be willing to take a little risk." He went to drape his arm about Avi in brotherhood, but Avi ducked away.

James could not stop laughing. He sat down hard in his stool and laughed himself to aching. The curtain flap twitched aside, and Jorah's wondering face appeared.

Avi was slinking away.

"Avi!" Nathanael reproached, arms wide. "Brother! I said I could get you an audience." His face lit in sudden inspiration. "We could practice on your friend! Find out exactly how long it takes him to bleed to death. What is your name? Joab? Come here, Joab." He traced a few practice swoops in the air.

Joab ducked out the door with Avi close behind him. Keturah ran to the doorway, where she stopped and yelled, "My coppers, you thieves!" Over her shoulder she flashed a smile at Nathanael and James, then flew out the door, shouting, "Stop, you thieving cheats!"

James went to the doorway and watched t
down the path. He laughed again delighted
"Look at them run!"

Mother joined Jorah at the curtain, smiling a mystified
smile at her boy. "What was that all about?" she said.

Jorah folded her arms and looked at Nathanael, who, with
a pleased grin on his face, twirled the adze between both fore-
fingers. James came away from the doorway, shaking his head
at Nathanael and chuckling.

"Too bad Judas missed that," James said.

"I don't know who you are," Jorah said to Nathanael, "but
I have not heard my brother laugh in forever. For that you will
join us for the midmeal."

Grinning, Nathanael looked from the adze to Jorah, and
his grin promptly faltered. James caught the look, and his own
smile finally came down. He knew well the look. Probably
how he appeared the first time he saw Keturah.

Jorah swept an up-and-down look at Nathanael, then
whirled away.

Mother nodded at the young man. "You must be the lad
Annika told us about."

Nathanael straightened and ducked his head respectfully.
"Yes, I am."

Mother folded her arms and, with her eyes twinkling, said,
"How do you like living with Annika?"

Nathanael darted a look at James. "I—she—"

"Annika is a wonderful woman, I am sure you have discovered," Mother said.

"That she is," Nathanael replied, not meeting her eyes.

"Do join us for the meal," Mother urged. She glanced at

James. "I want to know what made my son laugh." She disappeared behind the curtain.

Visibly relieved, Nathanael resumed his slouch at the workbench.

James went to the passage and held the curtain aside to watch Mother's retreat. Then he let the curtain fall back and turned to Nathanael. "Now, what do you *really* think of Annika?"

Nathanael snorted. "Sounds like you know her."

James straddled a stool at his bench and picked up the crooked piece of olivewood. "All my life. She is more of an aunt than a family friend. She is a grandmother to every child in Nazareth; they all adore her. The opinions of the adults are different."

Nathanael hesitated, then said quietly, "I have never met anyone like her."

James raised his eyes from the wood. He watched the lad look around the shop.

"My uncle never kept his place so neat." Nathanael shook his head. He jerked a thumb at Jude's bench. "The amount of tools you have . . . I have never seen so many, let alone so many sizes."

James pried off a piece of bark from the olivewood. "Tools are a hobby for Judas. We have a decent set for every bench. 'He who does not teach his son a trade brings him up to be a robber.' My father used to say that."

"My father is a drunk."

James pursed his lips, nodding. He broke off more bark. "Anything else?"

Nathanael folded his arms. "My mother is a whore."

James shifted his jaw, then offered, "My brother walks on water."

"Anything else?"

James studied him long before he could answer. He liked what he saw in those strange bright eyes, liked the defiant tilt in the chin. He liked this boy, and he already feared for him.

"Yes, I am afraid there is something else," James said, resting the olive piece on his lap. "Work for me, and you will regret it. You will be scorned and ridiculed, sometimes refused trade in the marketplace. Some cowards will throw things at you when you pass. They will spread rumors about you and shun you in the synagogue. Some will cross to the other side of the street when they see you coming, people you have known all your life. People who used to be friends.

"Your chances of a decent marriage will be ruined, unless you choose to marry one of the—seekers. You will have more interruptions to your work in one day than you will have visits to the brush. You will deal with fanatics and with fools. And if you are used to being liked, forget about it. Forget all about it, because you will be hated." He broke off to smile grimly. "Work for me, Nathanael, and your life will be misery."

A gleam came into Nathanael's eye, and with it a slow grin. "I have not had such an offer in a long time."

"I hope you refuse it. I like you."

Nathanael stretched his legs out and folded his arms. "Let me see . . . they won't have much chance to shun me in the synagogue since I am a bad Jew and do not go. If they throw things at me, well, I can hit a gecko at fifty paces—I will keep a rock or two handy. Being scorned and such . . ." He lifted his hands and shoulders. "My mother is a whore. I have been scorned since birth. So I hate to disappoint you, but I accept your offer."

James smiled. "You will live to regret it."

"From what you tell me, I can only hope so." He looked about the shop. "Where do you want me?"

James hesitated. All of the other apprentices had worked at Father's bench, or alongside Judas and James. The corner bench had been vacant for three years.

He had hoped . . .

Jorah called them from the courtyard to the midday meal.

Nathanael looked at James, who waved him on. "I will join you in a moment."

Nathanael set the gouge adze down on the corner bench and went to the passage. The curtain flap swished behind him.

James lingered to look at the tools hanging above the corner bench.

Sounds and smells drifted into the workshop from the almost-spring day outside: the bray of neighbor Eli's cantankerous donkey, some children shouting to one another, the fragrance of rain and of wet grasses and of early spring wildflowers. From the courtyard he heard Jorah laugh, heard the soft clatter of a lid on a cook pot.

He remembered the way it used to be. On a day like today it might be his turn to check the barley crop on their terraced strip of land. Or he might have gone to Capernaum with Jude. He might have been on the way home from the late-winter trip to Gaza, back when Jesus and James did much of the trading.

He had not taken a journey since the last one with Jesus, three and a half years ago. James could not even remember the last time he had walked their own land, one terrace up from Eli's. Simon had taken over the planting and weeding, and in the late spring and summer, the watering. And Jude went on the trips alone, or with Joses. James stayed here, under the sky within these four walls.

"Somebody has to stay," he whispered to himself.

"James, are you coming?"

"Yes." He cleared his throat. "Yes, I'm coming."

He tossed the crooked olive piece back into the carving box, set the box on the floor, and shoved it into the corner. He set his mallet on the pegs, then went to the corner bench, where he replaced the gouge adze on the empty peg just so, then adjusted it. He stepped back to look, because he would not see it this way again. Then he saw the tiny, tilted boat on the corner of the shelf.

On sudden furious impulse, he lunged for the toy. He ran out the doorway, stumbling as he went. He reared back and whipped the little boat as far as he could. It sailed long in the air, then bounced and skittered down the slope.

2

"Hear, O Israel, Adonai is your God. Adonai is one."

Gentle morning light suffused the workroom. James liked prayers here. The room had serenity at this time in the morning, so still and silent. The feeling nearly matched that of the synagogue. One step short of holy.

"You shall love Adonai your God with all your heart, with all your soul . . ."

The latest edict from Temple Jerusalem was not so bad: Anyone who held with the teachings of Jesus the Nazarene was to be banned from synagogue. The brothers decided not to go out of respect for Mother. Who cared what their absence implied? James did not care what the synagogue leaders thought anymore. He could never persuade them otherwise.

". . . with all your might. Take to heart these instructions, which I charge you this day. Impress them upon your children. . . ."

Keturah's face flashed unbidden in his mind.

"Recite them when you stay at home and when you are away, when you lie down and when you get up. Bind them as a sign upon your hand. . . ."

Annika had reported a thing his brother had said. He had criticized some of the Pharisees who wore their tefillin past the morning prayers. Had he stopped wearing his own for the morning prayers? Could he have gone so far?

". . . and let them serve as a symbol upon your forehead. Inscribe them on the doorposts of your house and on your gates."

With deliberate reverence, James slowly unwound the leather straps from his hand and forehead. He brushed his fingers on the leather packets attached to each strap. Father had copied the words from the synagogue Torah onto parchment years ago and slipped them into new leather packets.

If James said more prayers, if he did more pious deeds . . . would God hear and see, and maybe credit the excess to the account of Jesus?

Hear me, Adonai. Let the beat of my heart pray, because I cannot anymore. Help me, Adonai, I cannot.

James folded the tefillin and placed them in the willow basket on Father's workbench. He could not pray any more for Jesus. These three years, had he not prayed with every rhythm of his life? Hammer blows became *protect him, protect him, protect him.* Metallic chinks with the stone chisel became *help him, help him, help him.* And sometimes only the rhythm of his breath did the praying. *He needs you. Have mercy. He needs you. Have mercy.* Fear did the praying these days.

He found himself looking at the money box on the shelf above Father's bench, and he went to pick it up. Heavy as ever, though not for what it contained. The wood had to be ebony heartwood, a heavy wood indeed. James grimaced. Only a handful of coins, some silver, mostly copper, rattled in the box. He hoped Joses and Simon were able to sell the oak benches in Gaza. The man who had ordered them months ago had never returned to the shop. Simon's scrollwork, for which he was famous in Galilee, adorned the edges and supports of the benches. The man had wanted a replica set of benches Simon had done for a Greek family in Sepphoris. He had swept into the shop, placed his grandiose order, and never returned.

"Served us right," James muttered. They had been too easily impressed. They had taken on the job as they always had, on word alone. Long ago Jude had suggested they begin the practice of receiving half the payment in advance of the project. Of course, this idea came after Father died, and Jesus did not say much about it. Too bad. Half the amount Simon deserved would have been rattling in the money box by now.

He replaced the box and rubbed the back of his neck as he considered straightening the mess on Father's bench. Try as James could to keep it neat, it had become the catchall spot since it was the bench closest to the passageway to the home.

Sometimes tools or a current project would migrate to the courtyard—Mother and Jorah, especially Jorah, worked to make sure business stayed on the business side. Instead of scolding, Jorah would switch aside the curtain and stand until her presence was known; then she would stretch out her arm, holding the offending tool with the very end of her fingertips, and deliberately drop the tool onto Father's old workbench. She would ignore any shouts from the brothers—especially from Jude, who railed at her for being so careless with valuable tools—and lift her chin and whirl away.

When Jorah was old enough to begin keeping house with Mother, she had many ideas for doing things differently from the way Mother did them. "But Jerusha's mother puts the pots like *this*, so they can drain better." "I think we should eat our bread *after* we eat the vegetables; I hear it is better for the body."

Mother treated her revolutionary ideas with calm assurances: "Jorah, soon you will marry, and you will be able to run your household with all Jerusha's mother's ideas that you want."

But the marriage never came. Father died suddenly, while drawing water for the terrace. The dust had not yet settled from that aching loss when, almost one year to the day, Jesus decided to walk away.

Jorah was now seventeen. Devorah had already married and moved with her husband to Bethany in Judea. Most of Jorah's friends were having their second and third babies. He did not hear her speak of marriage often, which was rare with a girl as opinionated as Jorah, but he could only imagine the humiliation she had to endure among her friends.

Humiliation upon humiliation, for all of them.

"I saw Jorah at the well. She tells me we got another apprentice."

James jumped and angrily whirled on Judas, who came into the workroom with a large bag slung over his shoulder.

"I *hate* it when you do that."

"Good morning to you too."

"Why do you do that when you know I hate it?"

Judas shrugged and unshouldered the bag. "I don't do it on purpose. And my trip to Capernaum was splendid, thanks."

"Liar, on both counts," James muttered, but he went to Judas as he knelt to take the things out of the sack.

Judas held each item to the morning light before handing it to James. First came a new mallet, or rather a used one, very heavy. James tested the weight, knowing it would go to Simon, who was a fool for any size mallet for his carving projects. He set it aside and took another tool from Jude. He raised his eyebrows as he examined this one. Use the tool on one side and it was a mallet; turn it around and it was a hatchet.

"This is a handy thing," he murmured, turning it over in his hands. "By the way—welcome back."

"Got that from Shimron. Thought you would like it. We will see more of it, according to him. Causing quite a stir."

"Where is it from?" James tapped a stool with it. "Has a strange balance. Feels awkward."

"Shimron claims he invented it. Says he gave the idea to a smith in Decapolis."

James snorted. "Ha."

"Same old Shimron."

Judas pulled out two more mallets, a straight gouge, a sheepsfoot carving knife, and a chisel. He unwrapped a thick packet of four- and five-inch nails, most of them rust-filmed but straight. He handed them to James, then tossed the carrying sack onto Father's bench and brought the tools to Simon's bench to sort them.

Judas ben Joseph was the youngest of the brothers and the

thinnest, with a wiry work-hardened frame and a face with smoothed hollows. He had the same deep-purple puffiness below his eyes as Mother, making the line of his nose white in comparison. And though Jude was the youngest brother, already his hair was beginning to shrink from his forehead. James put a hand to his own forehead. He was the only one of the brothers with hair not yet retreating. Perhaps he would escape this family trait.

At Simon's bench, Jude took a mallet and a chisel and began to tap holes for another tool rack next to the one on the wall already filled.

"Simon and Joses back?" he asked.

"No."

Jude's mallet hesitated only a moment. "They should have returned before I left. I've been gone a week."

James sifted through the nails from the packet, trying to ignore the simmer in his stomach. Some days the pain was dormant. Other days it cramped and twisted, especially when thoughts of . . .

Softly he asked, "How did it go in Capernaum?"

Judas stopped the mallet halfway to the nail. He held the pose, then lowered the mallet and let it rest on the bench. "They tell me he is in Judea now. Northern Judea, they think."

James licked his lips. "What's the news?"

Judas sighed deeply and dropped the chisel and mallet onto the bench. He rubbed his face with both hands, and when he drew them away the hollows of his cheeks were deeper than ever.

"Rome is watching. Looks as if he has enemies on both sides now."

James dug his fingers into his stomach, but pain on

the outside did not lessen the pain on the inside. "What is happening?"

"They have been in the crowds. They are asking questions."

God of Israel . . . "What questions?"

Judas drew a breath. "Somehow they know he used to trade with Shimron. They came and questioned Shimron. They wanted to know if Jesus is associated with a man named Raziel from Kerioth."

The stool tumbled backward as James sprang from it with a curse. The curse came as much from the flash of fire in his belly as from the name of Raziel.

"Him again! He is all I ever hear of these days! Those stupid fool Zealots!" James paced the workroom, hardly knowing where he walked. Punctuated with language to make a centurion blush, he told Judas of the incident with Avi and his friend a week before. He waited, breathing hard, for Jude's response, sure to be an indignant one. But Judas merely regarded him with strangely saddened eyes. James became aware of the direction of Jude's eyes; he glanced down and saw that his own fist clutched his stomach. He jerked his hand away.

"It's getting worse, isn't it?" Judas said.

"I can manage," James replied tightly. "What are we supposed to do *now*, Judas? Rome, asking questions? That's the last thing we need!" He turned away from Jude, scrubbing the back of his head with both hands. "Where are Joses and Simon?"

"Maybe you should see Jesus about those pains."

"That isn't funny anymore, Judas."

The brothers used to joke like that in the beginning, when the reports first came filtering in. A brother would bang his thumb with a hammer, and one of them would call out, "Another job for Jesus!" Or one would wrap a belt around his eyes and stagger about the shop, hollering, "Have pity on a poor blind man! Lead me to Jesus!" It was great fun, until Mother put an end to it.

"I am not sure I am joking."

James froze in front of the fire pit. His mouth tasted of the ashes his eyes saw. "What am I—how am I supposed to answer that, Jude?"

"It is not what you think," Judas muttered. "It's just . . . you spend a week in Capernaum, you hear things. He does not stay in the house he used to anymore—he moves around too much—but the way they carry on in Capernaum, you would have thought he threw the stars into the heavens."

"What does Shimron think of him?"

"Shimron . . . believes."

"God of Israel," James groaned.

"James!" Judas hissed. "This has got to stop! This language of yours."

"Of course, it is only Shimron. He would believe pigs could fly."

"What goes on inside of you that such talk comes out?"

James spun around to glare at him. "What do you think? Our brother is heading for an appointment with a headsman or a cross! He will end up like one of those thousands on the roads, stuck up on a God-cursed Roman cross with 'Rebellion' written over his head. The Romans are getting wise. Finally, they say, 'What is this? A huge crowd and a single man who holds them spellbound?' God of Israel, what do you *think* goes on inside me, Judas? The same that goes on inside of you: *R-E-B-E-L-L-I-O-N*, in bright-red blood."

He quivered with rage. It came in waves from his feet; it colored his vision with red and black sparks. The rage, the language, the pain in his gut . . . all things acquired since his brother became the Prophet of Peace.

He grabbed the nearest tool from Joses' bench and hurled it across the room. It struck the wall near his own bench and sent chips of plaster flying. "I *hate* what he has done!"

Dimly, he was glad his mother and sister were at the well. They did not need this; they had to be kept from it. He stood still until the rage sparkles began to fade; he deliberately slowed his breathing. As ever, after one of these tirades, came guilt. He went to where the tool lay on the floor and picked it up.

"It isn't broken," he muttered, loudly enough for Jude to hear.

"How did you hear about Raziel from Kerioth?" Judas asked.

It was a fair question, and James understood his puzzlement. Jude knew he did not leave the workroom, except for visits to the brush and to haul in wood or stone stacked around the back of the house. He sometimes went to the rooftop but only after the sun had set.

"Oh, bits and pieces from the people who come here. I got an earful from Annika last week. She would think this Raziel was the latest savior of Israel if she did not think it of someone else first." Bitterly he added, "And of course, Keturah with her tour." He rubbed off the tool and took it back to Joses' bench. "Same old drivel. Nothing new around here."

Jude picked up the mallet and chisel again. "So Keturah was here."

"Do not worry; I'm over her. Besides, you know which of us she would have chosen. She did not ask *me* to teach her to carve."

"That's only because Jesus and Simon are the best. I have seen the way she looks at you."

Judas was trying to make up for James' fit of temper, which only made James feel more disgusted with himself. He strode to his bench and tried to busy himself with something before he made Jude's homecoming even more unpleasant.

Judas resumed tapping. James rubbed the back of his head, trying to order his thoughts to the day and the work before him. He wanted to work; he wanted to ignore the world and just work. With Jude back, he was stronger. Two against the rest of the world on the other side of the mezuzah. Two, much better than one. And when his other brothers came home, they would be four strong. He drew a long, slow breath and took his stool. He reached for the small jar of flint filings on his shelf and settled down to scrape the rust off the nails with the filings and a rag.

He remembered when Father taught him to scrape the nails, before James' fingers were work-roughened. Filings would work into his fingertips from the rags, making them sore, sometimes making them bleed. But, oh, the joy of working next to Father, the joy of finally being old enough to join Father and Jesus in the workroom. He never spoke of the pain for fear Mother would think him too young to begin the trade.

Father's bench was where each of them started, before they were skilled enough to earn benches of their own. The day came when a brother would come into the shop and find a brand-new bench, secretly made by Father . . . what a grand day it was. Each boy could organize his bench the way he wanted; Father never interfered with that. Over the years, tools accumulated on the pegs above the benches, tools perfected to each individual hand. And on a special shelf above each bench, every boy kept his nails and his treasures.

James glanced at his shelf. Four pots of nails on one side of the shelf, and the treasures of his twenty-nine-year lifetime on the other. A rock he found in a stream when he was nine, veined with gold. An exquisitely made wooden box, his own personal money box, the top of the lid carved in whorls and intricate convolutions. The lid was edged in carved braid work, as smooth as three thin snakes. A square in each corner had decorative crosscuts. Jesus made it for James' fifteenth birthday.

A ball-in-a-cage puzzle sat next to the box. After each son learned the rudiments, it was Father's first lesson in carving, an agonizing project. A carved wooden ball rolled between four slim bars, which ended on each side in a rounded, decorated knob. James could not remember how many times he had to start over because too strong a cut severed a slim bar.

Simon made his first ball-in-a-cage at the age of six with three balls instead of one—and not once did he sever a bar. It was the first sign of his gift, a gift Father made sure was brought to its fullest by introducing Simon to master carvers throughout Galilee, and some from Judea. Over the years some visited the shop just to see his work.

"How is Mother?" Jude asked. "I saw her at the well. She seemed good, but . . ."

"She has been—" James frowned at the nail he was scraping. "She speaks of joining the entourage of you-know-who to serve him and his followers."

The tapping stopped. When it resumed, the raps on the nail were harder.

James twisted to look at Judas. "Well? What do you think of that?"

"Does it matter what I think? When has it ever mattered what I think? When does what I think change anything around here?"

James set the nail aside and took another. He moistened the rag in the water pot, squeezed out the excess, and dipped it into the flint filings. The rust came off in dark amber, file-peppered smears on the rag.

"I will wager you-know-who asked her to do it himself," James muttered.

"You can say his name, James," Judas snapped. "He is still our brother."

"Barely! He prefers the company of strangers to that of his own family. You remember what he said, Judas, you heard it yourself. He disowned us, right in front of all those people. 'Who is my mother, and who are my brothers? Whoever does the will of my Father in heaven is my mother and my brothers.'"

James could barely utter the shameful words. They cut him more deeply than anyone could know. Only Joses and Simon and Judas could understand. They alone knew the shock, the humiliation, and worse, the finality of those words. With those words Jesus cut himself loose from his family, as if he had severed a mooring line. Didn't James have nightmares of watching his brother drift away into a tumultuous sea while his family stayed on the shore?

"We only wanted to talk to him. We only went to see if it was all true. He owed us that much," James muttered.

A storm, stilled. A blind man, seeing. A person mad with demons, made of sound mind again. The thought even now raised the skin on James' arm. All the crazy rumors that found their way into the shop were enough to make them pack a few sacks and fill a few skins and seek Jesus out to see if it were true. Healing a leper? It was not even lawful to touch one. *Forgiving sins,* sins not made against Jesus himself? Was this their own Jesus? Many bore the name of Jesus, as common a name as Judas. They had to know for themselves if this Jesus was their own. And they soon learned what Jesus thought of his own family.

Not long after came the gut pain.

"I do not want Mother trotting all over the countryside," James declared as he gave a nail a vicious swipe. "He should not expect that of her. It is his madness and none of her own. I wish . . . I wish Father . . ."

"So do I," Judas murmured.

"Why can't he heal the sick *here?*"

The brothers worked in silence, until James finally gave voice to what all the events demanded. It was hard; the words wanted to stay in his throat. But the time had come. "Judas . . . something has to be done about Jesus."

Jude did not answer.

Forget that Jesus left without so much as a good-bye. Forget that he never told anyone his plans, especially James, his traveling partner, his . . . friend. One day James came into the shop and found he was gone. James never knew, on that day, that his life would be forever changed. Never knew that everything familiar would begin to alter like warping wood.

It was hard enough to lose Father. Oh, God, it was hard, Father gone. Hard to come into the workroom, day after day, and hear the painful silence from the bench nearest the curtain flap. He thought he had had his fill of sorrow.

James remembered the way it used to be, Joseph the carpenter and his boys. Even after Joses married and built a room onto the home of his in-laws, it was still Joseph and his four sons. Joses, the first to marry though he was the third born, came to the shop every morning at dawn; nothing much changed, except for where he ate and slept. His new in-laws were Tobias and Sarah, who lived just over the hill past their land. The strip of land belonging to Tobias was one terrace up from their own; his daughter Abigail had grown up with Joses.

Joses and Abigail had their first child, a sweet-faced baby boy named Benjamin, Father's first grandson. Oh, how Father loved that child, and Ben adored Joseph. "Babba, Babba," Ben would call him. Joses was Abba, and Joseph, Babba. Ben was two when his grandfather died. Even now, four years later, the bench near the flap was "Babba's bench."

It was Benjamin who first brooked the question, upon hearing of all the wondrous things his uncle had done in places far from Nazareth.

"Why didn't Uncle fix Babba?"

"Did you hear what I said?" James irritably tossed the cleaned nail into a jar and took another. "We need to do something about Jesus. We cannot ignore it anymore."

"And what do you suggest?"

James chose to ignore that tone, soaked in sarcasm, and told his brother the ideas he had thought on since Judas had been gone.

"The countryside. We could take Jesus away to the country. We could stay with him, talk him out of this madness, hold vigils of fasting and prayer for him. When we are sure he has his senses again, he can come back to work. All the fervor will die down; they will all forget about him—eventually. We would have to put up with a few Zealots like Avi, sure, but we could do it, Judas." James set down his rag and nail. It was a tiny dream that often gave him a scraping of hope. It could happen; the brothers could do it. They would show mitzvah for their own kin, to their own hurt. They would restore Jesus no matter what it cost them.

"At the least we could take him to Qumran, place him with the Essenes. He could work out whatever fervor he is consumed with there, where he could do no harm." James glanced at Jude to see what he thought, but Jude's back was to him.

They would remind Jesus of the times they had had, of who he used to be when he was with them. The laughter, the joking. The friendship. James would remind him of the talks he and Jesus had on the trips down to Gaza, when it was just the two of them going for supplies. When they would camp together under the stars, lie side by side gazing into the sparkling blackness, talk of the wonder of the universe, talk of girls, talk of anything at all. Nobody heard James better than Jesus.

"We could make things the way they used to be," James told Judas.

"She asks about you in the marketplace now and then."

James blinked. "Who—what are you talking about?"

"Keturah. You cannot tell me she does not think about you."

James left his bench to stand next to Judas. "Have you not heard a word? Jude, answer me! What do you think of my plan?"

Jude would not answer, not right away. He was tapping nails into a new wooden tool rack. James was about to ask again when Jude turned cold eyes on him. In a tone to match his eyes, he said, "What do I think of your plan? I think it's too late. And I do not want to talk about it anymore."

James stood a moment, clenching his teeth, torn between agreeing with him and grabbing his neck to shake him senseless.

He growled and turned his back. So Jude did not want to talk about it now. Well and good. They would certainly talk when Joses and Simon returned. Jude could not ignore it anymore; none of them could. James had a strange, restless feeling that something was stirring. A feeling he could neither define nor ignore.

"What do you think of Keturah?" Jude said in a light tone that utterly dismissed their former conversation. "Did you get a chance to talk to her when she came with those seekers?"

"Why do you talk so much about her? Are you interested?"

"No. Her father spoke to me before I left."

James glared at Jude. "About what?"

"What do you think, sawdust-for-brains?"

James rubbed his thumb on a nail head, then noticed the crook in the nail. He took his hammer to try to make it straighter but gave up after a few blows. It would need the forge. True, Keturah and her father were among the few who did not look the other way at the sight of one of Joseph's tribe. He smiled in spite of himself when he remembered the look Keturah had given them before she lit out after her thieving cheats. It was a look of coconspiracy, us against them, the people of Nazareth against all the crazies out there who come only to fetch sawdust for their pockets. A rare glimmer of kinship in the Nazareth notoriety.

Judas mistook his smile. "Eh, you know it too. She likes you."

"That's not why I am smiling. You missed out on the best day of my life a few days ago."

James told him the whole story, from the way Nathanael swung his adze so that Avi had to jump, to the way he and his friend streamed out of the workshop like pigs on fire. Judas got to laughing, a rich sound indeed, until he finally settled down to ask, "Well, where is he? Our new apprentice?"

"He stays with Annika."

"One of her strays?"

"Something like that. I have learned he does not take to mornings so well. Stays out late with his new friends."

Judas frowned. "What sort of character is he? Father would have never put up with—"

"Oh, you will like him. Besides, we cannot afford to pick and choose these days."

"And what of . . . our reputation?"

"You know, I think he actually enjoys it. He takes it as a personal responsibility to show the door to anyone who does not have business here." James chuckled. "He does it differently every time. Quite an imagination the lad has. I almost look forward to the intrusions now, just to see what Nathanael's going to do."

"How long has he been here?"

"A week. He came the day after you left."

"Where did you put him?"

James dipped his rag, squeezed out the water. He smudged up more filings and applied them to the nail. "Corner bench."

From the corner of his eye, he could see Jude pause at his work and look at him.

Presently Judas said, "Cypress table done?"

"Nathanael finished it first day."

"How is his work?"

"Good. He is a hard worker. He has much to learn, but show him once, and he's on his way. Talks too much, but he has a quick wit."

Judas mounted the new tool rack on the wall pegs. He arranged the new tools on the rack and stood back to make sure they were aligned. "Why Simon, with his gift for carving, wants to be a scribe is between him and God only." He looked at James. "Why haven't they returned? A journey to Gaza has never taken this long."

"Mother is worried," James replied.

A form filled the entrance, the movement enough to make both brothers look. James started to grin, expecting to see Nathanael. But the one who filled the doorway was not the apprentice. James' smile disappeared. The way the man's eyes appraised the shop, the look on his face . . . he was no customer.

His eyes lit on James, and he began to smile. James looked away, scraping the nail with deliberate strokes.

With not much enthusiasm, Judas said, "Good morning."

"Good morning! This is the home of the Nazarene?"

"We are all Nazarenes," James muttered without looking up. He wished Nathanael were here. He would be laughing already.

The man nodded, fingering his gray-salted beard. "So you are. Forgive my imposition. You must receive many, ah, visitors."

James glanced at him. "We do."

The man had a rueful twist to his mouth. "I hate to class myself with them, though by showing up at your door I do just that. They come to my home and expect my Miriam to offer them a bowl for their feet. Perhaps even wine and bread."

James sat back on his stool. He and Jude exchanged a look.

"And forget about getting an honest day's work done," the man went on. He kissed his fingertips and touched them to the mezuzah set into the doorjamb, though he did not yet cross the threshold. The seekers were not this polite. They would stroll in as if they had the mitzvah to do so. "I had to go into seclusion just to finish one jar. Miriam took to what she called 'artful evasion' to keep them away from me. 'No, my husband is not here right now'—meaning I was not *right there*—'I will tell him you called.'" The man smiled a crinkly eyed smile.

But James was not ready to smile back.

"Tell me . . . do they take tokens here?" the man asked.

James blinked, then looked at Jude again. But Jude was staring at the man and nodding. "They do."

The man shook his head. "Odd, is it not? Miriam would get so irritated when they would make off with the silliest things."

"They take sawdust," James blurted.

"Pottery shards, at my place. As if . . ."

"As if their lives would be changed by cast-off wood shavings."

The man chuckled; then he shrugged and lifted his hands. "Ah, can you blame them? Belief and hope are in meager supply these days. We must not begrudge them a bit of sawdust. No harm in it."

James laid down his rag. He had not thought of it that way.

"I tell my Miriam, 'Where is the wrong done? These are hearts in need, hearts long encumbered, else they would not have troubled themselves to come to my place. If a bit of clay gives comfort or hope . . .'" He lifted his hands again. "Eh, let them have their tokens, and God bless them for it."

James rose from his stool involuntarily, the action nearly embarrassing him. He pretended to have to reach for the nail container on the shelf.

He nearly went to give the man welcome, as he would have a few years ago. Already he was drawn to the kindness he saw in the stranger's eyes. Drawn to the understanding. Something foreign these days, in these parts.

But time after time, each kind eye proved something in disguise. An arguer. A sectarian. A leader of Israel, all with a smooth approach and an acid finish. The only decent thing to happen around here in a long time was Nathanael. He suspected Nathanael did not care enough to be opinionated.

But Judas bought the stranger's act. He did what James did not and extended his hand, welcomed him in. The stranger murmured the house blessing as he crossed the threshold. James shook his head and slid a look at Jude. It was pathetic the way Judas strained at anything resembling humanness.

And truly, James' inkling proved out.

"Judas!" the man exclaimed after Jude introduced himself. "You are well-named indeed! It should not surprise me one of the brothers would bear the name of the Maccabee." He took Jude's hand warmly.

"I am called Raziel. Raziel of Kerioth."

3

Pain exploded in James' gut as Judas gasped. James lunged for the stranger and hauled him into the shop, casting a swift glance toward the road. He kicked the door shut and turned to seize Raziel by the tunic. "How dare you show up here!"

Judas went quickly to the door, cracked it open to anxiously peer down to the road. "Did anyone see you? Are you known here?"

James shoved Raziel, and he stumbled backward. He shoved again until Joses' bench on the other side of the room stopped the man.

Once-bridled rage now coursed freely in red-black waves. Filled with its release, trembling with it, James grabbed fistfuls of the man's clothing and yanked him nose-to-nose with himself. His fist would be the mallet, his fingers the vise. Crush his neck between his hands.

"James!" Jude shouted, a strangely dimmed cry.

Teeth bared, James hissed into his face, "What have you done—"

"James, stop!"

Everything precious—Jorah, Mother, the last of everything to him. Gone in one visit from a stranger. He could almost hear the footfalls of the soldiers.

"Let him go!" Jude's words were garbled, a shout underwater.

His fingers crept around the man's neck; his nails began to entrench human flesh.

"James, let him go." Her words cut through.

The red-streaked blackness began to abate. The roar in his ears became a rush. With Mother's voice came clarity.

"Release him, James."

Raziel's neck was between his hands. Nathanael stood at the entrance, poised as if to either help James or haul him off. Jorah stood near Nathanael, her face white.

He looked at his fingers, digging deeply into the man's neck. They would not release. Like the man in the story Father had told him as a child, the man who guarded the plot of beans with his sword. The sword had stuck fast to the battler's hand, as Raziel's flesh stuck in James'.

Mother laid her hand on James' shoulder. "Let him go, my boy," she whispered into his ear. Mother placed her hands on James' own, her fingers loosening his. She put an arm about his waist and tugged him away from the man. She took him to his stool, picked it up and righted it, and pushed him gently down to sit.

"I deeply regret causing any . . . it was not my intent . . ."

"One Roman!" Judas erupted. "It would take only one Roman to see you! They are asking if Jesus *knows* you. The Romans are *asking*!"

"No one saw him," Nathanael said quickly. "I followed him from Annika's; he took the ridge."

"Annika! He is staying with Annika? How could she . . . ?" That from Jorah.

How did Jorah know who this man was? How could she understand? She was only seventeen. Didn't James work daily to keep her from the craziness? *God of Israel, let me go insane.* Maybe things would make sense there.

"Annika does not know who you are, does she . . . *Samuel*?" Nathanael said in a softly dangerous tone, and James smiled. Insanity could wait. Raziel was in trouble, and James looked from hooded eyes to see.

Nathanael was circling Raziel. In an ominous singsong, he intoned, "Annika put him up for the night, didn't she, *Samuel* from *Hebron*? Annika thought he was who he said he was, a traveler come late to Nazareth with no place to stay."

"I am a traveler," Raziel said simply. "I did not use my real name to protect her." Raziel looked directly at James. "To protect Jesus, and your family."

"So you came right to our home," Jorah accused.

"What protection is that?" Jude spat.

Raziel did not answer and did not turn his gaze from James. What calm was this in those gray-green eyes? The red around his neck spoke of what the stranger risked to come here. He nearly got himself killed and was even now surrounded by hostility. Why the steadiness in that face? Four people—Mother did not count—would make him answer for nearly sending Rome crashing through their doors. Was it not enough to daily live their lives balanced on the edge of a cliff? What if someone in Nazareth knew who this man was? It would be the tiny push needed to send their lives sliding over the edge. *That which I have feared the most . . .*

"I should remove my shoes," Raziel finally said, "because I am not worthy to be in such company as this."

James felt his mouth fall open.

The gray-green eyes—intelligent eyes—were steady and peaceful. They reminded him of Father.

Raziel shook his head, looking at each person in the room in turn. "What you daily live . . . what you daily endure . . . my own circumstance is worthless in comparison."

"They daily endure people like you," Nathanael sneered on his circling march.

"Miriam sent me."

Nathanael reached for him, but James held up his hand. "Wait, Nathanael."

"'Tell them,' she said. 'They need to know. Tell them they are not alone.'"

Nobody, not one, could respond.

"'Tell them,'" Raziel continued softly, eyes brushing each face until they came to rest on James. "'Tell them we know what it is to be a daily affliction to all who see. Tell them we know the shame and the betrayal. They need to know.'"

A foreign sound broke over the silence of those who heard his words. It was not a pretty sound. It was a small and choking sound. Shock full on his face, James searched the workroom and saw his mother.

Her hands were on her cheeks, and from her lips rose a keen like an animal in pain.

"Know from this day you are not alone," Raziel said, voice heavy with weariness.

The wail rose, and Mother pressed her hands to her mouth. She choked and snuffled, and the keen stifled was almost worse. Never had he heard such a sound from her. Never such an ugly, awful sound.

"She is wise, my Miriam," Raziel murmured, eyes downcast, fingering his beard. He went to the doorway, put his fingertips to his lips, and touched the mezuzah. "I must leave now. More people will be about soon. I will take the back ridge again." He reached inside his tunic and brought out a small bundle wrapped in cloth. He set it down on the threshold. "My Miriam sent this for you, good woman." And he left.

Nathanael followed him out the door, muttering over his shoulder, "I will make sure no one sees him."

"He is not to leave until dark," James called after him.

The sounds from Mother crooned to silence. She took the end of her head covering and wiped her face. Except for its blotchiness, the face had returned to its normal, if weary, composure. The brothers, the sister, and the mother stood long in silence. At last Mary went to the threshold and knelt to pick up the small bundle. She unwrapped it, and fresh, silent tears flowed at what she saw.

She fingered the delicate fabric of the scarf, a fabric miraculously thin, with a satin sheen that seemed to change colors with movement. Tentatively, Jorah came beside her mother, gazing more at her mother, to be sure, but she did touch the fabric and murmured something appreciative.

Mother held the scarf across the front of her tunic, smoothing it down to admire it. And suddenly she laughed through her tears like a young girl.

James found himself shaking his head. One moment wailing, the next moment laughing as delightedly as a child. He would never understand women, his mother least of all. In her face was a happiness, if a weary happiness, one he had not seen in a long, long time.

"Isn't it lovely, Jorah?" she murmured. She lifted it to her nose and smiled. "It is perfumed. Such a lovely scent." She held it to Jorah to smell. Then she looked outside as if to see where Raziel had gone. But James watched her, and she was not looking toward the back ridge.

No, she was gazing south toward the Esdraelon Plain . . . toward Judea. Where *he* was. Her anguish from moments ago was replaced by a strange and glowing certainty. And James knew he was about to lose his mother.

She leaned against the door as she stared beyond Nazareth, hugging the scarf to her chest. At length she said softly, "I will be leaving soon."

Judas dropped his head. Jorah put the back of her hand to her mouth, stifling a sob, then whirled and ran through the room for the curtained passage. The sound of her cry retreated to the back of the home.

James stared at his mother's back; then he looked about for his stool. He pulled it to the front of his bench, settled down, and took up a rusted nail and a rag.

From the doorway he heard his mother murmur, "He has done mighty deeds with his arm; he has scattered those who were proud in the thoughts of their hearts."

He dipped the rag in water, squeezed out the excess, and smudged up filings from the jar. He rubbed the nail to a dull shine, then plinked it into the nail jar.

⁂

Far and away, many miles from Nazareth, an old man closed his eyes and turned in a circle until insensible of direction. Eyes tightly shut, he drew a breath and held it. He quieted his heart, smoothed his mind, and spread his arms wide . . . then slowly he raised an arm and pointed. He opened his eyes and gazed down the length of his arm. Fixing his finger to a spot on the horizon, he checked the position of the sun.

"So. Still we travel west and north," he said to the One True God. "Who is James?"

He could not help smiling as he squinted at the spot on the horizon. It looked like a tent slanted in the wind, from this distance.

"Oh, I will get no answers from you," he grumbled cheerfully to the sky. *Seek James.* An imperative not so very different from *Follow the star.*

He had heard Galilee was beautiful this time of year. If that was the end of his journey—and he had his suspicions—then this wasteland of crown after crown of upturned wasp nests would soon give way to hills clothed in spring green. His eyes ached for color. This barrenness looked as if the One True God had sniffed at it and turned away.

Balthazar knelt to retie the cloth about his flapping sandal. From between his big toe and the one next to it, he dug out a bit of greenery snagged from the brush. He examined the crushed leaf, sniffed it, rolled it between his fingers, and tossed it aside.

He rose and shouldered his sack again, then picked up his stick.

"Now. Where were we? Ah, yes. Melkor. You have yet to explain his presence on that journey, and from what I can see, we have all day."

The old man fell into the rhythm of his stride, the slanted tent on the horizon his next destination.

He shifted his shoulder strap and adjusted the pack to rest on his hip. "'Come, let us reason together.' Melkor was a woodenhead. Tell me why you chose him, and please, do not spare the details. I promise I will not tell a soul." West and north he went.

4

FAR FROM BEING put out with the stranger from Kerioth, Annika was secretly delighted. Not many fooled her, and fool her this one had.

Samuel—she smirked and amended it—no, *Raziel*, the famous Zealot from Kerioth, no less, sat meekly in a chair at her very own table. Across from him, his arms folded and face grim, sat Nathanael, magnificently indignant. She would not let him down. So from where she stood at the table, she made her scowl match Nathanael's and looked down with a cold, cold eye on Raziel.

Annika waved away a few fruit flies from the rim of the wine pitcher, then poured its contents into another pitcher half-filled with water. As she swirled the vessel gently to mix the two, she shook her head as if greatly disappointed. To hide her delight with the stranger, she would imagine he was her neighbor Esther at the well, screaming at her children as if they were pariah dogs. That vexing shriek could make the Almighty himself stuff his ears with wool. The memory of it must have done its work; one timid peek at her face, and the fellow's glance skittered away.

Annika pursed her lips and bit the inside of her cheeks to keep the smile in check. She would let this upstart simmer in his own sauce. Was she not a mother, and an expert at uncomfortable silence?

When Nathanael and Raziel returned from Mary's, Nathanael shoved the older man into a chair and told Annika the entire story. Annika listened in silence, allowing her face to go dark only when Nathanael expected it. Truth to tell, she had to step on her own toes to keep from laughing out loud, especially at the meekness in which the mighty Raziel now huddled.

To bring a threat of Rome to Mary's doorstep, no, that was nothing to laugh about. But heaven help her, that family needed something more than a daily plague of curious drift-abouts and indignant elders. James, in particular.

Poke him and prod him; it was all Annika could do. Hope for a little of the old James to show himself again. These few years that Jesus had been gone . . . daily she watched her James descend into someone she barely knew. Simon was bad enough, getting a smart mouth on him and goading James into his fits of temper. Several weeks back, James had finally let his fist fly—Simon left for Gaza with a bruise on his cheekbone. Truly, the boy had it coming . . . but it troubled her. James had never struck one of his brothers, not in his adult life.

That Simon. Annika allowed her thoughts to further sour her expression. (It would make dear Nathanael happy.) Simon and his Torah and the Prophets, Simon and this renewed fling of his to become a scribe. Yes, he had neat handwriting. But to deliberately ignore his God-given gift for carving was nothing but a slap in God's face. A nasty little defiance for all the unhappiness wrought on the family. Simon's own brand of rebellion.

As for Joses, she did not see him much anymore. He spent half his time at the shop and the other half helping Tobias farm his land. She wondered how he handled it. Did Joses work harder than he ever had; did he treat his wife any differently? Surely, with the absence of Jesus, Joses had been affected too; Annika just couldn't figure out how.

Judas, the youngest son of Joseph and Mary, certainly worked harder. He hid himself in work and pretended nothing was different; that, too, a defiance. Never an outgoing sort, he now treated Annika with more affection than he ever had, and that purely annoyed her.

Devorah was married and down in Bethany, gone a whole year now. She had seemed eager to put Nazareth behind her, and who could blame the girl? Maybe in Bethany Devorah did not hear much about what went on with Jesus. But Annika grimaced. If she did, she would probably pretend it was a different Jesus, not her own brother. Devorah had been the first to disown—or ignore—the doings of her older brother. Acted as though he did not even exist. The other siblings had not gone so far.

And Jorah. Her own sweet and willful Jorah, last child of Joseph and Mary, was different from all of them, from the stubborn fool brothers and Mary and Devorah alike. Jorah did not fail to openly question the activities of their oldest sibling. Annika saw the way the rest of the family dismissed Jorah, but in her eyes the child was the only honest one in the lot. Annika lifted one brow and shrugged, thinking. Mary was honest but did not voice her fears as Jorah did. Beneath that calm and capable appearance, Annika knew Mary was terrified. Annika sniffed. She did not care who Jesus was or wasn't; Mary was his mother, and his mother was going to worry. And with Jesus, God have mercy, the worry was fearsome indeed.

With James . . . here Annika allowed her face to go its measure in contempt. Didn't Mary have enough to kill herself in worry without James to salt the pot as well? The boy deserved a whipping for all the fret he dumped on his mother, but he was too selfish to see it. Annika herself would whip him if she were young enough to do it. She thought about Joseph, and wished again, time without number, that he were alive for this family crisis. Joseph would have held them together. Joseph would have known what to do. That the Almighty had seen fit to leave it to Annika herself was something she still shook her head over.

It was odd how she worried more about James than Jesus. She feared for Jesus, yes, and she prayed for him daily, but James . . . James.

Oh, Mary's firstborn had been her joy and delight all his life. How Annika *missed* that boy—how she missed him. She knew that half the villagers threw torment toward the family in payment for that day Jesus came home for a visit. But she also knew that the other half lashed out because they, too, missed him. Why did he leave? Why had he abandoned them?

How many times had she seen Jesus squat to speak to Mulaki, the beggar with no legs? Mulaki still asked about him, still did not understand why Jesus left him. Oh, Annika would have liked to strangle Jesus for the hole he had left in so many hearts . . . but didn't she see that he was bringing a part of Mulaki with him, to every village he went? "Blessed are the meek, for they shall inherit the earth. . . ." Mulaki did not seem blessed, now that Jesus was gone, nor in any real danger of inheriting the earth. But Jesus carried Mulaki in his heart, wherever he went, with those words. Jesus had not forgotten Nazareth, though its people did their best to forget him.

So, yes, with his gamboling about the country and his crazy turn-the-other-cheek ideas, Jesus had her fear; but James had her worry.

Sometimes when she looked at James it was as if she had the second sight. Sometimes she saw in him a strange, pebbled blackness. It did not happen every time she saw him, but it was occurring with more frequency. She almost didn't like visiting him these days, but she went because she knew she had to.

The pebbled blackness was not hate, of that she was sure, but somehow it was just as horrifying; it was as if a violence brooded in James. She had never seen this before.

Nathanael rose from the table, standing tall and fierce. With a fine manly sneer at Raziel, he declared, "Let me know if he leaves before dark. I will track him, find him, and gut him."

Gut him! Wonderfully put! Annika nodded gravely, and on inspiration added, "If he so much as sticks his little toe out the door, I will clout him with a pitcher."

Nathanael gave her a nod and with a last threatening glare at Raziel, strode out the door.

Raziel tried to call something to Nathanael. "Pardon, please, but we need to discuss the fact of—"

But Annika fiercely waved him silent, hollering, "And do not think this pitcher will break easily!" Gripping her apron with both fists, she hurried to the door to watch Nathanael stride quickly away. She turned on Raziel.

"But, madam—" Raziel began apologetically.

She waved both hands in the air. "Of course, of course. The Sabbath. You cannot leave at dark because it will be Sabbath. But who could ruin such a moment for him? Did you see the way he carried himself when he left? Magnificent!"

Raziel stared at her, perplexed, and his amazement grew when she took down two cups and plunked them onto the table.

"So. Because of the Sabbath you are my prisoner . . . *Samuel* from *Hebron*." But Annika could contain her amusement no longer. She put her fingers to twitching lips, then startled Raziel by laughing long and hard, her large frame bouncing. She finally fanned herself with the end of her head covering and, sighing happily, reached for the pitcher and poured the watered wine.

"Now, Raziel the Famous Zealot from Kerioth—and I do not give a dried-up fig who you are—you will tell me exactly your version of the story, and you will not hold back a single detail."

Raziel the Famous Zealot would not have dreamed of it.

❧

Know from this day you are not alone.

James added the last nail to the jar. Forty-seven nails

stripped of rust. When Nathanael returned, and once they had been assured that Raziel's presence seemed hidden from the villagers—"Only an old man saw us, and Annika said he was half-blind anyway—" they went back to a workman's day. All morning Jude showed Nathanael how to dovetail the mortises and tenons of a cupboard he was making. James half listened to their talk, surprised to hear Jude laugh now and again.

James went about the shop, adding the freshly scrubbed nails to the jars at the benches, including, for the first time in a long time, the jar at the corner bench. He added only a few to Simon's jar; Simon studied Torah with Saul more than he worked in the shop these days. He eyed ruefully a half-finished bowl, carved from olivewood, waiting for Simon's deft fingers to complete it. What he would not give for the smallest part of Simon's talent, yet Simon himself refused to use it. What arrogance was that? Why did he have to compete with Jesus? After all, was it not since Jesus left that Simon found himself seized with a compunction to be a scribe, and in particular, for service at the temple in Jerusalem? If Jesus had not left, James was sure the shop would be patronized with the likes of Pontius Pilate himself seeking Simon's work.

Know from this day . . . James turned away from Simon's bench as much as from Raziel's voice.

Idiots. They had been fool idiots. Surely the famous Raziel would not have come to the shop merely to bring Mother a scarf and spew a sentiment like "Know from this day you are not alone." That particular deception was insidious indeed; the Zealot had a motive, and it was not to align himself with the village pariahs.

But what motive? He came and he left. James frowned as

he swept flint filings from the bench to his hand. How far was Kerioth from Nazareth? It was deep south, that he knew, and west of the Dead Sea. A four- or five-day journey at the least, six if Raziel had taken the Jordan Valley way. No, the famed Zealot leader did not come to Nazareth to drop off a scarf. And was it any coincidence that an apparent disciple of his, Keturah's Avi, had been here only last week?

One day, the fame of the Zealot from Kerioth would surely outshine that of the Zealot Judas of Galilee—Raziel only had to wait for his own crucifixion to become better known. And Raziel brought something more dangerous, and potentially more powerful, to the many Zealot factions than Judas ever had. He brought unity.

James had been a baby when Judas of Galilee led a rebellion against the Roman legate of Syria. The legate had been sent to make an official survey of resources in Judea. The survey, of course, smelled of more taxation, and Judas had roused many countrymen to revolt. He told them they were cowards to pay tax to the Romans. Their slogan became "No leader but God"—and their brave effort was put down and brought to nothing. There were simply not enough Jews who rose up with him. Coponius, procurator at the time, saw to it that Judas and his companions received the full measure of punishment for the insurrection. Their bloody crosses lined the busy Roman trade routes as warning to other Jews who cherished foolish dreams of independence. Goliath prevailed that day, and all the Davids died in agony.

Now came Raziel of Kerioth. Not since Judas of Galilee had one garnered such support—at the least, an appraising eye—for the idea of another campaign against Rome. Raziel brought a sort of dignity to the Zealot factions; he brought order. He not only had some Pharisees and a few Sadducees listening but also some from the Essenes. At least, that was the news brought to the workroom over the years. Jesus had listened to the same news, and if he did not approve of the talk of a new rebellion in words, his silence did not necessarily condemn it.

Raziel had been brought up on charges more than once, under various procurators. The latest to occupy Herod's former palace in Caesarea Maritima was Pontius Pilate. Other than ordering short periods of imprisonment, primarily detainment for questioning, Pilate did not seem to be too concerned with Raziel. As militant as they were, Romans were fond of endless talk and elegant speeches. The rumors said this Raziel knew how to move in the Greco-Roman circles, with his smooth tongue and ability to appeal to reason. James frowned. Herod, the much-despised son of Herod the Great, also moved about easily in those Hellenistic circles. What did Raziel have in common with Herod the traitor, that they were virtually untouched by Rome?

"What are you up to, Raziel from Kerioth?" he muttered as he tossed the rag into the corner.

He shut the man away from his thoughts and rubbed his brow, considering his next project. Neighbor Eli had a broken plow, but acted as if his legs were broken too; he expected one of them to come and fix it instead of bringing it to the shop. "Plow's broken," he had called to James the other day—that was it. James had merely shrugged at him and turned away. Why was everyone so interested in getting him to leave the shop? He suspected Jorah had put Eli up to it.

He could contribute to the ready-made articles for market, though he was not in the mood to make a three-legged stool or a threshing sledge. Maybe a nice oblong bowl from the piece of sycamore. He was reaching for the carving box under his bench when the light dimmed in the doorway.

Keturah stood there, fingers absently brushing her lips and then the mezuzah. She unslung a sack from her shoulder as James' eyes met hers. He straightened. Jude and Nathanael looked up briefly, Nathanael with an ensuing frown when he recognized her; then both went back to their cupboard.

The beat of his heart used to suspend whenever James saw Keturah. The fact that it quickened now, if only for a moment, was something to think on later. She was as lovely as ever. Rivulets of hair made golden from the sun coursed through darker waves of windblown brown. She was not wearing her head covering, a habit she frequently employed. As she looked at James, the long slim fingers that had touched the mezuzah tucked a wayward strand of hair behind her ear.

Looking at her, and she at him, James felt oddly content. Something else to think on later.

"Did you ever catch up with your thieving cheats?" James asked.

Strangely, Keturah's face flickered with something James could have taken for—no, shame was too strong a word. Perhaps regret. That expression was replaced by the one he knew better, one of confident haughtiness. James kept back a smile—he liked that haughtiness.

"I did not come here to discuss those . . . Zealots," she

sniffed. She came to his bench and placed the sack upon it. "I came to discuss—" her haughtiness faltered—"employment."

James looked from the sack to Keturah. Why was she acting so strange? "You have something for me to fix?"

"I'm not talking about your employment." She opened the sack and one by one took cloth-wrapped bundles from it. She unwrapped each one and lined them up on his bench, then stepped aside for James to see.

The first was a bowl, carved from—he picked it up—sycamore. Beautifully rounded out, smooth as the curve of a river rock. A finish like honey satin. He replaced it and took the next item. A ladle. The handle was narrow at the scoop, widening to a carved line of roses. Next to that was a ball-in-a-cage puzzle, small and charming, with crosscuts on either end for decoration. He glanced at the other things. A beautifully carved box, much like the money box on Father's shelf. A set of spoons, various sizes.

"Whose employment?" James asked. These articles looked as though they'd been carved by Simon himself.

"Mine."

James blinked, then looked more closely at the ball-in-a-cage. He should have known. Those crosscuts were a favorite of Jesus.

"Cucumbers for carving," James finally said. "He taught you well."

Keturah nodded and pointed to one of the slender bars in the cage. "He did this one, made me watch every stroke. Then he handed it to me and told me to finish." She smiled. "I was terrified! Such a difficult piece. But somehow it came together."

"Father's first lesson in carving." James turned the fine piece over in his hands. "What did you use to stain it?"

"Fig and berry juice; isn't it lovely? I let it steep for two days, then rubbed in the oil."

He finished admiring it, then took the cloth and rewrapped the ball-in-a-cage. "Keturah . . ."

She whisked her hair behind her ear and spoke fast. "I know Simon will someday leave for Temple. It is no secret; my father heard it from Saul. Even now Simon studies with Saul two or three times a week. You need a carver to take his place."

James felt his shoulders come down. He hated to quell that earnestness. He couldn't meet her eyes as he put the ball-in-a-cage into the sack. "It would never work. You know that."

Keturah took the ladle with the exquisite handle and put it under his nose. "Look at that detail. Look at the design; look at the stain. Of course it would work. Show these things to Simon and ask him. Show him, James."

Why did she make him do this? Avoiding her eyes, he began to rewrap the other pieces. "Keturah . . . these things are beautiful. Better than I could do, better than—"

"He would have given me a chance."

His hands slowed for the space of a heartbeat as he rewrapped the box. "Jesus doesn't work here anymore."

"No, he does not," Keturah said icily and snatched the box out of his hands. With deliberate care, she folded the cloth over and around the box.

"What is that supposed to mean?" James demanded. Keturah leaned in front of him to get the carved bowl. The clean scent of her hair, like herbs and flowers and sun, drifted past. She was snipping back her reply, but strangely, James had trouble discerning her words. Until her anger made them perfectly clear.

". . . to rot on a shelf? 'She works with her hands in delight.' Is this not working with my hands? 'She makes linen garments and sells them.' What difference that my material is wood instead of cloth?" Keturah held up a carved spoon. "'Give her the works of her hands and let her works praise her in the gates.' *This* is what will praise me. Just because you don't have the sense you were born with—"

"Who denies you your carving?" James cut in.

"You think because I am a woman—"

"You are foolish, Keturah."

Blank surprise stopped her short. That look on her face—pure bewilderment—made James want to smile. How charming that expression, and how fleeting.

Scorn resolved in her face. "*Foolish?* James ben Joseph, if you think—"

Suddenly James reached and placed his calloused hand under her chin. Her eyes widened and another expression, one James could not place, dissolved the scorn.

"Keturah," James said quietly, "do you think I could bear to have you work in the same room with me again?"

Keturah's eyes, cast in a brown so very like the fig and berry shade, grew larger. She blinked, and color flared in her cheeks. James pulled his hand away. Did the color mean she was angry with him for being so forward? When he was angry, his whole face felt on fire.

Then James became aware of the silence from the other side of the workroom. Stifling a groan, he looked sideways to find Judas and Nathanael staring at them as if at a herd of camels walking backward.

"The cupboard is finished?" James snapped.

The two jumped and nearly scrambled to their task.

"Hand me the, uh, chisel," Jude said too loudly.

"You mean the rasp?" Nathanael asked, earning a scowl from Jude.

When James turned to Keturah, she was placing the last item in the sack. Without another word, she slipped the sack over her shoulder and hurried out the door.

James made to follow but stopped himself short.

"Go talk to her," Jude hissed at him.

"Shut up, Jude!" he hissed back.

He turned back to his bench. He picked up his mallet for no good reason, hefted it in his hand for a lesser reason, then, muttering no good words under his breath, threw it onto his bench and dashed out the door.

Once outside, he stopped short because there she stood, at the top of the slope, one hand on her hip.

"Foolish?" She picked up as though she had not left. "I am the foolish one?"

Feeling majestically idiotic that she had caught him running after her, and looking anywhere but at her eyes, James mumbled, "That is not the only reason. It is too dangerous for you to work here."

She followed his gaze down the slope toward Nazareth. "Of course it is dangerous, you woodenhead. But I am not interested in that reason. I want to talk about the other."

James swallowed. He could feel the sweat begin. *God of Israel, I am not good at this.*

"I—you were never interested in me," James managed to mumble, rubbing the back of his neck. How he hated this!

Keturah considered the view of the Esdraelon Plain, putting her head to one side. "No, I was not."

What was he supposed to say to that? He switched from rubbing the back of his neck to rubbing his jaw.

"When Jesus left, my heart went with him," Keturah said softly.

Now what was he supposed to say?

She contemplated the view as if to put it in memory. "Of course, once I realized why he left . . ." She airily folded her arms. "I am sure I would not like a prophet for a husband. Too much entertaining. I would have to be nice all the time, and *gracious*. I was not born for the kitchen. I was born to carve."

As though someone had pulled back the neck of his tunic and dumped cold water down his back, James felt a freezing curtain drop at the word *prophet*. Jesus managed to ruin everything. James pinched the bridge of his nose and wished Keturah away.

"What I cannot figure out for the life of me is why you hate him."

James dropped his hand to glare at her. Somehow she managed a look of condescension and sympathy at the same time. "Who said I hate him? How much do you think you know me, Keturah?"

"But you act like—"

"*He* acts like he is God's answer for Israel! He should be *here*, running the shop. He should be on the journey with Joses and Simon, collecting timber and supplies. Instead he is running around the countryside like some Zealot, embarrassing us all to ashes." Heat rose in his face. He did not want the anger now, not here, not with her. He fought to push it down. More importantly, he was saying too much. He bent to pick up a few stones and sent them singing through the air down the slope.

"Embarrassing you to ashes," Keturah repeated slowly, nodding her head in a way James did not like. "A few years ago I went to a talk your brother gave in Capernaum, before he came back to Nazareth for his—visit. Father and I went. We wanted to know what Jesus, whom we have known all our lives, had to say."

James was listening but did not want to seem interested. He folded his arms and sighed patiently.

"I watched Jesus heal a crippled man."

James' stomach rippled, and he froze his face. He would not let her see how he hated this talk.

"I watched him heal a crippled man," she repeated softly. "His leg, it was twisted at the knee. Broken as a child and not set by a physician."

He wanted to stop his ears, but dimly, from an ache inside, he wanted to hear.

"The man had not run since he was a child. I watched him run. I watched his wife nearly faint, she nearly had a seizure from astonishment. Then she cried, oh, how she cried, and rejoiced to bring the heavens down. Then she ran, James. She caught up with her husband, and they held hands and ran." She turned her face to him, eyes glistening. "A miracle, right in front of my eyes, enough for *me* to faint. How we all laughed for joy! But I will tell you the real miracle; it was the crowd. We had witnessed a thing so amazing, so impossible, and we were joined because of it. We did not even know this man, but we laughed and cried for his joy. It was . . . remarkable. It was not witnessing a miracle that changed something inside me; it was sharing it with those around."

James did not answer, for there was nothing to say.

The mountains of Megiddo in the far distance, south and west, were overlapping shadows of varied gray, barely discernible on this hazy day. The last time James had journeyed through the plain and past the mountains was for the last Passover at Jerusalem. The family did not know, but come Passover again, just over a month away, he would not go with them. Not this time.

Keturah suddenly gasped. "James, look." She pointed down the road to the village.

He looked and saw in the distance two figures coming their way. He straightened. Two familiar figures. A donkey between them pulled a cart, the contents covered by a tarp.

Relief gusted in a sigh. Neither walked with a limp; neither had any visible damage. No matter the trip had taken weeks longer than normal. They were home.

"Thanks be to God," he breathed.

"Thanks be to God," Keturah echoed.

Over his shoulder James called, "Judas! Get Mother and Jorah. Joses and Simon are back."

Jude appeared briefly at the door, face first anxious and then awash in relief. "Thank God," he said and disappeared to find the women.

"James, I am so glad," Keturah murmured as both of them waved to the travelers. They waved back, and one of them shouted a greeting.

"It's about time you decided on an honest day's work," James shouted down the slope between cupped hands.

"We found we have no talent for pillaging and thievery," Joses, the tallest of the brothers, called back. "We needed your leadership for that."

James gave a mocking laugh, loud enough for them to hear, then let his eyes enjoy the sight of them as they made their way up the slope.

Joses was tall and rugged, with a reddish brown beard and reddish brown curls, a grin as broad as it was lopsided, and eyes as kind as his smile. Simon was shorter and built like an ironsmith. Never as quick to smile, but fast with his wit. James would have him back, caustic comments and all. The bruise on his brother's cheek was long gone, he was glad to see. Both seemed thinner, perhaps, something Simon with his love of Mother's nut cakes bore well.

But the closer they came, the more clearly James could see the wear of the journey. Joses' eyes, though bright at seeing James, had a weariness that did not belong to this time of day. Simon's smile was faster to fade than usual, and he sent a few glances over his shoulder to the city.

James could not keep back the thoughts that set his stomach to simmering. At the beginning of Jesus' nonsense, customers with whom they had held a long relationship excused the silliness with grace. It was Jesus, after all. But time wore on, and with the passage of time the silliness should have gone. Now the things that had happened were enough to make the Sanhedrin at the Temple, and all the synagogues, shun Jesus and his followers. What had Joses and Simon encountered out there? How did the traders feel now, Jew and Gentile alike? Of course, no one cared much what the Gentiles thought, but in light of the Temple shunning . . .

Jorah suddenly streaked past, shrieking joyously, her over-dress billowing as the air caught her descent, arms flung overhead in that dramatic way of hers. She skipped down the slope and flung herself first at Simon, who laughed and staggered backward, catching her up in a fierce hug. She pounced on Joses next, one minute yelling, "How *could* you be so late!" and the next, "Oh, *Joses*, welcome home!"

Leaving the donkey and supplies at the foot of the slope, the brothers and the sister formed a chain of three, Jorah in the middle, and made their way to the house.

Judas and Mother joined James and Keturah, and Nathanael stood a respectful distance away.

"Where's my purple ribbon?" Jorah demanded of Simon.

"Ho! That is all she cares about, lads, not the welfare of her favorite brother!" Simon protested, but he pulled his arm from Jorah and produced a packet from a fold in his tunic. "Do you know how embarrassing it was to trade for that, surrounded by a bunch of fussing women?"

"Oh, you loved every minute of it," Jorah retorted, then reached up to put a kiss on his cheek. "Thank you, Simon."

Her face crinkled with beaming joy, fists on her hips, Mother declared, "So my young rogues are back." She opened her arms when they reached the top of the slope and took in her boys. She held them long, one arm tight about each of them. When they released one another, Mother's upbraiding started. "Four long weeks for a two-week trip? Joses and Simon ben Joseph, what were you thinking to trouble the woman who bore you?"

71

Though they chuckled and murmured at Mother's concern, James noticed the swift glance that passed between the two. And the fact that Judas instinctively met James' eye meant that he, too, was anxious to hear what news the trip brought. James hated the boil in his gut, hated the foreboding there.

But for now there were bread and wine to be fetched. For now, the domestic kind of necessary talk, which included and would satisfy the women. Nathanael had to be introduced and village news brought to the table. Later, they would speak of other things.

James did not notice when Keturah slipped away, only that when he thought to look for her, she was gone.

5

MOTHER WAS IMPATIENT to get going; Jorah had to be convinced.

"I know what you are going to talk about, and I will *not* be left out," Jorah announced to her brothers as Mother snipped some herbs for Annika from the pots outside the doorway.

"Jorah, fetch the water pots," Mother called.

"He is my brother too," Jorah stated, chin lifted and arms folded.

Simon pretended to examine the new tools at his bench. Joses squatted beside the fire pit, poking the embers with a stick. Judas idled with a stone chisel. Nathanael busied himself quietly at the corner bench, but James knew by now the apprentice's ears were as sharp as his eyes.

Jorah waited for someone to defend her presence, but no one spoke for her. Truly, James felt a niggle of guilt when he glanced at her face. If he sat and thought about it, he could muster enough pity to let her stay. But there was no time, and this was no business for women, especially his sister. He did not know what news Simon and Joses brought, but from the way they tried hard to act natural, it could not be good. Most of all, James noticed the odd way Joses seemed to ignore looks from Simon. And Simon's looks were anything but good.

"Jorah, please leave," James said.

"I want to know what is going on," Jorah replied evenly. James knew that tone—and knew better the set of her chin.

"Jorah," James warned, rising from his stool.

Jorah's cheeks darkened as she looked at each brother. Her eyes fell on Simon, her sometime ally, and she appealed to him.

"Simon . . . you know I have a right to hear news of him," she argued, and a note of pleading came into her voice. "Please, Simon. I belong here too."

"She is not a child," Nathanael muttered, earning instant scowls from the brothers.

"This is family business," James growled at him.

"You are not her brother," Judas added.

Nathanael kept his eyes properly downcast, fiddling with the strap of his sandal. James saw the quick sympathetic glance he threw toward Jorah, but he did not speak further. Smart boy. As hotheaded as Nathanael was, he could easily have argued on Jorah's behalf, yet he would not risk being thrown out to miss the news himself.

"Come, Jorah," Mother called from outside. "Annika will be so relieved."

Jorah waited, still imploring Simon with her eyes. He would not look at her.

"Jorah, obey your mother," James said quietly.

She folded her arms and pressed her lips into a white line. She waited a moment more, then all but stomped across the room to the smallyard passage and vanished behind the curtain. She reappeared with the two water jars and marched across the room to the doorway. On her way out, she slapped a kiss on the mezuzah, then said loftily over her shoulder, "We shall see who will fix your meals when Mother is gone."

Nathanael covered for his snort by coughing loudly.

Judas went to the door and watched them leave. Presently he turned around. "They are gone."

Each brother made for his own stool. News from the land had always been taken this way, as long as James could remember, each family member fortified at his own bench. Father would always snug his stool against the wall and rest his back there. Joses used to sit on his bench, not his stool, swinging his legs. Jesus would put his stool in the space between his bench and Simon's. Strangely, that was where Nathanael was seated now, tipped back on his stool. James was getting used to the presence at the corner bench. It was good to hear tinkering from that area again.

"Did you sell the oak benches?" Jude asked.

James did not like the way Simon continued to look at Joses, nor the way Joses continued to avoid his gaze. Simon took his glare away and muttered to Jude, "We sold them."

"Fair price?" Jude said.

As Jude and Simon discussed the sale, James rubbed his lower lip and regarded Joses.

It was no secret that Joses was not as resentful over the doings of Jesus as the rest of them. Joses was the quickest to come to his defense. Quickest to excuse the craziness. He sat at his stool, still as stone, staring blankly at a pile of drying wood near the fire pit. James could see he was not listening to Jude and Simon. But what was in that grave blankness on Joses' face? James pretended to fold his arms over his stomach, to cover for the fingers that dug into his gut.

". . . could have gotten more," Simon was saying with a shrug, "but we—"

"What happened, Joses?" James asked.

The question silenced Simon. He picked up the bowl he had left half-finished and turned it over in his hands. "Yes, Joses," he said as he inspected the bowl, "why don't you tell them?"

Joses raised his eyes to James. "I wanted to see for myself."

James looked from Joses to Simon. "See what?"

Joses' eyes fell back to the pile of wood. He rested his elbows on his knees and rubbed his hands together. "Three years now," he muttered, almost to himself. "It was time to decide my own mind about him."

His voice high with incredulity, James said, "Decide your own—what is to decide, Joses?"

"Oh, you would be surprised," Simon drawled.

James slowly rose from his stool. "Joses, if you tell me—"

"Sit down, James!" Joses snapped, which James did only from surprise. When Joses finished glaring at him, he again stared hard into the woodpile.

"This is bigger than we are," Joses said, talking to himself and his brothers at once. "That is what scares me. It is not the Romans, not the leaders of Israel. They do not matter anymore."

James turned his stare on Simon, who lifted his hands. "You see what these four weeks have been like?" he complained. "Half the time I did not know who he was talking to. He's getting as crazy as Jesus himself."

Joses went on as if he didn't hear. "It is bigger, I say. I don't know how and I don't know why. But stand back and look at it all, from the very beginning until now. There is a pattern."

"You see what I am saying? He is going crazy."

"Shut up, Simon," Judas said. To Joses he said, "What *are* you saying? We all know Jesus is not like us. Set apart, Mother has told us. We have known it since birth. He is destined to be a great prophet or a great leader." Jude narrowed his eyes. "But you are saying something else."

"How many great leaders do you know who raise the dead?"

Silence froze the workroom.

Joses could get no one to meet his gaze. He rose and began to patrol the room like a Roman, appraising each brother as he passed. "Come now . . . answer the question, anyone. By now you have heard about Lazarus." Joses leaned close to James' ear and whispered, "We cannot pretend *that* didn't happen." He pulled away and continued his tour, getting no one to meet his gaze except Nathanael, who could not take his eyes from him.

He came to stand in the middle of the workroom, where the awnings did not give shade. He looked oddly alone in this workroom of men. The ascending sun picked up the red in his brown hair. It also highlighted the weariness in his visage. When last had James really looked at Joses? The thought surprised him into studying his face. Did all the brothers look like Joses these days? That weary? That dispirited?

"We cannot ignore it any longer," Joses said in a near

whisper. "We cannot hole up here and pretend it isn't happening." His voice gained strength. "He is *healing* people. Our own brother is creating eyes for the blind. People lame from birth are walking—they are *walking*, James! Where in all our holy books has this happened through one man?"

The black acid in James' gut burgeoned, threatening to breach the perimeter of his stomach. He bit the inside of his lip to stifle a groan of pain.

"Tell me where it is! Not Elisha, not even Elijah, accomplished in a lifetime what Jesus has done in three years."

James winced at the mention of the two prophets. The family had heard enough about them the last time Jesus visited Nazareth.

"We need to do something," Judas muttered, rubbing the scanty beard on his jawline.

Joses barked an incredulous laugh. "Do *what*, Judas? What are we to 'do' about a brother who can smother a storm at the flick of his wrist? It is out of our hands. There is nothing left for us to do but decide if we are for him or against him."

James ignored that, flat ignored it, and said, "Jude's right. He is still our blood. We are still responsible for him, no matter what he is up to. Even if he abandoned us, we cannot abandon him."

"He did not abandon us," Joses protested.

James was on his feet in a bound. "What do you call it? He's the firstborn! When Father died, he became the patriarch. Some patriarch. He left us; he left Mother; he left the business." James flung his arm toward the doorway. "Call him Esau. He's as good as sold his birthright."

Nathanael suddenly spoke up. "So are you for him or

against him?" James was not sure if the question was for him or for Joses, but it gained a stare from all of the brothers.

"What is your name again, *apprentice*?" Simon scoffed at him.

"Don't you have some work to do?" James said.

The amber eyes narrowed, and Nathanael slowly reached for a half-finished stool, scowling at James as he did so.

James understood. Had not Nathanael protected the family this past long week? Had he not escorted Raziel back to Annika's with indignation not much less than James' own? He deserved more than dismissal, James knew . . . but the brothers did not know Nathanael the way James did. In one week, though James would not let the lad know it, Nathanael had entrenched a place in his heart as no one since . . . Well, making a new friend these days was a rare thing indeed. But with the others, Nathanael had not yet earned the right to be heard.

"If we could get him away from his band of followers, we could talk sense into his crazy head," James said. He tried hard to make his voice calm. Sensible. Joses was going in a direction that was anything but.

"Didn't we try that one other time?" Simon muttered. "We thought from the beginning that he had lost his senses. A rescue effort did not work then, and it is too late now."

"What do you suggest, James?" Joses asked. "Sneak up on him in the middle of the night, throw a sack over his head, and drag him away? Oh, that is good. His fishermen friends would not let us within five footsteps of him if they got a whiff of what we intended. One of them is the size of a bear and twice as mean."

"I hear one of them is a tax collector," Nathanael offered.

At the ensuing vicious glares, he quickly muttered, "I'm working, I'm working."

"We still need to do something," Jude said. "If we are lucky, we can slip him away to someplace in the country, and maybe all this fervor will die down. We will care for him until he regains his senses. Maybe stick him with the Essenes at Qumran."

James looked at Jude sideways; wasn't that his own idea?

Joses shook his head. "I still say it is bigger than that. It even runs in the family. Look at our cousin John."

"Exactly!" James declared and spread his arms wide, looking at the sky as though he had finally been understood. "And look where his nonsense got him! Excellent point, Joses."

Joses turned away from him and went again to the fire pit. He peered long into the slumbering embers. At length, he murmured, "'I am the voice of one crying in the wilderness, make way for the coming of the *Lord*.'"

James felt a chill rise on his shoulders and flush down his arms.

"We all know who John meant," Joses said, quiet and low.

God of Israel, how he wanted to press his hands to his ears. But here it was, the restlessness of three long years now come to a crest. His own voice tinny and hollow, James heard himself say, "Well, then, Joses . . . tell us what to do. Tell us what to believe. Tell us *how* to believe."

"Yes. Tell us, Joses," Simon said with a smirk.

"Shut up, Simon," Jude said.

"I am only saying, step back and look at the whole. Look at it from the beginning." Joses pulled his gaze from the fire pit, his tone becoming urgent. "We need to investigate this.

Investigate our own brother just as the ones from Temple investigate him. We need to speak with Mother and hear things from her own lips. We need to talk with the people who have witnessed the things he has done. We need to hear *exactly* what he is saying. We must get all of the facts and think logically and soberly. Then we must make our judgment, brothers."

"He dragged me all over the countryside with this nonsense!" Simon erupted, slamming his fist on his bench. Tools jumped, and one fell to the ground. "Thank God I am finally home! You two talk to him. He will not listen to me."

"Where did you go?" Judas asked, surprised.

"It would take less time to tell where we did *not* go," Simon said bitterly. "We spent only two days in Gaza, didn't we, Joses? From there we went east and north. Jerusalem. Bethany. Jericho. Ephraim. Oh, and while we were in Bethany, could we stop to see our own kin? Devorah's house was probably within a stadium, but no. No time. And on our way north, would he take the road closest to the Jordan? No. We went through Samaria."

"Samaria?" James demanded.

"'The water in Samaria is dirtier than pig slop,'" Nathanael quoted.

"One more word out of you . . ." Judas warned, pointing the end of his mallet at him.

"Ho, that is not all, lads," Simon continued. He crossed the room, put his arms about himself, and leaned his shoulder against the stone wall, glaring at Joses, who squatted at the pit. "By this time we were running low on supplies. We had not sold the benches yet, and we had very little food and no money to put up at an inn, so we had to inquire for homes to stay.

The first time we inquired, we made the mistake of identifying ourselves. Didn't we, Joses?"

A flush appeared on Joses' cheeks. "I make no pretense that the situation is bad. You blame me, Simon, but it seems I am the only one looking for answers."

"Oh, we got an answer that time, did we not? The man threw at us what he had handy—a bucket full of fish guts."

"Will you let him talk?" James said between his teeth. He kept his clenched fists fast at his side. He had promised himself he would never strike Simon again.

"I wanted to know what the people were saying," Joses said, rubbing his eyes, his voice weary. "The people, just the *am ha-aretz*. Not the leaders, not the ones trying to stir up another revolt. If I heard one more opinion from a scholar, or a scribe, or an Essene, or a Zealot—especially a Zealot—I would tear out my beard. Or tear out theirs."

James kept his surprise hidden. Joses too? Not gentle Joses.

Joses waited a moment before he continued, studying the embers. When he spoke, it was as if to himself. "It occurred to me on the road to Gaza that Jesus never really went to the leaders . . . he went to the people. I wanted to listen to them; I wanted to see if I could find some of the people whose stories we have heard right in this room. I wanted to look in their eyes. I wanted to hear it from their own lips."

"That makes sense." Nathanael nodded.

"And what did these people have to say?" Judas asked.

"Make a good collection of stories someday." Simon snorted. "I wish I had had my writing materials with me."

Joses turned to look Simon up and down. James watched carefully; it was Joses who now expected something out of

Simon, and Simon, incredibly, who caught a meaning from Joses' face and looked away.

"Simon, why don't you tell them about the fellow from Decapolis?"

The sour smirk on Simon's face gradually lessened. He looked down at his feet. One foot toed at some stone chips not cleared away from a newly made roof roller. He scraped the gravelly chips into a pile.

"Gone four weeks, and this place is a mess," he muttered. "And that with a new apprentice."

"From Gadarene in Kursi," Joses prompted quietly.

Odd, odd, *odd*, the look on Simon's face. James realized he was holding his breath. Simon did not act this way. Nobody cowed Simon. Nobody.

Simon shrugged and chuckled—a nervous chuckle—and said, "All the other stories could have been fabricated." His grin came down. "This one . . . I still do not know what to make of it."

Jude squinted at him. "Gadarene. Is this the one about the demon-possessed man?"

"Where the demons went into the pigs?" James added.

"I thought there were two of them," Nathanael put in. "Men, I mean." At James' look, he added, "Not two pigs. I didn't mean two pigs. This stool is almost finished, by the way."

"We only spoke to one man, right, Simon?" Joses said.

"Yes," Simon said absently, eyes on the stone chips.

"Joses?" came a thin call from outside. "Joses!"

"Abigail," Joses breathed, his weary face suddenly livened. He hurried to the doorway, quickly brushed a kiss on the mezuzah, and ran outside.

The rest of them followed Joses outside and watched the big man catch up his wife in a fierce hug. Two children danced around them—Benjamin, his head only reaching Joses' waist, and sunny little Hepsibah, three years old. Shrieking delight, the children jumped and plucked at Joses' tunic until finally Benjamin grabbed hold of his belt and scaled Joses' back. He wrapped his arms around Joses' neck and lay against his father's broad back, his short legs dangling.

Hepsi hooked her hands on Joses' belt and swung from it. Joses, laughing, released his wife and, putting his arms out, turned in a circle to the joy of the children.

"What is this?" he exclaimed. "Two little monkeys instead of my children? Where have my children gone? Benjamin!" he pretended to call to the hills between cupped hands. "Hepsibah! Where are you?"

"I am here, Abba, I am here," Hepsi piped, releasing his belt to tug on his sleeve.

"What? Where?" Joses looked all around, then down. "Oh, there you are!" He knelt to scoop her up.

James folded his arms and leaned against the doorway. It did not take long for Abigail, once she knew Joses was all right, to chide her husband about his long absence. With both children hanging from his neck, one in the back and one in the front, Joses pleaded with his hands while Abigail planted her own firmly on her hips. They started for their home, talking as they went.

Joses would be back in the early afternoon, after the midday meal. Sabbath began at sundown; there were the preparations, so he knew Joses would not tarry. James turned to look at Simon, who stood apart, watching Joses and Abigail leave. Soon he would learn of the news that had bested Simon. And Simon would learn of the visitor to the workshop this morning.

He watched the family head for the back ridge, which would take them to the path through the terraced strips of land. Poor Joses. Raziel from Kerioth might be the one to make him pluck his beard.

Joses' words were enough to make James pluck his own. That which James had ignored, that which had lurked since the beginning, was given form and could never be taken back. *There is nothing left for us to do but decide if we are for him or against him.*

6

What would his friends in Caesarea say if they saw him? He could hear Theudas and Zadok ben Zakkai now.

You may look like Nathanael, but our Nathanael would not bow his head before a meal. Our Nathanael would not think twice about uttering a curse word. And, heaven help us, our Nathanael would not kiss a mezuzah.

That last, of course, had been done when no one was looking. James was on a visit to the brush; Jorah and her mother were in the courtyard. Nathanael had been hauling a block of stone into the workroom, and suddenly he had paused at the rectangular metal ornament fixed onto the right-hand side of the doorpost, and even more suddenly put a kiss on it. The action had put instant fire in his cheeks, and he had glanced about quickly to be sure no one had seen him.

It was not the only thing Nathanael had surprised himself with these days. If he were not careful, he would end up religious. We are Jews of the land, he and his friends would fiercely declare, the *am ha-aretz*. Who needed all the baubles and bluffery that belonged to the religious?

But here was something different; he knew it the first day he came. It was not just this home, and it was not Nazareth . . . it was Annika. He had met her nearly two weeks ago, when he passed her in the street. Not that Annika herself drew his interest, but rather that she was talking to a beggar. That brought the second look. Nobody talked to beggars. You flipped a beggar a copper pruta, if the beggar were lucky that day. You stepped around beggars; you ignored them. You did not talk to them. Or talk *with* them. Annika had been sitting on her ample haunches, listening to the legless pauper speak. He would have taken her for a beggar herself, but for the fact that she was swathed in a fine weave of linen.

He knew fabric. His mother's "visitors" often gave her gifts of finely woven cotton from Egypt, sometimes silken lengths from the East. *Nathanael, lad, look at this color . . . have you ever seen a finer indigo? Nathanael, look at this cloth . . . doesn't it feel like milkweed down?* He had been with his mother on countless trips to trade for fabric, her face always veiled in frothy layers of multicolored scarves.

What if his mother could see him now?

He would sooner eat a stone roof roller, chip by chip, than admit to one of his friends that living with religious people was not so bad. In fact, despite the multitudinous precepts these poor people had to remember, Nathanael found the experience rather . . . nice. In a quaint, amusing sort of way, of course.

A mezuzah set in every passageway. Prayers before and after meals. Blessings said before the prayers. Wash your hands. (But they are not dirty.) Wash them anyway. Do not drink that water; it was standing uncovered. (But I am thirsty.) It is forbidden. Torah reading, Nathanael. (Didn't we do that already?) Twice, Nathanael. Twice daily. Prayers, Nathanael. (But we just . . .) Three times, lad. (He did not point out to them, as a testament to his longsuffering, that the *Shema* recited in the morning and the evening actually made the prayer number five times a day. For some reason they did not count that.) The obligations seemed to come just when he was at a crucial point in a project. At one time—not so long ago—the whole crazy situation would have sent him hollering into the hills . . . but at least these people were genuine, like old Thomas and Sarah back home, and that made it tolerable. He had a soft spot for genuine people, religious or not.

There were other things. Meals on time, as scheduled as the rise of the sun. Breakfast at Annika's, a light midmeal at James'—try as he might, he could not call the place "Mary's" as Annika did—and another meal when he arrived at twilight at Annika's. And the portions! Annika cooked for him as though he were three, and was offended if he did not eat in kind. He had learned to eat less at the midmeal to be extra hungry in the evening.

His missed his mother, to be sure. And Caesarea Maritima was a much bigger city than Nazareth, more to see, more to do. They had a *gymnasium* in Caesarea, and an amphitheater. And, of course, they had Herod the Great's famous harbor, as magnificent as the Piraeus in Athens. The Jewish enclave was smaller in Caesarea; there were more Greeks, more culture.

What was in Nazareth? Dirty sheep. Superstitious, backward farmers. Not much to draw a person here.

"More figs, Nathanael?" Jorah asked, offering a plate piled with dried fruit. He took a few and nodded to her, planning to whisk them into a fold in his tunic when she was not looking. She might not understand about Annika's meals. Sometimes it went that way with women; you had to insult one to please another.

He glanced about the enclosed courtyard while Simon droned on to James and Judas and the women about his journey. Nathanael gave a languid yawn and a stretch, and hoped Simon noticed his lack of interest. He did not like Simon. The man was a whiner, with no imagination.

Nathanael had planned to regale James and Jorah, and now Judas, with another tale from Caesarea, as he had every midmeal this past week. He had been thinking on what to tell early this morning, before the ordeal with Raziel. It was almost pathetic the way they had eagerly paid Nathanael attention for his stories. What tale he could not remember he made up, and the misadventures of his friends became his own. Anything to distract these people from what loomed beneath. He could always tell a story better than Zadok ben Zakkai anyway.

But this Simon had them plod through every step of the boring journey to Gaza, through every tiny insult suffered from people with as little imagination as Simon himself. James' somber face would have been bright if it were Nathanael they gave attention to. He gusted a sigh, which he hoped Mary interpreted as a happy-stomach sigh and Simon a bored, brainless one.

Who cared that Simon and Joses were refused a trade in

Gaza because Jesus had insulted a Temple leader? This family had better grow a skin as thick as the calluses on Judas' hands if they planned on surviving ritual humiliation. Was he not the son of a harlot? They didn't hear him whining about it. And after a while, it was not humiliation at all. It was life; you dealt with it. Sure, it stings at first, once you realize what the fools are saying. Blisters come before calluses. But you learn to be smarter than the fools who cast the insults, faster with your wit and quicker with your hands—it wasn't only a gecko Nathanael could hit with a rock at fifty paces.

He caught a glance from Jorah, and quickly looked away. Jorah he had not expected. She was different from most of the girls he knew. She had a sense of humor, and so far did not appear to be ridiculous. She could also make a man look twice with or without a fine weave of linen. Somehow Jorah managed to confuse his purpose here. With her, it was easy to imagine that he really was just a driftabout apprentice, fresh to Nazareth and looking for work, a man who had seen a bit of the world and would indulge them with a story or two.

He had not expected any of them.

Luckily for him, he had a friend who knew the carpenter's trade. The bit about his uncle was not true; he did not have an uncle. But he had spent enough time with his friend to gain a fact or two about working with stone and wood. He had enough handy memories to bluff his way into this shop.

His friends knew many things about him, but they did not know all. And this he could never have explained. How, one day when lounging about with his companions on the harbor in Caesarea, he had heard a voice his friends did not. They thought his newly pale face was from a stomach rebelling at too much wine the night before; they had chuckled as he stag-gered from the group, waving off the laughter that followed.

This he did not tell them, how the voice that day said, *Seek James,* how nothing he could do would make the compulsion leave, and how sometimes at night he would rise in a sweat to stand on a hill and gaze somewhere east. How one day he finally packed a few things and left, determined to seek until he found.

No, Jorah he did not expect. Neither kind Mary, who gave the religious as good a name as Thomas and Sarah—nor Annika, whose severe appearance cloaked a heart filled with a fierce, two-fisted goodness. Judas he had known barely a day and liked him already, and Simon he had known less than half a day and did not. Nathanael figured Joses to be the smartest one in the lot—the most *sensible* one, anyway, asking ques-tions and using his imagination to muddle through a hard family crisis—but James . . . James, though he had known him a week, knew him better than the rest and liked him best of all—James he could not figure out.

He looked at him now, seated next to Simon, scooping spiced barley with his bread from the bowl on the tripod table. His face dark, James chewed thoughtfully as he listened to Simon describe yet another snubbing. Nathanael threw a glare at Simon—why couldn't they talk about something else?—and resumed his study of James.

Though he had to be thirty years old, he supposed the girls would still think James handsome. Truth to tell, probably not as handsome as Nathanael himself. But he did have a brilliant smile, at the rare times he showed it, freshening up his whole face. And the dark-brown eyes, usually muddy with anxiety, sometimes glittered with an amusement Nathanael suspected was formerly common.

He would doubt his right hand sooner than he would doubt the compulsion to come here. He never doubted the compulsion. But the *reason*, yes, that he questioned.

He had only lived with Annika a few days before he confided his real reason for being in Nazareth. Something about Annika made him trust her. Something made him believe she wouldn't think he was crazy, and she didn't. After airily informing him that she never had believed his story of searching for a long-lost brother, Annika herself came up with the idea for apprenticeship. Nathanael had thought that the reason for *Seek James* would become plain as soon as he met the one whose name the voice had spoken. But nothing extraordinary happened the moment he met James. That didn't come until a Zealot named Avi walked through the door.

He couldn't keep a smile back as he remembered the way James had laughed like a child at the sudden departure of Avi and his friend. His smile came down. What James did not know, what James could not see, was the flush of indignation that had risen like a sudden storm and had carried him to Avi with the gouge adze. Placid as a rock on the outside, huge with fury on the inside, Nathanael had played his part as though born for it. That fissure of power he had felt within gave sudden shape to his reason to seek James.

Seek James surely had meant for him first to find and then to protect. What else could it mean? What else did the son of a whore have to offer, except muscle for expulsion and humor to lighten the load?

He never asked questions about the oldest brother, upon

whom it all seemed to pivot. There would be time for that later. Now was the time to obey the compulsion without question. James and the others thought the situation was bad. Nathanael glanced toward the curtained passage to the workroom and beyond; they had no idea.

Joses had said it was bigger, and so it was. He was the only one who seemed to sense it. Who cared if a few people came to insult them and be bothersome, or if others came to marvel and collect tokens? Tossing out those pests was the easy part. But what of the black clouds, which Nathanael thought he could see if he turned around fast enough? What of that?

"And then he gave me the haughtiest look and *turned his back on me*," Simon sniveled like a mewling babe.

Any other time, a person who irritated him like this spineless whelp would have gotten a fist in the face. Any other time, he would have called rude things to Jorah if he had seen her in the market with his companions. He shook his head ruefully. Simon's face remained intact, a marvel in itself, and God help the one who was rude to Jorah. He was a commissioned man, sent like a prophet of old. He did not have time for petty things like a whiner or a pretty face. He allowed himself a very small smile. Yes, his friends would be astonished to see him now.

"I want to hear about the fellow from Decapolis," Judas said to Simon. Nathanael smirked; if he himself caught the subtle taunt in those words, then surely Simon did too.

Simon shifted position on the low couch. He leaned to poke at the fruit on the tray and chose a fig. He shrugged. "What is there to say? You have already heard about it. The fellow stuck to the same story."

"Oh no," James said, folding his arms and fixing Simon with a determined grin. "Tell us, or we'll get Joses to."

But Simon didn't seem to hear. The hand with the fig lowered. He was remembering again, the same look on his face as when he complained about the stone chips Nathanael had forgotten to clean up. Nathanael rolled his eyes. Simon's reluctance to speak was nearly as annoying as—

"We talked to so many. I was purely sick of it by the time we got to Decapolis. Sick of trying to figure out who was exaggerating and who was not. And who was outright lying—we had seen that too. But when we met Kardus . . ."

Nobody dared prompt him. He wasn't acting his petulant self. He even spoke quietly.

"It did not take us long to find him. That was the problem with some of the reports. We would try to track someone down, only to find that that person was now among those who followed Jesus. Not always, but much of the time. This Kardus was not far from where Jesus had first found him." Simon broke off to reach for his cup of watered wine. He stared into his cup between sips.

Nathanael glanced at the others. Jorah sat on a carpet at the foot of her mother, who sat in a tripod chair. Each of them had a basket of work, Jorah a mending basket and Mary a basket of wool to clean. Jorah's sat in her lap untouched, and Mary's fingers absently worked the tufts of wool through an iron-toothed comb. James was on the low couch next to Simon, perhaps not aware of the fact that he was rubbing his hand over his stomach—probably ate too much—and Judas sat next to Nathanael on the other low couch against the stone wall, eyes as intent on Simon as the rest. Sunlight sneaked through a gap in the awning and made a golden arc on Judas' shoulder.

Nathanael did not want to waste his time with Simon's slowness to speak. He gazed about the courtyard and put his thoughts to other things.

Here in the courtyard the awning stretched over the entire area from stone wall to stone wall. Only at either end was the courtyard open to the sky, where Mary had her oven in the corner, and at the opposite side where the smallyard met the sleeping rooms and the workroom. Spring rains were slowing down. Soon the heavy awnings for winter rains would be replaced with the lighter summertime awnings to protect against the sun.

Nathanael would have a place like this someday. His mother lived in the city, one of the nastier parts of Caesarea, in the middle of a row of houses that shared a common courtyard. Here, there was serenity, not the ruckus of two dozen children, not four different ovens with a passel of chattering women making meals.

Annika's place was even worse. Ten or twelve homes bordered a common courtyard, with double that number in families. Many families lived in the upper rooms, either renters or relations of the house owner. James and his family did not know how good they had it. To enjoy a meal in peace, to be able to breathe and think. To be able to step outside and not smell the stink of the refuse pit or hear the argument of the couple next door.

Annika loved living in the city; Nathanael, he would live in a place like this if he ever got himself a wife. Might even take up carpentry; he wasn't half bad at it. He glanced down at his palms and traced his fingertips over newly forming calluses.

His gaze drifted to Simon, whom he realized still wasn't speaking.

"Simon?" his mother said softly.

"I was afraid."

Simon was staring into his cup, then noticed the silence. "Don't look at me like that," he said with a return to his former sourness. "Any one of you would have been afraid."

Nathanael could not stop his own smirk. Simon did not know him very well.

"But why were you afraid?" Jorah asked. "There was nothing to be afraid of, because Jesus cast the demons out of him."

"That's why I was afraid."

It made no sense to Nathanael, but from the looks on the other faces, it made perfect, if disquieting, sense to them.

Just when Nathanael wanted to hear more—surely there was more—suddenly no one expected anything else from Simon. Nathanael looked from face to face . . . this was ridiculous! What made the man act so strange? Didn't anyone else want to know? Or did the troubled faces mean they already knew?

Nathanael frowned. Surely this Kardus, this demon man, wasn't the same man his mother used to scare him into doing chores when he was a child. . . . *Nathanael, fetch that water, or I swear I'll feed you to the madman in the tombs.* Of course, the madman was on the other side of the Sea of Galilee, so the stories went, but even miles away in Caesarea his reputation had children wide-eyed with fascinated fear. The tales the children alone could conjure were enough to prompt them to obedience.

"This isn't the same man who lived in the tombs, is it?" Nathanael asked doubtfully. Nobody answered him. Somebody sighed.

He shook his head incredulously. The famous madman of his childhood? The man was a legend—their brother ended a legend.

"Mothers everywhere will need a different reason to get their children to do chores," he muttered.

"Shimron will have to come up with new jokes," Judas put in. "Remember what he told the man who had crossed from Kursi to Capernaum? The traveler said, 'Has anyone ever heard the commotion from the tombs near Kursi? Such awful screams and groaning.' And Shimron replied, 'Of course. The man did not pay his Temple tax.'"

Nathanael laughed with the rest, and if theirs faded faster, at least it was laughter.

"Why didn't you tell me about Raziel?"

Joses stood in the smallyard, holding the curtain flap aside, breathing hard. The tinge of red in his dark beard matched the ruddy color in his face. He still wore his prayer shawl from the midday prayers, fallen down to his shoulders.

Simon sat up. "What is this?"

Joses glowered at the brothers. "It should have been the first thing you told us! What were you thinking, not to tell us right away?" The awning did not stretch over the smallyard. Sunlight made the prayer shawl glow next to the shade. Joses looked like an angry religious fanatic.

"How did you hear about Raziel?" James asked.

Simon stared at them. "Raziel? The Zealot?"

"Abigail told me," Joses fumed. "Seems he paid the shop a visit this morning."

"He *what*?" Simon exploded.

"*I* told Abigail, when we went to the well," Jorah said, chin lifted. "She is family. She had a right to know."

Judas turned on her angrily. "Who else did you tell?"

"Do you think I am stupid?" she snapped back.

"Why didn't you tell us right away?" Joses demanded.

"We were going to tell you. It only happened this morning," Judas muttered. "It didn't seem right, just when you came home."

"If *I* had been allowed to stay, it would have been the first thing we discussed," Jorah declared, folding her arms.

Simon rose from the couch, glaring at James. "Raziel the Zealot was here, and just now we find out?"

"He was here very early, and not for long," James said. "Nathanael escorted him back to Annika's."

"Annika's?" Joses groaned.

Simon's glare came to rest on Nathanael, and he rose to meet it.

"You do not have anything to worry about," Nathanael said evenly, looking from Simon to Joses. "He came to Annika's under the cover of darkness last night, and he will leave in the same fashion tonight."

But the mother was shaking her head, face fixed with either worry or . . . "No, he will not be leaving tonight."

"But—"

"Sabbath, Nathanael. Raziel cannot leave because in a few hours Sabbath begins."

Nathanael watched the reactions. A hissing intake of breath from Jorah, a groan from James, an expletive from Judas that earned only a murmur from his bleak-faced mother. And a cold glower from Simon, shared with Joses.

Their reactions were confusing enough, and to top it all, Nathanael could not help but feel an odd sense of responsibility. The Zealot stayed at Annika's, after all. He had slept in the same room, on a pallet rolled out beside Nathanael's bed. "I will make sure he leaves, Sabbath or no," he began to assure them.

"It is forbidden, apprentice." Simon scowled at him. "Did we hire a Gentile?"

"No. You hired an *am ha-aretz*." He might get a fist in the face yet.

Simon looked him up and down. "What's the difference?"

"I am as Jewish as you are, whether you like it or not, you—"

"Travel is forbidden on Sabbath, Nathanael," Jorah broke in.

"But surely in this case—"

"It is forbidden," Mary said quietly.

Nathanael tried to take it in, tried to make sense of it. He stared at each of them, one by one. "Let's make sure we're talking about the same thing: Raziel brings an immediate threat to your household—and owing to his reputation, Rome could think you and he are up to something like, oh, an insurrection. And you allow him to remain in Nazareth one more second because of custom?"

"It is more than custom . . . it is law," Joses said wearily from the passageway.

"Whose law?"

"Our law," Simon stated scornfully, as though Nathanael should know. "Jewish law."

"A Jew may not travel more than two thousand paces on Sabbath. That is the length of a Sabbath day's journey," Joses explained.

"He knew this," James growled from the couch, his tone low and feral. "Raziel knew the danger."

Nathanael felt a flash of anger, at many things at once. Customs and—he shook his head in pure disbelief. He wished he had a chance to tell this Jesus what an uproar he had caused. If Nathanael had brothers and sisters of his own, would they have felt as strongly about him as these people felt about their precious Jesus? He wished he could catch up with the man just to tell him how lucky he was.

"How about if I set this Raziel on your donkey and lead him out of the city myself?" Nathanael reasoned. "He would just be sitting, not traveling—exactly. It's all the donkey. And if that's not enough, you can tell God it's my fault."

It was a perfect solution, but nobody seemed eager for it.

"Remember what Father used to say?" Judas muttered. "'The rules for the Sabbath are like mountains hanging by a hair, for Scripture is scanty and the rules are many.'"

Surprisingly, Mary chuckled at that. "He learned that from his friend Saul." She glanced at Nathanael. "Saul was a Sadducee. The Sadducees do not hold much with the oral traditions."

"But that sounds like an oral tradition," Nathanael pointed out with a small shrug.

Mary surprised him again by another soft laugh. Then she stood and set her basket aside. She smoothed down her tunic, then clasped her hands in front and raised her face. She gave a small sigh, then said, "Children, I am leaving."

Dead silence. Nathanael saw Jorah's fists, tight and white in her lap, and he watched the expression on James' face harden to cold stone. But Mary . . . he blinked, and his breath caught.

What was this face? What was this look? Did all mothers look like this for their children? He watched in wonder. Those eyes, stricken, yet filled with . . . had his own mother ever once looked this way? If she had ever looked like this for him, even once, he could forgive her anything. God his witness, he could.

"It must be hard for you," Nathanael said suddenly to Mary. "Jesus needs you. These here need you."

She turned eyes filled with misery upon him. "Yes," she whispered.

James' voice splashed cold and wet. "So, Mother. Tell us . . . when are you leaving?" He put his feet on the little table and folded his hands over his stomach. He settled his insolent look on his mother. "Anytime soon?"

Nathanael's fingers slowly clenched.

"Two days," Mary still whispered, brushing at a tear. "Eli is taking me."

James nodded, his jaw thrust to one side as though considering which tool to use for a job. Nathanael held his breath. *So help me, James, say the wrong thing to her and I will—*

"Why not leave now if you want to leave us so badly?" James drawled. "Leave with Raziel tomorrow morning. He brought you the scarf, after all. Perhaps he tires of his wife. Maybe he is looking for another."

The shouting commotion raised by the brothers and the

sister was enough to billow the awning, and that was commendable, but only Nathanael strode to James at the couch and lifted him from it by a fistful of tunic. He pulled James' face into his own, noted the surprise in the dark-brown eyes, and dragged him over to the dye pots in the corner of the courtyard. Purple, with the sodden hyacinths? Or yellow, with the bobbing rounds of onion? He chose purple.

Before James could guess what was coming, Nathanael swung him facedown into the pot of purple and dropped his knee between James' shoulder blades to hold him there. James' frantic struggles sloshed the water and threatened to tip the pot, but Nathanael held him fast. He gave it a three-count, vaguely wondering why the family were not pulling him off, then yanked James up. He thrashed blindly to grab Nathanael, coughing, sputtering, choking in air as well as chunks of hyacinth, which made him cough harder. Nathanael swung him into the water again, gave it another three-count, and hauled him up in a shower of purple. Then he dragged him to the center of the courtyard to Mary.

He allowed James to bend double, coughing and snorting, spitting out flower clumps.

At last the coughing stopped, and James held his position, bent with hands braced on his knees, gulping air, dripping purple. True, it was not as deep a purple as Nathanael had hoped—he had not steeped him long enough—but he knew the top half of James' undyed tunic would dry at least to a light lavender. Nathanael's mother often dyed her own fabric. He picked hyacinths with her every year.

James slowly straightened. His beard dripped. His eyelashes dripped. His hair, like a black sodden sponge, sent tiny streams of dark water down his neck. Wet bits of hyacinth clung to his beard, and some spotted his cheeks. One clump sagged from his eyebrow. He slowly reached to brush it away, eyes ever on his mother. And as Nathanael watched the two regard one another, a strange tightness gripped his chest.

The mother's tears dripped down to wet her clothing. Her son, Nathanael could see, tried to keep the tears in his eyes from falling.

"Mother . . ."

"It's all right, Son," Mary replied in a whisper. She reached and brushed flowers from his cheek.

"I am so sorry, Mother."

"It's all right."

Nathanael slowly backed away. He brushed past Joses in the smallyard, who gave him an unreadable look as he passed. Nathanael hunched his shoulders up, an old belligerent habit he had had since he was small, and stalked through the curtained passage. They would let him go for this. And what reason would he give Annika for coming home so early?

He paused in the doorway and gazed past the slope at the mountainous hills of Nazareth. In Caesarea, they had more culture. They had the Great Stadium and Herod's harbor. Nathanael's tunic was more fashionable than those of these poor rustics. Nobody here wore the thin leather straps about the head as they did in Caesarea.

His fingers were on something smooth. The mezuzah. He ran his fingertips over it; he pressed his palm flat against it. His fingers curled around it as if to dig it from the stone. He pushed off from the doorway and started for the back ridge to Annika's. He broke into a trot, then hard and furious into a run.

7

HALF HIS TUNIC clung wetly to him, and the other half was streaked and spotted with damp purple. He shook his head to one side to loosen water in his ear. Simon stepped back at the ensuing spatter of drops.

It was Simon who finally broke the silence in the courtyard. "What are you going to do, James?"

James looked down and picked bits of hyacinth from his shoulders. He fingered his beard and removed anything he found. Stems, pieces of bark. Fortunately he wore his beard short, in the Roman style.

"I am going to change my clothing." Unfortunately his other tunic was soiled. Washday was the day after Sabbath.

Jorah came close to examine the new color. She fingered the wet fabric. "James, I could dye the rest of this."

"I was not talking about your clothing," Simon stated. "What are you going to do with your apprentice?"

"You think I am going to wear lavender?" James asked Jorah. "I will donate this to Annika's poor box first."

"I could finish the rest in the purple, then soak it in the yellow. Then it will turn to a sort of—" Jorah cocked her head to the side—"dullish brown. Maybe gray. What do you think, Mother?"

Mary murmured something in agreement. She, too, fingered the fabric and sent a swift glance to James' face. James cracked a tiny smile that only she could see.

Simon waited, but James did not answer. Ideas were plentiful, of course, especially when his face was pressed at the bottom of the pot. He touched his nose and wondered if it was bruised. Why did this dunking not ignite the rage? Strangely, his stomach was peaceful, as if filled with warm milk.

"I do not know what I will do with Nathanael," James answered. "I will think on it." As he shook out his tunic, he quietly asked his mother, "Where are you going? Where will you stay?"

Mother went to the basket of soiled laundry against the wall near the smallyard. She rummaged through it until she came up with James' other tunic, wadded and rumpled. She shook it out and brought it to him—holding it away from her, with her nose wrinkled.

"I would not wear this around Keturah," she commented with a small smile.

James felt his jaw come down. "What . . ."

"Oh, James, don't be ridiculous," Jorah chided as she fussed about, picking flowers from his tunic. "Everybody knows."

"Knows what?" Simon and James demanded at the same time. James felt his face grow warm. Fortunately, neither Mother nor Jorah replied. But they did trade a look with each other. He grimaced and all but snatched the tunic from Mother. He ducked into the storage room at the back of the courtyard, pulled off the wet tunic, and tossed it out near the pots. He struggled his wet body into the dry—he wrinkled his own nose—and smelly tunic, then joined the others.

"Where will you go, Mother?" Joses asked.

Mary drew a breath. "I plan on going to Bethany to stay with Devorah until I can find out where he is. Then I will join him."

She had gone to him before these past three years, especially when he stayed around Galilee. A few weeks at a time, once an entire month. But she always came back. This time, her announcement had finality.

"Why don't you wait until we all go for Passover?" Judas said. "It is only a month off. We could travel together, stay at Devorah's again the way we did last year."

"Devorah's first child will come soon. I want to be there for her." Mother folded her arms, and her gaze drifted. "I need to go now. I must go now."

No, being forced into a dye pot like an armful of wool did not sizzle his stomach but talk of Passover did. James tried to smooth out the rumples in his tunic, glancing at the others. Passover was not a popular subject with any of them these days. What used to be a joyous occasion, something much anticipated, was now a source of worry, even fear.

"What is it going to be like *this* year?" Judas muttered as he handed a cup to Jorah, who had begun to clean up.

"Everyone thought he would declare last year," Simon said, crossing his arms and leaning against the whitewashed wall. "And the year before. What will happen this year?"

"Who knows what he will do," Judas said darkly.

James snorted. "We know what he will *not* do. I only wish those poor fool idiots realized it as well. Save them a whole lot of time and dreaming. They could pick out someone else to be their messiah."

"Like Raziel," Joses said. He sat at the cistern with the dipper in hand. He drank and replaced the dipper, then folded his arms and asked wearily, "What happened?"

"He came all the way from Kerioth to bring Mother a scarf," James told him. "Gave us some nonsense about— what did he say?—knowing what it was like to be the village pariahs."

"It wasn't nonsense, James," Jorah protested.

"You mean you believed him?" James gave a hard laugh. "Think, Jorah. Avi and his friend, both fanatical followers of Raziel, show up on our doorstep one week ago. Now Raziel. What does it say to you? You are the one who always wants to be included. You figure it out."

Simon frowned. "Two of his disciples, here last week?"

"Nathanael chased them clear to the plain," Jorah said with a small smile.

"Yes, just who is this Nathanael?" Simon demanded.

Joses waved him quiet. "We can talk about him later. I agree with James. He could not have come all the way from Kerioth just to bring Mother a scarf. That makes no sense."

"Where is Kerioth?" Jorah asked as she stacked cups together and placed them in a willow basket. She took the platter of dried fruit and slipped it into its hanging net near the bread cupboard.

"South of Hebron, west of the Salt Sea," Judas answered.

"It is a great distance," Jorah said slowly, fingers resting entwined in the hanging net. "Farther than Jerusalem."

"Kerioth," Joses murmured.

"I don't like that Nathanael." Simon brooded in a slouch against the wall. "He is disrespectful and rude. Father would never have tolerated—"

"Father would never have tolerated your own rudeness," Jorah snapped at him.

"God have mercy on us. What can it mean?" Joses whispered, staring into the air. His hands gripped the prayer shawl still draped about his shoulders.

"Joses . . . ?"

Joses said, "One of his disciples is from Kerioth. And rumored to be a Zealot."

Simon straightened. "One of whose disciples? Jesus'?"

Face white as his tallith, Joses nodded. "His name is Judas. Judas Ish-Kerioth."

Simon sat down heavily at the low couch. Judas began to pace. Jorah whispered, "What can it mean?"

"It means we go see this Raziel *now*," James said. "We find out what he is planning."

"He is using Jesus," Joses said in a voice of quiet wonder.

"Who is?" Simon asked, frustrated. "Raziel or Judas?"

"Raziel," James said at the same time that Joses answered, "Judas."

Joses went on, shaking his head, speaking as if to himself. "One of his closest friends . . . planning to use him."

"We do not know that, Joses," Jorah said. Doubtfully, she added, "Maybe Raziel and this Judas do not even know each other."

"Both Zealots? Both from Kerioth?" Simon demanded.

"He did not seem like a person planning an uprising," Jorah said. She appealed to Mother. "Did he, Mother?"

James groaned. "Jorah, if you are going to plan a rebellion, you are not going to *seem* like it."

"We have to stop it." Joses rose from the cistern. "They cannot use him like that; it is not what Jesus is about. That we know." He put both hands to his temples. "This cannot be happening. Jesus must be told. We have to warn him."

Jorah turned angrily on Joses. "How do you know there is a plot against Jesus? Stop talking like that! I liked Raziel. I do not think he would do anything to hurt Jesus!"

Joses came close to Jorah. "Jorah, Passover is only a month away. Jerusalem will be flooded with Jews. The Zealots see that as an opportunity to launch a campaign. With the great number of Jews, they can make it look as though we are all united against Rome. These Zealots will do anything—anything, Jorah—to get as much support for an uprising as they can. Numbers are what they need. A few months before Passover is when they are at their busiest . . . they travel all over the country, agitating the people to—" he opened his arms, gesturing for the word—"passion, or at least hope for the return of our land. Then, at Passover, all they have to do is shout the loudest." He took her shoulders and searched her eyes. "Don't you see, Jorah? They will use Jesus. Not from spite—I do not really believe that. But because they believe so deeply in their mission."

"'The cause is everything,'" Simon muttered. "It is their battle cry. We got an earful of it on the road. They even display it on signs, with other things like, 'Jews for the Land. The Land for the Jews.' When the Romans are not looking, of course."

"Only one of us must go to Raziel," Judas said, frowning and pinching his lower lip. "If we all go, it will look too suspicious."

Suspicious? James wanted to laugh. If the Romans knew Raziel was in Nazareth . . . and that one of Jesus' own disciples was from Kerioth . . .

"I will go," he said, his own voice hollow.

"You?" Simon asked, one eyebrow arched. Simon knew of James' reluctance to leave the workroom.

"Yes, me," James snapped, glaring at Simon, daring him to say something else. Simon shook his head and looked away.

"You should leave now," Judas said to James. "Sabbath is only a few hours off. Take the back ridge. Most people will be hurrying to finish work or busy with Sabbath preparations. It is not likely you will be noticed."

Simon snorted. "They noticed Joses and me. 'There go two more sons of God,' one of them yelled. Another said, 'Come, Simon, perform a miracle for us. Surely it runs in the family.' The louts."

"Devorah is the only one who had the sense to escape," James muttered, siding with Simon in spite of himself.

"Devorah does not have a soul," Jorah declared.

"Jorah!" Mother gasped.

"She doesn't! The only thing Devorah ever cared about is Devorah."

Jorah was right, and somehow it did not surprise him to hear her speak so plainly. It seemed everyone spoke plainly these days. Why hold anything back when your brother was Jesus of Nazareth?

"I will wager a month of wool sales that she was never even in love with Matthias," Jorah went on, arms folded. "He was her passage out of Nazareth."

"Jorah of Joseph, I did not raise my daughter to speak so," Mother said, drawing herself up.

"You raised your daughter to speak truth, Mother!" Jorah protested, coming to her side to plead with her hands. "All Devorah ever wanted was a perfect life. If things did not go perfectly, then she pretended that they did. She could never handle anything that threatened her idea of a—"

"She loved Jesus," Mother protested.

"Of course she did, Mother. But if anything unpleasant ever crossed her world—"

"She was the first to deny him." It came from Simon, and it surprised them all, that and the fact that it was the truth.

He sat at the couch, elbows on his knees, absently rubbing his hands together. "She denied him by ignoring him. My, but she had a talent for that. It was one of the reasons why I wanted to visit her when we were in Bethany. I wanted to see if she could ignore him now." He looked up at the attention on him and cracked a bitter smile. "Lazarus, you know."

"You never told me that," Joses said, quiet and surprised. "You never said that was your reason to see her."

Simon half chuckled. "You never asked. You had your own plans. I wanted to see how Devorah could ignore him now, with Lazarus in her new hometown. What a joke. She could not escape Jesus after all."

James' mouth was suddenly as dry as Mother's newly cleaned wool. Was it as bizarre to anyone else, speaking so casually of a recent event that most people denied and the rest refused to speak of? Just like the day Jesus came back to visit Nazareth. Nobody spoke of that day. Not the villagers, not the family, nobody. "This Lazarus was on your list of people to look up?"

"He was," Joses said, then added a touch too quickly, "But we could not find him. Neither Lazarus nor his sisters."

"We did not look very hard, did we, Joses?" Simon said, turning his gaze onto Joses. "Something I could not quite figure out, as hard as you sought for the truth."

But Joses would not answer. James had his suspicions . . . a man once mad with demons scared Simon. Maybe a man risen from the dead was enough to scare Joses.

James would ask later; he was wasting time. He took a cloth belt from the dirty laundry basket and wrapped it around his waist. He spared only a moment to send a swift glance at his family, then headed for the passageway.

"Godspeed," Simon murmured.

"The back ridge," Judas called after James as he trotted from the courtyard.

❦

The One True God's response brought him to an abrupt halt.

"That is why you chose Melkor?" Balthazar shook his head. Who could have known?

113

He glanced over his shoulder toward his homeland, where the sun soon would disappear. Melkor was from Arachosia, much farther east than Susa. He had been a fellow keeper of the flame of Ahura Mazdah. Another man singled out, tempest-tossed into the maelstrom that had swept across a sun-baked land, plucking others along the way, gathering them into its vortex, depositing them in a hapless little town called Beth-L'hem.

There would be others this time. Who would they be? Which unlikely ones had the One True God chosen now? Balthazar chuckled. Ever fond of choosing the unlikely ones, he was.

He faced westward and started walking, glad for the coming of twilight, comfortable with the stars.

❧

It was nearly springtime in Galilee. The skies were clearer now every day, and the heavy winter rains left behind a countryside awash with the first suspicion of vibrant color. The land from the ridge fell away into valleys that rose again into other hills, and those hills were cloaked in lush green. New flowers would soon decorate the cloak, embroidering it with yellow and red, purple and white. The breezes were growing gentler, filled with fragrance and a hint of the warmth to come.

From where James walked on the ridge, he could see down into the homes that grew in number the closer he got to the village. With the coming spring, most activity moved from the inside of the homes to the courtyards again. Summer shade awnings were beginning to replace winter rain awnings. Rooftops were ready to be smoothed from the season of rain in preparation for a season of baking in the sun.

When had he last walked this ridge? To go to synagogue, maybe, sometime last summer. It was always nicer to take the ridge down into the village. Longer, yes, but the ridge rode some of the highest parts of Nazareth, and you could see far from here. Mount Carmel, in the distance near the Mediterranean, on a clear day. The mountains of Megiddo and beyond.

James' reason for the ridge was not only for anonymity. His eyes scanned the land that fell away to the left; he would be upon Keturah's home soon.

Keturah lived with her father, just the two of them. Her mother had died at Keturah's birth, and her father, Therin, never remarried. He raised his only child with help from his sister until she left to marry and have her own children. Therin had been a close friend of his own father. Mother used to ask Therin and Keturah to come for a meal.

He came upon the rocky outcrop that meant her home was a glance away. He paused, deliberately gazing to the right, south toward Jerusalem, as if enjoying the view. He avoided looking straight down; below the outcrop was a ledge, a ledge Jesus had had an appointment with nearly two years ago. He had escaped that appointment, and to this day nobody knew how he had done it. Only that, James was told later, one moment Jesus was on the edge of the cliff, and the next he had passed through the entire crowd. Passed through an angry mob, untouched. James did not see it happen; he was back at the synagogue.

The sun fell in the west, and in an hour or two the shofar would sound. He knew he had to hurry. Of course, the Law did not prevent travel within one's own hometown, but the implication was there. Sundown meant Sabbath, and Sabbath meant home and family. He would soon have no business arguing with a Zealot in a home not his own. James studied the cloud streaks in the pale sky and kept his back to Therin's home. He thought about not looking.

He did not see her at first, but then there she was. Seated on a step at the back passage of the home. She had something in her lap; he could not tell from here what. Maybe she was mending something. Maybe carving.

He should be watching from the safety of one of the ridge trees, but even if Keturah saw him she could not recognize him from this distance. At least he didn't think so. He was on the verge of leaving, feeling increasingly uncomfortable staring at her in this secretive way, when suddenly Keturah looked up and directly at him.

He froze, and the foolishness he felt warmed his cheeks. If he dashed away, as instinct told him, he would look guilty . . . spying on her from on high, like David with Bathsheba. He made himself give a wave, then started on down the path. But Keturah called out, "Wait!"

James clenched his fists and cursed, first in Aramaic, then in Greek. Nathanael had taught him a few interesting expletives, which he had learned from some Roman soldiers in Caesarea. Somehow cursing in a different language didn't seem wrong at all. He practiced the words as he watched Keturah hastily set aside whatever was in her lap and hurry to the slope.

She first took the path that wound up through their strip of terraced farmland. Then, holding her skirts with one hand and using the other for balance, she made straight up the hill for James.

"Stupid idiot," he growled at himself. Now what was he going to do? He had to get to Annika's! He had no time for foolishness with a . . . beautiful young woman.

Keturah's face was flushed from exertion by the time she reached the top of the ridge. She stood breathing hard, looking at James, and pulled up her apron to whisk sweat from her face. Her hair was not covered, as it should have been. Had Keturah a mother, she would have worn a covering all the time. Then again, maybe not. James kept his lips from a smile. After all, this was Keturah, master carver. No one told her how to be.

"What are you smiling at?" she said, smiling herself.

"I thought I wasn't," he answered. "And I am smiling at you. You are not wearing your head covering."

She pulled some wayward hair behind her ear and hastily smoothed down the rest. "I am at home. Why should I wear one around the house?"

"You never wear one."

A delicate eyebrow came up, making James flush. He had as much as admitted he noticed.

"I have to be going," he mumbled. "Good Sabbath, Keturah. Good Sabbath to your father." He started away.

"Going where?"

He stopped, looking out to the hills. Over his shoulder he said, "I am—taking a walk."

"May I join you?"

"No! I mean—I have to go talk with someone before sunset."

"Oh."

But he did not leave. He stood with his back to her, looking out on the spring-filled hills. How would things be different, this day, if his brother had never been born? James blinked. Could he take his thinking so far? A thought for Jesus to never have been born? Is that what he wanted? He was close enough to the edge to be able to see several feet down to the ledge; he made himself look at it now. What if Jesus had died that day, as the crowd and the leaders had intended?

"Were you here that day, Keturah?" he asked softly. "The day they brought him here?"

Keturah came beside him and gazed at the ledge. It was a ledge that had caught many lawbreakers thrown down from the top. The distance—"not less than the height of one man, not more than the height of two"—was far enough for bone-breaking damage upon the fall, but not always far enough to kill. The ledge bore the lawbreaker while stones finished the job. Four or five others had been dragged to this precipice in James' lifetime; twice his father had been among the crowd for the righteous judgments. One had been a murderer, one an adulteress.

"I was weeding the garden," Keturah murmured. "It was a quiet morning, and I was angry that I could not be at the synagogue. I wanted to hear what Jesus had to say. I knew Father would tell me later, but—well, I heard something in the distance. I remember standing up, looking around, trying to figure out what the sound was. It was coming closer. And then I realized it was coming from the ridge."

Keturah moved to the edge of the cliff, directly above the ledge. She looked down at it, arms about herself. A gentle breeze from the valley caught her long wavy hair, lifting it in a swirl for a moment. She sat down and looked up at James, and patted the ground next to her.

God of Israel, he did not want this. Why was he doing this? Why was he reliving a day he had tried hard since to forget? But he was moving to the edge, and he was sitting down beside her. And he was looking at the gray rocky ledge below.

Keturah crossed her ankles and folded her hands in her lap. "It had happened twice before, that I remember. I would always feel such . . . pity . . . horror . . . for whoever was being condemned. Knowing that the condemnation was just did not make it better. Those other times I had run around the side of the house to cover my ears against the screams. When I saw the crowd this time, I wanted to run again. I was ready to—and then I saw Joses."

Joses had gone with the crowd. James was . . .

"He was on the outside of the crowd, trying to get to someone in the middle. He was screaming, and—" She put her fingertips to her lips, perhaps to make them stop trembling. "He was beside himself. They would not let him in."

James had been on the ground in front of the synagogue. Gravel imbedded in his beard and cheeks. Dust in his mouth, the taste of the crowd that dragged his brother away. The memory came back in relentless strokes.

"Tell me what happened, James."

He thought he had seen his brother for the last time, and so he tore his tunic down the middle in a torrent of grief and rage.

He realized Keturah had spoken and heard what she said. "Why?" James snapped. "Why do you want to know what happened? You already know. Everybody knows."

She shook her head. "James, the explanation my father gave is no explanation at all."

"What did he tell you?" He had seen Therin in the crowd. Therin had turned on Jesus too.

Keturah drew her knees up. She rubbed a water spot on her sandal, then sighed heavily. "He said Jesus deserved to die for the shameful things he'd said. That was it. He does not speak of it, will not permit me to ask questions about it." She paused and said reluctantly, "And since that day he changed his mind about Jesus. He used to support your brother. Now he will not even speak of him."

James nodded slowly. Pretty much the whole village changed after that day. And though Keturah seemed embarrassed for her father, at least Therin was one of the few who still treated the family with a . . . determined sort of normality. Perhaps to honor the memory of Joseph.

"Keturah, you and Therin are rare. Not many want much to do with my family."

"Father is a good man. Most of them are good, James; they have good hearts. They simply do not understand Jesus."

James shook his head. "You are wrong, Keturah. They understand him perfectly. That's why they wanted to kill him."

"Tell me, James," Keturah insisted, turning her dark eyes full on him. "Tell me what happened that day."

And so James told her.

The paradox was that it started out as the finest moment in the whole of Jesus' mission. Sitting in the synagogue that day, listening as Jesus spoke . . . in those moments an idea formed in James' mind, in the minds of all who were in the synagogue that day. For a short and wondrous time, the mission of Jesus seemed clear, and hope rose.

The brothers had sat together, the five of them, as they

used to, in the same old place on the same old bench. After a whole year, it was so *good* to have Jesus back again—but it was more than good; it was time. It was a day for answers, and if Jesus had not exactly promised he would explain himself at last, why, it was more than implicit. Expectation lit the faces of all who attended. Jesus, their own son of Nazareth, had returned to set down once and for all his purpose and his plan.

"Take gracious pleasure, O Jehovah our God, in thy people Israel, and in their prayers. Accept the burnt offerings of Israel, and their prayers, with thy good pleasure."

The blend of male voices had resonated in the room. They were all together again, save Joseph. All the brothers, one in voice, one with the rest.

"And may the services of thy people Israel be ever acceptable unto thee. And, oh, that our eyes may see it, as thou turn in mercy to Zion. Blessed be thou, O Jehovah, who restores his Shechinah to Zion."

James had glanced about the room, tense with emotion; pride, of course, that his brother sat next to him; anxious that he would say the right things. James himself did not know what Jesus would say; he only hoped that it was . . . right. That the elders would approve.

James cast a look down a row of men; some were scholars, one or two were sages, and all were the chosen of Nazareth, Jews who had kept the faith—often at great personal cost. They were men he had known all his life, good men whose familiarity brought comfort, whose presence brought security and sane thinking to a world of Roman violence and Gentile godlessness. Men who took care of their families, men like neighbor Eli, sitting behind Joses, who once found

James when he was lost as a child and carried him home to his mother. Men like gentle old Rimson, who carried sweets in his pockets for children. Jotham, whose family had often shared Sabbath meals with them. Benaiah, the father of a girl James once liked. James could relax when he saw those faces, once Jesus said the right things.

They had every right to expect a full report. All the things they had heard these past several months . . . of healings and grand speeches to hold a crowd spellbound. Why, the fame of Jesus had spread to even the distant places of Galilee. This son of Nazareth had much to explain, and today every man present would discover at last what he was about. After all, these things had not happened in Nazareth, had they? Surely there was a reason for it.

Pride and anxiety, hope and worry, joy and anticipation. All of this, and the Sabbath service too. James had to force himself to keep from fidgeting like a little boy. The service had proceeded as usual, with measured deliberateness, as if the attendants would not brook a casting off of piety in favor of excitement over this famous son of Nazareth. They would allow Jesus to speak at the proper time. But glances from the attendants themselves joined the stares from everyone in the assembly . . . attention always came back to Jesus and the brothers. Sometimes James would share a nervous grin with one, with Joses in particular. He remembered the way he and Joses had looked at each other and the way Joses had looked at Jesus. With confidence. Assurance.

The *Shema* was recited, as well as the other prayers and blessings. Then the readings began. The first reading came from Torah. Then came the reading from the Prophets. The leader who was designated to read that day turned instead to Jesus. The brothers exchanged looks as Jesus rose; to offer the reading to someone else was an honor. It signified acceptance. It recognized piety. The day was only getting better. After nearly a year of uncertainty, it seemed as though things at last were being righted.

They handed to him the book of Isaiah, and the passage scheduled for that day seemed providential at the least. Jesus found the text and began to read.

"'The Spirit of the Lord is upon me, because He anointed me to preach the gospel to the poor. He has sent me to proclaim release to the captives, and recovery of sight to the blind, to set free those who are oppressed, to proclaim the favorable year of the Lord.'"

James remembered how very small he had felt, because those words loomed large. They set his skin to tingling, coming from the lips of Jesus. Did anyone else feel the same? To be sure, a reverent hush had come upon them all. As transfixed as James, the men in the synagogue watched as Jesus gently rolled up the scroll, smoothed his hands reverently over the outer cover, and gave the book back to the leader. He took his seat, and they could not take their eyes from him.

And then Jesus spoke, firmly and clearly. "Today this Scripture has been fulfilled in your hearing."

There it was. Exactly what they wanted to hear.

The collective pent-up breath was released, and astonished murmurs rose. James closed his eyes briefly, then turned to look at his brothers with a weak smile. In their eyes he saw what he felt. Relief. Wonder. Awe. And the murmurs around him were a balm to his soul.

"Fulfilled? Why, yes—of course! The healings . . . the miracles!"

"This is Joseph's son, is it not?"

"Yes, blessed be his memory. Would that he had lived to see this day!"

"His own boy . . . our own Jesus!"

There was time enough for imaginations to kindle. There was time enough for expectation to brighten their senses. There was time enough for James to hear things spoken in the rushing ebb and flow around him, things to lift his heart and, for the first time in a year, to change the wistful fear inside to something more like hope. Something more like belief.

"All the marvelous things he has done . . . it has truly been a sign of God's hand upon him!"

"Could it be that he fulfills the words he just spoke? Release for the captives? Think of it!"

"The days of Rome are numbered!"

"Then . . . Isaiah wrote those words for this time, this place . . . astonishing!"

"That I have lived to see the day of Israel! The freedom of our people!"

His own brother. *God's hand upon his own brother!* It was enough to make James sag in his seat, to exchange wondering stares with Joses. Recovery of sight to the blind. Freedom for the oppressed. And oh, God, most of all, release for the captives.

All about him imaginations ran riot; speculations came fast and thick. Was it the beginning of a new era? Time at last for the end of all foreign domination? For Israel to rise again? And would Nazareth—think of it!—be at the heart of it all?

They would all be famous! Those in Jerusalem would come to see their Galilean brothers not as the rustic provincials they supposed, but as the chosen of God.

Yes . . . yes! Nazareth would be the headquarters. Jesus ben Joseph would be their leader . . . their Prophet! And the people of Nazareth would be like David's mighty men of old. A rush filled the room, a force of heady power that left James trembling. God was on the move! God was going to really, truly restore Israel. Through his own brother.

They were the last moments James remembered being happy.

Everyone was so busy whispering and murmuring and imagining that no one had taken notice of Jesus himself until a single voice rose above the murmurs.

Clear and resonant, new words came. "No doubt you will say to me this proverb: 'Physician, heal yourself.'"

Jesus is speaking again! Quiet, everyone!

"And 'Whatever we heard was done in Capernaum, do here in your hometown as well.'"

What is this? Shhh, I cannot hear him! What is he saying now?

"Truly I say to you, no prophet is welcome in his own hometown."

The murmurs fell away.

Confusion came.

And what had begun in the synagogue that day, as the mighty swell of a single wave, what should have ended as a magnificent crash upon the shore, instead stopped short of the land because Jesus did next what he always did—he took it too far.

"I say to you in truth, there were many widows in Israel in

the days of Elijah, when the sky was shut up for three years and six months, when a great famine came over all the land; and yet Elijah was sent to none of them . . . but only to Zarephath, in the land of Sidon, to a woman who was a widow."

"No," James whispered.

But his brother went on, relentless and calm.

"And there were many lepers in Israel in the time of Elisha the prophet; and none of them was cleansed . . . but only Naaman, the Syrian."

Silence like a tomb seeped over the assembly. They waited, stunned, for him to explain, to justify, to retract. But, implacable, he sat next to James and did not speak again.

It did not take long for the implication of his words to penetrate. Mutters swept the crowd. Was Jesus saying he would bypass them in favor of Gentiles? Naaman was a Syrian, a hated enemy of Israel. Was Jesus saying he would go to the Romans? Heal their lepers, bypassing Israel's own? Go to their widows, despising the widows of Israel? After all Rome's cruel tyranny and oppression? What effrontery was this? Who did Jesus think he was? His words rang discordant in their ears, and not long after, a growl like low thunder rose.

Look at him, so haughty! He performs his mighty works elsewhere, but should not Nazareth be his proving ground? Why would he ignore Nazareth? Because they all knew how ordinary he was? Look at him! What is so special about him? He is not like David, is he? He is not like Judah the Maccabee. He is a weakling compared to the mighty men of old! Naaman the Syrian, he says? A Gentile pig widow, he says? Touch not the unclean, the Torah says! He is not for us but for our enemies.

James and the brothers twisted in their seats, quickly assessing the furious rise of emotion in the assembly, looking to Jesus to assuage the crowd. Do something! Take it back! Tell them you didn't mean it! Implacable, he remained.

He is not for us but for our enemies! He is a traitor!

You have got to take it back! Make it right! Quickly!

Open your eyes, brethren, it is a trick of Satan! He does his miracles to lead us astray from God and the Law. We have been deceived!

Jesus! For God's sake, say something! Do something!

"Physician, heal yourself"? Come, let us give him a chance.

James and the brothers were on their feet, instinctively forming a circle around their brother. They had to get him home, out of this hothouse of emotion. Let it die down and—

The low thunder kicked up into a roar of fury. The good men of Nazareth rose as one, spurred by righteous anger. James saw flashes of faces he knew, young and old, heads covered in prayer shawls, hands gripping garments as if to tear them, people he had known all his life, people he loved and trusted —all bearing down upon his brother.

"Simon! Joses! We must get Jesus—"

A hand dug into his shoulder and pulled him aside, and the crowd streamed into the breach.

"No—Jesus!"

Shoved aside, pushed back and jostled, James tried to struggle back into the crowd, but the distance between him and Jesus grew. He jumped to see, and the flash of view revealed Jesus—someone was tearing his prayer shawl from his head. James jumped again, using shoulders to pull himself up—someone had a handful of Jesus' hair, was dragging him to the synagogue door. Another jump . . . Simon! He was still at Jesus' side, arms trying to shield, wide shoulders taking a blow meant for Jesus! James felt an insane moment of hope, because Simon was there and fighting.

But the next leap revealed Simon going down.

And the tidal wave of human wrath swept Jesus away.

"Jeee—sus!" James screamed. Oh, God, this was impossible!

"To the cliff!" they shouted.

"No! Listen to me—listen to me! He is innocent! He does not deserve a death like that!"

"The cliff!"

"Not a death like that!"

He scrabbled after them, clawed his way into their midst, only to be recognized and beaten back. He rose and stumbled down the synagogue steps, to be again forced back. He fell, and a foot ground his cheek into the gravel, filling his mouth with dust. The foot held him there, and he watched the crowd surge away while he screamed things they did not hear.

You do not know him as I do . . . no, he is good! Oh God, he is good. . . .

The roar faded into the distance, and James struggled to his knees. *Please . . .*

⁂

Keturah wept softly. James' chest felt compressed, as though held in the grip of a giant. Numb, he rose, staring down at the ledge. Then, without a word to Keturah, he stumbled away, lurching in the direction of Annika's.

8

How much time had he wasted? The sun dropped closer to the far-off sea, a melon-colored discus near the horizon. The rest of the sky darkened with early twilight. James quickened his steps. How could he have lived that day again? Now, of all times?

The ridge came to a slope that descended into the village of Nazareth.

Annika's neighborhood was a noisy one, and he could hear the bustle long before he reached the aftgate of the common courtyard. Mothers scurried to finish tasks before the setting sun brought Sabbath. They issued curt orders to their children. "Straighten the blankets. Fill the cruses with oil, lad, quickly. Trim the wicks. Bank the fire. Fetch the water."

Why had Jesus come back that day? The thought made James pause outside the aftgate to the courtyard.

It made no sense, none that James could see. Jesus had come back to all but declare that his mission was to the Gentiles—or had he? Why, then, did he continue to speak to mostly Jewish crowds in the two years that followed? And the new words he spoke seemed in direct contradiction to what happened in the synagogue that day. The new words claimed he was sent to the lost sheep of Israel. James heard that Jesus had balked at healing the daughter of a Gentile woman—balked, after all his talk about Elijah and the Syrian! The woman was from the same pagan area Elijah had gone to. It was crazy, confounded crazy. How differently that day should have gone.

What was the point for Jesus to alienate his hometown brethren with his preaching about the Gentiles, only to take up again with the Jews? None of his disciples were Gentiles. Sure, most of them were rustic rabble—but they were Jewish rabble. All of this grandiose talk of God sending his Son for the whole world made no sense when his disciples included none from a pagan race.

"Why did you come back?" James whispered, hand on the gate.

"Well? Are you going to come in or are you going to stand there?"

A woman waited in front of James for him to move. He hurriedly opened the gate and stepped aside, and she swept through, arms laden with a large bucket. Something for the refuse pit, by the smell of it.

He gazed upon the busy commonyard. At the old sights and sounds around him, he could almost forget why he was here. He could imagine—it wasn't hard really—that it was an ordinary visit in an ordinary time. He took a breath and entered the gate.

It had been a long time since he had been to Annika's. He thought he had not missed it, but the sight of the people around him, people who probably could not recognize him for their hurried preparations and the coming dusk, made him almost glad he had come. When had he last seen such activity, so many people all at once? It was not any wonder Nathanael stayed here with Annika. He was used to such comforting clamor, being from a busy place like Caesarea. All the stories Nathanael told . . . the lad would be bored senseless if he had to live in a home like James'.

He kept close to the houses as he headed for Annika's place, the fifth and last one on the left of the commonyard. A row of houses flanked each side. The foregate opened to an alley, which led to a main street and the marketplace; the aftgate led to the garden patches and chicken houses of the homeowners, to the refuse pit, and to the back ridge beyond. Staying closer to the houses meant James walked in the shadow beneath the balcony of the upper rooms, homes built upon the lower houses. James skirted a man who stood on a chopping block, working to patch a hole beneath the balustrade. He gave the man a quick glance and a nod, and was relieved to earn barely the same in return.

His steps slowed as he watched the busy, wonderfully normal commonyard. Smaller children played, some of them creating elaborate little villages with cast-off pieces of lumber and stone, broken pieces of pottery, and old bits of string. A trio of children squatted over tiny buildings, happily chattering and arguing. Ben and Hepsi sometimes came with Joses to the shop; they loved to take scraps from projects and create the same sort of villages. Jesus and James used to do it when they were children, playing at the foot of their father's bench.

Some women shook out carpets or beat them with a stick. Some gathered laundry from lines. Some pulled out laden dishes from the ovens or waited in turn to do it. Older children helped their mothers or minded smaller siblings. He watched a young girl, not more than eight or ten, upbraid a small child who had a telltale ring of brown about his mouth. At the same time she bounced a fretful baby in her arms; the baby reached futilely for a harried-looking woman at one of the ovens.

A fig tree grew in a corner of the commonyard, its fruit belonging to a miserly man whose name James could not remember, second house on the right. Two common-use, dome-shaped ovens were in the center of the yard, next to a common grindstone. The harried mother waited with an impatient grace for another woman to remove a dish from one of the clay ovens. James had to stop suddenly when a man darted out of a doorway, chased by his wife, who shrieked over his mud-caked sandals. She retreated, her complaints disappearing with her into the house. The man gave James a rueful glance as he leaned against a balcony post to take off his sandals. James heard the sandals slap together behind him as he continued on.

At the end of the walkway beneath the balcony, an older, heavier woman was snatching tunics from a laundry line strung up between Annika's home and the foregate.

Beyond Annika's home, on the other side of the alley, was

the home of Hananiah, a Pharisee who was a member of the local Sanhedrin and one of the synagogue leaders. James used to tease Annika to send Hananiah some of her honeycakes. She was a widow, he a widower. They had been neighbors forever and had exchanged enough good-natured insults over the years to make for a couple already. Why not make a match of it? Annika would always retort, "And why ruin such a nice arrangement? I like Hananiah too much to marry him." Women seldom made sense to James, and Annika least of all. She seemed to enjoy not making sense.

As he came closer to Annika's, he realized that the woman taking laundry from the line was Annika herself. And how easy it was to imagine he was not here for Raziel at all.

He sidled up to her and said into her ear, "Doing Hananiah's laundry now? Why don't you just wed the man? It's not decent, Annika."

Annika turned, and on seeing his face she dropped the laundry into a basket and set her fists on her hips in surprise. She glanced about, though, and did not exclaim out loud as she might have.

"Why, James ben Joseph, finally you show yourself at my doorstep," she declared quietly, reaching up to give a gentle tug to his beard. Then she sniffed, and her face soured. "It appears I should be doing your wash. And what is this, wearing your beard so short? Are you turning Roman?"

"God forbid, no. I like the style. Especially when I get to pick out fewer hyacinths."

"Hyacinths?"

He enjoyed the perplexed look on her face, a look of disapproving surprise. Annika always looked as though people surprised her, and not for the good. But James liked that old familiar suspicion. It was a face any street merchant thought twice about cheating, and a face any beggar in Nazareth knew for a friend. Most beggars, that is—Annika could tell a fraud from across the street, and James once saw her drag a new-comer from an old-timer's corner by his ear. "The fool forgot to change his fine sandals," she had told James.

She regarded James' face and seemed to decide she did not like what she saw. "What troubles you, lad?" she asked softly. Any illusion of normality drifted away at the concern in her eyes. No, it was not a normal visit. Nothing was normal anymore.

"I need to speak to a guest of yours," he said in a low tone. He could not help but throw a glance at Hananiah's home.

"Would this be the guest who cannot leave because it is Sabbath?" Annika murmured back. She flicked a glance at Hananiah's home as well and pulled a towel off the line.

"It would."

"He is in the back room. Nathanael will be surprised to find he is not gone."

James had started for the doorway but stopped. "Nathanael is not here?"

Annika turned from her laundry line. "No. Should he be?"

"He . . . left a bit early. There was a . . . confrontation."

Annika drew herself up. She was the only woman James knew who could look down on a person though she was shorter than everyone. "What confrontation? What did you do to my Nathanael?"

Why did everyone take the side of the apprentice? His own family took his side by doing nothing while James steeped in a pot of herbs. Of course, he deserved it, but . . .

"Your Nathanael," he said in her face but pressed his lips together and drew back. "Talk to him later. It is nearly sundown." He ducked into her doorway to avoid more words. He kissed the mezuzah and paused at the threshold to gaze at a kitchen as familiar to James as his own workroom. Raziel, yes . . . but this kitchen . . .

The old oak table beneath the window that looked on the commonyard . . . how many times had he sat at this table, with or without a brother or sister, for a meal or a treat or for prayers or news of the land? How easy it was to imagine old Simeon, Annika's husband gone these few years, seated at the table, mending a harness or sorting grain for Annika. Reading Torah from the old leather scrolls, rocking in the gentle rhythm of worship, arms wrapped with old, cracked-leather tefillin. Gentle Simeon, with that warm, crooked smile.

The table was set for Sabbath. Upon a white linen tablecloth, small dishes held mashed olives and dried fish and oil and salt. There was a platter of dried fruit and a dish with roasted new barley and one of Annika's famous spiced nut pies. Candleholders held ivory wax candles, waiting to be lit by the woman of the household. Two Sabbath cruses filled with oil, wicks trimmed, also waited. James' fingertips brushed the tabletop, and he looked to the corner of the room. . . . His expectancy faded when he did not see the scrolls. Of course they would not be there. They would have gone to the household's only son, Judah, who lived a few miles away in Sepphoris. *Simeon, Simeon, with your crooked smile. How you are missed.*

Raziel, yes . . . but the cupboard on the right, next to shelves recessed in the stone wall. How many times had Annika whisked from there a spiced nut pie or one of her honeycakes when James came to visit? It was a cupboard his own father, Joseph, had built. James had always suspected they had given him the business during a lean time; they had no need for a cupboard, with as many built-in shelves as their home had. The top recessed shelf was not even used. Annika would be mortified at the layer of dust it held. She wasn't tall enough to see.

James looked past the cupboard to the sleeping rooms in the rear. A short stone passage led to a curtained doorway.

Stomach lurching, he started for the curtain. Wild thoughts flickered. Did Jesus ever heal someone with fearsome gut pain? Had James really worn this smelly tunic around Keturah? What was Jesus thinking, to make his younger brother confront one of the most famous leaders of the Zealot factions?

He trailed his fingers on the nicks carved in the limestone on either side of the passage, nicks marking the growth of children. The nicks on the right were for Annika's children, and for the children of Joseph. First were the nicks for Judah, Annika's son, reaching to James' present height. Then came the marks for their daughter, Leah—tragically, they stopped waist high. Leah died when she was five. Then began the nicks for Joseph's tribe, starting with Jesus, ending with Jorah at the end of the passage.

Nicks dotted the other side of the passage as well, varying in height. James did not know to whom these nicks belonged. Some of the marks were fresh.

He stopped at the doorway, his jaws clenched like his gut. Quietly he said, "Raziel?"

He heard a scraping, perhaps the legs of a chair against the hard earthen floor. Then the flap was pulled aside, and James had his answer to the absence of Simeon's scrolls. Raziel held one, and beyond him James could see the others on the bed in the corner. A large cruse of oil, especially for Sabbath use and probably freshly lit, sat in a small recess in the stone wall. Strange, the rustle of emotions James felt all at once: anger that Raziel had overstepped himself, violating the memory of Simeon by daring to handle scrolls that had belonged to him; a certain comfort that they were being used; a further comfort that this Zealot leader was righteous enough to wear the tefillin—his own, James noted, not Simeon's—and read the Law and the Prophets.

Yes, it was strange to see this sect leader as a guest at Annika's house, reading the scrolls of her dead husband, but stranger still was Raziel's greeting.

"It is you," Raziel breathed.

Momentarily speechless, James glared at him. What was this? Raziel looked at him much the way some of the seekers did, with a mix of awe and respect. It could not be that this Raziel was just another seeker. It could not be! Not after his words this morning. Then why this horrible greeting? Why this eerie look?

It disappeared as quickly as it had come. Raziel covered for it by stepping aside and gesturing widely, with good grace, to the room. "Please, be you welcomed."

James would sooner brawl with the man than be treated by him with such continued respect. Feeling every inch of the awkwardness now sweeping through him, he kissed the mezuzah posted inside the doorway and entered the room.

The room was divided by a curtain wall. On the left, on the other side of the curtain, was Annika's room. On this side of the curtain, a bed stood in the corner, with a chair next to it. A rolled-up pallet lay against the wall near the bed, with a collapsible three-legged chair against the pallet. A bundle lay near the pallet . . . the wooden object on top identified it as Nathanael's. James went to the bundle and picked up the crude ball-in-a-cage puzzle and turned it over in his hands. Truth to tell, James' first ball-in-a-cage, at the age of six, was better than this. It was evident Nathanael had not spent much time with his woodworker uncle. But still, despite cuts too deep or not deep enough, the lad showed promise.

"I could not leave at sundown because of Sabbath," Raziel said quietly behind him. "This you know already."

James replaced the puzzle. "You should have left right away once you remembered the Sabbath." James turned to him. "I doubt your face is as well-known as your name."

Raziel pursed his lips, studying James. Finally, he said, "I was instructed not to leave until dark. Why are you here? You had to know I would keep hidden until it was safe to leave."

James took the collapsible chair and folded it out. Joseph had made the chair, by the look of it. The ends had been rounded in the smooth scallops so reminiscent of the hand of Joseph. Thick leather, stiff and in need of a good coat of oil, made the seat. He planted the chair a formal distance from the chair near the bed, then sat, folding his arms over his stomach.

"I need answers," he said to the Zealot.

Raziel went to the other chair and faced it toward James. He reverently laid the scroll on the bed next to the others and unwound his tefillin. He removed his blue-striped prayer shawl, wrapped the tefillin in it, and placed the bundle on the bed near the scrolls.

"Those are Simeon's scrolls," James commented as he gazed at the old familiar books. He owed to Simeon some sort of protest, however mild.

Raziel nodded as he sat, arranging the folds of his outer robe around him. "Beautifully done. An honor to read them." He added, "Annika asked me if I wanted to."

"My brother Simon wants to be a scribe." The thought escaped into words, and James wished for them back. He shifted in his seat. Raziel did not seem to notice his discomfort.

"Annika tells me that Simeon used to tutor your Simon with these scrolls," Raziel said with a fond look at the books.

That surprised James. "But Simeon died four, five years ago. I thought Simon wanted to be a scribe only because—" James cut himself off. "I am not here to discuss Simon. I'm here for answers."

Raziel lifted his shoulders along with his hands. "To give answers, I need questions."

"Why are you here? You did not come to bring my mother a scarf. What nonsense was that?" It felt good to demand. It felt good to be in control again.

But Raziel was not to be ordered into an explanation. A strange expression crossed his features. By his squint, it seemed Raziel was trying to decide something. James felt picked over like a bowl of grain by that look.

For all the world, Raziel from Kerioth looked like a sage, with the scrolls on the bed beside him and the contemplative look on his face. The gray in his beard and the clench of his eyebrows, the purse of his lips and the wrinkles at his eyes . . . he was no longer young and not yet old. In some ways he reminded James of Joseph, but for the color of his eyes. James was used to eyes the deep-brown cast of oak bark. Nathanael's eyes were light amber, Raziel's were the color of an unripe olive, gray-green. The unusual color, and the glint of light therein, only reinforced his reputation as a fanatic.

The way the look now flickered away from his own gaze made James sure that Raziel was hiding something. The notion made James' back even stiffer.

"You know who I am," Raziel began. "Of all people, I can understand what you and your family have to endure—"

"That is a lie!" James shouted, then quickly lowered his voice. "That is a lie. You did not travel all the way from Kerioth for that. We want to know why you are here. Your devoted follower Avi was at our doorstep not one week ago. My brother Joses tells me one of the disciples of Jesus is a Zealot from Kerioth. And now Raziel himself shows up. What are you plotting? Just how do you intend to use Jesus?"

By the subtle change on Raziel's face, either James had given Raziel information he did not have, or Raziel realized James had come to proper conclusions. Satisfied, James folded his arms and sat back. But it wasn't enough to make Raziel speak.

James rose from the seat and began to pace, arms folded, eyes ever on Raziel. "You are planning something. This Judas is in on it with you, but what you do not know is that you are making a big mistake. We know Jesus better than you both. Let me save you a lot of trouble, and probably your own crucifixion. Jesus will never proclaim himself." James stopped to emphasize it with a glare. *"Never."* He began stalking again, hardly a thought for his boiling belly. "You put lives at risk by being here. Stop whatever you are planning, now. Go back to

Kerioth, and take your Judas with you. Go ahead and carry out your rebellion—but leave Jesus out of it. I don't want his name even whispered with yours."

"What have you decided about your brother?"

James' stomach plunged, and he lost his pacing rhythm. "What do you mean, what have I decided? It does not have a single thing to do with what I decide."

"It has everything to do with it." Raziel's eyes narrowed. "You are miserable because you have not decided, for or against him."

Rage rippled through James. What did this stranger know of him? Raziel was suddenly behaving strangely. He had his hand on his chest; he was looking down at it, gasping, blinking rapidly. Was his heart failing? Alarmed, James snapped, "Are you all right? Raziel?"

The man shook his head as if to clear it. Then it was as if it had never happened. In fact, his intensity doubled. He raised his eyes, and with his hard new stare came sharpness to his tone. "You are miserable, boy, because you have not decided. You have taken the coward's way." His chin lifted. "Pick a side, James. Fight from there."

Before James knew it, he had lunged across the distance between himself and Raziel. Should he seize him by his robes and hurl him against a wall? Beat him bloody?

Raziel rose to meet his fury, gazing calmly into James' eyes. "I will not be bullied by your anger. You are acting like a child."

That should have been the spark to set ablaze the wrath, but instead it quelled his anger. Joseph . . . he could only think of his father. He could only think of the boundaries his father had set when he lived, boundaries James had known since childhood. Boundaries that, as a child, he would not breach lest he earn himself an appointment with a switch; boundaries, as an adult, he would not breach lest he dishonor his parents. Joseph would never have tolerated the rage James allowed. And this Raziel . . . somehow, he reminded him of Joseph.

James gulped a breath.

Raziel's nod was slight, and he took his seat again. James, after a moment, went back to his own. But he would not look at Raziel.

"You are not like other Zealots," James grumbled, reaching over to take the ball-in-a-cage puzzle. He turned it over, watching the crudely carved ball tumble back and forth.

Raziel inclined his head. "That is reasonable. Every person is different."

James frowned at him. "But you are supposed to be a leader. I have never heard of a Zealot leader like you."

"Perhaps you think I should be a brawn-without-brains camel driver? Would that better fit your idea of a Zealot?"

"That's not what I—"

Raziel waved him silent. "You are not alone. Any brute with a club in his hand is a Zealot. Anyone considered rebellious is a Zealot. If you are sick and tired of foreign rule and wish to do something about it, you are a pillaging Zealot. Nothing more than a brigand infesting the hillsides. Full of hatred for anyone who does not look like you or worship like you."

James shifted in his seat, not from impatience this time. He had never heard a Zealot speak this way.

Raziel spread his hands, a reasoning gesture so like Joseph. "By those definitions, no, I am not a Zealot. The Zealots merely come closest to what I believe. I do not care what I am called. It would not change who I am or what I believe."

"What do you believe?" James asked, surprising himself, because suddenly he wanted to know.

The light in the gray-green eyes sharpened. Raziel lifted his chin and fixed James with a mesmerizing gaze. "I believe, above all, in the God of my fathers. I believe he is for Israel, not against. I believe in our land, that God intended it for us, and to us it must return. To not actively pursue the return of the land is to sin against God with our indifference. And I believe, James, in our people. I believe in their passion, be they Pharisee, Sadducee, Essene, Zealot, *am ha-aretz*. I believe, James, that these many passions of Israel can be united into one. I believe in unity."

It was no wonder the man could command the following that he did. James wet his lips and swallowed. No, he was not like any other Zealot he had known.

"How can we be united?" James began doubtfully. "Is there such a thing as two Jews who agree? There are even divisions in our divisions." It was part of Jewish heritage to not agree. James half-smiled, ruefully and with affection. It was said that to ask ten Jews the same question would get you eleven different answers.

"I believe it is possible to be one in purpose," Raziel said. "Find me a Jew who does not believe this land is Israel and belongs to the Jews. On that point, we all agree."

"Yes, but the method of regaining our land . . ."

Raziel leaned forward eagerly. "Ah, now you see it. 'Come, let us reason together.' Therein, James, is the heart of our problem: How do we Jews become one, one enough to overthrow foreign rule and regain what the Romans call Palestinia? I believe it can be done; further, I believe it can be done in the middle of our personal differences."

James shook his head. "Whatever else you are, you are crazy."

Raziel's brows lifted. "My hope comes from your own brother. He has a personality to capture a crowd, but I tell you, any lout can do that. It is his philosophy! It very nearly mirrors my own. He is what separates me from the Zealots."

James tried to muster a response, but Raziel continued, edging closer, his fists balled in passion as he spoke.

"I keep waiting for him! He is so close, I . . . when I listen to him, I am stirred with what I hear. His words are full of power. He—" Raziel visibly calmed himself and continued with a quiet eagerness. "He embodies our people, James. He has the gentleness of an Essene . . . the discipline of a Pharisee . . . the confidence of a Sadducee . . . the passion of a Zealot. And because he is daily with the people, mingling with those most would rather forget, he is every inch of him an *am ha-aretz*."

"You say you are waiting for him. What are you waiting for?"

Raziel sighed and placed his hands in his lap. He studied them a moment. "I am waiting for him to be our liberator from without. If he is to be our liberator from darkness within, as he proclaims to be, he must first be our liberator from without. Can the heart be saved if the body is destroyed?" He gestured to the scrolls on the bed. "One of these scrolls is an account of the Maccabean uprising. Our people were nearly destroyed from within by the Greeks. Corruption of the soul.

But with the Romans we face a danger more immediate. We face the annihilation of our race."

"But they have not declared open war on us. They do not wish to destroy us, only to dominate us."

"Tell that to the thousands who have already lost their lives. Tell it to their families. Have you lost a brother to Roman domination? Have you lost a cousin or an uncle? I make war with words, young James. I go to Rome, and I try to make my voice heard. The Romans make much of being a people of decency, of great reason. It is not so. Do you know what they call their mighty Publicani, the ones to whom we pay our blood in tax?" He lifted his hands and fluttered his fingers mockingly. "'The ornament of the state, the strength of the republic. The most upright and respected of men.' I have heard it with my own ears! Such vile lies that I tremble and look to heaven to see whether God will not immediately consume them with fire! These upright and respected men employ the publicans, James. They employ the ones who squeeze blood from rocks. Usury and corruption! Our bellies are full of it; we stagger from it. Upon the backs of the Jews are the scars of their great reason and decency."

James gripped the ball-in-a-cage. One who ran with Jesus was a publican, a tax gatherer ranked by the rabbis with harlots and heathen, with murderers and highwaymen. They were not even considered Jewish. Justifiably so. No decent Jew could do what they did. The publicans worked for the Publicani and usually received a percentage of what they collected, so their methods of collection were often cruel indeed. And publicans could arbitrarily name someone's tax; that person could appeal it by law, sure, but only a fool did so. The judges were paid by the Publicani too.

James himself had witnessed a woman, a grandmother, quietly plead with a publican who must have had a previous glimpse of the old woman's granddaughter. He named the tax to the woman, waited while she blanched and stuttered, then murmured a solution. By the look of horror on the old woman's face, James knew the suggestion was to give her own granddaughter to the man as a mistress. James had been young at the time, but not so young that he did not understand what shameful thing the publican suggested. What he remembered most vividly was the rage on the face of his own father, who had stood in line behind the woman, and the way Joseph had dug into his own purse and slammed the price of the grand-daughter on the table. James remembered the rage on the face of Jesus as well; he had gazed at the publican with the same furious contempt as his father. The old widow had kissed the hands of Joseph, weeping her thanks.

Joseph did not get off easy for his kindness. The publican, cheated from his pleasure, charged Joseph twice what he origi-nally owed for his own household. Worst of all, Joseph could not pay; it took two years to work off that tax, a debt that had become a personal loan from the scoundrel publican himself. And interest . . . the last bitter bite was that interest on this two-year debt took another half year to pay.

God of Israel, why a publican? Why did Jesus choose a pub-lican? How could he align himself with the worst of humanity? Raziel was still speaking, and James tried hard to bring his thoughts about. But so much had happened this past week, so much to drag forth questions long dormant. Did not the proverb say, "He who goes with him will be like him"? How could Jesus blacken his reputation by choosing one of them? How could he bring to nothing Joseph's act that day long ago?

"It is no wonder the rabbis and the leaders do not like him," James said beneath his breath. He felt the smolder of his gut on his face, but if Raziel noticed he did not say. The older man continued in a harangue all his own.

"The Romans poke and they prod, and like Antiochus Epiphanes, they will drive us into a corner and demand of us that which we can no longer accommodate. Antiochus, may God erase his descendants, did the same. Concessions were made by our people, here a little, there a little. Then he did the unthinkable, and our people could bear no more."

James looked away in discomfort. What God-loving Jew did not know the story? How Antiochus pushed the Jews, perversely demanding ever more until he did the unthinkable. In smug arrogance, he entered the Temple—a pagan, marching into the Holy of Holies—there to offer upon the altar a pig for sacrifice to his demon god. Then he wanted the Jews, whose first command from their God was to have no other gods, to do the same: He demanded that the Jews themselves offer pigs to his gods.

Raziel intoned, "One arose who said, 'No more.' Mattathias the Maccabee rose in holy indignation and said no more. What courage he and his sons displayed, may their memories be blessed to a thousand generations, to rise as King David and say to Goliath Antiochus, 'No more!' But today we face something worse than Antiochus. We face the end of our race with the Romans. We thought that Rome delivered us from the Greeks . . . but it was only a matter of time. Out of the cook pot, into the flames, and Jews, once again, are made guilty. Guilty for wanting their own land—what God himself gave them! Jews will always be guilty in the eyes of the world. It will never end.

"But, James . . . we did not remain silent. We did not keep still. Judah the Maccabee rose up after his father, and for a time deliverance was won. Others came after, and with brave Hasmoneans like Alexander Jannaeus, deliverance remained. Then we gave it all up because we could not agree among ourselves. The land that was reclaimed with precious blood was lost—" Raziel drove his finger to the sky—"lost to the Romans!

"I say, let your brother rise up now, and as surely as I stand before you, God himself shall rise with him! Time grows short, James. Rome grows impatient with our ways. They have only Jewish pretenders in power. No Jew in power today represents the heart of Judaism. Not one! I would take one passionate *am ha-aretz* over Herod's pig family any day."

Raziel fell silent, but his words continued to hiss and pop, like a fire pit doused with water.

A corner of James' mouth came up. Jesus shared the same sentiment about Herod the philanderer—called him a fox. Herod's brothers, who ruled over the other provinces, were not much better. James could not think of a single Jew who had less than contempt for those in power today. Some of the Sanhedrin, they were good, to be trusted. But not these rulers. They were not for Israel. They were for themselves.

"Your brother steps into a time when we have never needed a great leader more. He needs to wake up to see it, for the sake of our people! Jerusalem is a dry box of tinder, and Passover is only a month off. Jewish nationalism will be at a peak—now is when your brother must lead. James, your brother is good, but he is young. He needs to be reminded of the valor of the Maccabees. He needs to—" Raziel drew his balled fists to his chest, then continued more quietly but with no less earnestness.

"If he is allowed to continue on his course, James, he will die, and we will look for another messiah." Raziel raised his hands and let them fall into his lap. "There it is, and it is the truth. He will end up on yet another Roman cross, all for nothing. Have we not learned from Judas of Galilee? His trouble to defy Roman taxes earned him and his followers crosses, crosses that lined the highway as warning to others. Jesus needs to use not only his heart but his head. All he has to do is say the word, and he will have the backing of thousands! We all watch him, James. From the Sanhedrin to the *am ha-aretz*." Raziel put his palms together, finally pleading. "We sin against God by refusing to pull together. In your brother is great hope."

Raziel stood suddenly to gesture at the curtained passageway. "Did you see all of those people out there, James? Good people! Innocent people! People who scrape for a living and have good hearts and an honest faith in the One True God amidst people who worship gods who are not gods. These people are the ones who do not much care what is played out daily in Jerusalem and Rome. They are concerned with bread for the table and shoes for the feet; they are concerned with scraping together the next tax. They don't think much about what goes on in Rome . . . but I care about them. And your brother cares. We are the ones who have gifts from God to lead." Raziel came close to James and crouched to gaze into his eyes. "But we cannot lead if we refuse to be united."

"I wish my brothers could hear you," James said before he could stop it. These words, this passion . . . here was more sense than he had heard since Joseph was alive.

The light in Raziel's eyes could kindle a brush fire. "I wish only one brother could hear me."

James pulled back, mostly from reflex. So many had wanted an audience with Jesus, as if James could personally grant one. But no one before had spoken like Raziel.

"You give me much to think on," James said slowly. He rubbed his hand absently over his belly, thoughts gusting. Before he could begin to put them in order, Raziel took his seat and pulled it close. He put his hands together, touching his fingertips to his lips.

"Talk to him, James. He will not listen to me. I have tried. I will go to my grave knowing I did what I could. But you . . . you could be the one to make him see. I have heard that your father was a good man, respected by all in the community. Annika speaks so well of him, of his goodness and how he tried so hard to raise his children to walk in God's ways. What would your father say today? Would he approve that his son does not take his leadership gifts to the lengths God intended? James, I feel great pride in Jesus, as if he were my own boy. I think many Jews do. He is a young man with great passion and great wisdom who is simply misdirected. He needs fatherly advice. You know it, James, I see it in your eyes. I appeal to you, as a father to a son."

James looked away. Why did he—how did he know?

"James, listen. Judah the Maccabee fought back. Mattathias and his sons, they fought back . . . and they won. Look at the similarities. Mattathias and his five sons. Joseph and his five sons. Perhaps it is history playing itself out again. Perhaps we are given a chance by God to make it right this time, to take back our land and make a lasting peace, one to endure for the generations of our people. James, listen—Joseph is here no longer, but God help me, unworthy as I am, I am here. Ready to do what I can, to offer everything I have. It comes to this: We Jews will either be assimilated or annihilated. That, and soon. Now is the time, James."

James found he was nodding but stopped. No, no, he could not agree yet. He could not commit to anything. Confusion and frustration made him scrub his nails in his scalp. How was it he even considered the words of this man? And yet . . . in three years . . . this one spoke James' heart like no other.

James dropped his hand into his lap and sighed heavily. He said quietly, "I don't know what I can do. Jesus knows his own mind. He does not listen much to others, even his own family. But—I will think on it." He swallowed. "I will speak to my brothers."

Raziel sat back. "Do what you can, James. It is all God ever asks of us."

James rose and suddenly felt uncomfortable at his leave-taking. He managed a weak half smile at Raziel. "When I came, I wanted to kill you."

Raziel rose too and returned the wry smile. "And now, perhaps, we depart as friends? Only God."

"Only God."

"I will be here until dusk tomorrow night. Contact me if you and your brothers come to a conclusion that we can, perhaps, discuss."

James nodded and started for the passageway. He stopped

when he realized he was still holding the ball-in-a-cage and went back to place it on Nathanael's bundle. He wiped his hands on his tunic, glanced at Raziel, and went through the doorway. He threw a last look over his shoulder at the older man, who stood holding apart the curtain. When James would see him next, he did not know. Oddly, he had a feeling he would miss him.

⁂

Raziel watched until James disappeared around the corner at the end of the passageway, then let the curtain fall back into place. He had not lied to the lad. For this he was grateful, though he would have lied if he had to. The cause was everything.

Raziel turned from the doorway, fingering his beard. Well, where was the harm in his speech? That boy needed a little passion in his life. He needed a chance to get his focus off himself. Raziel had watched what went on in those dark-brown eyes. James had listened and had put good hard reasoning to harder issues. Raziel had seen it hundreds of times; he had seen minds change course through words Raziel himself was inspired to say. He knew his gifts. It never failed to exhilarate and to humble him. What power in the spoken word!

What power, too, in the unspoken words. Raziel could not help but chuckle as he began to gather the scrolls together. If James had pressed him for the reason for his presence in Nazareth, what would he have told the boy? *Seek James* was not a sensible option.

He had left Kerioth in a hurry, in a flush of confusion,

unsure of where he was going, only knowing he had to go. He had sensed that the name was far off, and he'd packed for the journey as if it would take a week. So it did. He was slowed on the way by early pilgrims heading to Jerusalem for Passover. Hostels were filled, inns were filled; Raziel often had to inquire for a home to stay in, or put up a tent and risk it on the roadside.

He never once dreamed that the James of the mystical injunction would turn out to be the younger brother of Jesus the Nazarene.

Oh, he had heard young Jesus speak, on several occasions. All he told James was sincere, though Raziel, in truth, had long given up on the man from Galilee. Jesus had an authority in his gifts that Raziel knew all too well; Jesus knew what he was about. He would no sooner give up his mission than would Raziel himself.

Raziel folded up the tripod chair and set it against the wall. So, one who ran with Jesus was a Zealot from Kerioth? That was news to him. Ah, let James think there was a plot to strong-arm Jesus to nationalism. No harm in it. He hoped it would make James face reality. Think on important things. Maybe even prompt him to join the cause. To do what his brother would not. Such a pity. All those powers.

He sighed. No, Jesus himself would not be Israel's messiah—not the messiah they needed. Either way, the poor fool would earn himself a cross for being different, for stirring up passion, and Raziel hated Rome even more for it. He liked that lad, liked his revolutionary ideas and his kind and compassionate ways, and he did not want him to die. For the inevitable fate that awaited gentle Jesus and his followers, Raziel would one day make Rome pay. Yes, they would pay. But he knew better than to try again with the turn-the-other-cheek peace lover from Nazareth.

What a paradox indeed. At one time, it would have been Jesus to bring him so far north, had he conceived to pay the family a visit to persuade their brother for the cause of Israel. Nothing could make him leave his Miriam, or his work for Israel. Nothing but a voice that exacted obedience, a voice that demanded that he *Seek James,* a voice he knew at his core. It was more than a voice; it was a presence, *the* Presence, the life force that he could sense in a hot wind sweeping in from the Negev, or in a beautifully formed vase. Miriam, in the end, had insisted he go, lest he torture himself with another sleepless night. The decision to take the journey made him sleep like a baby for the first time in a week, and the next day he left Miriam at the doorway, wondering if he would see her again.

The things he had told James' family early this morning—no, Raziel was not proud of those things. He'd had to devise something, because *Seek James* was not tidy. It was raw and echoing; it came with no buffering advice. It left Raziel to come up with a reason for his presence. He had told them things Miriam had never said, but she might have. Those words were very like Miriam. She had only given him her scarf so he could take it out and breathe deeply of her fragrance when he needed to. How he missed her! How he longed for her wise counsel and her companionship. The things he would have to tell her when he returned.

Miriam, you were right. I found James, and you will not believe who he is. Miriam, I thought I had failed on my outlandish mission . . . but James came, and with him, one more chance by the One True God. And strange, Miriam, do you know when I was released? When I told him he was miserable because he had not decided. I spoke those words, and the great stone on my chest gained wings and flew away.

Laughing, Raziel lifted his hands and turned in a joyous circle.

I come, my love, I come! It is out of my hands, and I am lighter than a down feather. Set a candle by the window for me, my love. I come.

9

THEUDAS WOULD BE refilling his cup. Zadok ben Zakkai would be boasting of another exploit with one of the servant girls from Pilate's palace. Bargil would be eyeing every passerby with cold suspicion, and Ephrem would be joking with Philo. It didn't take much imagination to figure out what his friends were doing right now.

He could shout himself purple at the God of the compulsion, but it would not do any good. He could rave and foam and spit like the demoniac from—Nathanael snorted. That fellow wasn't foaming and spitting anymore. Well, he could scream anything he wanted to the God who said, *Seek James,* but Nathanael somehow knew that this cursed compulsion would not leave.

In the darkness he brooded on his haunches in a thicket of trees on the ridge, looking down on the neighborhood below. He had seen James come and, half an hour later, had seen him go. James never saw him. If he had been looking for Nathanael, he took a long time at Annika's to do it. Was it possible he went to speak with Raziel? Nathanael was too far away from James to see his face when he passed. He would have liked to know what—

No. He was done with this crazy family. Done with Nazareth. His mother probably missed him . . . maybe she did . . . and his friends, well, at least he'd have a story or two to tell them when he got back. When he got—back.

He scratched his neck and tossed another pebble into the little pile he had been building. The only thought more miserable than staying was going back. Back to Caesarea. Back to friends who, a few weeks ago, he could not imagine being without. Now the very thought of lounging about with them on the harbor made him want to writhe for the suffocation of it.

"Where does that leave me?" he growled at the deeply violet sky. "You were the one who brought me here. You were the one who sent me on this adventure. I was supposed to be like one of those men of Israel. This was *your* idea, not mine." He punched his fist at the stars. "*You* got me into this. Why don't you take your *Seek James* and—and give it to Zadok ben Zakkai? He is the son of a priest. What were you thinking to choose me? The son of a whore." He shook his head in bitter amazement.

The fact that the compulsion remained, unchanged, not a whit stronger or lesser for all his anger, made him even angrier. He felt the compulsion with every breath. He felt as though someone had given him a dose to hear better, see better, think better. It felt like an . . . awareness. Stitched to his soul, with no hope of tearing it out. With it came the sense that someday it would leave, but it would not be on Nathanael's terms. And that part made him livid.

In the back of his mind, like the rustle of Mother's wind chimes, was the thought that he had a choice in this. He could leave Nazareth, go back to Caesarea, and eventually the compulsion would die out. He knew how it would go . . . the way Theudas would holler from the top of Sebaste's Cliff and leap off into the Mediterranean surf . . . a strong, clear shout would become a descending cry, no less strong but dimmer for the distance. *Seek James* would descend within him, dwindle away to silence. It horrified him.

He did not want it to be a choice. He wanted someone to blame. And really, what choice was there? He had never felt more alive in his life. Never more full of doubt, never more scared, and he would sooner die than admit that to his friends. He had never had a burden like this. He did not want it to leave.

He squeezed a fistful of pebbles. Those sons of Joseph, they didn't know how good they had it. Spoiled brats, the lot of them, and that Jesus included. How could Jesus leave behind everything he had? Brothers, a sister, a mother who—

Jesus left behind a normal life. He left behind scheduled meals and tidiness and nice neighbors. He left behind order. Didn't Nathanael have the hardest time of all behaving as if all this wonderful life about him was normal?

Jesus left behind a home full of good memories, for all the things James had told him this past week, all the things Annika said. That Joseph, he was a good man. A righteous man, the good kind of righteous, and Nathanael knew the difference. Folks like Joseph were rare. Nathanael would have liked him, he knew. Nathanael liked anyone who treated people with dignity. Annika never remembered he was a bastard; Zadok's father, Zakkai the priest, never forgot.

He let the pebbles drain through his fingers. Nathanael had a feeling that Joseph would have liked him, maybe. Joseph would have seen something in him, that he was honest—that he tried to be—and most of all that he was loyal. Joseph would have treated him as Mary did. He had never met anyone like Mary.

He did not want to compare his mother to Mary; it wasn't fair. Mary surely had had a perfect little childhood, adored by her parents; his mother had scars on her legs given her by her own mother. Mary grew up in a cushion of love. His mother grew up with a drunken father, whose favorite thing to do was to cuff her on the back of the head when she wasn't expecting it. To avoid the blows, she tried hard to be a good child. But it did not matter if she was good or not, and to this day, anytime a hand moved suddenly around her—to swat a fruit fly or scratch a nose—she would flinch. Nathanael hated his grandfather, hated him in his grave. He would have killed him, old man or not, had not the wine already done so. He hated his grandmother too. She treated Nathanael nicely but treated his mother with an insidious amount of contempt—not enough for his mother to throw her out when she came to visit, but enough to make Nathanael wish his grandmother would stay away.

Mary had the childhood his mother deserved. It was not

Mother's fault she was the way she was. Nathanael was very sure she would be . . . different today . . . if her own mother had been like Mary. Or Annika. He had never known anyone like Annika. A pity, that one could not choose one's own grandparents.

Nathanael slowly pulled up his tunic, inched it above his knees. The scars on his thighs, bumpy horizontal stripes like terraced stone walls on a hillside, were old now, turning white. It was not Mother's fault. If she had had a childhood like Mary's . . . if she . . . it was not her fault . . . she never meant it . . . and the only tool Nathanael could not bring himself to touch, in that grand assortment of tools at the carpenter's shop, was the razor.

The tunic fell back into place, and Nathanael picked up another handful of pebbles. Caesarea or Nazareth. Caesarea or Nazareth. The family probably hated him now, dunking their precious brother. Spoiled, contemptuous brats, the lot of them. He hated every one. James, next time he saw him, would fire him on the spot. No use showing up at the shop tomorrow. No—it was Sabbath. Well, no use showing up at the shop the day after.

He glanced over his shoulder into the murky night. He had a scratchy feeling of late, that the night had eyes. He sometimes felt a gaze upon him even in the daylight, but when he turned to look, no one was there. The other day he even thought he saw—what was his name? Avi?—with his friend in the marketplace. But when he looked harder, they were gone. He grimaced, and the pebbles ground against each other in his fist. The suspicion was probably joined in some way to the compulsion. He was hounded, from within and without.

Caesarea or Nazareth. *Seek James* or a dwindling shout. He gazed at the candlelit village below and squeezed the pebbles till they squeaked.

☙

"'Out of my way, old fool'? You cannot do better than that? Use your imagination, boy. How about 'Out of my way, you with the breath of a thousand camels'? Or 'Out of my way, you donkeyless pile of wrinkled age spots'? If you are going to insult someone, make it interesting."

Of course, the young man with the unflattering scowl, who had jostled him as he passed, could not understand a word he said. Not many knew the tongue of Persia in these parts, even fewer knew the dialect of his village. Oh, Balthazar could speak Aramaic. It was simply nice to let loose in a good scathe of a decent language now and then.

The sun crept up the horizon, heading toward a cap of gray. Not many were on the roads today, contenting Balthazar. Well, he missed their songs of ascent, to be sure. Today he passed parties camped beside the road, and sometimes he caught a snatch of music. It would be good to hear the fullness of the joyful sounds tomorrow. But for today, he would enjoy a road less traveled, less congested with caravans of people on their pilgrimage to Jerusalem. Today was their Sabbath, emptying the road, and today he would leave many miles behind him.

He greatly delighted in the sights that accompanied the bustle of the roads these days. He loved to watch fathers point out places to their sons, surely telling them of the ancient events that had happened at the spot of their fingertips. He watched them openly marvel at the wonders beyond their villages, at the historic places and ancient monuments. They did not hide the thrill of journeying to their holiest of cities.

Balthazar found himself humming one of their psalms of ascent. *I will lift up my eyes to the mountains; from whence shall come my help? My help comes from the Lord, Maker of heaven and earth.* Wonderful words with a richly resonant tune. Sometimes the pilgrims would break into a sort of skipping dance; how he longed to join them at times, to celebrate with them under the loving gaze of the Creator. He chuckled to think of it, imagining the looks on their faces. A pagan, matching joyous fluid steps to their own—a Gentile, the Unclean, uniting with them to fling arms to the sky in a grand celebration of the One True God. They, to celebrate their Passover, God's great and terrible deliverance of his Jews from cruel bondage. He, to celebrate being chosen again.

He wondered if there were psalms of *de*scent; soon his direction would veer from that of Jerusalem. Yesterday he had crossed the Jordan River and had passed the ancient city of Jericho. He had chosen to rest near the remains of a fortified tower, hundreds and hundreds of years old. He made sure he was near enough to a family so he could hear what the father said to his seven children, whom he had gathered about him, seating them near him on the ground.

The young father had told the story of Joshua and the trumpets of Jericho. Balthazar had listened and nodded, thoroughly enjoying the sweet young faces of rapt attention. He watched the attentive mother, the patient and earnest young father. What a beautiful sight it was, family. How much his people could learn from these Jews.

Enchanted, he had forgotten himself yesterday and had

offered one of the little ones a stick of cinnamon. The mother, though polite and smiling, had whispered gently in the ear of the little one. The child, dark eyes solemn and wide, ducked behind his mother's skirts, but peeped out long enough to catch Balthazar's wink. Balthazar had nodded to the young woman and withdrawn the offered treat; he understood perfectly and felt a little abashed at the slip. Strict Jews could accept nothing from the hand of a heathen, not without a purification rite.

Perhaps he had made them uncomfortable too, by eating so close. Jews were not allowed to eat with the heathen. So Balthazar picked up his things and moved himself farther away. Sadly, it was out of the hearing of the young father, but it was for the comfort of the family. He continued to watch them as much as he could without appearing to stare openly; it was simply that the road was long and lonely, and this lovely family so very vibrant.

The thump of his stick was hollow on the Roman road. Balthazar adjusted the pack on his shoulder and wondered if the family had reached Bethphage yet. The young man had told him he had cousins there, to stay with during the Passover celebration. The strictest of Jews did not even converse with the heathen, but fortunately for Balthazar the young father did not seem to hold with this particular tradition. While he replaced articles from their meal into their basket lashed to the donkey saddle, he called amiably over to Balthazar. "You are traveling far?"

"Yes. Far. Galilee, I am thinking."

"Ah, Galilee is beautiful in the springtime. In a few weeks the rains will pass, and the almond trees will blossom. Beautiful white flowers. Looks like snow from afar."

Balthazar had nodded from where he lounged against his pack, eating his bread. "We also have almond trees where I am from. Nothing like the sight of a grove of blossoming almonds."

"You are from the East? Very far?"

"Very far. Have you heard of Susa?"

The father paused at his pack. "That is far. How long have you been on the road?"

Balthazar had chuckled as he glanced at the wide stones used to pave the roads. "A very long time, but on this one, not long enough. Would that the Romans could pave every byway. Makes for a faster and easier journey. You are going to one of your feasts?"

The young man nodded.

"Tell me," Balthazar mused, "is frankincense offered to your God for part of the sacrifices of this feast? I see the lambs with the caravans; I know these are for your sacrifices . . . but I wonder about the frankincense."

The man shrugged. "It is used in grain offerings, but it is not specifically a part of Passover. Why do you ask? Do you sell it?"

Balthazar had given the man some sort of response; he did not remember what—he did not wish for the young father to know he had been a pagan priest. He had actually wondered if Mary still used Baran's box for frankincense. Though he was familiar with some of the customs of these people—he snorted—enough to make him an expert on Jewish affairs back home—he still was unsure what part frankincense played in worship. In his own country, frankincense was a typical offering to Ahura Mazdah's flames. Baran's gift was appropriate for a man who wanted to be well represented to the new . . . to the ancient . . . Deity.

Perhaps it would not rain today. He surveyed the cloudy sky, striated with gray but broken here and there with patches of blue. He would like a day to dry out down to his skin. When he had started the journey, he had not given thought to protection from the rains; the winter rains had not yet begun. He had traded spices for a cloak coated with beeswax somewhere near Babylon, but the wax was now cracked and crumbling. He had spent an entire season on this road.

Balthazar's walking stick thumped the paved road in dull hollow thuds, rhythmic and comforting. He wondered how the nice young father and his sweet family were doing. Humming one of their songs of ascent, he made for Galilee.

"Hear, O Israel, Adonai is your God. Adonai is one. You shall love Adonai your God with all your heart, with all your soul, with all your might. Take to heart these instructions which I charge you this day. Impress them upon your children. Recite them when you stay at home and when you are away, when you lie down and when you get up. Bind them as a sign on your hand and let them serve as a symbol on your forehead. Inscribe them on the doorpost of your house and on your gates."

"Amen," murmured Joses, Judas, and Simon.

James glanced about the workroom at the brothers and settled on Joses. He nodded at him, and Joses took up the benediction.

"True it is, that you are Jehovah our God and the God of our fathers, our King and the King of our fathers, our Savior and the Savior of our fathers, our Creator, the Rock of our salvation, our Help and our Deliverer. Your name is from everlasting, and there is no God beside you. A new song did they that were delivered sing to your name by the seashore; together did all praise and own you King, and say Jehovah shall reign, world without end. Blessed be the Lord who saves Israel."

"Amen," responded James, Judas, and Simon.

James glanced at Judas and nodded. Judas took up the first eulogy. He cleared his throat and began.

"Blessed be the Lord our God and the God of our fathers, the God of Abraham, the God of Isaac, and the God of Jacob; the great, the mighty, and the terrible God; the Most High God, who shows mercy and kindness, who created all things, who remembers the gracious promises to the fathers, and brings a Savior to their children's children, for his own name's sake, in love. O King, Helper, Savior, and Shield. Blessed are you, O Jehovah, the Shield of Abraham."

"Amen," said the brothers. James glanced at Simon.

Simon intoned the second eulogy. "You, O Lord, are mighty forever; you, who quicken the dead, are mighty to save. In your mercy you preserve the living; you quicken the dead; in your abundant pity you bear up those who fall, and heal those who are diseased, and loose those who are bound, and fulfill your faithful Word to those who sleep in the dust. Who is like you, Lord of strength, and who can be compared to you, who kills and makes alive, and causes salvation to spring forth? And faithful are you to give life to the dead. Blessed are you, Jehovah, who quickens the dead."

"Amen."

All four brothers offered the final eulogy. "You are holy,

and your name is holy, and the holy ones praise you every day. Selah. Blessed are you, Jehovah God, the Holy One. Amen."

The prayer shawls came off; the phylacteries were removed, kissed, and folded. The tefillin were unwound, kissed, and placed with the phylacteries into the shawls. The shawls were folded into bundles, and the bundles placed in the willow basket on Father's bench.

A lifetime of going to synagogue was not an easy habit to change. Sometimes James ached to be back. It felt foreign not going. It felt wrong.

"You did not come home until very late," Simon said, not looking at James, as he took his stool at his bench and picked up the half-carved bowl.

"I had much to think about," James said as he slipped onto his own stool. He hooked his legs around the stool legs.

"Did you see Nathanael?" Jude asked. James squinted at him. His tone was too casual.

"No. I didn't."

"I waited long, James," Joses said quietly. "We all did. I finally had to go home to Abigail. Where did you go last night?"

James inspected a ragged thumbnail and turned in his seat to look at his hanging tools. He took down the rasp and went to work on the nail. "After I spoke with Raziel, I went for a walk."

Simon put the bowl back and folded his arms, his thoughtful gaze on James.

Simon was not a tall man, but he had the chest of a wine cask, big as a barrel. His arms were as thick as a metalsmith's. He was considered the best looking of the lot. He had square, strong lines in his face and brown eyes set in thick, long lashes. Though his eyes were often cold and mocking, the girls in the village still gave him a second look. James supposed they still did.

It was not fair that Simon, even Simon, was denied a normal life. Only Joses and Devorah were married, raising children for an inheritance. Simon and Jude and Jorah were all denied the happiness of married life. Nobody wanted to be united to the family of the Galilean preacher. James had never really wanted to be married, himself. The only one he wanted had wanted someone else. If she even had a wisp of a thought toward James; well, he was second choice. He would not be second choice.

Simon, he could have had his pick. Heaven help the woman who would marry him, but still . . . it was not fair. As much as Simon irritated James, there was the flashing memory, not thought of in a few years, not since late yesterday afternoon. Simon, his broad shoulders protecting. Simon, taking a blow meant for Jesus.

James raised his eyes to Simon. "I never knew you studied Torah with Simeon."

Simon gave a small shrug. "What of it?"

James went back to his nail. "Nothing."

"Raziel—" Judas broke off to lower his voice. James could understand, too, his quick if irrational glance toward the doorway. But what Roman or Israelite would be strolling about close enough to hear on the Sabbath? The men of Israel were in the synagogues, and the Roman soldiers stationed in Nazareth considered Sabbath their day of rest too. It left them only the pagans to keep an eye on, cutting their work by half.

"Raziel is leaving at twilight?" Jude asked quietly.

"Yes."

"Well, James? Why are you so hesitant to speak?" Simon

said less quietly. "What did you learn from Raziel? Is there a connection between him and this Judas who runs with Jesus? What about Avi and his friend? Why were they here? What does Raziel know about that?" He lifted his hands and dropped them. "Is there a plot against Jesus? You seem very reluctant to talk about any of it."

James replaced the rasp on the peg behind him. He straightened a few tools that were not perfectly aligned. He dreaded this moment, dreaded it and was ready for it. Three long years, and he was finally ready. For last night, after leaving Annika's home, he went and did what Raziel suggested. He sat down to choose a side and fight from there.

He had not walked the ridge at twilight in a very long time. The skies were clear, and the night was a glittering cloak of comfort. With the setting of the sun he was finally at ease, able to relax in the concealing darkness.

He went to his favorite place as a boy, the highest point on the ridge, past his home, past the terraced strips, past Eli's place, and past the home of Tobias and Sarah, Joses and Abigail. It was a quiet outpost, one of the highest places in Nazareth, with a solitary olive tree near its peak. There James settled down, back against the trunk, and there he gazed on the flickering lights in the valley below. From here he could look to the East and see the mound of Mount Tabor. If it were a clear day, he could turn to the west and see Mount Carmel, near the coast of the sea. There it was that Elijah had engaged in the contest of power with the priests of Baal. The very tree he leaned against was hundreds of years old; perhaps this very tree had witnessed the sight.

Father once told James he thought the tree had been around when King Solomon built the first Temple six hundred years ago.

It existed when Nebuchadnezzar sacked Jerusalem, destroyed the Temple, and carried off most of the inhabitants to Babylon. It was here when Cyrus the Great allowed the captives to return. And it was here when, south in a place called Modi'im, a man named Mattathias the Maccabee said, *No more*.

Joseph had taken a peculiar liking to this tree. He came yearly to prune it and had placed a ring of white stones about it. The stones were still there, a few out of place. James knew why Joseph liked the tree. It was representative of Israel—of the Jewish people. It endured; it survived. Half the tree was stunted from an oval scar the size of a cistern cover. Where the trunk suddenly stopped, limbs branched beneath and curved toward the sky. It was a tree that would continue to grow, no matter what devastation had caused the scar. And it was there, with the tree to brace his back, that James made up his mind.

At first he had wanted to convince them. Raziel's fire, he could feel it burning now within, but now he did not want to convince them at all. He had decided, and that was that; he would leave the rest of his family to their own decisions.

"Simon, last night at some point, those questions did not matter anymore," James said with a sigh. "They were what drove me to Raziel, but I came away with something different. I was not planning to go up to Passover this year, but I have changed my mind. I will go and speak with Jesus."

"About what?" Simon demanded.

"We will warn him about the potential plot against him," Joses broke in, daring James to say differently. "Of course that is why we will speak to him."

"I want to speak to him about why he is here," James said, ignoring Joses. "About his gifts. About his obligation to Father."

"Oh, you know what he will say," Simon sneered, shifting on his stool. "He will talk about his *heavenly* Father. You of all people, James."

It didn't even bother him. Something had happened last night. In deciding, an unexpected balm had come to his stomach. It had not left.

"What exactly will you say to him, James?" Joses asked from where he sat on the ground near his bench with his back against the wall.

"I will tell him that I am on his side."

Simon's stool tumbled backward as he suddenly stood. "What did that Raziel do to you?"

"What do you mean, you are on his side?" Judas demanded. While he and Simon yammered protests, James slipped a glance at Joses. He remained silent, watching James.

"Be quiet, and I will tell you," James said.

Simon shook his head, muttering, and grabbed the stool to drop it into place. He snatched the bowl from his bench. He selected a small gouge adze, sat down heavily on his stool, and began to chip out the bowl.

"Simon . . . ," Judas warned, watching the pitch of wood chips.

"Shut up, Judas."

No one else offered any recrimination about work on the Sabbath. Simon's back was to James. Fine with James; Simon could hear him front or back.

"Raziel only spoke aloud the things I have long felt. He convinced me of nothing; he merely gave voice to the things of my heart."

Simon grunted, and the chips flew.

"What things of your heart, James?" Joses asked.

"Oh, the honesty is thick this morning," Simon sneered. "I think I am going to be sick."

"Shut up, Simon," Judas said. "What things, James?"

James did not want to push Simon over. He did not want to throw anything at him. He marveled on this a minute before answering Jude.

"We know him. As no one else does, we know him. What we know most about him is that he is true."

"According to him, *the* truth," Simon muttered.

"The . . . extraordinary gifts he has . . . how he heals . . . and brings hope. . . . I believe that God's hand rests upon him."

"Who can argue with that? Snap your fingers and calm a storm. I wonder what would happen if he sneezed."

"Simon . . . ," Joses warned.

"He would wipe his nose on his sleeve like the rest of us," Jude said. "Continue, James."

"But I think his compassion is misplaced. At least, I think it is premature. He has allowed his heart to get in front of his head, because the issue, as always, is the foreigner. The foreigner, brothers." James spread his hands. "This land is ours. It was given to us by God. The prophets and the great men who came before us were all about the land—to dwell in the land and to possess it. It's God's command. Then Jesus comes, and as they say . . . no one has ever spoken like him before. He says things that, that—strike us within for the truth of it . . . and that is good. But, brothers, he speaks different things. He is not about the land, which to me is not Jewish. And that is not good."

Simon, at his stool, was shaking his head. James pushed down a ripple of annoyance and continued. He would give them what he felt, toss it into the middle of the workroom, and leave them to their own decisions.

"Deliverance from within must be preceded by deliverance from without. We must do what our fathers before us have not been able to do, what David himself was not able to do. We must fully root out the foreigner. After that, let the kingdom of Israel truly begin. After that, let . . ."

Simon's shaking his head was more than annoying; it was distracting.

"After that, let Israel flourish and become what God intended Israel to be. This is where Jesus comes upon the scene. Jesus has been chosen by God to be our leader, to liberate with his powers and his words. He must be made to see that his kingdom is indeed of *this* world. Simon, what do you find so offensive about this?"

Simon looked up, the expression on his face one of mock surprise. "Me? Nothing at all. By all means, continue, James."

"If Jesus can be made to see that Rome is an interloper, not something to be tolerated, that Rome represents a test of some kind by God to see whether we will *unite* as one and—Simon, why don't you take your insolent head shaking and—"

"Better yet, Simon, tell us what is wrong with James' words," Joses said from his place at the wall.

Chips flew from decisive cuts. "Why don't you take yourself to Jesus, James? Let him heal you of your blindness." Before James could sputter a single word, Simon continued. "You are a fool. You bought into Raziel's talk, which is nothing more than another distraction from the real issue."

Joses folded his arms and cocked his head. "And the real issue is . . . ?"

Simon turned in his seat to glare at James. Anger made his face harder than ever. He was so full of it the words came out between tight lips.

"You are a coward, James. Like Raziel. The only honest people around here are some of the Pharisees and Sadducees, because they hear what Jesus says, and they are not afraid to confront him. People like Raziel would seize him and make him king. The *am ha-aretz*, who are thrilled to see someone align himself with them, would seize him and make him king. The leaders are not happy with what Jesus says about himself, but at least they are honest. They take him to task for the things he says, and *that* is courageous honesty."

James rose from his stool. He would not allow this, not when he had finally figured it out. He knew where he stood now; he knew what was right. The fact that the gut pain strained at the balm meant nothing.

"Simon, you are only full of poison because he ruined your chance to serve at the Temple," James said evenly.

Simon looked him up and down, nodding, his lip curled. "You would believe that."

Anger oozed from under the lid, coating James' stomach, breaking a sweat on his brow. No! He would not let Simon goad him. He would not go back. "It's over for me. I have chosen which side I am on." He looked to Joses. "You were the one who said we had to decide if we were for him or against him. I have decided—I am for him. I am on his side. There it is; you can take it or leave it."

Simon gave a long, mocking laugh. "You are on his side, though you want what he does not? Sounds like you are on your own side. Why can't you look something in the face instead of always running away? The issue, James? The real issue? He says he is the Light of the World. He says horrifying things like 'My flesh is true food, and my blood is true drink.'"

James made his hands into fists to prevent himself from clapping them over his ears. His decision threatened to unravel, when finally he had firm footing, and James hated Simon for it.

"The issue, James—"

"Enough!" James screamed.

Simon rose and tossed the bowl and the adze onto his bench. "The issue, James? Jesus said, 'Before Abraham was born, I am.' The people see his miracles; the leaders hear his words. And what they have heard is blasphemy."

Black and silver spots skittered on the periphery of James' vision. No matter how much he gave, no matter how hard he tried, no matter how far he allowed himself to go, it always came back to this. Blasphemy, blasphemy. And so it was.

Simon looked at each brother, then turned and walked out the doorway. Odd how James noticed he did not kiss the mezuzah. Such a little thing to notice.

After a moment, Judas followed Simon, kissing his finger-tips and touching them to the small metal plate. Joses drew his knees up and rested his arms on them. James slowly made his eyes look into the eyes of his brother, who was already looking at him but not at his eyes. James looked down to where his hands clutched his stomach.

It was blasphemy. That was the accursed misery of it.

10

"Nonsense. Why, I have not heard such a tale spun from—"

"Who is telling this story? Stop interrupting me. So we were standing in this pantry, this huge pantry, the size of my mother's entire home, and Bargil is looking in jars, and Theudas is saying, 'Come look what the baker made—anyone want pastries?' and I'm nearly on the floor laughing, and Ephrem is stuffing his pockets with anything he can find—figs, dates, pistachios, you name it—and all of a sudden Zadok comes racing into the pantry, face white as linen, and he whispers, 'It's Pilate!'"

"No!" Annika pushed back from the table, her mouth agape in horrified delight. She immediately pulled herself back. "Then what happened?"

"For the worst moment in our put-together lives, we just stare at each other. Then we all dive for the nearest hiding place. Bargil ducks behind a wine cask; I jump behind a huge sack of barley; Zadok throws himself onto a pile of skins and pulls one over himself. Theudas, who lost his mind for a moment, first crawls onto one of the shelves, then realizes it's no good and throws himself next to Zadok and covers up with a skin."

Nathanael took a moment to press his fingertip to the crumbs on his plate from Annika's spiced nut pie. He luxuriated in Annika's astonishment while he licked the crumbs from his finger. Wasn't he better at telling stories than Zadok ben Zakkai? Timing was everything. He had to allow his listener—listeners, since Raziel was in the back room and probably listening—time to imagine any number of ghastly outcomes.

"Well?" Annika demanded. "Did Pilate find you?"

Nathanael brushed his mouth and shook out crumbs from his tunic. He set the plate on the table and leaned back in his chair. Then he grinned.

"No. But we had to listen to him scold the cook for half an hour while we basted in our sweat. Then Pilate's chief secretary, Orion, comes and takes up where Pilate left off for another half hour. We thought we would die."

Annika sat back, shaking her head as if scandalized. Then her plump frame began to shake gently with chuckles, and then she laughed out loud.

Nathanael laughed too and reached for the pitcher of watered wine. He topped off Annika's cup and refilled his own, then settled back and looked appraisingly at Annika. He swirled the wine in his cup and said, "Do you miss him?"

Still smiling, she took a sip, then pressed the cup to her cheek, squinting at him. "Miss who? There are a lot of hims for me to be missing."

"Which ones do you miss?"

Her gaze drifted to the window that looked out on the common courtyard, darkened with twilight. She sighed, and her tone grew soft. "I miss them all. Simeon the most. I miss him when I'm not even thinking about him. I miss my boy; he lives too far away. I miss Joseph, the Lord love me. And that Jesus." She shook her head. "He carved a hole out of this old heart when he left. And I miss James and Simon. The way they used to be." She smiled at Nathanael. "You see how blessed I have been? A person is blessed to be missing so many." She set her cup on the table, and her brisk tone came back. "And whom would you be missing, Nathanael?"

"Nobody."

"Nonsense. There must be a pretty girl back in Caesarea who has her heart in bitty pieces right now. Tell me about her."

"There is no one." One shoulder jerked in a shrug. "Well . . . once there was. Almost as pretty as some of the girls around here." Her name was Zipporah, Zadok ben Zakkai's younger sister. She had a shy, sweet smile—but it did not matter anymore. She was married now. Nathanael hoped his grin didn't look fake. "I wasn't good enough for her."

Annika looked at him thoughtfully. "What about your mother? Do you miss her?"

Nathanael drew a breath and thought on this. No one had asked such a question of him. If anyone else had asked the question, they would have gotten a different answer. But this was Annika. She was what his grandmother would never be.

"I miss her when she's had just enough wine but not when she's had too much."

"She is not nice when she has had too much?" Annika asked quietly.

"No." Then he added abruptly, "But I love her."

"Of course you do. She is your mother."

"No matter—"

"Of course not." Annika folded her arms. "She is precious in the sight of God. Made in his image."

He gripped his cup. Crazy, what Annika managed to bring out in him. Dumbstruck relief and pure provocation at the same time.

"She has done a lot of—" his mouth worked—"terrible things. Things I would never do to my—that is, if I ever—"

Annika suddenly reached across the table and put her hand over his. "We are all of us six different colors of ugly, in one way or another. Thanks be to God for his mercy on us all."

Nathanael bit the inside of his lip just short of drawing blood. When he could, he said quietly, "It is still there." He touched his hand to his belly. She would know what it meant. He glanced over his shoulder to the hanging curtain at the end of the passageway. That, he did not want Raziel to hear.

Annika nodded, patted his hand, and withdrew her own. She glanced down the passageway, then said as quietly as he, "What do you suppose that means?"

Nathanael frowned, hunching his shoulders, gripping his cup again. "Means I will never understand the Ruler of this universe to save my sorry life. That is, if it came from him."

Annika gave him a sour look. "Of course it did. We have been over that." A glint of mischief came into her eyes. "James did not mention his appointment with the dye pot. What he said about hyacinths now makes perfect sense."

Nathanael could not help a grin. "I'm as good as fired, but what a way to go."

Annika pointed a finger at him. "We have been over that too. I know that family like nobody else does. If you are fired, why . . . I'll propose marriage myself to Hananiah."

Nathanael let an eyebrow come up. "That sounds like a wager." He spread his arms and looked about. "I feel more at home all the time."

She squinted at him, lips pursed. Then she gave a brisk nod. "It is a wager. If you are fired, I will propose to Hananiah. If you are not, then you will stay on at Mary's. None of this back-to-Caesarea nonsense. You have a mission, my boy, like Jeremiah."

"Jeremiah . . ." Nathanael chuckled.

"That is what I said. Well? Is it a wager?"

"It's a wager. I do feel at home. That, and the fact that I heard you say a very unpleasant word when one of your cakes broke apart as you took it from the pan."

Annika drew herself up. "That was one of my six colors of ugly," she muttered haughtily. "I'm working on it. You did not hear two words, did you?"

Nathanael grinned wickedly. "One of your other colors will probably come out when you have to propose to that bloated old wineskin over there."

The savagely indignant look delighted him, but her next words snuffed the delight. "For that, I am adding to the bet. If you are not fired, you not only have to stay on at Mary's, but you have to ask Jorah to go for a walk on the ridge with you."

He almost bolted from his chair. "No! I would never—and they would never allow it. And you can't do that—you can't add to a wager. It's illegal."

Annika sniffed. "Since I have never made a wager before, the rules do not apply."

"That doesn't even make sense," Nathanael snapped. He scuffed his hand through his hair.

"For a man who is certain he will win, you do not look very happy," Annika pointed out demurely.

He glowered at her. "All right, if you are adding to the bet, then so I am. If I am fired, you not only have to propose to Hananiah, but you have to do it—" his mind raced— "shouting from the middle of the courtyard. At dinnertime, when everyone is here."

"Done. Are we supposed to shake hands? Or spit or something?"

Nathanael grimaced. She either really wanted to marry that man, or she was certain he was not fired. He pointed at her. "If we shake hands, that's it. No more adding to the bet."

"No more adding." She offered her hand. Nathanael looked at it warily.

"I mean it, Annika," he warned.

"I promise."

Muttering, he took her hand and they shook. He did not care one whit for the utterly satisfied look that came over Annika's face.

"More wine?" she offered sweetly.

"I've had enough, thanks," he grumbled at her. "Or maybe not nearly enough."

Annika planted the heels of her hands on the table and

pushed herself up. She went to the cupboard near the built-in shelves and pulled out a wooden serving tray. "Nathanael, would you be a dear and bring some refreshment to Raziel? And I think you should take yourself to bed early this evening if you plan on escorting him out of the city before dawn."

Nathanael turned in his seat to regard the room at the end of the passage. "At least he was true to his word. He has not even visited the brush today, not since early this morning."

Annika followed his gaze. "Men like Raziel are hard to find. If he were ten years older and not married, why, I would shout that proposal to him."

He turned from the curtain to look at her quizzically. "Because he can hold his water all day?"

She gave him a soured up-and-down grimace. "Because he is a man of honor. I wish James could see it."

"I can't see it. I can only see that he is the one who caused all the mess at James' place. He's the reason I am in a kettle of boiling water."

Annika's eyebrows lifted. "I thought your own foolishness did that." Her look flickered back down the passage. "I can't say I agree with all his notions, but my, my . . . a woman would be proud to call him her man."

Nathanael had no interest in the political doings of this Raziel. Besides, he did not understand much of it. He only cared that Raziel had set off James' family like a hot spark on chaff.

"Tell me something," Nathanael mused. "What makes a fellow like that come all the way here to Nazareth simply to offer . . . encouragement? To people he does not even know? What a waste of time."

Annika leaned back from the cupboard to give Nathanael her look of surprise mixed with disapproval. He took a sip of wine to hide his smile.

"A fine one you are to speak of coming to Nazareth for—" she looked him up and down—"less than deliberate reasons."

He grimaced and glanced at the passageway. It would not do to have Raziel overhear that. An important man like a leader in the Zealot faction would never understand *Seek James*. He was glad only Annika knew his secret. Nobody else would understand.

As if she could listen in on his thoughts, Annika said, "Does anyone back home know why you are here?" She slipped a piece of honeycake onto a plate and set it on the serving tray, then folded a linen napkin and placed it next to the cake.

Nathanael snorted. "That's a fine joke. There is nobody to tell."

"What about your mother?"

He stared at her. Hadn't she been listening this past week when he told her about his mother? "She would not understand. More than that, she would not care."

Annika took a metal cup holder and placed it on the tray. From the top shelf of the cupboard, she reached and took down a thick glass cup. She blew on it and polished it with the end of her head covering. The glass was a cloudy greenish blue, in the shape of a funnel. She slipped it into the cup holder and took the pitcher of wine to fill it.

"Why didn't I get the nice cup?" Nathanael teased.

"Rile up James as much as this Zealot leader, and you will have your wine in a nice cup," Annika told him. She looked thoughtfully at the tray, then took a small saucer from the cupboard and set it next to the cup. She went to the hanging basket near the cupboard and dug into a small sack. She placed a handful of roasted almonds on the saucer.

"I thought I did rile up James," Nathanael said as he rose and took the tray from Annika.

"You didn't rile him enough."

"How much is enough? When will I know?"

"When he does not want to kill you." She shooed him toward the passageway. "Off with you. Visit the brush and get to bed. I will wake you early tomorrow."

"There's been a great mistake, Annika," Nathanael muttered. "Somewhere a Roman officer is wondering why he is not as commanding as he should be. Poor fellow doesn't know the cosmos gave most of his share to a woman in Nazareth."

Annika reached up and tugged a lock of Nathanael's hair. Her lips twitched to prevent a smile, and as if she could not come up with a single caustic remark, she settled on flicking her fingers at the thin headband circling his hair.

"Fashion these days." She sniffed and turned back to the kitchen.

Nathanael went down the passageway, glancing at the small marks gouged into the limestone on either side of the passage. Just yesterday a skinny little urchin had stood solemnly against the wall while Annika laid her hand on his head and observed the new distance from the last mark. "Well, look at that, Jotham. It appears you have been eating your good oats and barley."

Jotham had turned to study the placement of Annika's hand, then gave her a small smile. She had made a mark in the limestone with her thumbnail, then fetched a small chisel and hammer and tapped a new nick on the wall. They must have had an arrangement; Jotham followed her into the kitchen and waited expectantly while she rummaged in a small wooden box. She drew out a copper pruta, looked down her nose at him, and with ceremony placed the copper in Jotham's waiting palm. He stared at the coin, then smiled that slight smile and looked up at Annika.

Later Nathanael remarked, "You pay him to grow?"

And Annika had responded, "No. I pay him to eat."

Nathanael paused at the curtain and looked over his shoulder toward the kitchen. But Annika was standing at the passage entrance, leaning against the stone wall, regarding him. Her look was plain and honest, and for the first time in his life, he loved another person in this world.

"My mother would like you," he whispered.

"I like her already," she whispered back. "She gave this world a fine boy."

He said louder, "Raziel? Come see what Annika has for you. Seems one of us rates a nice glass cup around here."

⚜

She was leaving tomorrow. The silence in the workroom spoke of it; the bundles at the doorway spoke of it.

All morning Mary passed through the workroom from the courtyard to the doorway, adding another bundle or package for the journey. She would murmur things as she did. "For Devorah's little one," and a small parcel was stashed in a wicker basket. "Spices for Devorah's mother-in-law," and a packet went into the side pocket of a burlap bag. She spoke perhaps to fill the silence, or to buffer her leaving.

"James, make sure Jorah remembers to water the potted plants. The mint should be watered every other day. She will forget otherwise."

"Yes, Mother."

"Simon, please replace the goatskin on the churn when you get a chance. That old one is just about done in."

"Yes, Mother."

Nathanael came well after sunrise. His coming brought welcome relief from the chore of ignoring Mother's leave-taking.

He stood at the threshold for a time before anyone noticed. James looked up and straightened when he saw him. Judas followed his gaze and straightened from his work too. Joses was already at market, trading for purpleheart brought back from Gaza, but Simon wasn't. He looked up from his bowl and once he recognized the lad, turned a deliberate look on James.

Mother came through the curtain and hesitated only a moment on her way to the bundles. "Good morning, Nathanael," she said pleasantly.

He nodded respectfully and murmured his greeting.

"You have seen Raziel out of Nazareth?" James asked, his voice low.

He nodded, sending a fast glance at Simon. "He is well on his way. Left a few hours ago when it was still dark."

"Are you going to finish that chair for the widow Esther?" Mother asked him as she rearranged a few parcels in a tall willow-branch hamper. "She asked about it at the well this morning."

James gave her a wry glance. He would miss the way she . . . smoothed . . . the goings-on around here.

Nathanael licked his lips and glanced uncertainly at James.

James let him sweat a moment while he took his nail jar from the shelf and rummaged about in it.

"Simon, I need a four-inch. Do you have one?"

Simon dragged his stare from Nathanael to his own shelf.

James poked some more in his nail cup, then looked again at Nathanael as if surprised to see him still lounging at the doorway. "I pay you for dawdling? The widow Esther wants her chair."

"Sorry," Nathanael murmured and hastened to the corner bench.

Simon slapped the nail into James' palm, making sure he saw the displeased look on his face. It was almost worth ignoring Nathanael's misdeed just to annoy Simon. On inspiration, James tossed the nail onto his bench and went to Father's bench to pick up the heavy money box. He removed the lid and studied the coins until at the corner of his eye he saw Simon looking his way. He selected a Tyrian shekel and a silver dinar, replaced the cover, and set the box on the shelf. Then he strolled to Nathanael in the corner.

He placed the coins on the bench. "Your wage. You did not stay around long enough to collect it." Ignoring the surprise on Nathanael's face, he strolled back to his own bench.

But James passed Mother on her way to the bundles, and by the small smile on her face, he saw that she misunderstood. He had only paid the lad to spite Simon. Nathanael deserved a dunking of his own for his insolence. He probably deserved to be fired too.

He sent a quick glance at the boy, who stood looking at the coins. He deserved to be fired, but James would have hated to see him go. Nathanael made him laugh.

"James, could you carry the hamper to Eli's?"

He picked up the four-inch nail, scratched off a rust spot, and dropped it into his nail cup. "Yes, Mother."

❧

"What do you have in here?" James grunted as he labored with the tall hamper on the path to Eli's. "Iron serving ware for Devorah?"

"This and that," Mother murmured, her arms full of smaller packages. She stopped suddenly, and James went a few steps farther until he looked over his shoulder. He set the hamper down. Mother simply stood on the path, gazing around her. She looked long at the view falling away before them, the Esdraelon Plain giving way to the Megiddo mountains. She turned, and James watched as her gaze traveled along the way they had just come, up the slope to home. Wind swept up the slope from the valley and gently lifted the back of her head covering.

"He built the shed when Jesus was three. Jesus helped him. He loved to work with his abba."

James wiped the sweat from his forehead and peered at the sun. The rains were ending. Good to see the sun stay around for a while. He would have to remember that sentiment come midsummer.

"He built the stall onto the shed when you were little. Then it was you and Jesus, helping Abba."

James rubbed his lower lip. He hoped this would not turn into a discourse on every child of Joseph. She could go down that path by herself. He picked up the hamper.

"Mother, Eli is probably waiting."

When she turned to James, she was blinking back tears. "It is time to let him go, my son."

James let the hamper drop with a thud. "You say that on your way to join him?" He shook his head and looked away.

"He has to go his own way, James." She looked again south, toward where he was. "We all must, one day."

"Whatever you think, I let him go a long time ago."

Mary shook her head. "No. I do not think you have yet. You have waited these three long years for him to come back. He is not coming back, James."

"Apparently, you do not listen in at curtain flaps as Jorah does. I have come to a decision, Mother, one that may please you. I have given it a great deal of thought and have concluded that I am on his side. I am for him, not against him. I support him. There. Are you happy?"

But the troubled look in her eyes discounted everything he said. He felt a wave of anger. He raised his arms and let them drop. "Why does everyone around here think I do not know my own mind?"

"How far will your support take you?"

"Meaning . . . ?"

She regarded him a long moment. "Only that every little bit of your support for him will be tested. As it has been for me since before he was even born."

He followed her gaze that had gone again toward Judea. He decided to tell her the one thing he had not told the brothers. If he could. He pressed his lips together, wanting to. Trying to.

She was not aware of it. She gave a sigh at the view, then turned to look at the hamper. "I think Devorah will love the cradle Simon made for her. It has a line of roses carved into the headboard. So very beautiful. I wrapped it in the blanket Annika made for them. Strange, Simon refused to let anyone else see it." She started forward on the path again, then paused when she realized James had not moved.

"James?"

"I—"

He had her full attention now. As was her way, she waited patiently. He looked down, wishing for the courage to say it. He toed pebbles on the path with his sandal. In the end, the courage came from his own mother. She was risking everything, again, for him. But he could not say it looking at her. It was enough to say it. He fiddled with the leather strap on the hamper.

"Mother . . . I am less sure of who he is than who I was when he was here."

It did not make sense, but there it was, the whole truth. He busied his fingers with the strap some more until he risked a squint at her.

The broad smile on her face startled him. And she never did reply. She just kept that smile on him until it faded, then took up the path again for Eli's place.

11

LIFE FELL INTO uncertain routine. Uncertain because one never knew what to expect with Jorah as the new woman of the household.

Mary had been gone a week now, though Jorah's changes started the next day. First she rearranged the courtyard. The tripod swing that held the newly replaced butter skin was no longer in the corner James knew from his birth, but on the opposite side of the yard. The dye pots were now lined up on the adjacent wall, though James could not see any good reason for it. Jorah had plans to put in a mosaic floor in the smallyard, and was often found with slate and chalk, busily at work designing it.

The brothers took most of it in good humor. Jorah had

been denied her own household. Who could begrudge her a few changes? So they kept any murmurs to themselves and endured all the reorganization with general good cheer—until the day of the bread.

"Midmeal!" Jorah called from behind the curtain flap. Simon, James, and Judas all exchanged glances. Late again, six days running. Ben and Hepsi had come to fetch Joses over an hour ago.

Jude propped a plank against the wall and went outside to call Nathanael. James untied his leather apron and set it on his stool. He and Simon traded a wary look.

"I wonder what it will be this time," Simon muttered as he replaced a tool on the pegs.

"Minted barley?" James grumbled back. "Dried fish with a 'nicely spiced' relish?"

"Date cakes—made with cumin instead of cinnamon?"

"Have mercy on us all," James groaned. He was about to push aside the curtain flap when he spied a fat ball of uncleaned wool on the floor near Father's bench. He picked it up and followed Simon through the entryway.

The brothers washed their hands in the bowl near the cistern, wiping them on the towel from the nearby hook. Simon gave the towel a look before he handed it to James. James looked at it and curled his lip. Funny how he never noticed before that the towel was always clean when they used it. This looked as if it hadn't seen the inside of the washtub since Mother left. He took the towel with him to toss into the laundry pile.

Jude and Nathanael came through the passage, chattering as they came.

"Then what happened?" Jude asked.

"Theudas grabbed the man by the robe and said, 'I *am* a Roman citizen.'"

"Wait!" James protested. "I haven't heard this one. Save it for the meal. And if you want your hands clean, wipe them on your clothes."

"Hello, boys," Jorah greeted them pleasantly when they came in from the smallyard to the courtyard. "I hope you're hungry."

She had rearranged the couches again. They were no longer near the wall in the center of the courtyard; they had been dragged closer to the far wall, near the storage alcove. The low table was between the couches, spread with the midday repast. James paused at Mother's—at Jorah's—wool basket on the way to the couch. He waited until he had her eye, then held the fat ball of wool at arm's length with only his fingertips, and let it drop into the basket. She did not think it funny.

"Sit," she ordered with a lapse in the gracious-hostess tone. "It's getting cold."

"What is getting cold?" Simon muttered, only loud enough for James to hear. James pressed his lips together to keep back the smile.

"Today we are having fish soup flavored with horehound and fennel," Jorah announced with clasped hands, "and bread made with four different kinds of grain." She beamed and gestured to the couches.

The men seated themselves, none too eagerly. After the thanksgiving, Jorah passed out the pottery bowls and began to ladle out the soup. Jude sniffed doubtfully at the steam rising from his bowl and looked at James. James took a tiny whiff and glanced at Simon. Simon ventured putting his nose over the steam, then pulled back with a grimace he barely managed to hide from Jorah.

"Smells good," James lied.

Jorah smiled as she passed out the spoons. "Thank you, James," she said demurely. She passed the breadbasket, and everyone took a small loaf. It felt heavier than usual in James' hand but looked safer than the soup. After a glance at the others, James took a bite. It crunched. Loudly. Jude's eyes widened, and he stared at the loaf in his own hand.

James chewed arduously, crunching down on something with every bite. Simon blanched and dropped his bread into his soup to let it soak. Nathanael seemed miraculously unaffected; spoonful after spoonful of the soup went into his mouth. He tore off a chunk of bread and ate unconsciously until he noticed the looks on him. He stopped mid-chew, glancing at them suspiciously.

"Good soup?" Jude asked him hopefully.

Nathanael shrugged. "Fine," he said with a full mouth.

"Try it, James," Simon encouraged. James held up his loaf and continued to chew for his answer. Simon peered at his bowl.

"How is the bread?" Jorah asked.

"You know me," Simon said with a weak smile, holding up his bowl to show his bobbing loaf. "I like to dip my bread."

"James?"

He held up his loaf and continued to chew. But, lying, he wiggled his eyebrows approvingly.

"I got the recipe from Jerusha's mother," Jorah said, satisfied. "It didn't seem quite right so I added, oh, a pinch of this and that. Same with the soup." She took her own bowl of soup and tried a spoonful. She frowned in concentration, glanced at the soup kettle, then tasted it again. "Maybe I added too much horehound. Just a little too much. Do you think?"

Jude tasted his soup. His narrow face seemed even more pinched as his mouth worked over the soup. He took his napkin and wiped his mouth. "Maybe just a little," he managed, his voice oddly strained.

"Jorah, is there something wrong with the grindstone?" James asked when his mouth was finally free. "Do you want me to adjust it?"

"No. Why do you ask?"

He cleared his throat and regarded the remains of his loaf. "It appears the flour has a . . . coarser texture than usual."

"I did that on purpose. Jerusha's mother says a coarser grind is better for you."

"Oh."

The meal progressed in silence until finally James sat back and summoned any strain of diplomacy he could possibly possess.

"Jorah," he began, "I think you are working too hard."

She looked at him in surprise, holding her spoon over her bowl.

James gestured about the courtyard. "You have double the work since Mother left." The overflowing pile of dirty laundry testified to that. Never before did it take two large baskets to hold it all. Jorah seemed to think the extra basket solved the problem. "You are taking care of all of us, doing an—" he swallowed and would not look at his brothers—"admirable job, but I think you are troubling yourself too much."

Troubling herself? How many hours did she spend scribbling on that slate board, plotting out intricate mosaic designs only to erase them and start over? How many times did she rearrange the furniture? And since when did the kitchen area look the way it did? Dirty bowls all over the place, dirty spoons, spilled flour, opened spice jars, the chopping board still littered with vegetable peelings . . .

"Thank you, James," Jorah said, pleased. "It's nice to be appreciated."

James wet his lips and glanced at the others. He got no help from his brothers, the cowards, who stared hard into their soup and probably silently cheered him on. With any luck, he would be a hero after this day. "What I am saying is this: Owing to how much work you have to do—"if it weren't for James, all the potted plants would be dead by now—"why don't you ease up on yourself and prepare meals for us that are more . . . plain?"

"Plain?" she said flatly.

"Not every meal," he quickly said. "Just now and then. Just some dried fish . . ."

"With plain old bread," Simon added wistfully.

"Roasted grain with a little salt." Judas sighed.

"Some olive oil to dip the bread in," Simon said and added quickly, "You know how I like to dip my bread."

"But Jerusha's mother says too much olive oil is—"

James cut her off. "Enough with Jerusha's mother!"

Jorah drew herself up and gave James a stare frosty enough to chill wine. She set her bowl on the table with a clatter.

"Jorah, I love you," James pleaded. He gestured with both hands at his bowl. "But I cannot eat this soup."

"The honesty is thick this morning," Simon muttered. At James' ensuing glare, he swallowed and added, not looking at Jorah, "James has a point."

"You truly have an . . . imaginative way with cooking, Jorah," Judas said gently, "but I think we all prefer meals that are less . . . adventurous."

"More plain," Simon agreed.

"Like Mother used to make," James added, then could have bitten off his tongue. "Not that we are comparing your ways to—"

"What are you talking about?" Nathanael said, his face bewildered. "There is nothing wrong with Jorah's cooking."

James sent Nathanael a smoldering look that Jorah could not see. It was obvious the boy had been born with no sense of taste; that or he had spent too much time in that grand amphitheater in Caesarea, learning the ways of those travel-ing pretenders. Or it could be another reason. The same day he came back to work, a red-faced Nathanael had stammered his way through a request to take Jorah for a walk on the ridge.

Jorah folded her arms, and the look on her face grew darker and darker. James braced himself for the blow, but instead, the brothers watched as the crimson shade lessened. Then, horribly, Jorah's eyes began to fill and a tear escaped down her cheek.

"It's not that bad," Judas protested quickly.

"I'm eating, I'm eating," Simon said and shoveled soup into his mouth.

"Now look what you've done." Nathanael glowered at James, with the same hooded look that preceded the dunking in the dye pot. "All she does is work herself crazy for you boys, and this is how you—"

"Jorah, *please*," James said helplessly. "I am so sorry. I did not mean—"

Jorah waved him off and quickly brushed away the tear, jerking a shoulder. "It does not matter. It is not your fault. I do not blame you."

"Jorah," James said miserably. Why couldn't he keep his mouth shut? He could live with dirty laundry, with unpalatable food. To see his sister cry . . . he would endure anything to—

"Why did she leave?" Jorah whispered. The courtyard grew still.

Simon stared at nothing; Jude studied his bowl. James and Nathanael kept their eyes on Jorah.

"Everybody leaves," Jorah said as more tears slipped down her cheeks. "Father. Jesus. Devorah. Mother. There was a time when everything was perfect. I remember that time, like a dream. I keep—I keep trying—" Her face tightened. Her voice went up a notch. "I keep trying to understand. I try to make it work, you know, in my head." She gulped a breath. "'God's will,' I keep saying to myself. God's will. But how could he will so much misery on us?" Her face contorted. "Why does everyone leave?" She dropped her head to bury her face in her lap. Her choking cries were the only sound in the courtyard.

His face stinging with shock, James watched the shoulders of his sister shake as she sobbed. He had never seen her cry like this. His own breath came faster. No, this he could not endure. Not Jorah. Not his sweet sister, who laughed easily, lived wholeheartedly. Not Jorah! The precarious calm he had nurtured since he spoke with Raziel . . . it had the strength of a spiderweb against a swinging cudgel.

The fury rose within, streaking black and red. In one move he rose and hurled the pottery bowl across the room, where it exploded against the wall, spraying soup and shards. Another explosion went off in his stomach, bending him double. The pain stoked the fury insane.

Bellowing rage, he overturned the table, raised a couch over his head, and heaved it. He screamed things vile and exhilarating to the God who had wreaked his will on them. *What did Jorah ever do? You could not pick another family to inflict with scandal and shame?* Suddenly the pain in his gut was not near enough; he spun to the wall and drove his fist into it, then dodged from hands that tried to catch him.

Jorah says this is your will—then maybe it's time for me to serve other gods! He slammed a dye pot against the wall and kicked over another. *Why shouldn't I say such things, Jorah? It is truth! My brother is the truth!*

He needed pain as he needed breath. He sidestepped a charging Nathanael to try to drive his fist into the wall again, then raged at those who tried to quell the fury. He could never quell it himself, not until it was done. Who were they?

Convulsions bent him double, and he vomited a river of bloody bile. He staggered, then slipped in the gore, collapsing in it. He drew his knees to his chest and wrapped his arms about them. Through a sticky haze, past someone's legs, he saw a battered dye pot on its side. Jorah's anguished face replaced the pot. She was crying his name, but her lovely cheek was spattered with his blood. He reached trembling red fingers to brush it away.

*Who I was when he was here who I was when he was here who
I was when he was here who I was when he was here who I was*

※

"I have seen it before. A sickness of the body tied to a sickness
of the soul. Mix this into warm milk, Annika . . . not sure how
much good it will do . . ."

Who I was when he was here who I was

※

"I *know* he can heal him! We can at least give it a chance!"

"Simon, we do not even know where he is."

"Passover is three weeks away! He must be near Jerusalem.
All we do is look for the crowds—keep our ears open and look
for the crowds."

Who I was . . . Passover is not three weeks away, it's four.
Four . . . should be preparing for the journey . . . should be on
the road by now . . . bundles by the doorway . . .

※

"Who was that, Simon?"

"Some old man looking for James. Wanted to know if
Mother still had some box, crazy old fool. I sent him away.
How much milk did he take today?"

"Nearly a cup. We need more of the powder."

"I will send Nathanael."

"Tell him to fetch an extra tunic for me. Tell him to give a
pruta to Jotham."

I am less sure of who he is than who I was when he was here.

I know that doesn't make sense, Mother. Nothing much does these days. I miss you, Mother.

❧

"Been a while since I have seen those beautiful brown eyes. With any sense in them, anyway. Oh, don't give me that look. They *are* beautiful. A certain young girl who has been here every day would agree."

He was looking at the bottom of his own bunk. That meant he was in Jude's bed. He turned his head to see Annika settled in a chair next to a small table with cups on it. She looked tired. She was not wearing her head covering. Gray wisps framed a face pleasantly wrinkled, pleasantly round. Achingly familiar.

"Good to see you, Annika," he whispered.

"Good to see you too."

Tears pooled and spilled over his nose. He was so ashamed he could not even say it. Making them worry, clean up a grisly mess. Broken pottery, broken couch, broken kettle. He turned his head from her to the wall. Jude had etched his name in the limestone when he was six. James reached to touch the name and saw the bandage covering his hand. Three fingers were splinted. The things he had shouted, the things he called God, the things he called his mother, and Jesus. He closed his eyes.

"I would like to see you get more than a cup of milk down today. The physician says the powders may help knit your stomach back together. The powders will account for the taste you have in your mouth."

Why didn't he die? He was not worth Annika's ministrations. She took care of widows and orphans as though unaware she was a widow herself.

"Hepsi picked you flowers. They're over there on the shelf. Look, James. The first flowers of spring."

Couldn't she see what he was? He brought down grief and pain on this family. The rage, he could not control. Joseph would be ashamed of him. Jesus would be ashamed. He never used to be like this. His temper had vexed him since he was a child, yes, but not like this. The only time the rage let him alone was when he gave it free rein . . . then he had release . . . and then, when it was done, he hated himself. Why could everyone control their tempers but him?

"Milk first, for a few days. Then we will mix in some honey. Then eggs. I think some olive oil will help buffer your stomach too."

"Go away, Annika."

Did he really pick up that couch and send it to the other side of the courtyard? He squeezed his eyes shut. The shame came in weighted billows.

Annika was saying something else; he didn't listen.

Jorah . . . how could he even look at her? Didn't she have enough to worry about? Nathanael was right. Nathanael was the only honest one around here. He had hoped the boy would one day be his brother-in-law. But he was not worthy of it. Nathanael treated Jorah and Mother better than he did.

He could not hear what she was saying, only the babble of his own shame.

❧

"Again?" Annika gusted a sigh. "He vexes Simon to madness. Let me talk to him this time. James is not up for visits from his own family, let alone a vagabond from the East."

❧

The room was dim. Muted light came in from the window near the ceiling. It had to be close to twilight. He lifted his hand in front of his face. The splints were gone. He remembered ripping them off a few days ago . . . maybe a week ago.

How many days had he lain here? How many days since . . . ? He did not ask them.

He would create fancies in his mind; with any luck, the physician would make a mistake, give him a powder that hastened death. Annika said he should be up and around by now. They were preparing for the journey to Jerusalem; didn't James want to go? Then he'd better eat more eggs. Better drink more milk. Better try and take some bread.

He would soil himself in the bed, if it didn't cause them more trouble. At first he needed their aid to visit the brush. He would totter, leaning on an arm, through the cool stone passage to the smallyard and through the workroom. One day he could finally shed the indignity and go himself, always shambling back to Jude's bed. He didn't miss the pain in Jorah's face when she thought he didn't see. He didn't miss how quiet the workroom got when he passed through. He just didn't care.

He wondered where everyone was. Though he didn't really listen to the daily sounds around him, he was aware of them. Now he heard nothing at all.

He would hang himself, but that would cause them more work; they would have to take his body down, go through the purification rites for touching a dead body. He could not do that to them; he was not worth more of their trouble. Someday he would be strong enough to make it to the ridge. To the same place where they wanted to cast down Jesus. He chuckled at the mockery in it. Trouble was, the fall did not always kill. He would have to make sure to launch himself headfirst.

He became aware of the figure in the corner gradually, the hair prickling on his arms when he realized someone was there. Dim in the shadowy corner, swathed in folds of indigo, head trussed in crisscrossing folds of white, the figure sat motionless. His gray beard tumbled down his chest. His eyes glittered, set deeply in sockets with wide purple crescents beneath. James could feel his skin rise an inch, his neck hairs prickle.

"I am Balthazar." The man inclined his head and touched his fingertips to his forehead. His dark face had marked him as a foreigner, but his speech made certain of it.

"What do you want?" James whispered. His eyes darted to the passageway.

The man's shoulders and hands came up in an elaborate shrug. "Ask the One True God."

"Where are—where is my family?" Horror crept over James, and he tried to keep his mind from ghastly things. He had heard of the things some foreigners did. Offered humans as sacrifices to their demon gods. Why didn't he hear anyone? Who could have allowed this stranger—this Gentile—into the room of a sick man? James pushed himself to a sitting position, kicked away the blanket, and set his feet on the ground.

He didn't like it that he could see the man better. The indigo robe was grubby with stains. The edges of it were frayed. He could smell the man from here—sweat and dirt, foreign sweat and dirt, greasy and strange. The turban was not white; it was gray with grime. A walking stick was propped against the wall.

"They are at the Sabbath meal at the home of your brother, the one called Joses. Precious children he has. They like my cinnamon sticks."

"Annika . . ."

"She is with them. Are you thirsty?" Balthazar went to a small table set with a pitcher and cups and a jar with the powder. He poured a cupful and brought it to James. James took the cup, noticing as he did so the deep, ugly scar on the top of the man's hand. Hair did not grow there, and the scar pulled the skin tight so the man could not fold his fifth finger. He noticed James' observation.

"I was too close to an oil libation for Ahura Mazdah," Balthazar said as he started back to his seat. "'Trust the one with the scars,' Reuel used to tell me. 'The scarred ones know.'" He chuckled deeply. "It was the last oil libation I offered."

He paused at the little table to pick up the jar with the powder. He sniffed it, took a pinch of it, and rubbed it between his fingers. He tasted of it and nodded. "Blueblade. There is someone around here who knows herbs. You must have a nasty taste in your mouth—this explains your breath." He set the jar down, then settled himself in the chair and arranged the folds of his soiled robe.

He smelled bad?

The old man rested his chin on his knuckles and kept an odd little smile on his face as he gazed at James, a smile that did not do much to settle the prickles on James' skin. What does one say to a stranger in one's room? How could he know for sure the family was at Joses' place? Balthazar spoke before he did.

"Amazing, is it not, the confines of a miracle? It was once an animal trough. Then, for years, this place."

That did nothing to settle the arm prickles.

"How did he know when to leave? Was it spoken in the wind? Whispered in the rushes?" the man mused. He looked at James' bunk, set with beams into the wall. He looked at Simon's bed next to the wall. He looked past the bed to the curtain of Mother's—of Jorah's—chamber. He looked at the animal skins on the floor, at the tunics folded neatly and placed on the recessed shelf. He tapped his fingertips against a slight smile and gazed at the oil cruses set in a smaller recess.

He looked at the ceiling as though he had never seen its like; it made James peek up. Sycamore beams overlaid with rushes, packed down with clay to support summer activities on the rooftop—like every other home in Israel. What was so amazing? But this Balthazar took in the entire room, from the ceiling to the floor, with the curiosity of—a seeker. His eyes finally rested on James.

"Forgive my sense of wonder. It has never left me. Did she keep the box?"

James stared at him, tensed to spring for the doorway.

"It may be presumptuous of me. She may have given it away long ago. I inquired of the others; they know of no such box. Not even Annika." The man made the shape of a box with his hands. "It was silver. The cover was inlaid with the finest lapis lazuli. Perhaps you have seen it?" he asked hopefully.

Should he shout for his brothers? But he heard no sounds from the courtyard, none from the workroom.

Balthazar sighed. "Perhaps it was not the box at all. Perhaps the memory of a time long passed has somehow fuddled itself with today. It would have been nice to see it again." He briskly tapped his head. "I am getting old, you know." He grimaced at the ceiling. "Perhaps I am the only one who cares about that. Old to be making long journeys." A smile began and deepened. His teeth shone white in the darkening room. "But I like the journey. You do not like the journey until you are older. Tell me, James, are there songs of *de*scent?"

"I want you to leave."

Balthazar nodded. "Of course you do. But I cannot, not yet. Are you sure you have not seen the box? Silver? Inlaid with—"

"The finest lapis lazuli. No, I have not seen the box. I wish you well on your quest. Please leave."

"It was filled with frankincense."

James cocked his head a fraction. A memory rustled.

"It was Baran's gift. I never thought to bring my own. Reuel would have, but then I never wanted to go. Baran's was the gift of a dying man." He tapped his fingertips to his lips. "I never told her that, you know. It seemed . . . inappropriate at the time."

"Never told who?" James asked slowly.

"Your mother. I never told her the frankincense was from a man who died on the way."

The cup slipped from James' hand. He was on his feet so fast his head exploded with sparkles. He grabbed the top bunk, staggered backward from the man. The back of his knees caught Simon's bed, and he sat down heavily.

"They were only stories! How my brother was born under an omen, and . . . and . . . how there were visitors. They were . . . only stories."

The old man leaned forward in his chair, concern full on his face. "You have been sick many days. Be at ease, James."

"I heard the stories all the time when I was a child, very young. But people mocked us. Then Mother did not want to talk about it anymore. She said she treasured things in her heart, best left there." James looked Balthazar over. It was impossible.

"Perhaps I will fetch Annika. She told me to get her if you—"

"She said there was a star."

Balthazar sat motionless. Then he gave a single nod.

"There were other gifts," James said, his throat suddenly dry. "Gold . . ."

"From Gasparian. A golden plate."

"Myrrh . . ."

"From Melkor. In a fine enameled amphora."

"They were given by visitors from the East." James licked his lips. "Some said they were reputed to be kings."

Balthazar chuckled softly at that.

James shook his head. "Even if it were true . . . they were supposed to be kings." He looked Balthazar over, top to bottom. Someone who looked less a king, he could not imagine. "Are those the garments of a king? What kind of a king wears the clothing of a travel-stained vagabond?"

Balthazar thought on that, and an enigmatic smile came. He tapped his lips musingly and nodded. "Yes, James. Exactly." Then his head came up, and the smile faded. He blinked several times, put a hand to his stomach, then said in surprise, "It is time for me to go." He drew a deep breath, held it as if testing it, then let it go. "Yes, it is time. I will fetch Annika before I leave."

He rose and took up his walking stick with a flourish, gave

the room one last gaze, and went to the passageway. Then he stopped abruptly and turned.

"Another thing Reuel used to tell me, young James. 'Consider it all joy, Balthazar, when you face your many trials; tested faith is faith to endure.'"

He inclined his head, touched his fingertips to his forehead, and was gone.

12

TRUST THE ONE with the scars. It was a hazy thought between the dreaming and the waking, something his father used to say. James had noticed the scars on the back of Joseph's hand one day and traced his fingertips over them. Joseph looked down at James and patted his shoulder, and said, *Trust the one with the scars, boy. The scarred ones know.*

Sunlight spilled through the rectangular window near the ceiling, made a rectangular patch of brightness on the brown and black goatskin on the floor. It was a dream. That man in the corner, the strange things he said . . . Things like that belonged to dreams. His eyes traveled from the goatskin to Simon's bed. Something beneath the bed caught his eye, and then his breath. A cup.

James sat up quickly, eyes fixed on the cup. He tossed aside the covers. "Annika?"

He didn't wait for her to answer. He got to his feet and headed for the passage, pausing a moment for the sparkles in his sight to go away.

He walked down the three long steps in the passage to the smallyard and swung himself around the corner to the workroom, as he had done since he was a boy. The corner of the passage was worn smooth from many hands swinging around. He pushed through the curtain and paused at the sight of the workroom. Nathanael alone was there, working on a donkey saddle at his bench in the corner. He looked up when James came in.

James was about to speak when he noticed the bundles near the doorway.

"Passover," James whispered. He looked at Nathanael. "We are preparing for the journey to Jerusalem?"

Nathanael eased the donkey saddle against his bench and straightened. The look on his face was one of wariness. "Yes." He looked James up and down. "How are you feeling?"

James thought about it. He touched his fingers to his stomach. Tender at the press. Then he held his hand in front of his face; new pink scars covered his knuckles. He flexed his fingers. They were stiff and felt sore. He vaguely remembered the pain in his hand, remembered soreness these past many days. But he felt better than he had in a long time.

"Better. When do we leave?"

Something in Nathanael's face shifted. "I am to remain here with you. The others leave tomorrow."

Stunned, James said, "Tomorrow?"

"Judas said this is the latest they have ever left for the festival. He said if they make good time they should be there for the first day of the feast."

He had lain around in that bed for three weeks! But he had no time to deal with the shame of that as well.

"Where is everybody?"

"Simon has gone to purchase the Paschal lamb. Jude is getting the tents out of the storage barn. Jorah is right behind you."

He turned. Jorah stood holding apart the curtain, her face pathetically hopeful.

"James? Are you feeling better? You are looking better."

When last he saw her, really saw her, the flawless skin was splattered with his own bloody bile. She seemed thinner but no less beautiful. He could never say how sorry he was for all he had put her through. That shame he would have to bear. And he would, for her.

"I am better. Thank you, Jorah."

"Are you hungry? Come, have something to eat."

Meekly he followed her. He paused at the curtain to look at Nathanael. The amber eyes were filled with coldness. He had never seen coldness there. Anger, yes, but not this. He let the curtain fall into place to obscure it.

James washed at the cistern and dried his hands on a clean towel.

The butter swing was back in the old corner. Dye pots, one much battered, lined up in their familiar place. The couches, too, had been restored to their positions, though one of them was more lopsided than it used to be. There were no longer two laundry baskets, only one, and that empty. Bunches of herbs hung upside down from nails. Propped against the wall was a slate. A blank slate.

He could not say he was sorry. It would diminish his guilt, and he at least owed her his guilt. He could only wish the place was the crazy way Jorah had wanted it. Wish for a chance to eat that fish soup again.

She gestured to the couch and quickly went about preparing a tray. It hurt to watch how eagerly she sliced bread, scooped butter from a crock, filled a cup with watered wine. He was not worth it, he wanted to tell her, but it would only hurt her. He would not hurt her again. God help him, he wouldn't.

How many times had he promised himself that?

He would never strike Simon again . . . how many times had he broken that one? He would never curse when he bruised himself in the shop; he would never think unchaste thoughts about Keturah; he would never wish murder upon those who tried to cast Jesus down the precipice. He would never want to kill Joses for that calm superiority of his; he would never . . . And he had broken them all. Again and again and again. He knew he could hurt Jorah again, and probably would. He could not rein in the anger. He had tried and failed so many times. He was weak against himself, another accursed misery.

She set the tray before him, clasping her hands, eyes flitting over the tray. Then she said, "Oh! A napkin," and dashed to get it.

She gave him the napkin and stood expectantly, that pathetically eager look on her face. She mistook his not moving and immediately sat beside him to take his bread and butter it.

"No, Jorah, I can do that," he pleaded gently, and took

the bread and knife from her. "Thank you. It looks good. It smells good." And so it did. She waited until he had taken a mouthful; then he looked at her in surprise. "It is good, Jorah. It really is."

She beamed her pleasure. "Like Mother used to make. I never liked Jerusha's mother anyway." She whirled away from him with a lightness he had not seen since Mother left. She went to the water pots in the corner and took up the largest.

"I have to go to the well. Call on Nathanael if you need anything." She headed for the curtained passage.

"Jorah—"

She stopped. But he could think of nothing to say. How could he tell her how much she lifted his heart, lifted it and weighted it both, with the reminder of his deeds? How could he tell her how much she meant to him?

"Not everyone leaves," was all he could say.

The sudden sweet smile gave off more warmth than the sun. She blew him a kiss and disappeared through the curtain.

The bread was delicious. The butter sweet and cool. The wine tasted better than any he had had before, even that day at Cana, and this was watered.

"You don't deserve them."

He looked up to find Nathanael leaning against the doorway, arms folded, eyes cold.

James chewed and swallowed, forcing the bread down. Strange to hear his own phantom thoughts spoken aloud, not by himself.

"I know."

Nathanael must have been looking for a fight, because by his sour grimace, the answer disappointed him. He pushed off from the doorway and went to the water dipper near the cistern. He removed the cover, dipped a ladleful of water, and drank, then lowered the ladle to peer at James.

"What did that old fool say to you?"

James set his bread down. "Then it wasn't a dream."

"Not if dreams are smelly and walk about saying, 'Have you seen the box? Silver with the finest—'"

"Lapis lazuli. How long ago was he here?"

Nathanael looked at him as though he was crazy. "Just yesterday. He left just before sunset. While it was still Sabbath, I might add."

James nodded. It felt like yesterday that the old man was here, but he wasn't sure. The days fell behind him like dreams best forgotten.

Nathanael wiped his mouth on the back of his sleeve and replaced the ladle on the hook. He slowly strolled toward James. "You will not make the trip. You are not strong enough."

"How do you know I am going?"

"The look in your eyes."

James looked away. Nathanael's eyes made him uncomfortable. He studied his bread, then peeked up again.

Nathanael kept coming. It made James send a quick look to the dye pots—they were not filled. But he would not dunk a sick man, would he? He glanced at the amber eyes. Oh yes, he would. James shifted on the couch and tried to concentrate on the bread. He picked bits from it and stuffed them into his mouth.

"You fixing the donkey saddle? Making it ready for the journey?"

"I will show you something I have never shown anyone.

Not even Annika, and I trust her the most. *Not anyone.* If you think for a second I show it for pity, I will kill you. That you have forced me to do this is—" He broke off, his face full of loathing, his lip high in a sneer, and his eyes full of the closest thing to hate. "I show you only because you are the sorriest thing I have ever met. Because you have it all and you are stone-blind to it."

Nathanael propped his foot on the low table and pulled his tunic above his knee. There, striped on his thigh, were scars that graduated all the way up. A whole line of them, each one inch apart from the next. Each scar was a palm-span wide.

"My mother has the same scars. She promised herself when she was a child that she would never do it to her own."

"God of Israel," James whispered.

He felt the horror on his face like a slicked-on mask. He wanted to recoil but stared, transfixed, at the bumpy lines. They were deliberate. Perfectly, hideously placed. This, done to a child? To Nathanael? The bread fell from his fingers, and he clutched his gut. How could a mother . . . ?

Nathanael leaned forward. "So you see, James, I will never understand how you can treat your mother and your sister the way you do. I defy you to tell me your mother ever gave you a scar."

Numbly, James jerked his head no.

"Do you know what it has been like for me this past month, living with people who are kind and decent and—" He broke off with a derisive snort. "No, you wouldn't understand. You would not know heaven on earth because you've had heaven all your life and have nothing but contempt for it. I lied about having an uncle, James. I have a demented mother who is a whore and a grandmother I wish were dead. Do you pity me, James?"

The scars were a soft, silvery white. Emotion he could not name bunched up inside him. James looked away from the scars to the glistening amber eyes. He tried to make an answer but could not. Tried to make words come, but they stuck fast in his throat. Pity? How could he pity one with such passion in his eyes? He would never be equal to it.

No, Nathanael, I do not pity you. How I envy you.

The boy pulled his foot off the table, and the tunic mercifully dropped past his knee. He stood for a moment, then turned away and walked toward the workroom. James opened his mouth but still could not make words. And when he did, Nathanael had already ducked through the curtain to the workroom.

"Trust the one with the scars," James whispered.

He rose and went to the passage, pulled aside the curtain. But the workroom was empty.

Jorah pulled up another bucket and emptied it into the jar. Their own cistern was full from the rains—indeed, they had to reroute the drainpipe from the roof lest they flood the small-yard—and Jorah wanted to keep it full. When they came back from Jerusalem in a few weeks, she wanted a full cistern to scale the mountain of laundry that would accumulate on the journey. She grinned in delight —two weeks without the loathsome laundry task! Two weeks, maybe more! Once there, perhaps she could sweet-talk the boys into visiting longer with Devorah and Mother. They could find things to keep themselves amused, could they not? They could work with Devorah's husband in his shop. Maybe they could take along some of their own tools. But then they would know Jorah's plans, and it wouldn't do to try and convince them to stay longer now. Perhaps she could select a few tools and secrete them away in the baggage for the journey. She would have to be careful about the selection; the boys were unaccountably fussy about their tools.

She had nearly danced to the well today. For one thing, she came late enough that Jerusha and her loathsome mother would not be there. For another—James! He was walking about, with the same old light in his eyes! Well, nearly the same. And in not many days they would see Mother and Devorah and Jesus. She could shout for the joy of it.

Passover in Jerusalem. The hope, the expectation of every Jew in the land. To see the magnificent Temple again, to gaze in wonder at the busyness of the great ancient city. So many people in one place, especially at Passover! Once she had been to Jerusalem when it was not Passover, when crowds did not choke the city streets. It was fascinating then, to see Jerusalem as it was every day, without the influx of Passover pilgrims. All the foreigners and tradesmen, the Roman officials and soldiers, the constant parade of things captivating and strange. Merchants lining the crowded, narrow alleys, some who were bold with their selling, some who merely watched others and made change. Women with their faces painted, wearing exotic clothing; important-looking men who talked with other important-looking men. The squalling of animals and babies and children. All of this, multiplied by tens of thousands at Passover.

She set the draw line in the rope-worn groove in the stone

and lowered the bucket again. Only one thing could possibly dampen the joy today, something she had ignored the past several weeks—they would not *all* be together. James was not going. And because James was not going, it meant Nathanael—Of course, he would not have gone anyway. He was so proud of being an *am ha-aretz*, a Jew of the land. One who wore his ignorance of the Law like a prized medal. He would not even want to go.

But James was up and around today, and a teeny, tiny hope began to grow. Maybe . . . just maybe he could go. And if James went, then . . . well, if Nathanael was a tiny bit interested . . .

She angrily yanked on the rope and pulled it hand over hand. It was James who mattered. James was her own brother. She should be ashamed of herself, thinking of a certain boy with the most beautiful light-brown eyes she had ever seen. Eyes to make a girl look again just to see if that amazing color was what she really saw. And that smile of his, so full of mischief, so . . . charming. She abruptly realized she was not pulling the rope anymore and jerked on it to make up for her silly—

"Jorah."

She looked up and yelped at the sight of him, releasing the line. Rope fibers sprayed as the line sawed on the groove, then instantly stopped as the bucket splashed at the bottom. Horrified because she had yelped, she ignored him and furiously worked to pull the bucket up.

"Jorah, walk with me."

She let go of the line again to stare at him, barely noticing the bucket's splash. She glanced around, but no one was there. "Nathanael . . ." But as she said his name, she finally noticed him. He was breathing hard as if he had been running. His face was flushed and had a shine of sweat, and nowhere was the grin.

The day he came back to the shop, after the famous dunking he had given James, he had asked her to walk on the ridge. Then, he would not look her in the eye and was blushing so furiously his cheeks would rival any shade of crimson cloth. Now, he looked her plainly in the face. Then, her heart had skittered from excitement. Now, it began a slow, strange pound. He held out his hand, and she took it. Then, they had not held hands.

She left the jar and followed where he led; she knew where they would go. He had taken a liking to the olive tree her father had ringed about with stones, the one on the ridge. He had been fascinated by the tree and, interestingly, more so when he knew Joseph had cared for it.

He kept a fast pace and did not look at her once. His grip was firm, and she held on as tight.

Joseph's olive tree was at an outcrop just before the ridge crested. The crest was one of the highest places in Nazareth. Nathanael let go of her hand and went to a white rock that had been dislodged by rain. He pushed it back into place, then looked at the tree. Half the tree was stunted by a large, disc-shaped scar. Limbs meant to grow where the scar was grew instead straight out, then up.

"I wish I knew what happened here," Nathanael said softly, smoothing his hand over the empty place.

"Lightning, maybe," Jorah said, eyes fixed on him. She took the end of her head covering and wiped a film of sweat from her face.

"Hundreds of years old, maybe a thousand. Maybe more," Nathanael murmured. "I wonder how many pruned it before your father. I wonder how many people this tree has seen. Jews, Gentiles, the way this land goes back and forth. Tended by the hand of a Jew, taken up by a Gentile . . ."

She found a smooth spot of scrub grass a small distance apart and settled on the ground to watch him. He was getting close to what he wanted to say.

"You are not wearing your leather string today," she said.

"My—? Oh. My grimlet. I forgot to put it on."

"Grimlet?" She wrinkled her nose. "What a funny word. Is it Latin?"

He dropped beside her and drew his knees up. "Latin?" he repeated, eyes tracing the line of the tree. "No, it is not Latin." He wiped sweat from his brow with the heel of his hand.

His eyes were still on the tree when he said, "There is so much I have to—so much I want to say to you. I don't know where to start, or if I should at all."

"I would not mind."

He chuckled. "Not mind what?"

"I would not mind if you started. And I do not mind where you start."

He looked off to the distant hills. "I did not expect you, Jorah."

"I do not think I am going to like what you have to say to me," Jorah said quietly. He turned to her, and she looked into the vivid eyes. So much in those eyes. Pain, and such a longing to belong, a longing he disguised with his wit and charm. Loyalty, that was plain. But what else was there? What was there for her? How she wanted to reach out and touch his cheek, brush his eyelashes with her fingertip. She should have looked away at that thought, not because it was improper, but because she was not ready for more pain. She could not look away; she did not know how much longer she could look.

"I have to go."

"Then James was wrong," Jorah whispered. "Everyone does leave."

Misery filled the amber eyes. Jorah did not often see men with tears in their eyes.

"I don't want to leave."

She did not answer, because it would not make a difference. It did not matter how good she was, how bad she was, how anything she was. They all left. All the ones she loved, and now this one too.

"I wish—I want to—" he stammered. He reached to take her hand and pressed it to his cheek. Her heart should have leapt, but instead it filled with stones of dread. "Jorah . . ."

"Don't go," she whispered. She should not ask him to stay—everyone seemed to have a good reason to leave—but there it was. "Please, Nathanael. I could not bear it."

She would have imagined it this way, if she had let herself. At the tree, how perfect, of course the tree. Here was the place to make their hearts known. She had loved him the first day he made James laugh.

"I will not ask why," she said softly. "I only ask you to stay. I did not ask the others. I never had a chance with Father or Jesus. But I cannot help asking you."

Nathanael let go of her hand. His face darkened as he glowered at the tree. He rubbed his hand over a tight fist and descended into a private brood.

"I did not ask for this," he muttered. "Why him, of all people? Why did it have to be him?"

No tears flowed. How could her heart splinter this way with no tears to show for it? She felt as hollowed out as a hive emptied of honey.

The color in his face lessened, and he sighed heavily. "I want to stay. I truly do. I feel a—" he flicked a glance at her— "compulsion to stay. But your brother does not make it easy. He makes me question it all the time. I have never met anyone who can make me so angry." He chuckled bitterly. "The strange thing is, I really like him."

He spoke of James. A bond rested between the two, something she could not understand but knew was there.

"He likes you too," she said absently. Then, "If you leave, will you start walking on water?"

A laugh burst from Nathanael. That beautiful grin on the heel of such gloom. He slipped a sideways look at her, eyes dancing. "You think maybe I should give it a try? Maybe Jesus and I can be partners. He can do the healing; I'll walk on water and raise the dead."

Her lips twitched as she tried to restrain a smile. "No. There are beautiful women out there. Jesus is not handsome, but you the girls would fall in love with."

Nathanael snorted. "I do not think many would fall in love with a man who raises the dead." He was quiet a moment. "They are probably terrified of him."

They sat in silence for a time. Then Nathanael started a rock pile. He began with a layer of larger rocks, then piled on smaller ones. He scraped up pebbles and added them to the heap. Jorah helped, tossing on a pebble here and there.

"Not that one," Nathanael said, and took the white-flecked one she added and tossed it aside.

Her brow came up as she looked at him and, keeping her eyes on his, she reached for the pebble and put it back on the pile.

"Stay, Nathanael."

Nathanael very slowly reached to flick her pebble off the pile, then looked behind himself to find more. By the time he turned around, Jorah had put the pebble back. He picked it up and set it delicately on the toe of her sandal, then put more rocks on the pile.

"I am tired of trying to be patient," he said. "Tired of trying to understand."

She took a handful of pebbles from his rock pile, tossed them toward the olive tree, then took the white-flecked pebble from her toe and placed it on top of the diminished pile.

"Then just stay."

He took her pebble and studied her a minute, then reached and tucked it under the cloth covering her forehead. She rolled her eyes up trying to see it.

"I don't think you like Caesarea, as much as you brag about it," Jorah said, still trying to see the pebble. "I think you would like it much more in Nazareth."

"I don't brag about Caesarea."

"'Have you ever seen an amphitheater? Herod built a fine one. Have you been to his great port? Have you been to a gymnasium?'"

"I am not sure I am meant to stay."

Her eyes dropped to his. "How can you be sure you are meant to go?"

Nathanael looked at the rock pile. He drew his finger in the sand around it. "I suppose I am not sure." He looked at the olive tree, then let his gaze drift. "I do not know where I would go."

"You would not go back to Caesarea?"

"No." He studied his sandals, then noticed the rock pile again and found a few more pebbles to toss onto it. "I hate it there. I hate the way the Jews hate the Gentiles and the way the Gentiles hate the Jews. They are all such fools. Some of my best friends are Gentiles, you know that?" He shook his head. "The fights that happen. You haven't seen that kind of thing here, Jorah. There is not as much open hatred here as there is in Caesarea. The dividing line is much clearer back home."

"Maybe a clear dividing line is not such a bad thing," Jorah murmured.

"That it is there at all is plain stupidity. All these people hating each other . . . my Gentile friends see only the fighting and the squabbles. Then my Jewish friends see the Gentiles act the very same way, full of fuss and rage. Full of hate. Ha. They are more alike than they think." He held out his hands, and his tone grew incredulous. "And then you know what? I see on both sides people who would give you the sandals they stand in. People who would go hungry to make sure you had a meal, but can they see it in each other? Oh, no. It makes me angry. I'm so caught in the middle. I belong to both, and to neither."

He scowled his blackest. "So there you are, Jorah. I do not want to go back to Caesarea ever, not this side of the sun. Perhaps . . ." He dropped his eyes and trailed his fingers in the sand. The scowl disappeared. "Perhaps, if it is all the same to your brothers, I will come along to Jerusalem." He shrugged a tiny shrug. "James is surely going, and I have never been.

I would like to see the Temple, I've heard much about it." He threw a mischievous grin at her. "Of course, Herod built Caesarea before the Temple. But at least a journey like that would give me time to figure out—" He stopped short, groaning, holding his head. "Oh, how I need to talk to Annika. Things make sense when I talk to her."

"And they don't when you talk to me?"

"You least of all."

She let one eyebrow rise. "That is either a good thing, or it is not."

Nathanael did not answer. He was lost again, deep inside himself, frowning and adding more pebbles to the pile. He ran out of pebbles and pulled up scrub grass to sprinkle on the rocks. Despite the grimace on his face, and for the first time since she had seen him at the well, Jorah felt she could breathe again. One minute he was leaving her, and the next—maybe he would go with them to Jerusalem? *Annika, Annika . . . tell him the right things. My heart depends on you.*

"Perhaps we should get back," Jorah murmured.

"Let them wonder," Nathanael said with a small grin as he sprinkled the grass.

"Wonder? Nathanael ben—" She broke off. "What is your father's name?"

"I don't know."

"What is your mother's name?"

He hesitated, then, "Rivkah."

"Nathanael ben Rivkah, maybe in Caesarea they can wonder, but they cannot wonder in Nazareth. I will not let them wonder." She got to her feet.

"Perhaps I should kiss you."

Jorah felt her eyes widen and her cheeks flame as she gaped down at him.

He squinted at her against the sun, his cheeks dimpling in a grin, and gave an innocent shrug. "What? If they are going to wonder, we should at least give them something to—"

"I said we will not let them wonder!"

He offered his hand as if he wanted her to help pull him up, but she folded her arms. He got up and dusted off his hands, then wiped them on his tunic. He surveyed the tree with his hands on his hips, squinting in the sun.

"These trees survive many things, don't they? Fire, James said. Catastrophes, like whatever befell this one. All manner of weather. Amazing."

"They do not have olive trees in Caesarea?"

"Sure, we have olive trees. I just never noticed them until I came here."

They started for the ridge path, but Jorah stopped. She felt for the pebble in the fold of her head covering, then turned back and placed it carefully on top of Nathanael's rock pile. She whirled to face Nathanael. He rolled his eyes and started straight for the rock pile.

"It stays!" she shrieked, laughing and pushing him away.

"All right, all right," he grumbled, holding up his hands. "Who can argue with one of Joseph's tribe?"

On the way back, they spoke about what had to be done yet to prepare for the journey. They spoke about the provisions, what they had, what was yet needed. They spoke about what had to be done to the house to leave it for a few weeks, and Jorah even confided her hope that they could stay in Jerusalem—in Bethany—a little longer. On the way back, they did not hold hands. It gave Jorah more hope than ever.

A gentle wind swept up from the valley, rounded on the ridge, stirred about the scarred old olive tree. Gray and green leaves fluttered in the delicate breeze, releasing drops that still clung from an early morning rain. The wind briefly rocked the white-flecked pebble on the pile, then left the tree and coursed along the ridge, down the hill, rustling the head covering of Jorah ben Joseph, ruffling the hair of Nathanael ben Rivkah. It caught their laughter and swept on, tumbling down to the valley below where it first began.

13

FROM THE INSIDE of the cave, Joab sat and watched his friend brood on his haunches, watching the road below. Occasionally, Avi carved a piece out of the hunk of moldy cheese and stuffed it into his mouth. Cheeks bulging, he chewed away as he studied the road. Joab did not think Avi knew how unflattering it looked, the way he always stuffed his cheeks so full. Why not take normal bites, like a normal person? Maybe Avi thought it looked manly.

Joab grimaced and looked at the dried-up fig in his hand. It worked up more of an appetite to chew the things than it was worth. Might as well chew a piece of goat hide. "Bah," he muttered, and tossed it aside.

Normal food. A normal night's sleep. A normal day, with

normal people. He had given up much to take up with Avi. But the cause was everything. It's what Avi said all the time. The trouble was, it was not as exciting now as it had been at the beginning. Scrounging for food. Sleeping like vagabonds. Joab scratched his ear, sure another flea had found a home. He was getting tired of the whole thing.

He should be in Jerusalem now, helping his father pick out the Paschal lamb. This was the first Passover Joab had ever missed. But what would Avi think if he voiced his silly sentimental feelings about Passover? The cause. The cause was everything.

Somehow it was important to the cause that they seek the carpenter's apprentice. Joab scratched his other ear. He wasn't sure how, but Avi was the smart one. Avi called the apprentice a "pretty lad," with those strange bright eyes of his. Joab shook his head. He had no desire to look in those eyes again. He did not say this to Avi, of course; Avi had called him a coward once. He would not give him cause to do it again.

"Avi, what if we missed them? What if they are not even planning to go up to the festival?"

Avi did not answer, which meant Joab had said something stupid again. Avi told him once he would not waste his breath answering stupid questions.

"How much money do we have?"

It was the first thing Avi had said to him all day. And Joab had learned not to remind Avi that the money was his own. When a man joined the cause against Rome, all personal possessions became common—the cause was everything. He stifled a sigh; used to be, his pockets always jangled with coins when he had worked for his father at the dye works.

"I only—we only have two silver dinars and a few coppers." The cache had become seriously depleted with the first side trip to Nazareth. The whole point of their journey, when they had started it over a month ago from Hebron, had been to meet with the Zealot leader Jonathan of Gush Halav, near the Phoenician border. To veer off and see Nazareth on the way had been Avi's idea.

Joab privately thought that if they had not diverted into Nazareth, they would have never wasted so much time or money—but Avi had insisted on visiting the home of the Teacher.

"We may have to pick up a job here or there," Joab said ruefully as he slipped the coins back into his pocket.

After meeting for several days with Jonathan, whose zeal for the land would put Raziel to the test, they began the long journey south to report back to the enclave in Hebron. But Avi could not get the apprentice out of his craw. They left the Roman road, which traversed the land from Phoenicia to the Sea of Galilee, and veered west—again—to Nazareth. Joab stifled a sigh. They could have been in Jerusalem by now. They could have made it to Passover. He wondered what would have happened if they had never stopped to visit Nazareth the first time. They could not hold out here much longer.

"Maybe they decided to go through Samaria. Quicker by a day or two," Joab said.

Avi did not answer.

Joab shrugged to himself. Maybe it was a stupid suggestion, but it made sense to him. The Galileans had fewer qualms about traveling through Samaria than the Judeans. They almost seemed to welcome the danger, as suited their uncouth natures. Joab's father did not hold much with Galileans. Galileans had the beauty of the land, it was said, but Judeans had Jerusalem.

Avi rose smoothly from his haunches. "We go back to the crossroad. I will watch the road to Beth Shean; you will watch the road to Shechem."

Joab's eyes widened. Did Avi think Joab was right? He scrambled to his feet, glad for some action, if only for a different locale. He grabbed a burlap bag and began to stuff it with their bedrolls and meager provisions.

Avi's voice was a mere mutter as he stood with his hand against the cave wall, gazing at the road below. "Nobody makes a fool out of Avi ben Aristobulus."

Joab hesitated, clay plate in hand, then wrapped it in a dirty towel and stuffed it into the sack. He didn't know why they were doing this, but Avi knew what he was about. Surely a mere grudge could not distract Avi from the cause. It all worked into the plan somehow.

He barely caught the next words Avi whispered, and ignored the ensuing chill at the back of his neck.

". . . shall see who the Teacher has to heal. If you don't bleed to death first."

❧

Consider it all—*what?* James snorted to himself as he brushed the bread crumbs off the plate and stacked it on the others in the cupboard. Consider it joy to face trials? Last he heard, a trial was something difficult. Something like controlling your temper or giving up Keturah. Consider that joy? What kind of craziness was that? He shook his head as he wiped the serving tray and slid it into its place next to the cupboard. Balthazar's Reuel was a strange one indeed. But then, he was a foreigner. Perhaps it was a custom of theirs to relish pain as some kind of sacrifice to—what did the old man call his god? Ahura something-or-other.

Murmuring the post-meal blessing, he went to the small-yard and washed at the cistern. But he could not get the words out of his head. They were not only baffling but irritating. He pushed through the curtain and went to his workbench.

He was embarrassed by its neat appearance. A workbench only looked this neat when a brother was away on a journey. Simon had a finished olivewood bowl sitting on the side of his bench, apparently awaiting a second coat of stain. An inkpot and a parchment lay next to the bowl. Was he planning to take his writing implements to Jerusalem? Was he still learning from Saul?

Jude's bench was strewn with an assortment of things. Hairy twine, an awl that had come apart at the handle, scraps of goatskin, and two new tools James did not recognize. James looked away. Three weeks. He had been in that bed three weeks.

He turned to look at Joses' bench and to his surprise found it neat. No wood chips or white stone dust on the floor near it, no project awaiting completion, every tool in its place. James' gaze drifted from the bench. He vaguely remembered overhearing something in the past week or so. Had Joses left for Jerusalem already, with Abigail's family? Yet another shame for those hazy weeks of dullness; they were surely waiting for James to recover, something that should have reasonably happened two weeks ago. Every year since Joses had married, the two enjoined families had made the pilgrimage to Passover together. Neighbor Eli went too, and Keturah and Therin, and Annika and Simeon. Safety in numbers and great enjoyment too.

In recent years, the traveling company had changed. Simeon died first, then Joseph. Then Jesus left, and soon after, Devorah. James did not know why he had expected everything to remain the same. Of course things would change. He was just never ready for it.

Consider it joy when you face your trials. He could not think of a more stupid, foolish notion than that.

"Consider it *joy*?" he said angrily. Why? What was the point? Joy that Jesus left, plunging the family into three long years of tumult? Joy to see Keturah and not to be able to tell her that—

A sweat broke on his brow. Breathing hard, he braced himself against his bench. Unaccountable panic began to trickle over him, as though he stood beneath a thin waterfall. He wanted his bed. He could not do this. He could not deal with *anything*, God help him. Just his bed, just to bury himself beneath the blanket.

"I cannot do this," he whispered hoarsely. He gripped the edges of his bench as the trickle of panic increased. Anger, and now anxiety? Fear? Was he going mad? His breath came in short gasps. The bed—all he wanted was his bed. He was safe there. Safe, if only he could get there.

No! He had to go to Jerusalem. For some reason he had shaken off the lethargy of the past weeks and he—he had to warn Jesus. Surely, as Joses suspected, there was a plot against him. He had to tell him of the plot and that he, James, was on his side. He was, wasn't he? But all he wanted was the safety of his bed. He couldn't move.

"James, you all right?"

Simon was at his side.

"S–s–s—"

"Here, let's set you down. Easy, now." His brother's arms came around him, helped him let go of the bench. Simon pulled out his stool and helped him sit. "Easy, James. That's it. That's better."

The panic began to abate. Focus came. Simon was sitting on his own stool in front of him.

"You all right?" Simon asked again. James wet his lips and nodded. He felt trembly, sweaty as from a broken fever.

Simon looked at him closely. "You are better, somehow. You look—well, terrible, but you seem . . . different."

James nodded. If he only knew. He felt just a hairsbreadth from insanity, and yet . . .

"Simon . . . I'm sorry."

"About what?"

He swallowed hard to wet his throat. "Everything."

Simon studied James. "Good to see you up."

James nodded and looked away. "Did you get the lamb?"

"Yes. It's tethered outside."

"I want to go."

He had not thought far enough ahead to fear this moment, because surely his brothers would try to talk him out of it, in his condition. He was the reason they were leaving so late, perhaps forcing them to take the quickest route through Samaria. That they had not left at all amazed him.

"I was counting on it. The donkey can spell you when you get tired." Simon looked at him evenly. "You will make it."

James blinked, momentarily speechless. "Thanks for waiting."

As was Simon's style, he would not let the honesty get thick. He stood and glanced outside. "Have you seen that apprentice of ours? The four-wheel needs to be gone over; the railing came apart at one of the corners. I need to get to the granary for a sack of feed for the donkey."

"Are we going through Samaria?"

"Yes. It will be all right. If we keep our eyes open at all times, we should not have a problem."

"Whom are we traveling with?"

Simon hesitated. "Just us."

"Us, meaning . . ."

"You and me, Judas and Jorah. Maybe we can talk Nathanael into coming. It would not hurt to have an extra pair of eyes."

Or an extra pair of muscles. James frowned. If it were not for him, they would have traveled much more safely, in the company of Joses and his family, along the Jordan Valley route. "When did Joses leave?"

"Last week. Joses—"

James waved him silent. Who was he to hold up the entire party? "They were right to leave. You should have left with them."

"Joses wants to find Jesus as soon as possible. He wants to warn him."

"About that disciple?"

"About both of them, Judas and Raziel both. Joses is worried. I wish he would let it go. I have had time to think on it, and I—" he flicked a look at James—"I think Jesus knows what he is about. This Judas has been with him for three years. Three years. That is a long time to plot, especially for a Zealot. Maybe Judas went into it thinking he could—"

"Change Jesus, as everyone else does. Then he learned better." In the bright of day, without the unaccountable panic, the notion of a plot against the Prophet of Peace seemed a little ridiculous. But it was time to change the subject, because it had been a long time since he had agreed with Simon about anything. He would not ruin it. "What of Therin and Keturah? Did they go with Tobias?"

"Yes."

James nodded. He looked at the pile near the doorway. "Well, what do you want me to do? What needs to be done?"

Simon glanced at him uncertainly. "James . . ."

"I can do some." He needed to do something. "I will stop when I have to."

His brother nodded. "All right, then. The bitter herbs need to be gathered. Jorah has them drying in the courtyard. The tithe needs to be—never mind, I will take care of that. Perhaps you can check the awnings; they need to be secured before we leave." He rubbed the back of his head. "We need to fill the waterskins. Oh, and sandal tacks. Pack a bag of them, with the tack mallet."

"Did Annika go with Tobias?"

"Annika is not going this year. She says she is too old for the journey."

This was a surprise. Women were not obligated to make the pilgrimage, but they usually went. Why would she not want to go?

"Annika will never be too old for the journey. I wonder what her real reason is."

Simon shrugged. "She says she has too many things to take care of in her neighborhood. As if it would fall apart without her."

"It probably would. She will be missed."

"What will you miss more?" Nathanael said as he strolled in the doorway. "Annika or her honeycakes? Myself, I am torn betwixt the two."

Nathanael went to his bench and picked up the donkey saddle. He looked it over, found the place he wanted, and laid the saddle across his bench. He looked over the tools on the pegs above the bench and selected a sharp awl and a mallet. Then he launched into one of his sailor songs, learned from the harbor at Caesarea, and set to work on the saddle.

Changeable as the Sharkiyeh east wind, that one. One minute stuffing James' throat full of his own sin, the next as placid as the Sea of Galilee after a storm.

"Nathanael, when you're done with the saddle, the four-wheel needs to be fixed," Simon said. "A corner came apart at the rails. Check the wheels, too, and put together a repair kit."

Judas came in, wiping sweat from his face with a grubby towel and at the same time kissing the mezuzah. "Tents are airing. We had a few winter guests in there. A mama scorpion made a nice home for her—" He stopped short when he realized James stood at his bench. He looked from James to Simon and back. "James?"

"Risen from the dead," Simon quipped.

James grinned. "Call me Lazarus."

Judas squinted at him warily. "Are you—?"

"I'm fine." James glanced at Simon. "And I am going."

That made Judas throw a fast look at Simon too. Something unreadable flickered between the two. Strangely, Simon wore a look of satisfaction. Jude still had a wary frown, but it gradually faded into something like relief.

"It's about time you got your carcass to work," Jude muttered as he tossed his sweaty towel at James.

James snatched it in the air, threatened to throw it back at him, but instead slung it at the apprentice. It caught him full on the face and snuffed his raucous song.

❦

For the third time in his life, James performed the ritual belonging to the head of the house at the time of Passover.

Those who remained of the tribe of Joseph in Nazareth, plus a scrappy apprentice from Caesarea, stood outside the doorway to the home. The bundles and packages lashed securely to the four-wheel made the donkey appear hitched to a small mountain at the foot of the slope. Jorah was already softly humming a psalm of ascent, though she probably didn't realize it. She had spent the morning patrolling the grounds with her slate, like a Roman centurion inspecting a departing cohort. Ever fond of lists, Jorah consulted the slate and made a fat line through every item when the task had been completed. She had snapped out commands like a field general—"Simon, lock the shed. James, stow the feedbag. Judas, put the pay for Jotham under the rock by the plants. Nathanael, make sure the cistern drainpipe is secured. All of you, visit the brush before we leave."

Nathanael had seemed almost eager to go, once asked, and preparations made yesterday fly. The pile at the doorway had diminished as one by one the bundles were stashed in the cart. The house was swept and the workroom tidied. They had got to bed late last night, each dropping exhausted to his bunk.

Faces scrubbed, hair combed, wearing their favorite and

most comfortable traveling garments, the five were anxious and ready to depart for Jerusalem. First, though, came the obligation for Passover. James took the candle and raised it to Jude, who lit it with a burning twig. James drew a breath. He had rehearsed the words all morning long, the words that had long belonged to Joseph. Then, once, to Jesus.

"Blessed art thou, Jehovah our God, King of the Universe, who has sanctified us by thy commandments, and commanded us to remove the leaven."

He crossed the threshold, paying careful attention to the wavering flame of the candle, and slowly walked through the workroom to the courtyard.

"But why does he have to do it with a candle? He can see just—"

Nathanael was hushed by three different voices. The search had to be conducted in pure silence.

Of course, Jorah had already used up the leaven for the pile of loaves she had made for the journey. James wasn't sure leaven was ever found by the head of the household. The women had enough respect for the command to make sure they had their cupboards cleared by the time the candlelit search came through.

But he went to the courtyard anyway, opened the cupboard, and carefully passed the candle near the space where Jorah kept her crock of leavening. He lifted the lid and found the crock meticulously emptied. He passed the candle near the bread shelf. The space was empty, not even a crumb. He shut the cupboard door.

Slowly, he made his way back to the workroom, but before he got to the doorway, he stopped and looked around. Every bench was neat and tidy, the only time of the year it was so. The only time the fire pit was carefully smothered. The only time a project did not wait for completion.

He looked as long as he dared, before they had time to wonder, and oddly, as he gazed at the empty benches, the words of a travel-stained vagabond came. *Consider it all joy . . . Consider it all joy . . .*

He turned to the doorway, kissed the mezuzah, and joined the four gathered outside.

He held the candle aloft in front of them and intoned to the sky, "All the leaven that is in my possession, that which I have seen and that which I have not seen, be it null, be it accounted as the dust of the earth." He brought the candle close and blew out the flame.

The door was pulled shut and locked, the key tucked safely into a pocket fold in Simon's tunic. A Gentile boy from the village would come and check on the place while they were gone, make sure the crops were watered, the goats fed.

The laden cart at the bottom of the hill had a space in it made for James when he needed it. Nathanael ben Rivkah, and James, Judas, Simon, and Jorah ben Joseph all made their way in silence down the slope. Simon gathered the reins and clicked his tongue at the donkey. With an occasional glance flicked back to the solitary house on the hill, the five young people began their pilgrimage to Jerusalem.

14

THE HILLS OF NAZARETH gave way to the flat basin of the
Esdraelon Plain. Though the terrain had become easier to manage, and especially on a Roman road, the eyes of the travelers
grew sharper as they began the descent into Samaritan territory.

The Esdraelon Plain was not the place for wariness, not yet.
The land was flat; there were few places for brigands to hide.
It was a broad, spacious place that produced most of the land's
wheat crops. They passed farmers in the fields, who often gave
them no more than a glance from their work. Behind them, a
few travelers followed about half a mile back; ahead of them,
about the same distance away, a large caravan of pilgrims filled
the road, in Jude's estimation numbering about twenty-five,
including children.

"They probably came late to the road, like us," Simon
murmured as he pressed his sleeve to his forehead to clear it

of sweat. The day had more of the feel of midsummer than spring. For the first time since winter passed, that James noticed anyway, the sky was cloudless.

The presence of the large caravan was a comfort, though no one spoke this out loud. The trick was to keep the distance between them constant. Move when they moved, camp when they camped, and hope they did not dawdle. There wasn't much chance of that, given the fact that the fourteenth of Nisan was a handful of days away; the caravan had so far kept a fairly brisk pace.

They had picked up the other travelers just before Kfar Otnai, near where the road broke east for Beth Shean in Decapolis. And if a few of the five sent a wistful glance toward that Jordan Valley route, well, who could blame them? Many memories lay on that well-traveled road. All in all, it was probably best they went to Jerusalem via Samaria. Why not take change by the plateful instead of by the morsel? Besides, it was not so uncommon to take the Samaritan road for travel to the festivals. Many did.

What would happen *this* time? What would happen *this* Passover? What if by some miracle Raziel's words had gotten through to Jesus? Would he, indeed, proclaim himself? Restore the kingdom to Israel? Jesus sometimes seemed as fickle as the pitch of an unanchored boat.

Those were wild thoughts James rarely allowed himself to muse upon, but he used them to help block out other ones. With nothing to do but walk, and mostly ride, thoughts were as treacherous as highwaymen. Thoughts that came in the voice of Raziel. *Pick a side; fight from there. You are miserable because you have not decided.* Thoughts that took on the foreign accent of the stranger from the East. *A golden plate from Gasparian.*

Myrrh from Melkor. Frankincense, the gift of a dying man. And above it all the drone of his own voice, just to make it a mad mess. *I am less sure of who he is than who I was when he was here.*

At times it was hard to discern what the pain in his stomach was. Was it hunger or the gut ache? Presently, Nathanael helped him decide. The lad shielded his eyes with his hand to gaze at the caravan in the distance. "Do they have plans to stop for the midmeal? My stomach is knocking on my backbone."

"Just a little farther," Simon said over his shoulder. "If they don't stop soon, we will take a rest."

James had managed to keep a steady walk for about two hours, then had to avail himself of the space on the cart, next to the lamb. The lamb had trotted behind the cart until it lagged to the point where there was no slack in the tether. It touched his pride a bit to ride atop the cart next to a panting, drooling lamb, but better to make it to the festival than not. James glanced at the lamb; one eye stared one way, the other lolled at James. "What are you looking at?" James muttered at him.

Nathanael strode beside him. Apparently, ambushing thoughts seemed to afflict the others as well—the apprentice, at least, was full of the oddest questions. He once asked James why, if the farmers in the fields were Jews, even Samaritan Jews, why were they not on the trek to Jerusalem for Passover? ("Samaritans are not allowed in the Temple, Nathanael." "Why on earth not?" "They would not *want* to go—they consider Mount Gerizim the holy place to worship, not Temple Jerusalem." "Why?" Why, why . . .)

"That mezuzah," he said now, in a voice James suspected was carefully pitched for his ears alone. "Why do you kiss it? What is the purpose of it?"

It was hard not to show amazement. Truly, Nathanael seemed more a Gentile than a Jew. "Purpose? It is a command by God, written in the Law."

"I know, I know. I grew up in a Jewish community, remember? Well . . . on the outskirts. I mean, why? What is the significance?"

James thought on it. It was not easy to put into words something that had been a part of him since birth. But he was beginning to enjoy the challenge of Nathanael's questions. That he wanted to learn was heartening.

"It is said, 'As the words encompass the home, so his Word encompasses our lives,'" James slowly quoted the oral tradition. "Within that metal plate is a tiny parchment, and upon the parchment is written these words, what we call the *Shema*: 'Hear, O Israel; Adonai, your God, Adonai is one. You shall love the Lord your God with all your heart, with all your soul, with all your might.'"

"That is what is in there?" Nathanael said, amazed. "That thing we say every morning and night and every time we cough, sneeze, or visit the brush?"

James could not stop a small chuckle. "Yes, that and more. The *Shema* is also in our tefillin and phylacteries, because it is written, 'Bind them as a sign on your hand; let them serve as a symbol on your forehead. Fix them on the doorposts of your home.'"

Astonished, Nathanael said, "It's in your leather things too?" He frowned, thinking hard, then nodded. "Yes, of course. It makes sense. God is smart."

"What do you mean?"

"It makes sense to wear it. Makes sense to stuff it in a

mezuzah and recite it every time you wipe your nose, perfect sense. It is much to ask."

"What is much to ask?"

Nathanael took his eyes from the road to give James a look that wondered if he was joking. "The *Shema*, of course. What did you think we were talking about?"

James stared at him, then shifted in his place. "I don't think I understand."

"What is not to understand? 'You shall love the Lord your God with all your heart, with all your soul, with all your might'? That, James, is much to ask."

If James' eyes could go wider, he knew his eyeballs would fall out. "Nathanael," he sputtered, "it is more than a request. It is a command."

Nathanael shrugged. "Command, request . . . whatever. It's much to ask."

James was not sure if this conversation was borderline blasphemy or not. At the least, it made him uncomfortable. He shifted in his place again, then glared at the lamb, who still had that eye on him.

Nathanael did not share his discomfort. He poked at the roadside brush with his walking stick and cheerfully fired another question. "Why did you make a parcel out of those herbs? Last I heard, harkhavina isn't very tasty."

"Uh, bitter . . . they are bitter herbs, for Passover." Of course it was much to ask . . . it was a command, was it not? "Horehound, harkhavina, succory, lettuce, endive."

"But *why*, James? Why do you do that for Passover? Do not tell me you are supposed to eat it."

"Yes. With vinegar."

Nathanael soured his face. "Why would you—"

"Let me explain, Nathanael," James said. Despite the great amount of long-suffering this lad incurred, a stir of enthusiasm came. Did the rabbis feel this way? He could almost hear Joseph's voice speak with him. "It is said, 'Whoever does not explain three things in the Passover has not fulfilled the duty incumbent on him. These three things are the Passover lamb, the unleavened bread, and the bitter herbs. The Passover lamb means that God passed over the blood-sprinkled place on the houses of our fathers in Egypt; the unleavened bread means that our fathers were delivered out of Egypt in haste; and the bitter herbs mean that the Egyptians made bitter the lives of our fathers in Egypt.'"

The scowl on Nathanael's face meant he was thinking on it, and James gave him time. Then James said, "That is Passover in an inkpot, the rudiments. Of course, there are other rituals and obligations that go along with it—"

"They have stopped," Simon said over his shoulder. He peered behind them, then cupped his hands around his mouth and called to Jorah, who seemed to examine every spring wildflower along the way. "Jorah! It is time for the midmeal."

"At last," Judas sighed. He braced against the cart to remove a stone from his sandal. "I can taste Annika's cakes already."

"I'm glad she sent along so many," Nathanael added. "Of course, since I live with her I think I should be the one to hand them out."

When Jorah came trotting up, Simon said, "Don't fall behind, Jorah. I don't care if it is the plain; you stay with the cart."

"I was looking for—"

"Just stay with the cart." Simon put his hand over his eyes

to peer beyond her to the travelers in the distance. She turned to follow his gaze.

"Only two of them, Simon," Jorah said. "Perhaps we should ask them to join us. It would be safer for them."

"They are stopping too." He dropped his hand. "If they ever catch up, they are welcome to join us." He tugged on the back of her head covering. "But you still stay with the cart."

Jude waited until Nathanael was on the other side of the donkey saddle, then unfastened the food hamper at the same time as Nathanael unfastened the hamper containing the wine- and waterskins. They eased the hampers down at the same time to avoid upsetting the saddle. James pushed himself off the cart and fetched the feedbag for the donkey.

He fastened the bag to the bridle and scratched the gentle animal on the forehead, then lifted his head when his ears caught the strain of music. The caravan ahead had taken out instruments. He smiled slightly as he recognized the tune, one of the songs of ascent.

"Behold, bless the Lord, all servants of the Lord, who serve by night in the house of the Lord. Lift up your hands to the sanctuary and bless the Lord. May the Lord bless you from Zion, he who made heaven and earth."

Jorah came beside him, smiling too, and hummed along with the music. "Isn't this wonderful, James? I feel so . . . free."

"No laundry . . ."

"Not until Bethany. No sweeping . . . ," she said.

"No fixing meals . . ."

She folded her arms and said airily, "No grinding. A girl could get used to this."

"You would take to the road for a life of vagrancy?"

She flung her arms out to take in the plain and the mountains in the distance. "Look around you, James! Isn't it beautiful? Look at those flowers! At least I would be a happy vagrant. All this beauty and no responsibility . . ."

"You would miss me too much. Or somebody else," he said, with a deliberate glance at Nathanael.

"Keep your voice down," she hushed him but smiled just the same.

❧

The willow basket with their tallith, tefillin, and phylacteries came out after the meal. James caught Nathanael's eye as he wound his tefillin about his forearm.

"Yes, Nathanael," James said to him with a grin. "Even on the road. 'While you are at home and while you are away . . .'"

Nathanael shrugged. "It only makes sense."

James felt his grin slip at that. He had never before given thought to the fact that the *Shema* might be hard words. They were words that were Law, to be obeyed without question. It was who they were; they were Jews. The Hebrews of Abraham, the rescued of Egypt. Called out by God and commanded of him. The Law separated them from the rest. The very first of the Ten Commandments set the course of separation in a land of pagans who worshiped a multitude of gods: "You shall have no other gods before me." This command alone had brought bloodshed for the obeying.

The *Shema* was recited, along with additional prayers for their safety on the road. For the safety of Joses and his people, and of Mother, and of Devorah and her kin, and of Jesus. Long ago, Nathanael had refused to wear the leather straps and bands.

He had muttered the prayers if he knew them, with reluctance, and seemed relieved when any form of religion was set aside for the time. Now, while Judas prayed, James watched as Nathanael studied the tefillin Simon had on. He stared at the phylacteries as if he had never seen them before. Oddly, it annoyed James.

The caravan ahead was packing up.

＊

James had a question of his own. The midmeal had revived him, and the earlier ride on the cart had spelled him, so he walked beside Nathanael, occasionally leaning on his walking stick.

He glanced to make sure his brothers did not hear. Jude walked in conversation with Simon, who led the donkey. Jorah trailed behind the four-wheel, stopping occasionally to whisk a wildflower from the brush for examination.

He was not sure how to put the question, which was really more of a comment.

"You said something earlier," James began. "About the *Shema*."

"Yes?"

James grimaced. "I have never heard anyone speak like that."

Nathanael glanced at him in surprise. "What did I say?"

"That the words were much to ask." He could hardly say it. Such a preposterous notion. "That is . . . a very new thought to me."

Nathanael gave an expansive shrug. "What is so remarkable about it? Is it wrong to question things?"

"No! That is—" James drew a deep breath. "I don't think so."

"Have you even considered those words, James?" Nathanael

asked incredulously. "They are astounding. Astonishing. Impossible."

"They are Law. They are to be obeyed."

"Look!" Jude called, pointing south and east. "Taanach." It was the largest city they had seen since passing through Kfar Otnai. Taanach was about as far as they would go into Samaria to trade. James gave it a quick glance, then turned to the apprentice.

"How can you obey a command to love?" Nathanael reasoned. "You either do or you do not. How can someone *tell* you to love?"

James nearly choked. "The Someone you are talking about is God."

"Do you love God?"

The question made him speechless. Temporarily. "Of course I—what kind of a question is that? Of course I do."

Nathanael shrugged. "Then I envy you."

James looked unseeing toward the city of Taanach. Each new thing the apprentice said baffled him more than the last.

Jorah rushed up to James' side and thrust her palm in his face. "James, is this gold?"

He stared a moment at the lump of rock in her hand, then he mumbled, "No. Try again." To Nathanael, after Jorah had whirled away, he said, "Do *you* love God?"

Nathanael, with those bright and clear eyes, simply replied, "I do not know him well enough to love him."

It was all he could take. James stopped walking.

Nathanael turned to speak, then realized James was not there. He looked behind himself and stopped. "James? Hold up, Simon. I think James has to visit the brush."

James could only stare at Nathanael. He began to shake his head slowly, and he began to laugh.

"What?" Judas demanded. "What did I miss?"

The longer he laughed, the harder he laughed, and he set the others to chuckling. When his laughter was finally spent, he wiped his eyes on the heel of his hand and strolled to Nathanael. He clapped him on the back and said, "Nathanael, you must meet Jesus. I think you would like him. I know he would like you."

❧

It was long past Taanach when the party ahead stopped. Now the real danger began. The Valley of Esdraelon posed no real threat; it was at the northernmost part of Samaritan pig territory, too close to Galilee for Samaritan pig comfort. No, it was as they got closer to Beth Haggan and Ibleam that they kept constant watch on the roadside and a firm grip on their walking sticks.

"They've stopped," Avi announced and halted. "We make camp here."

Joab unslung the pack and rubbed his shoulder wearily. Avi had not told him the plan yet, but that was okay. Avi was one of the trusted ones. Raziel trusted him. Jonathan of Gush Halav trusted him. Avi conferred in hushed tones with great leaders of the Zealot movement, and Joab tried hard to keep a proper and constant sense of respect for him. Trailing after this family worked into the plan.

Avi's implacable gaze, a gaze Joab knew was for the apprentice alone, also worked into the plan. It did, somehow.

15

Any other girl he would have kissed by now. But he had never felt this way about any other girl.

What held him back from an attempt now was not the brothers—they didn't scare him, he had dodged brothers before—but instead a crazy, odd notion indeed: What did the Torah have to say about it? Nathanael nearly laughed out loud. Well, it was a curious thought anyway. The Torah and the Prophets and the oral tradition seemed to have everything in it, from the way James talked. Why not advice on the timing of a first kiss? First kiss with the most beautiful, remarkable girl he had ever met.

He tilted his head considering. Most beautiful? Apples to apples, no. Zipporah was more beautiful. Zipporah was . . . He watched Jorah straighten from the small kettle that hung on a tripod over the campfire. Zipporah was a droopy-faced crone next to Jorah ben Joseph.

He sighed and dropped his gaze. Wouldn't do to let Simon see him watching her. It was prudent to keep the peace. James, maybe he would not care, neither Judas. But Simon would stick him on a spit and roast him dry for even a wayward thought about his sister. He smiled ruefully at that; if Jorah were his sister, he'd do the same.

Nathanael settled back on his elbows and looked to where the sun had set. Even the colors in the sky made him feel content. Listening to the faint strains of music from the caravan ahead . . . camping on this roadside . . . watching Judas and James converse near the fire. Watching Simon tease Jorah . . . it was easy to see Simon was Jorah's favorite brother, a much mystifying fact . . . Now if only Annika were here to tell a story to, to fuss at him for not eating enough . . . no, he had no right to wish for perfection. What he had this evening was enough to content him for a year. If he could top it off with a single kiss, he would call it the best day of his life.

He looked over his shoulder to the two travelers behind. They did the same as Simon—they stopped when the party ahead stopped, moved when it moved. It showed they were smart; wary, as they should be, and safe with the presence of strangers a comfortable distance apart. He wondered if the two had a party behind them, keeping the same equidistance. He wondered what it looked like from a cloud, to see a ripple effect when dawn came, to see the caravan farthest ahead on the road arise and lead a much-scattered march to Jerusalem.

A pity the two were only two. They would enjoy a larger company, like the one he traveled with. They would enjoy Jude's occasional comments; he did not talk as much as Simon or James, but when he did he had something to say. Something to make Nathanael laugh or think. And the two strangers would side with him about Simon, that he was smug and full of himself. An easily offended whiner. Perhaps they would see, too, the way Simon looked at James when James did not notice, ready to spring to his aid or order him to the cart. Twice he had made James ride the cart when he thought his brother had walked long enough. And James, strangely, had complied without protest.

What would the strangers think of James? Nathanael watched him study Judas as Judas talked quietly with his hands. How would Nathanael himself perceive him, if he did not have *Seek James* plastered to his soul?

He stood and stretched, then let his arms drop as he glanced again at the strangers. He knew what it was to be on the outskirts, to be a small number looking on. He didn't like people to be afraid. Maybe in the morning he would take them one of Annika's spiced cakes. Maybe he could invite them to join their number, if the others were open to it. People should not be afraid, not when there was no reason to be.

Whistling the tune he had heard earlier, he trotted down the slope and went to the four-wheel cart. He pulled out his bedroll and the sack with his personal belongings. Maybe tonight Simon could show him what to do with the knot he had come to in the piece of sycamore he was carving. Simon's deft fingers could make a knot look as though it was meant to be there. Nathanael shared Annika's sentiment; why he wanted to be a scribe, with the astonishing gift he had, was purely baffling.

Nathanael noticed the lamb tethered on a long rope to the back of the cart. It was curled up in a short thicket of brush, legs tucked underneath, sleeping peacefully. He usually tried to ignore the lamb, uncomfortable with its fate. He glanced about at the others in camp, then rummaged in a bread sack and broke off a bit of honeycake. Glancing around again, he set it near the lamb's nose, where it would find it when it woke.

❧

Joab pulled his blanket over him and rolled into it. If the days were softened with spring, the nights were still bone cold. Avi was squatting at the small campfire. He had first watch. Joab closed his eyes but opened them after a moment.

Avi was considering the blade of his short knife. He thumbed the edge, then stuck it point down in the sand. While Avi stared hard into the flickering flames of the campfire, he turned the knife by the handle. The rotating blade caught the glint of the firelight.

He had finally told Joab the plan.

Not long after meeting with Jonathan of Gush Halav last week, Avi changed his mind about the Teacher. They all had had such hopes for him, Jonathan told Avi, but once Raziel walked away it was only a matter of time before the rest did too. Jonathan had all but forgotten Jesus and was well on to other plans. He told Avi he should do the same.

Avi came to the conclusion that the Teacher's family was a worthless lot. They needed to be taught a lesson. They had to be made to see that Roman violence begat violence, that the Roman presence created nothing but misery for all. Ultimately, it would be a generous act. He was going out of his way to offer a lesson that he hoped would reach the ears of the Teacher—one last chance to get his attention. Perhaps this would be the event to turn the heart of the Teacher, and his powers, to the cause.

Once Avi and Joab arrived in Jerusalem, they would spread the heartbreaking news that Roman soldiers had not spared violence even on the family of the gentle one from Galilee. Jesus would hear and would rise in rage for revenge.

Joab felt confident again. He knew Avi had a plan, had it all under control. Joab closed his eyes against the flash of the slowly spinning knife and, after a moment, opened them again.

16

THE CHILL ON HER NOSE probably woke her, though she had been snugly warm in her thick wool blanket all night long. The sky showed a first hint of dawn, like an eyebrow raised.

Jude and James slept on either side of her, both of them scrolled securely in their blankets like tight rolls of carpet. Jude snored softly, and James slept openmouthed. She pushed herself up to watch them a moment; she did not often see her brothers asleep and found it rather charming. They were usually up before she was, despite the ideal in Solomon's proverbs of women rising while it was still night. James had a little patch of dried spittle at a corner of his mouth, which was not charming at all, but the rest of his face was peaceful, his brow smoothed from the tension of the day.

She turned to look at Simon, who slept by the—but his bedroll at the campfire was empty. He was probably visiting the brush. She settled back down and laid her cheek on her arm to watch the sleeping form of Nathanael on the other side of the campfire. He slept on his stomach, his backside hiked in the air, his face pressed against his bedroll, mouth puckered from his pressed cheek. She giggled softly; he would never willingly allow an expression like that. It made him look like a little boy.

She had thought maybe he would kiss her last night; goodness knows, she had given him an opportunity. She had called him to the cart to ask him to help her find the money box, which he had replaced after they bought a packet of roasted grain from a roadside merchant at Taanach. Of course, she only asked him after she was sure her brothers were planted about the campfire, entertaining themselves with one of their heated debates. They barely noticed when he got up in response to her call.

Nathanael actually thought she had wanted the box. Why would she want it at this time? He seemed a little distracted, as though he would rather be in on the debate. She even had the shamelessness to flip a bit of the tarp over the box when she spied it before he did.

"I know it's around here somewhere," he had muttered with a glance over at the three seated at the fire.

"What are you talking about over there?" she had asked, pointing to an opposite corner of the cart for him to search. Utterly shameless!

"The usual. Jude is making a great point right now. He said that if all Jews were really for the land, if that were the main of Judaism, why are so many dispersed abroad? More live outside of Israel than in it. A very good point. And I said, 'If Judaism were only about the land, then why would God bother with things like the mezuzah?' Got a nasty look from Simon on that one."

Jorah had forgotten the box and looked at the three. Why did they always reserve such conversations for when she was doing things like washing dishes or making preparations for the morning meal?

"I asked James if they were less Jewish for not living in the land of Israel," Nathanael had said with a self-pleased grin. "That did not make James very happy."

"Do you enjoy not making him happy?"

The grin had vanished. "Of course not. Is that what you think?"

"I wonder sometimes."

The two regarded each other until Jorah finally remembered why she had called him over, and looking into his eyes brought sudden shame. Her cheeks bloomed with heat, and she hoped the twilight concealed the color. Funny, once she realized she did not really want to lure him into a kiss, that she wanted it to be his idea, it suddenly seemed it was.

His face registered a subtle change; he had forgotten about the debate. The look made her suddenly notice the beat of her heart. Her eyes widened; he leaned closer . . . and who knows what would have happened had not Simon called at that moment.

"Jorah, could you bring the wineskin?"

Not sure if she was relieved or not, she called back, "I—yes, Simon. Coming."

Now Jorah glanced at Simon's empty bedroll. Was it only a coincidence Simon wanted the wine at that moment? His distaste for Nathanael was obvious.

Her gaze wandered back to—and Jorah's breath caught. Nathanael had opened his eyes and was looking straight at her. The puckery look disappeared as he lifted his head and gave her a sleepy smile.

"Good morning," he whispered.

"Good morning," she whispered back.

Who knows what would have happened if Simon had not returned that moment.

❧

Simon checked the rope that tethered the lamb, then dug his hand into the donkey's bag of feed. He scattered a handful of the grain in front of the lamb, who nibbled up the feed with scrabbling black lips. Simon dusted off his hands and looked to the caravan ahead. They should have been moving by now. He sighed and lifted a corner of the canvas to tuck the feedbag into the cart. He pulled the canvas tight and cinched it.

"They have more people than we do," Nathanael said when he heard Simon's sigh. "They are not as mobile."

Simon flicked him a look. The apprentice always had a comment handy. On his way to the remains of the campfire, Simon paused next to Nathanael as if to limber his arms with a morning stretch; it never hurt to remind the little woodenhead that Simon was the much bigger of the two.

James was packing the tallith, phylacteries, and tefillin in the willow basket. He passed the basket to Simon, who handed it to Nathanael. "Here, put that in the cart," Simon ordered the lad. But if it would have prevented the boy's next comments, Simon would have done it himself.

Nathanael looked into the basket as he slowly lifted a corner of the canvas tarp. "It makes you wonder if he loves us the way we are supposed to love him," he mused out loud.

Simon turned to him. "Who?"

"God."

From the front of the cart where she was checking the donkey's bridle, Jorah lifted her head to look at Nathanael. Jude's tinkering under the cart, where he lay on his back inspecting the axle, stopped—meaning he was all ears. And James got that rabbi look on his face, one of hopeful expectation, as he turned from smothering the campfire to regard the apprentice. Simon rolled his eyes.

Nathanael said, "Can you imagine being loved by God with all his heart, with all his soul, with all his—"

"Nathanael!" Simon said sharply.

The boy looked at him in surprise.

"That is enough," Simon snapped. "Do not provoke the Lord your God. You are too free with your—observations."

"What a fascinating thought," James murmured as he tossed a handful of sand on the fire.

Nathanael gave Simon the closest thing to a glare. He hunched up his shoulders in that sullen habit of his and muttered, "I was only trying to imagine a way that God remembers us. Does he have a mezuzah in his doorway in heaven?" The look on the lad's face went from sullen to almost wistful. "Does he wear things on his arms and forehead? We have constant reminders of our command to love him . . . but does he return the favor?"

Simon stared, momentarily speechless.

"Does he *love* us?" the boy said mostly to himself as he finally tucked the willow basket into the cart. "Turnabout is fair play, my mother always says."

Simon wanted to remind him that his mother's opinion did not count, owing to her profession, but oddly, he stopped himself.

Fortunately, the apprentice himself changed the subject. He looked behind him to the two travelers far in the distance. "I have been thinking . . . should we ask them to join us?"

They were at least half a mile back, barely visible near a rocky outcrop in the road. They, too, seemed to be waiting. They had camped at the same place Simon had nearly chosen. It was a pass through the trough of a cluster of hills, a cozy place, snug in the surrounding rock. There were no caves that Simon saw, but after careful inspection he did not like the feel of it; brigands could easily descend upon them in the night from the sharply sloping hills. Besides, the caravan kept moving. Only when they were half a mile beyond the pass did the caravan stop.

"We should have asked them already," Jorah said, scratching the donkey's muzzle as she followed Nathanael's gaze. "They might feel safer, sleeping around more people."

"I have had my belly full of entertaining strangers," James muttered. "We have been doing it for three years."

"Our obligation does not end," Simon reluctantly reminded him. Was it not written that to entertain the stranger and alien found favor with God? Besides, not long ago Simon had been the stranger, thanks to Joses' desire to get the full story on Jesus. "Jorah is right. We should speak with them." He added,

"We do not have to tell them who we are or where we are from. On this road, we are the same as they—just pilgrims on the road to Jerusalem."

"I will go," Nathanael said cheerfully, and pulled back the tarp to rummage in the bread sack.

"I will go with you," Jude said from under the cart.

"He should go alone," Simon said. "They will feel threatened if two approach."

Nathanael held up one of Annika's loaves. "One whiff of this, and they will know us for friends." Whistling a tune from a psalm—and Simon was surprised he knew it—the apprentice started off for the two travelers.

❧

Simon examined the rock. "No, Jorah. It is not gold." She handed him another. "No." And another. "No. Try again. Find us a fortune."

Nathanael was taking his time. Not surprising, Simon figured, as chatty as that one was. He was probably regaling them with one of his braggart stories from Caesarea. Or one of his notions about God.

The caravan ahead was packing up. Simon frowned and threw a sour look behind him. Just like the boy to—Simon straightened as he gazed toward the pass. He squinted under his hand; he did not see Nathanael. He did not see anyone.

He sighed and dropped his hand. "James? The caravan is packing up. They will be rolling in half an hour. That apprentice of yours had better be back shortly or we will leave without him. He can catch up after he is done talking himself blue to anyone who will listen."

Judas came out from under the cart, wiping his hands on his tunic, looking toward the pass. "I wonder where they are."

"Perhaps asking a group behind them to join up with us too," Jorah said, poking through the rocks on her palm. "Wouldn't it be fun to have a group as large as the one ahead? Maybe they even have instruments."

❧

James had busied himself with a chunk of olivewood from the carving box. Finally, a chance to carve, and yet he had spent the last half hour trying to figure out what he wanted to do with it. He had removed the outer layer, taking his time in hope of inspiration, but so far none had come. He had himself a smooth, shapeless piece of wood. Simon would have had ten ideas and be half-finished with one of them by now. He tossed the piece back into the box.

"We can wait no longer," Simon announced and rose from his squatting position. The caravan had left moments earlier. "He will have to catch up."

James put the box into the back of the cart and pulled the tarp over it. He took up his walking stick. Judas joined him to look back. "Where could he be?" Jude murmured.

Simon took the donkey's bridle and clicked his tongue. The cart lurched forward. They had busied themselves as much as they could, waited as long as they dared. Simon had checked everyone's sandals, replacing some tacks and securing others. Jorah had picked a bouquet of flowers, a few of which she entwined, with giggles, into the donkey's bridle. James and Jude had thrown stones at a boulder in the distance until Jude tired of it and went to tinker under the cart some more.

James did not like it that Nathanael took his time. It did not do much for his status with Simon. It seemed an unspoken thing between Judas and James and Jorah that Simon be made to like Nathanael, that he see in Nathanael what they all did. But the apprentice did not help things when he provoked Simon with dawdling and—

Seek Nathanael.

"James?"

Fear rushed through him in a torrent, drenching him with dread.

James yelled, "Simon! Stop the cart!"

The foreboding spun him about. The walking stick dropped from his fingers, and James began to run for the pass.

Jude matched him pace for pace. "What is it?"

"Something is wrong," James breathed.

❧

They approached the trough in the hills and saw nothing at first, but the inner cry rose to a shout. James' body was giving out; his skin was slicked in clammy sweat. Jude ran on ahead and disappeared around the rocky outcrop.

Nausea rose from the exertion. James stopped and braced his hands on his knees, panting and dripping sweat, then vomited on the side of the road. Trembling, he wiped his mouth with the back of his hand and staggered forward. He came around the corner and stopped short.

First, he saw a young man he vaguely recognized, but his face was contorted in soundless anguish, arms wrapped over his head where he sat on the ground rocking back and forth.

An eerie wail rose from his throat. James followed his eyes to the still form of one he was sure he recognized.

Avi, the young Zealot who had visited that day, lay in the road, face slack, eyes dull. James' gaze stopped at the knife stuck handle-deep in his chest. The blade tucked fabric into the center of a red stain. Beyond Avi . . .

Jude was crouched over a form. James could see the legs of the apprentice.

"No."

James felt his chest begin to heave. Weak with dread, he came around Judas, then fell to his knees beside Nathanael. The inner cry came out in a whimper.

Nathanael's chest was sodden red. The fabric of his tunic was sliced in several places, gaping in some spots, wetly closed in others. One, two, five places on his chest. Jude's hands were moving over him, unsure, trembling. "James . . . we've got— we must stop this bleeding. We have to stop it! Get some cloth, quickly." Whispering under his breath, Judas gingerly tugged at the bloodied fabric. He put his fingers into a fabric hole and began to carefully tear the tunic apart.

James rose and stumbled to the body of Avi. Numb in what he did, he worked the knife from the chest, then plunged the blade into the lower half of Avi's tunic, ripping the cloth as he sawed. The knife fell from his fingers. He wadded the cloth and hurried back to Jude, where he dropped beside him, shoving the cloth at him.

The apprentice had fought, and fought hard. Three deep scratches curved from the bottom of his neck into his jaw. His lower lip was split and growing thick; one eye looked like a ball of swelling dough. The other eye was fixed on James. His lips, faintly blue, were moving. James scrambled around Jude and dropped close to hear.

Nathanael weakly patted James, whispering.

"What, Nathanael?" James whispered back, close to his ear. He took Nathanael's hand and bent to listen.

His chest rose and fell in irregular rhythm. He labored for breath, speaking only on the exhale. "How about—that. Still there."

"I'm still here, Nathanael."

Nathanael dragged his hand from James and placed it on his own stomach, beneath the fearsome wounds. He grimaced in pain at the inhale, nostrils flaring for air, and on the exhale he patted his stomach and rasped, "Still there."

Jorah's scream tore the air, carrying with it a bit of her soul. From around the rocky outcrop, she ran toward them, Simon running behind her, yelling and lunging for her.

"Get her out of here!" James screamed and swung his body to block her view.

"Nathan . . . Nathan . . . ," she gasped. Simon seized her and dragged her back.

Judas had finally worked the fabric free from Nathanael's chest, and James wanted to howl at what he saw: methodical cuts! God of Israel! He slammed one fist on the ground, for nothing to punch, and growled every curse he could think of as he glared at Nathanael's mottled chest.

"That makes me—feel better," Nathanael pressed out. "Try it in—Greek."

Jude took the wadded cloth and pressed it to the wounds, pulled it back, pressed again. He waited a moment, then removed the cloth and bent closely to examine the wounds.

"Not deep here . . . not here . . . not deep." He hissed, then said grimly, "Deep here. Deep here." Jude raised his white face to James. "We need Jorah's sewing kit." Jude was the one to sew up their small cuts. He had sewn James' thumb when he cut it on a grape scythe. James stared at the wounds, fighting a wash of nausea; these were not nicks from a grape scythe.

Nathanael fought for his breath, nostrils flaring. Every pore of him sucked for air, the skin about his neck pulling inward at his gasps. And as he strained with every inhale, a horrible sucking noise came from the lowest wound, just below his ribs.

"Couldn't even—cut it out." His hoarse voice was full of wonder. Then he grimaced in pain and tried to touch his chest. James held his hand back, but Nathanael groaned and began to shift; then he rolled to his side and vomited. Jude frantically followed his movement, keeping the cloth pressed to the wounds. James held the lad as his body convulsed. When it was done, he eased him to his back again. Whispered prayers replaced the curses, and James gently wiped blood and bile from the corner of Nathanael's mouth with his sleeve. Jude peeked under the cloth and groaned.

"What do you need?" The other young man stood over them, fingers fiddling, face desperate. "What—needle and thread? Avi has—I will get it!" Gravel skittered from his sandals as he ran to a pile of camping things near the roadside.

"Do you need me, Judas?" James said, his voice hollow in his ears. "If you do not, I need to go and pray."

"Pray here!" Jude snapped. "Don't you leave me! God have mercy, I have not done this before."

"That *really*—makes me—feel better."

The young man skidded next to Jude and thrust a small

packet at him. Jude's fingers fumbled to open it; then he cursed at what he saw. "This is a tent needle! For canvas!" He threw it aside and sat back, pressing a bloodied hand to his forehead. "Go, James. Pray."

"He has to—pray?" Nathanael managed a chuckle, producing a bit of bloody spittle at the corner of his mouth. "This gets better—all the time."

"There is a caravan not far behind us." The young man was already running. "I will hurry!"

James rose, turned from the horror, unsure where to go. He looked to where Simon held Jorah, who beat against her brother, wailing, "I want Nathanael. I want Nathanael!"

He walked a few paces, then dropped to his knees. He began to rock back and forth in the rhythm of prayer. Something on the ground caught his eye.

Annika's spiced honeycake lay broken on the ground, half of it crushed underfoot. The *Shema* already on his lips, James closed his eyes and fell into himself to pray.

❧

Despite her large size, the woman arrived on the run with her sewing kit, the young man on her heels. Eyes small and sharp, set in a red puffy face, she glanced at the body of Avi as she pushed up her sleeves and knelt beside Nathanael.

"Let's see what we have, lad," she panted. "Old Beca will set you straight." She pulled aside the cloth. Her breath caught, and she pressed her lips tight at the sight of the wounds. She lifted a dark face to Jude. "This was torture," she said angrily, breathing heavily. She gestured at the cuts. "Five of them? All horizontal? All on the right side? What demon work is this?"

She leaned to Nathanael's face, and her tone instantly became crooning. "Trust old Beca, lad, I will have you—" She broke off, eyes on Nathanael's lips. She seized his hand to examine his fingernails, then dropped it to probe the wounds. She clicked her tongue at the lowest one.

"This we must plug." She looked at Avi's friend. "A burning candle, boy. Quickly." He sped off, and she rummaged through her sewing kit, glancing at Jude. "Can you sew?" Pale-faced, Jude nodded. "Good." She bit off a length of thread and handed it to him with a needle. "Go to work on the upper wounds. I will take care of these two."

She looked to where Simon sat with Jorah. "You there! No, not you. The girl." Jorah sat straight up. Her face was swollen and red, and miserably eager. "Come, girl. Speak to him while we work." Relief broke in a fresh sob as Jorah scrambled to her feet. She gave her face a fierce swipe with her sleeve, then ran and sank to her knees at Nathanael's side. She sent only a glance to his chest, then ran her hands along either side of his face. She smoothed his damp curls and smiled down at him, eyes filled with tears, though none fell. His one eye was now purple and swollen shut, but the other returned her gaze. Dusky lips curved in a smile.

"You are not wearing your silly grimlet," Jorah softly said.

"We should have—let them talk."

"Enough with *your* talking."

Beca threw Simon a sharp glance, then snorted as she licked the tip of the thread and squinted at the needle. "We are tougher than you think."

17

SIMON SAT AT THE roadside up on the hill, rubbing his hand over his fist and watching the activity in the camp below. It would be just like the weasel of an apprentice to die now. Just when Jorah's heart was beginning to mend from all those who left her. Just when Simon was beginning to—heaven help him—like him.

They had to get him to Jesus. Before, it was James. Now Nathanael.

He shifted his jaw. What would the others say if he voiced this sentiment? It had to come from James or Jude—anyone but him. Though the woman and Jude had done the best they could, the lad was plainly not going to make it.

He had watched as they worked with tense swiftness to sew

the wounds but had to look away when the woman dribbled the wax. Presently Nathanael's color began to pink up. His lips lost their bluish hue, and his breath came easier. But blood continued to seep from some of the wounds, making crimson stains on the white linen bandages wrapped tightly about his chest. Once during the middle of their work, Nathanael had to roll to the side to vomit, causing a fresh, hard flow of blood.

"Don't you dare die, apprentice," Simon growled under his breath.

The woman's kin had arrived in a caravan close behind her, two large families traveling from Beth She'arim. On the periphery of the horror, Simon noticed their concern. The men, at least a dozen, had joined James to offer prayers on behalf of Nathanael. Simon and Joab had seen to the body of the young Zealot.

What a waste, Simon had thought bitterly when they added the last stone to the unnatural mound on the landscape. Had Avi ever dreamed his end would come to this? No funeral, no one to say prayers at his burial? God help him, Simon could not say the death prayers. What sort of a man would do to Nathanael what he did? And what sort of man was this Joab, who first was party to the unthinkable, and then took the knife himself and plunged it into the chest of his friend?

Though Joab had spoken in halting snatches, what had happened was still not completely clear. He stuttered something about it being for the cause, that Jesus was supposed to hear, that his powers belonged to the land. The babble of words from the distraught lad put a thorn of fear in Simon's gut.

He gripped his fist. What if it were true? What if this were part of a widespread plot against Jesus, to—to blackmail him into using his powers to take back the land of Israel? Would the Zealots go so far? Thoughts tumbled forth, each blacker than the last. Was Judas Ish-Kerioth a spy? Were there more people on roadsides, dying like Nathanael, victims of an unthinkable plot? A plot at Passover . . . of course. What better time for attention, with thousands upon thousands stuffing the streets of Jerusalem. *Joses . . . maybe you were right. Find him, Joses, and God grant that he will listen to you.*

After removing Avi's body, Simon helped the others move Nathanael to the roadside to allow travelers to pass. A line of scars on Nathanael's thigh showed silvery white when his tunic slipped aside. Simon stared in sick horror at the scars, then saw James glower at them in a way that said he already knew about them. When he caught James' eye and tried to ask, James cut him off with, "It's his to tell."

From where Simon sat, it appeared that the lad had either fallen asleep or lost consciousness. His face was waxen white save for the thick purple gash at his eye. What of this young man—not many years younger than Simon, really—born of a Jewish whore and raised as a Gentile? How came he to them, to capture the heart of his sister and speak things to make Simon want to—rattle him senseless, or . . .

He rubbed his fist and looked away. Jude or James should bring it up soon. They had to get him to Jesus. To Jesus, the blasphemer. They had to . . .

He squeezed his eyes shut. He tried hard to keep it a buried memory, undisturbed, and he did not know why it would choose to come now, but it came. Brutal and swift and relentless.

Gadarene, Decapolis. Simon and Joses found his home not in Kursi but south of it, near Hippos, and Simon had been the one to knock. For once, he knew what it was to knock.

"We seek a man called Kardus," Joses had said.

"I am he. Come inside," the man had said. "Be you welcomed." From habit they went to kiss the mezuzah; there was no mezuzah.

"You must get many visitors," Simon had mumbled. "We are sorry."

"I never tire to share my story."

He brought water to wash the dirt from the journey, and wine and olives and bread. Simon could not take his eyes from him. "Do not worry—they are all gone," Kardus had said with a merry sparkle in his eyes. "The demons. In case you were wondering."

They sat in the home of a pagan and broke bread with him. Simon would not believe this Kardus was the one, save the directions of the villagers. He was kind, and gracious, and droll—and sane.

Kardus told a tale of a man's descent into madness. He told of inner torment to make Simon wince and Joses go white. He told of a man driven to the far corner of his being, trapped there by a lashing horde who tortured him without measure.

The demons were agitated, Kardus said. They made him pace the shoreline, muttering gibberish. In the distance, a boat came. The demons began to thrash and wail, and one was dispatched for help. Help came: A storm rose, crashing and violent, a malevolent masterpiece. The demons cheered, and Kardus capered about with their glee. Then, as suddenly as it had risen, the storm died. When the curtain of raging water dropped, when the spray diminished, when calm came, they saw what he did. Still the boat came, more relentless than the storm.

"Then he stood on the shore and inside me I wept. He came for me. He crossed the lake for me." Joyous tears streamed. *"I wanted to shout and wave and show him I was in there, but he knew. He saw them, and past them, he saw me."*

Simon could listen no longer. He rose and stumbled for the door, ran from the house as fast as he could. And when he could run no longer, he found a solitary place to weep as he never had.

"How did you know?" Simon whispered, gripping his fist to pain. "You had no reason to cross the Galilee. How did you know?"

Did he actually hear Kardus' pain? Did he raise his head, fall silent in the middle of a teaching, look over his shoulder across the sea? For some reason, that was the picture Simon had in his mind. Jesus raising his head, looking over his shoulder, the wind blowing his hair across his face. He brushes it out of his eyes to gaze at that distant shore. What was he thinking at that moment? What was he hearing?

Did the torment of the one pull him from the many? That thought alone could keep Simon from sleep, long into the night.

How could the still form of the apprentice make him think of it now? Those old silver scars on his legs, sickeningly precise, and the fresh wounds on his chest . . .

"Jesus . . . ," Simon whispered against his fist. "Hear the torment of this one."

❦

Judas climbed the short distance to Simon and sat beside him, drawing up his knees. The sun slipped behind the hills, still sending up its luminous spray. The moon was on the rise, nearly full. In a few days, it would be Passover. First full moon of spring.

The caravan had moved on a few hours ago. Simon had watched as, in the midst of their stashing and stowing, a constant trickle of their number came to pay respect to Nathanael. A white-haired one had brushed what was surely a mixture of oil and water and wine over Nathanael's forehead. Simon had heard his resonant prayer from here.

He had watched the woman, Beca, give instructions to Jude. Watched as she drew Jorah aside with an arm about her shoulders. Beca spoke briskly to Jorah, arranging the girl's hair as she did so, and ended her talk with a broad smile. She waited until she got a smile in return; then she patted Jorah's cheeks and embraced her tightly. What Jorah did not see was how quickly the woman's smile faded as she watched Jorah return to Nathanael.

"We cannot move him," Judas said. His voice was hard and weary like his face.

"How is he?"

"I don't think he will live."

"Jude . . . if he has a chance, it is because of you. You and the woman. I could not have done what you did."

When Jude did not respond, Simon looked to the aura of sunset over the hills. A noise brought him back to Judas. His face was now drawn tight. He dropped his head and squeezed his eyes shut. A gasping snort came. Simon looked away.

"Simon, I am so . . . angry."

Simon stared unblinking at the ground between his feet. Had he not time to think on it these past several hours, not moving from this spot? "What do we do with Joab?"

Jude rubbed his face on his sleeve, leaving it ruddy. "I don't know. Bring him to the Temple; let the Sanhedrin decide. I think he is eager for punishment."

"He needs to be questioned when he is of the right mind. What brought him to such a thing?" Simon murmured. The lad had sat on the outskirts of the prayer circle, praying in rhythm yet perhaps feeling unworthy to join. His face would sometimes crumple in anguish. And like Jorah, he did not stray far from Nathanael. Simon shook his head as he gazed at the lad now. "What a putrefying world we are part of, Judas."

"Hidden reefs . . . clouds without water. Doubly dead. Uprooted."

Simon felt a prickle on his skin. What were these words Jude muttered?

"An illusion of brilliance, but instead, wandering stars."

Simon swallowed. Was his entire family going mad? He looked to where James sat in a brooding crouch, apart from anybody, face dark and staring. He had heard James mutter strange, bitter words when he passed him on the way up the hill. *Consider it all joy.* And, *Trust the one with the scars; scarred ones know.* James had spit the words like curses. It had chilled Simon then . . . the way Jude chilled him now. *Hidden reefs? Clouds without water?* Maybe Jude needed to talk, but Simon could not listen, not to that. Someone had to stay sane.

Briskly, he said, "Can Nathanael be moved? We can make a place—"

"I have never felt so helpless."

"Jude—" Simon broke off and held still. He suddenly knew why Kardus held hostage his thoughts. Nathanael's legs. Like the demoniac's arms.

All over Kardus's arms, and perhaps the rest of his body, were scar upon scar upon thick and ridged scar. As though fingernails had ripped his skin. As though teeth had torn off ovals of flesh. Scars from gashes so numerous that Simon had whitened at thoughts of what caused them. *Scarred ones know.*

Kardus had described with vivid words the hugeness of the storm. Sudden. Violent. Crashing. Angry. And despairing—he could no longer see the coming boat.

But still he came . . . more relentless than the storm.

Simon did not know he had spoken the words aloud until he realized Jude was staring at him. Wonderful. Now he was the one to babble.

"Can he be moved?" Simon asked sharply.

Jude wiped his nose and gave a bleak shrug. "Sure. He can be moved because it does not matter. He has lost too much blood."

Simon rose and rubbed his lower back, then sighed heavily. So Jude would not say it. And James would not say it, not by the lost look on his face. Why did he have to be the one?

"Then we take him to Jesus," Simon said. "If he dies on the way, he dies. But we give him a chance." He nearly had a grim chuckle at that; whom were they really giving a chance? Nathanael . . . or Jesus?

He waited until Judas rose, and together the two made their way down the slope to the camp below.

❧

Every jostle of the cart, however small, made James wince. He knew Simon watched the road carefully, avoiding stones and ruts. The roads were always prepared for heavy travel months before Passover, but it was now nearly the end of the time for pilgrimage. The wear of the road from thousands of carts and donkeys and horses and camels and feet was apparent.

The roadsides were littered with evidence of pilgrimage. James frequently saw cast-off items, worn-out sandals, broken parts of wheels, rotted peelings from fruits and vegetables, empty spits with charred bits left on them. They passed scuffed-over fire pits and places that stank, perhaps a popular spot to visit the brush.

They traveled in silence. The supplies had been piled up on the side of the cart, their bedrolls spread and laid on top of each other. Nathanael was placed on the bedrolls. Two embroidered cushions, gifts for Devorah, were tucked snugly on either side of his head to keep it still from the cart movement. Jorah walked ahead of Simon, working endlessly to kick away rocks and animal droppings. She had kept at it for nearly two hours now, since they had left the pass early this morning. Jude and James walked on either side of the cart, never more than a few feet away. Joab walked a distance behind the cart with his pack slung over his back and the lamb across his shoulders. What had happened back there was still unclear. Nobody spoke to him.

And nobody had slept much last night. Nathanael was restless and once in the third watch had roused the camp by the alarming sounds of his vomiting. Jude had to reseal the bottom wound. They had settled him down again, and he drifted into a fitful doze, but no one else slept after that.

Songs of ascent eluded them. The dismal quiet of the party caused more farmers to stare instead of glance. James exchanged a gaze with one man who had straightened from a thresher. The man was a Samaritan, one of the despised race. James did not feel hate for the man, nor did he sense it in return. The man looked to the cart and back at James. He kept his gaze on them as the party passed, then bent again to the thresher.

Consider it joy? James flicked a glance at the white face secured between the cushions. What sort of god did Balthazar serve?

Whenever Judas checked on the wounds, James leaned to see as well. The woman Beca had given Jude admonition to keep him as still as possible to keep the seal unbroken. They had to help Nathanael visit the brush with the utmost care. Should the seal break, a candle was at the ready to be lit from the bucket of ash-banked coal.

James gazed at distant hills as he strode beside the cart. The hills were dim with haze; the morning held promise of thick warmth for the afternoon. Flies were coming up thick, and James held a long sheaf of grass, ready to whisk them from Nathanael. Two walking sticks secured in the front corners of the cart propped the tarp over the lad to shield him from the sun.

The road wound through the troughs of hill after hill. Some hills were striped with terraced farming, like wide stairways to the top. Some hills were covered with trees, some with rock; some had equal amounts of both. Even now they were passing a rock quarry, where stonemasons were at work chiseling blocks from the bedrock. Surrounding trees and plants and ground cover were coated with the white rock dust.

James was not sure which bothered him more, Nathanael's lapses of silence or his talk. With his one good eye on James,

Nathanael took up conversation again after an hour of silence. "How did you know?"

It was the one question he feared. James shook a pebble from his sandal. Who could understand *Seek Nathanael*? It came and left in a whirlwind, an impression more than a voice. He was not even sure it really happened, if those were the exact words. What he remembered was the dread.

He realized Jude was looking at him too. "I don't know," he finally mumbled. "You thirsty?" They had settled a waterskin next to him, where he could drink as he wanted.

"No."

James did not like to look at him long. The purple gash on his eye and the whiteness of his face kept James' gut at a constant simmer. And the thoughts Simon had confided last night—they could keep his stomach stewing until Jerusalem. Nathanael, maybe the victim of some blackmail plot? James glanced over his shoulder at Joab. The entire family at possible risk because of some fanatical Zealot notions? If he did not look sharply to the hills before, he did now. The only thumbnail of hope was the last thing Simon had announced last night: They were taking Nathanael to Jesus.

We head for Bethany. He will most likely be there, at Devorah's or at the home of his friends Mary, Martha, and Lazarus. Wherever he is, we will find him.

James remembered with quiet astonishment. Simon, of all people. He who never ceased to remind them, with or without words, of the blasphemy of Jesus. Simon had left the campfire soon after that, muttering about seeing to the lamb. Jorah and Jude and James had exchanged glances, eyes glittering in the firelight.

"Why don't the Samaritans go to Jerusalem for Passover?" Nathanael said weakly.

"Remember? I told you. They are not allowed in the Temple."

"Whyever not? They are Jews too."

James and Jude exchanged bemused looks. Nathanael and his indignation. At least it was good to hear him speak. Jude answered this one. "It was said a Samaritan had once come at night and strewn bones in the porches and throughout the Temple to defile the Holy House." He glanced to either side of him before he said in a low tone, "Leave it to the Samaritans. Another reason to hate them."

"Do you? Hate them?"

Jude shrugged. "They despise us as much as we despise them. Makes us even."

"Makes no sense," Nathanael said drowsily.

Judas sighed, a sound as close to exasperation as the usually placid Jude could get. "It is more complex than that, Nathanael. They claim to be the true representatives of Israel. They say Mount Gerizim is . . ."

James pressed back a smile as Jude held forth. Was Nathanael taking advantage of his condition to argue so freely with those who were his employers? No. It was simply Nathanael, every inch of him. He always put himself on equal footing, which is why he was always in trouble with Simon.

Nathanael did not respond to Judas, and James glanced at him. He had drifted off to sleep again. At the times Nathanael slept, it was as if each took up brooding thoughts again, and conversation stopped altogether.

Last night's moon was a thumbnail from full, putting today

at the thirteenth of Nisan. Passover began at sunset tomorrow evening. James was supposed to be in the Temple compound tomorrow, as he had been for the last two Passovers, to slaughter the lamb and have the priest collect the blood. While Jesus played the rabbi for the past two Passovers, James had taken over the abdicated position of head of the tribe of Joseph. What would happen now? If Jesus knew James was not there, what would he do? Would his conscience prick him to take responsibility at last and offer a lamb for their household himself?

You owe us at least that, James thought bitterly.

"Simon, can we stop and get some figs?" Jorah asked over her shoulder, ever vigilant to kick away stones. Her cheeks were flushed and perspiration shone on her forehead.

They were coming into a more populated area where smart merchants had set up stalls along the road to take advantage of the burgeoning traffic at festival time. Simon led the donkey to the side of the road and went to the cart to find the money box. He glanced at Nathanael, then Jude. "How is he?"

"He needs to drink more," Jude answered, a pucker of worry between his eyebrows. He leaned over the cart side to lightly rest his hand on Nathanael's stomach. "His belly is swelling," he said mostly to himself, the pucker becoming a frown. "I don't know what that means. Maybe he bleeds on the inside. Maybe it is infection."

"It's too early for infection," Jorah said quickly, standing on her toes to look in the cart. She looked at Jude. "Isn't it?" Jude did not answer.

Simon worked the lid from the money box. He tossed a coin to Jorah and went to replace the lid. He hesitated, then took a coin and slipped it into his pocket.

"James, have Joab water the lamb. I need to see about supplies for . . ." But James did not catch what Simon mumbled over his shoulder as he strode to a cluster of merchant stalls.

❧

The dropping sun made long shadows of the trees on the ridge. They stretched across the road, thin limbs streaking up the hill on the other side. Her chin on her knees, Jorah watched orange butterflies flit in the greenery growing on the bedrock beside her. Like huge dollops of gray porridge, bedrock was cropped in lumps on the green. She would have picked up the stone next to her to look it over carefully, but she was just too tired. Simon had stopped the cart to make camp, and she had enough strength to slip onto this boulder. She should be helping to unload the cart, to put together a meal. She could not move.

Not far south lay Shechem. They had hoped to reach it before nightfall but had to negotiate with great care a washout of rock from a recent rain. Other caravans passed their little party, bumping over the stones with never a care. Jorah looked at the stone beside her. It would only take one of those under the cart wheel to break the seal on Nathanael's wound.

Shechem. The place of God's promise to Abraham. "To your descendants I will give this land." She heard James tell it to Nathanael, who had kept up his questions all morning. In the afternoon, the questions came less frequently, then stopped altogether. As if to fill the silence, James began to offer to Nathanael all sorts of information about the places they were passing through. Was it more painful to hear the silence from Nathanael, or the efforts from James to ignore it?

Nathanael grew weaker by the hour. The last time they sat him up to go to the brush, he nearly fainted. Was it from the pain or from the loss of blood? Jorah tightened her arms around her knees. Maybe both. Early in the afternoon, James had leaned close to hear something Nathanael was saying, then shouted to Simon to stop the cart. Nathanael had been straining for breath, and his lips were darkening. He himself did not realize the seal had been broken. Jude had scrambled to reseal it.

She would not have blamed Nathanael if he had cried out at the pain from the wax, dribbled and smeared over the lowest wound, or from the heinous wounds themselves. But no, he took it with nothing more than a teeth-bared grimace now and then. The only time she had heard him groan was when he vomited. Jorah dug angrily at a slipping tear. Men and their stupid fool bravery. Why was it so important to face pain in silence?

That their journey had come to this was bad enough; worse was that one traveled with them who could have prevented it. She had not even looked at him, not once. Now Jorah looked over to where Joab fussed with the lamb.

Had she ever hated before? She had not hated in these past few years, not when the insults came or when trades were refused, not even when they were banned from the synagogue. She watched Joab timidly approach the donkey, where it stood with its feedbag fastened on, his nervous glances all for the brothers, who ignored him. She watched him quickly dip his hand into the bag, then slip to where the lamb was tethered by Joab's shoulder pack. He spilled the feed onto the ground near the lamb and stood back to watch him eat.

Jorah put the bloody slashes on Joab's chest, made his face white and his lip fat with a blow and his eye swollen and—

"Mother," Jorah whispered. She rested her cheek on her knee. A tear rolled to the tip of her nose and dripped away.

She had seen the crushed loaf Nathanael had brought to Avi and Joab. She could not get it out of her mind. Its image brought wave after wave of—was this what it was to hate?

They were helping Nathanael from the cart. For the first time, as they eased him to a sitting position, a groan escaped his lips. She was on her feet and running for the cart.

❧

James watched Simon in the distance. He had gone to a place where the waning sunlight was not blocked by a hill, taking with him his bundle of writing implements, and another small bundle he had purchased on the road. He found a smooth boulder and with his back to the group, settled down to work. On what, James could not see.

While they helped Nathanael to the brush, Jorah dragged the bedrolls from the cart and arranged them on the ground, near a smothered fire pit from earlier travelers. It would be the second night they all slept in extra clothing instead of their bedrolls, but it was nothing to Nathanael's comfort.

Joab was off refilling the waterskins from a well in a settlement not far up the road. Jude was rummaging in the supplies, probably for something to use for fresh bandages. Jorah was already asleep, curled on the ground on the other side of the fire pit, her back to them. James set about making a small coal fire; wood was scarce, the place picked over from pilgrims.

They had brought kindling but had not reckoned on an extra day to make it to Jerusalem.

"Tell me about your brother," Nathanael murmured, words slurring from fatigue.

"Which one?" James answered, eyes going to Simon.

"The one you are taking me to."

James' hand froze midway to the coal bag, only for a moment. He shoved his hand in, pulled out two chunks, and tossed them onto the others.

"I can still hear," Nathanael said, answering the question James did not ask.

James glanced over at him. The apprentice was too peaceful, as though the fight had gone out of him. His cocky manner had mellowed into something that made James want to . . . tear things apart.

"You should not worry so much," Nathanael murmured. He looked down and touched his fingertips to his swollen stomach. "It's still there."

"*What* is still there?"

But Nathanael only smiled, a smile as weak as it was mystifying. Then he said, "James . . . if we do not make it to your brother in time, I want to tell you—"

"You want to know about Jesus?" James broke in quickly. "What do you want to know?"

"—how much it has meant to me, being a part of something . . . normal."

James forced a short laugh. He dug in the metal ash bucket with the tongs until he found a smoldering chunk. "Normal? You call this family normal?"

"I have never been . . . more happy in my life."

James built the little pile and coaxed it into a fire. Once he had it going, he sat back, then flicked a glance over at Nathanael. A tear had left a glistening trail down the side of his face. *God of Israel . . .*

James bit the insides of his cheeks to keep the emotion in place. Normal, yes, normal. More so than ritualistic scars on a child's leg. Than life without a father, and with a mother who . . .

"You want to know about him?" James whispered. "He was my best friend."

"I thought so," came the slurred reply. Then, "What are you . . . so afraid of?"

James stared into the fingers of flame. He rubbed his hand over his fist. "Afraid," he murmured. "I am afraid of . . . terrified of . . . who he may be."

❧

The sun had set, leaving behind a sky lavished in color. Stars began to light the night, and the rising moon was one day from full.

Joses stood outside the city gate of Bethany, eyes ever on the people entering the town. But most of them were pilgrims who had already settled themselves in the tent city on the slopes surrounding Bethany and were merely visiting relatives in the town. Joses could not share the festive mood prevailing in the city.

He scanned the road. Where could they be? They should have been here by now, with or without James.

An arm came about him, settling on his hips, and his own arm responded to circle about his wife.

"You should have seen Hepsi dance," Abigail murmured, eyes on the road, where Joses' were. "She's the sweetest thing alive."

"Are they to bed yet?"

"No. They are with Jesus and your mother at Mary and Martha's."

The two looked long down the road.

Simon and Judas did not know, unless by some wild chance they had heard of it on the road. They did not know of this, the latest act of Jesus. Well that it was for Joses to see it, and not the other brothers. Especially not James, God have mercy. The near-belief in Jesus that Joses had long nurtured, like a tender seedling in the desert, came to its greatest test the day before yesterday. Joses himself did not know if the seedling lived or died.

Joses had followed Jesus about since his arrival in Jerusalem. The arrival alone brought back memories of the short-lived time of acceptance in Nazareth. Jesus was feted like a king— given palm branches to walk upon! People impulsively tore off their coats and settled them just in front of the advancing donkey. And Joses had cheered with them all, cheered himself hoarse. He had tried to catch Jesus' eye, to let him know he was there. Jesus did not see. And, strangely, Joses thought he saw tears on Jesus' face. Thought his face looked—anguished. It was only a glimpse, and the crowd did not seem to notice; they continued to cry out and rejoice. Many of them spoke loudly of wonderful things Jesus had done, things they had seen or experienced. That was a moment Joses wished with all his heart for his brothers to see and hear.

But everything changed, as it did with Jesus, sweet milk

going sour. His heart large with hope, Joses had followed him through the thousands of people packing the ways of Jerusalem to the Temple compound. They supposed him to do as any rabbi would, to sit with his disciples assembled about him and teach. Once again, Jesus did what they did not expect.

He strode with determination, mouth compressed, face unreadable, to the tables of the money changers and those selling animals for sacrifice. Joses stood on his toes to see, but first he heard. Crashes and yells. Then a voice thick with rage crying out, "It is written!"

It is written . . .

Shock waves rippled the crowd to near silence, and his brother's voice carried across the compound.

"It is written! 'My house shall be called a house of prayer!' But you have made it a robbers' den!"

The words echoed through the crowd, repeated over shoulders to the fringes of the throng who did not hear.

Who is that?

It's Jesus, the Galilean from Nazareth.

Who does he think he is?

On whose authority does he . . . ?

Where is someone from the Sanhedrin when you need him?

"Do you regret it, Abigail?" Joses presently said. "Do you regret marrying into this family?"

"Yes, of course I regret it."

For the first time in a long time, he smiled. His gaze at the road slid down to his wife. "You do, do you?"

"Every single day. I say, 'Abigail, you fool. What were you thinking?'"

Joses tightened his arm around her, and she wrapped her

other arm around to encircle his waist. She settled her head against his chest and sighed as she looked down the road. Then she glanced at movement on their left. It was Keturah, looking with them down the road.

Abigail whispered to Joses, "One day, I hope, this sweet little thing will regret marrying your family too."

Joses looked to catch Keturah's eye and smiled at her. She smiled shyly back, whisking her hair nervously behind her ear. The shy smile disappeared as she returned her gaze to the road.

Though Keturah and Therin stayed within Jerusalem's gates, at the home of Therin's sister, daily she came out to Bethany to wait with Joses and Abigail. She visited with Devorah and Mother and Devorah's new baby, and went to the home of Mary and Martha to hear Jesus speak with his followers, always wandering back to Bethany's foregate. Joses had already told her—offhandedly, trying hard not to imply anything—that likely James would stay behind with Nathanael. While she did not deny that it was James for whom she looked, like him she didn't seem to believe he would stay home.

Joses frowned. How could he tell the brothers? It would only seal Simon's belief that Jesus was nearing insanity. True it was that the act at the Temple did not make sense, none that Joses or Tobias or the other elders could see. The money changers offered a service to the festival attendees, because nothing but the half-shekel of the sanctuary could be received at the Temple treasury. Was it usury Jesus railed against? Jesus himself knew the Law fixed the rate the money changers were allowed to charge. And the others, who sold the animals for sacrifice? A service too, for the pilgrims who traveled far and were burdened enough with provisions for a long time away from home. Why was Jesus so angry?

And why, when he had begun to court their trust, did he do confounding things like this? It was no different from the day he came back to Nazareth, raising hopes only to squash them himself.

Believing in Jesus was like . . . tapping your chin to invite a blow.

18

JAMES WOKE TO THE sound of soft weeping. It was a low and crooning sound, broken by snuffled gasps. When he finally realized it was Jorah who wept, he jerked his head up.

"Jorah?" he whispered thickly, fumbling out of his extra tunic. He looked to find Jorah crouched at Nathanael's side near the fire pit where the brothers had laid the apprentice last night. He reached past Jorah to feel Nathanael's forehead. Too warm to the touch.

The lad moved his head side to side, murmuring weakly. James yanked aside Nathanael's covering to look at the wounds. But it was not quite dawn and too gray to see. James reached to shake Judas awake, where he lay curled in a ball not far away.

"What is it?" Jude said, instantly alert. He shook out of his own extra tunic and came to Nathanael's side. He felt his forehead, then peered at Nathanael's chest, running his fingertips over the bandages. "James, bring a candle."

"Jorah?" Nathanael said hoarsely. He looked at the faces over him, bewildered. "What? No, Jorah. Don't cry . . . it's still there. Annika would say . . ." His words drifted away.

It took too long to coax a flame out of the sleeping embers, too long no matter how he hurried. Cupping his hand around the flame, James went to his knees beside Nathanael. He held the candle over Nathanael's chest while Jude gingerly pulled back the bandages. The first three wounds did not receive more than a glance. Jude stopped at the second lowest. Even James could see the fluid seeping between neat black stitches. Jude placed his fingertips very lightly around the wound, then winced. "It's warm."

"But that doesn't look like infection." Jorah's voice wavered. "It's too watery." She lifted her face to Jude. "Isn't it? Too watery?" When he did not answer, the crooning came back, and she sat back on her heels to weep into fistfuls of her head covering.

Jude rubbed his forehead, then pinched between his eyes. He dropped his hand and whispered, "I don't know what to do. I am not a physician. A poultice? What would we put in it? Would it even draw it out?"

"There's a settlement ahead, and Shechem is only a little farther," Simon's voice came from behind. Joab was awake too, and though he hung back, his eyes were wide with anxiousness. "Should one of us go find a physician?" Simon asked.

"I will go," Joab quickly said.

"Annika . . ." Nathanael muttered.

"No." James spoke as he stared at the restless form of Nathanael. "There is no time. We pack up and make straight for Jesus. We can make Bethany by nightfall if we leave now and do not stop."

A moment of silence followed; then as one they moved to break camp.

***

He came in and out, rousing to fire a question at James, only to fade before he heard the answer. The quickened pace made the cart jostle more. It was something they had to risk, though they all winced at the hard jolts, as if wincing would ease it for Nathanael.

They left Samaritan territory and came into the province of Judea.

Before leaving Samaria . . . *Mount Gerizim, Nathanael. The holy mountain of the Samaritans, the place of their temple; remember what I told you?*

As they came into Judea . . . *Look off to the East, Nathanael, see there? Shiloh. It is where Samuel was called to be a prophet of God.*

Halfway on the Judean road to Jerusalem . . . *East again; it is Bethel. There Jacob had his dream, a ladder full of angels. Think of it, Nathanael . . . angels.*

His one good eye drifted and watched and drifted again, as if he tried hard not to sleep. He listened to what James said, though James hated the way he listened . . . too placidly, too peacefully. He listened as if trying hard to commit what he heard to memory. It made James unaccountably angry, made him ache to see it. What made him ache, perhaps, was the freshly cut tefillin Nathanael now wore.

Before they set out, as a slice of sun just topped a rocky ridge, Simon had gone to Nathanael with a wrapped bundle. They had just settled him in, tucked the cushions at his side. He was weakly joking that he was being pampered like an Egyptian princess and wouldn't it be fine for his friends to see, when Simon pushed a bundle into his hands.

Nathanael glanced at the bundle, then at Simon. His one good eye on Simon, he slowly pulled aside the wrapping, then looked to see. The wrapping fell from a small leather packet threaded onto a long, freshly cut strap of leather. Nathanael fingered the strap, then closed his hand on the packet. Slowly his gaze came away from the tefillin to Simon.

Simon's awkwardness was evident. He kept his own eyes fastened on the tefillin. "Do you know how? Here, let me help you." He pulled himself up on the cart and helped Nathanael put them on. "You wind the strap seven times around the arm, three times around the hand. Always on the left arm."

But Nathanael's one eye was not for the tefillin. It stayed on Simon until he slid off the cart and went to take the donkey's reins. Simon clicked his tongue and the cart started forward, with everyone in the usual places. Nathanael rocked slightly side to side with the cart, gazing at the tefillin wrapped around his arm. James kept close and reached in to pat Nathanael's shoulder.

"What are the words again, James?" Nathanael whispered.

"'You shall love the Lord your God—'"

"'With all your heart,'" Nathanael whispered with him, "'with all your soul, with all your strength.'"

Exertion asked its price, and Nathanael's good eye began to close. Before he drifted to sleep, he chuckled, his fingers curled around the leather packet, and murmured, "Only makes sense."

❦

They stood in line in the clogged Temple courtyard, if there was order enough in the press of people for it to be called a line. It was early afternoon, and at sundown it would be another Passover without Jesus. The first without the rest of his brothers.

Joses stood with his father-in-law, Tobias, who kept the lamb on a short rope next to him. They had come later to the courtyard, hoping at the last to see Judas and Simon and Jorah arrive, maybe with James. They never showed, and Tobias urged Joses to join him.

"What of my father's household?" Joses had wondered on the way from Bethany to Jerusalem. "Who will offer the lamb for them? I have not seen Jesus since yesterday, and Simon and Judas are not here."

"We will offer another on their behalf," gray-haired Tobias had assured him. "We will purchase a second at the courtyard. If we cannot . . ." The old man spread his hands. "I think God will allow for this lamb to cover us all. Eh, Joses?"

"Yes, Tobias," Joses had murmured, with a reluctant glance over his shoulder to the city gate.

Roman soldiers were stationed at strategic spots in the maze of streets in Jerusalem, eyes ever on the press of people about them. They usually stood taller than those around, as one of the requirements for serving in the Roman army was to be at least six feet in height. Pontius Pilate was in town and had brought with him extra soldiers from Caesarea to display strength against any notions of uprising. Herod Antipas, for all his Gentile ways, was in town for the festival too, staying in the Palace of Herod. Everyone was in town. Everyone except his brothers.

Jerusalem normally kept Joses bright with interest; the Antonia Fortress Herod the Great had built, though it had none of the beauty of the Temple, was a sight to see, if a disquieting sight. Part of it loomed over the Temple, as if to remind the Jews that Rome ever saw, Rome ever knew. Still, the architecture was impressive. Many faces from the smother of bodies in the courtyard (bodies in need of a bath from days of travel) would bide the time gazing up at the soldiers stationed on the Praetorium walls, who gazed in turn upon the Temple courtyards, ever on the alert for the merest hint of insurrection.

Any part of the Temple itself could be studied for hours, marveled at and admired for its beauty and design. Even the colors of the Temple stones were beautiful. One arch in particular had always captured Joses, since he was a child; it was the stone above the center arch from the Court of Gentiles, on the north side near the Antonia Fortress. The stone was a solid piece of marble with foamy colors like a wave of the sea. Joses could look on it for an hour without losing interest.

So much Jerusalem had to offer, especially at Passover, so much to engage and to mesmerize . . . but Joses only wanted to be somewhere else.

He gazed unseeingly at the Temple sanctuary, where soon Tobias would slay the lamb, and a priest would collect the blood. Where else could he possibly want to be on such a holy day? He was in Jerusalem, God's Holy City, the heart of every Jew. If it belonged—temporarily, he reminded himself—to foreign hands, it was still Jerusalem; it belonged to the Jews. He was here, with his beloved wife and his children. He was—

"Isn't that . . . ?" Tobias asked, pointing.

"What?" Joses said. "Who?"

"The fellow over there, talking with those priests. Isn't he one of the disciples of your brother?"

Joses looked where Tobias gestured and felt a rustle in his gut. It was the one from Kerioth. He spoke with a few priests, with some from the Temple guard looking on. While he spoke, the fellow occasionally cast a glance about; he was a man who either did not want to be recognized or did not want to be overheard.

"What's he doing with them?" Joses frowned. Why wasn't he with Jesus? The disciples never went far from their beloved Teacher, save for things like provisional errands. What was this man doing?

After a week in Bethany, talking with different people, Joses had learned something the other brothers did not know. It was a fellow named Simon who was rumored to be the Zealot among the disciples of Jesus. There wasn't much to learn about this Judas Ish-Kerioth, save that he took care of money matters for the group. Joses' relief at finding that the man did not seem to be connected to Raziel had left him nearly weak. It was one of the reasons he waited daily for the party from Nazareth. He waited with this good news . . . and with news like the Temple incident.

Joses sighed deeply and turned away from the little

gathering. Was it his business to understand the doings of the disciples? He had a hard enough time understanding Jesus.

❧

He could not cry out. He would not. The latest cut was a streak of fire, but he would not let her see him cry. To release the wickedness, she said. To let the evil out. It was his only hope.

"I will run away!"

"The madman in the tombs will get you. He likes to have little boys for lunch."

Mustn't let her see him cry . . . never that. The streak of fire, it ached so. She always cried later, cried and cried, and bandaged the wound with salves. Why not this time? Why did she let it keep hurting?

Mother . . .

"Nathanael?"

He opened his eye to a canopy of canvas and to James peering anxiously inside. The streak of fire was not one but several, the pain making them one. He held back a groan as he shifted to see James better.

The cart was not moving. "Where are we?" Nathanael croaked. He touched a thick tongue to dry lips.

The cart creaked as James hoisted himself in. He took the waterskin, loosened the fitting, and dribbled some water onto Nathanael's lips. Then he helped him up to take a real drink and eased him back onto the bedrolls.

James took a drink himself and replaced the fitting. "We are somewhere near Ramah." He gave a grim half smile. "The going is about to get rough. We will leave the Roman road to take the shortest route to Bethany. Through Givat Shaul, then

Nob. We should arrive in Bethany in a few hours if the road is not too bad." He reached to touch the back of his fingers to Nathanael's forehead. "How do you feel?"

"Better than this morning." It was an easy lie. He could talk, if not walk. Sitting up to drink was enough to make the cart spin, and thoughts of going to the brush could set him to whimpering. He figured if he did not drink, he would not have to go. But he was so thirsty.

He hated to see the worry on James' face. If he only knew, he would not worry . . . but Nathanael could not tell him. He would think he was out of his mind, in delusion from the wounds on his chest. But as long as *Seek James* was there, settled in his gut like a second soul . . .

"Where are the others?" Nathanael asked.

"Resting. Eating. How about some of Annika's cake?"

He hadn't eaten anything since—that morning. Fear of the unholy pain of vomiting had taken care of his appetite. And now he was too warm to eat, uncomfortably so. The sun must have mistaken this spring day for summer. He was about to refuse; then he noticed James' face. "Sounds good. A few bites."

James turned to rummage in the supplies, which had been shoved and stacked to the other side of the cart in a jumbled mess not like these people at all. It looked like his sleeping room back home in Caesarea. His sleeping room at Annika's was as neat as the rest of her house.

James produced a loaf of bread and broke some off. Nathanael reached for it, lest James entertain any notions of feeding him. He wasn't that bad off. Not yet. He ate one bite and tried for a second but could not. Faint nausea was enough to fear him into not eating. He took another drink instead.

James was unusually quiet. He remained in the cart, half in the sun where the canvas did not cover him and half buried in the supplies to make room. His gaze was drifting about, then came to rest on the tefillin still wound around Nathanael's arm. Nathanael lowered the waterskin and squinted at him. The movement cost him pain in the bad eye, but James caught his look and glanced quickly away.

"What, James? Am I that bad off?"

"You do have a fever," James replied absently, fixing his eyes instead on one of the cushions. "And a wound is infected. Second lowest."

"That's not it."

"No," James answered, rubbing his hands together. "I have wanted to tell you something. For a long time."

"Maybe I don't want to hear it. Not if you think you have to tell me before I die. I am not going to die, James." He had not spoken so much in . . . devil take him, he was getting tired. He sagged dead weight into the cushions. This was not the time to convince James he was ready to chop wood. His heart skittered as though he had just sectioned an entire tree.

"I said I've wanted to tell you for a long time. Ever since I knew that—" He broke off.

"What?"

James picked at his thumbnail. "Since I knew that . . . your mother . . . you know."

Nathanael could feel himself stiffen, and his tone went flat. "What about my mother?"

James would not look him in the eye. "It's a story I heard, Nathanael. You up for a good story?"

Coldly, "What does it have to do with my mother?"

James settled back on the piled-up provisions. He folded his arms and this time looked right at him. Nathanael noticed his sunburned face, his thinner-than-usual cheeks. James had been the sick one not so long ago.

"The story goes that there was a woman. A woman who was caught in the act of adultery."

Nathanael's stomach tightened, and he forced a wry smile. "My mother is not an adulteress, James. She's a flat-out whore."

"This woman was dragged to the Temple by religious men to another man."

He could feel his jaw clench, bringing a spasm of pain. Avi had a good right. "This man wouldn't be your brother, would he?"

"They said to him, 'Teacher! This woman has been caught in adultery, the very act. The Law of Moses commands us to stone such a woman. What do you have to say about it?'"

What was in that face? Pity? Sympathy? He would kill him if it were so. "Well? What did your brother have to say?"

"Nothing, at first. The story goes he ignored them. Settled down and wrote in the dirt with his finger."

"Why would he do that?" Writing in the dirt. What kind of crazy was that? "What did he write?"

"The religious men kept pestering him for an answer until finally the Teacher stood. He looked at them, every one, and said this: 'The one who is without sin among you—let him be the first to throw a stone at her.'"

Nathanael stared. He couldn't have heard what he did. "Say that again."

"Let the one without sin be the first to throw a stone."

Silence. "He said that?"

"So I heard."

"What did they say to that?"

"Nothing. They dropped their stones and left."

Nathanael studied the leather packet on his hand. Quietly, he said, "The woman . . . what did she do?"

James drew a breath. "Well. Story goes he said to her, 'Where are your accusers? Is there no one left to condemn you?' And she said, 'No one.'" James paused a moment. He cleared his throat. "And he said, 'I don't condemn you, either. Go home now. Sin no more.'"

He did not know how long he stared at James. He stared until . . .

. . . a strange sensation began to sweep up from his toes.

It swirled around him like a gentle wind, briefly fluttering his senses until he closed his eyes against the faint dizziness. Then the gentle wind was gone. . . .

. . . taking with it . . .

Seek James.

His eyes flew open, and he looked down. His hand went to his stomach.

"Nathanael . . . ?"

"It's gone," he breathed.

"What is gone?"

He slowly raised his disbelieving face to James.

"I never came for you," Nathanael whispered.

James was backing away. "Judas? Jude!"

"I never came for you."

"Judas!"

"What's wrong?"

"I don't know!"

I never came for you.

"James?" Nathanael slurred. "Tell Jorah she can worry now." His fingers closed around the leather packet on his hand. He had even more impossible words to clutch now.

Where are your accusers?

"Simon!" Jude shouted. "Simon, we have to go!"

Neither do I condemn you. They were the last words he knew before the silken haze enfolded him.

19

THEY WOULD NOT make it to Bethany, not today. The sun was ready to dip behind the hills, and no one had the heart to push farther. The cart's jostling was unforgiving. The wounds showed the wear of the journey, three of them seeping now, the lowest breaking the wax seal more than once. And more than once, James heard from him a faint groan.

Simon stopped the cart at the roadside and went off to the brush. Jorah crawled into the cart to nestle next to Nathanael. From where he sat on a rock, James watched her trace her fingertips over his eyebrow, smooth a curl of hair thickened with grime.

Didn't Jorah see he was dying? She whispered to him as if he could hear her. She took a daisy from the posy she had fixed to the canopy where Nathanael could see it and drew it playfully over his nose. She acted as though they were lovers in the grass on a picnic, and Nathanael was only sleeping.

The infected wound was frightfully hot and no longer oozed water but fluid tinged in yellow. Jude tried to draw it out with a poultice he had concocted from plants alongside the road, but Jude was a carpenter, not an herbalist. He and Joab had gathered a doubtful assortment and drawn it up in a square of coarse cloth cut from Joab's tunic. Jude soaked it in water and settled it on the wound. The only thing it seemed to do was leak murky water down Nathanael's sides. But it made Jude feel better; it was something he could do. All James could do was watch him die.

"Caesarea or Nazareth," he heard Jorah murmur to Nathanael. "Neither, let's leave both behind. Wherever we go, we will have the sweetest little place where I will plant jasmine bushes. You will have a shop, and you can make things ready-to-sell for market. I can make mosaic plaques. Perhaps we can visit Caesarea for a time and I can study with Theron. He is a great mosaicist and lives near Father's cousin. And we can come back and visit Father's olive tree if you wish. I think Father would have liked that."

Jude came next to James. He wiped his brow free of sweat with his sleeve. "We are sending Joab to see if he can find someone to sell us unleavened bread. Have you seen the money box in that mess?"

"No. Jude—I'm worried about Jorah."

Jude frowned and said in a low tone, "That's why I'm sending Joab. Have you seen the way she looks at him? I've never seen her face like that."

James saw. He hoped Joab could find bread. James had gone through the cart less than an hour earlier, holding the candle aloft in search of the sack of leavened bread made by Jorah and Annika. No one would have guessed the trip would have taken an extra day. Passover would be upon them at sundown.

"Come on, help me look for the box," Jude said. They went to the back of the cart and began to rummage.

"Jorah, are you lying on the money box?" James asked.

"No," she murmured, blowing away a fly from Nathanael's nose. The swelling there had gone down, as well as the swelling in his eye. In moments of consciousness he could open the bad eye to a slit; the white of his eye was now crimson, a jarring contrast to the amber.

Jude pulled out a rolled-up tent to prop alongside the cart. "Well, we'd better find that box if we want to eat. We only have some figs left. I hope we didn't lose it somewhere."

Article after article came out of the cart. James pulled out a mess of tangled rope and dropped it onto the heap growing next to him. "Jorah, are you sure you're not on the box? Is it behind Nathanael?" She didn't seem to hear him at first, then gave a disinterested glance around.

"Oh, wait—here it is." She pulled it from under a wadded bunch of clothing in the corner. James snatched it from her, glowering. They didn't have all day! In fact, they had about half an hour before sunset. Nobody would sell them bread on Passover. He set the box on the edge of the cart to open it, but it slipped and tumbled to the ground. Coins scattered in the dirt. With a curse, he bent to retrieve them.

"Watch your tongue, James," Jorah said absently.

The box had fallen on its edge, and the lid had come free. He picked up the lid, then looked closely at it. A shard of wood had chipped from it at the fall. There was something . . .

"What is that?" Jude asked, leaning closer to see.

"I don't know. Get me a knife."

James pried at the edge of the lid, breaking off another shard. He brought the lid closer to his eyes. He worked another chunk off with his thumbs, barely noticing when a splinter went in beneath his thumbnail.

Simon had returned from the brush and came close to see. "What's going on?"

"I don't know. Look at this; the lid isn't one piece. Looks like there's a veneer."

Jude came with the knife. James set the lid on the cart rail and worked the knife into the edge of the lid. He pried until a chunk of wood snapped up. Revealing . . .

"What *is* that?"

"What's going on?" Jorah asked. She sat up and crawled to the side of the cart.

James worked at the lid, snapping off piece after piece until what was left in his hands was . . . a thick, tarnished silver square. Embedded with . . .

"My money says you're looking at the finest lapis lazuli," Nathanael croaked groggily.

Simon took the lid from James and put it in a patch of waning sunlight. He looked at it closely, then slowly raised his eyes to Nathanael. "It is lapis. How did you know?"

"The box, James," Nathanael murmured, but he was already closing his eyes. "The box the . . . crazy old . . . crazy . . ."

"That driftabout from—?"

"The East," James finished for Jorah. His arms and his neck and his scalp prickled with chill. He dared to look at Judas, who dared to look back. Yes, Jude remembered what was unspoken. The family had agreed not to speak of it anymore, for all the trouble it brought. So what was unspoken drifted into story, and what was story drifted into vague childhood memories.

Simon picked up the rest of the box and hefted it, then carefully examined the edge where the lid fit. "This is all veneer too." He shook his head wonderingly. "No wonder this thing is so heavy. Never for the money in it. I always thought the wood was purpleheart or ebony heartwood."

"He stained it the color of ebony heartwood," James said in quiet surprise. He took the lid from Simon and began to pick away the remaining bits of wood stuck in the tiny crevices.

"Who stained it?" Jorah demanded.

"Father." When James had cleaned off every scrap, he blew his breath on the lid and polished it on the front of his tunic. Then he held it up for the others to see.

Tarnished, to be sure, smudgy black with it, but the workmanship was evident. Square-cut stones of lapis lazuli nestled in ridges of silver, arranged in a pleasing, symmetrical design.

"What a lovely pattern for a mosaic," Jorah breathed. "Why would Father hide such a thing?"

Nobody answered. Simon took the box with the knife to the rock and sat down to go to work freeing it of the veneer. Jude followed to stand behind him and watch. Joab even ventured near to see what was going on. James folded his arms and rested them on the cart, watching Simon.

"Why would Father—?"

"I imagine he fashioned a disguise for it for the journey to Egypt," James replied. Simon's knife paused at that. The three brothers traded looks; then Simon went back to his task.

Jorah's eyes narrowed. After a moment of studying James, she said warily, "Journey to Egypt? I don't think I—"

"In that box was the frankincense." Saying it dried out his throat. James troubled waters long still with those words. He took a great paddle and stirred up memories probably different with each child of Joseph. How did Jude remember it? How did Simon? Was Simon ever ridiculed, as James was, when he told other children about the entourage to visit his brother? About the angels? How they laughed. Jorah was the youngest; she would have only the vaguest memory of the stories, because by then they had stopped talking about it altogether.

"Balthazar said he got it from a man who died on the way. He said the others brought myrrh. And gold. To Bethlehem, Jorah." He glanced at her, and she was shaking her head.

"Stop it, James," Jorah whispered.

Judas kept his eyes deliberately fixed on the lid and said, "Did he . . . did Balthazar say anything about a star?"

"Yes," James and Simon said together, then glanced at each other.

"Stop it!" Jorah suddenly shouted. She climbed out of the cart, took a few steps back, a few steps forward. "Isn't it enough that we are taking Nathanael to him? Those stories are in the past! Best left alone. Best forgotten."

"I thought you always wanted to be included," Jude snapped. "This is what it's about, Jorah."

"You spoke with him?" James asked Simon. "He told you about the star?"

"I spoke with him," Simon answered grimly. "He hung about the shop for two whole days, waiting for you to come around." He handed the box and knife to Jude to have a go at it.

"What did he say to you?" James asked. When Simon didn't answer, he said, "Well? What did he say?"

Simon scratched behind his ear and gave a halfhearted chuckle. "Oh, nothing much."

Doubtfully, James said, "He had plenty to say to me." But Simon would not answer no matter how much James prodded him, until finally he said he didn't want to talk about it and got up and walked away.

Suddenly, James noticed Joab. He didn't like it that Joab found the whole thing so wide-eyed interesting. This was family business, not belonging to a stranger. James looked at his feet where the coins had fallen from the box and picked up a shekel. He dusted it off and tossed it to Joab. "Here—see if you can purchase some bread from the settlement ahead. Be quick."

Joab caught the coin and, with a backward glance at the box in Jude's hands, hurried off.

"I don't know why he travels with us," Jorah said darkly.

James looked from the box to Jorah, then to where Jorah's smoldering gaze went. "He travels with us because he is lost."

"I hate him. I wish he were dead."

The words were a hand slap on his cheek. Jorah never said such things. She did not know James was staring at her until she caught his look when she turned from watching Joab. She lifted her chin. "Well, I do. He could have prevented it."

From where he sat on the rock, Judas muttered, "Hate isn't pretty on you, Jorah."

Her lips trembled. She pointed at the cart and said tightly,

"That isn't pretty. Anyone who could let something like that happen deserves to die." She turned to walk away, then broke into a run, head covering fluttering behind her. Jude stood up to go after her, but James said quietly, "Let her go." They watched her leap the ditch next to the road and run for a grassy knoll. She scrambled to the top and disappeared down the other side.

⁂

Have you seen the box? Fashioned of silver, inlaid with the finest lapis lazuli.

Simon whipped a stone at a distant boulder, pale bright in the moonlight. Crazy old man. Filthy foreigner. He smelled as bad as he looked, and Simon had to assure himself more than once that a mallet lay handy—any man who babbled as he did was unpredictable at best.

He had hung about in the workshop for two straight days, waiting for James to waken. Two days! He watched Simon work with those dark glittering eyes; he possessed the corner of the shop like a brooding shadow. He was eerie, he and his words.

Amazing, the confines of a miracle, don't you think? Once, a manger. For years, this place.

He did not speak much in those two excruciatingly long days, but when he did, his words were anything but mere talk.

What chafes you, Master Simon?

What *chafes* me? You do! What business sends you to a man who is broken in his bed, perhaps beyond redemption?

He brings change, Simon. Change will always chafe.

Change? What would you know of it? I was once a respected carver. I once went to synagogue.

How is it a foreigner knows your own prophecies better than you do? You should see what is written in our holy books.

What prophecies, you mad old vagabond? You think we do not search the Scriptures? Daily, we do! Many times daily!

Does it chafe that he came as no one expected? That the One True God chose pagans to herald his coming? He remembered the Gentile, Simon. We, too, are in his image.

Herald his coming? I will—I will throw you out for your blasphemy!

Blasphemy, Simon? The answer is simple. Either it is blasphemy—or it is not.

"What of that box?" came a timid voice behind him.

Simon closed his eyes. Joab rarely spoke on this journey; why did he have to choose a time like this? "I don't know," Simon answered wearily, opening his eyes to gaze upon a moon luminous and full. "I don't know about the box. God help me, Joab, I don't."

Did any of the other brothers get a switching from a Hebrew teacher for informing the other students of Jesus' . . . interesting . . . birth? Did any of the other brothers have his mouth scrubbed out with a cake of ash soap for speaking blasphemy?

"What of Nathanael?"

Simon made fists. To hear the lad put the name of the apprentice on his lips . . . "What of him?"

"Where is he from?"

"Caesarea Maritima."

"Who is his family?"

"He has none. Save a whore for a mother."

"What is . . . her name?"

Simon spun to face him. "What do you care?"

Joab shrank from the disdain in Simon's voice, clutching flat loaves of bread to his chest. The shivering little coward. Hateful worm.

Simon snarled, "Get out of my sight." He watched Joab slink away toward camp. He wished he would creep all the way to—Rome, for all Simon cared. He could never be far enough away.

He picked up another handful of rocks and began to whip them at the boulder in the moonlight.

20

PASSOVER

"Arrested?" Joses demanded, rising from the breakfast table. "On what charge?"

Devorah stood in the doorway, twisting her hands, face full of worry, near tears. "I don't know! It's so confusing; nobody knows what is happening. He was arrested last night. They say he is being detained at the home of the high priest."

"Joses," Tobias breathed, rising next to him.

Joses tossed his napkin onto the table. "Where is Mother?"

"Matthias took her to Jerusalem to see what they can find out. She and some of the other women."

"They choose now to arrest him, on Passover?" Joses came away from the table, walking the room, hardly knowing where he went. "What charge, Devorah? What charge? Is it what happened in the Temple the other day? Is it—blasphemy?"

Abigail was at his side, her hand on his arm. "She does not know. Go with her, Joses."

Joses stopped. "He was arrested last night? They waited until night to do it?" Bewilderment made him stare; fury made him glower. "But he was in the Temple daily with them! He hid nothing!"

"Go with your sister, Joses. We will watch for your brothers." Tobias hurried him to the door. He snatched Joses' outer robe from a peg and pushed it into his hands. "We will send them on when they come."

Joses pulled the robe over his tunic, then stopped in the doorway to look over his shoulder at the table. There sat his mother-in-law, Sarah, and Tobias' brother and sister-in-law, faces anxious and grim. Hepsibah and Benjamin, faces solemn and eyes wide. A brown ring circled Hepsi's lips, honey syrup from the unleavened cakes.

"Pray for your uncle, children," Joses urged quietly.

"We will, Abba," Ben said.

"We will, Abba," Hepsi echoed. She turned to her brother. "How come Uncle Jesus was 'rested?"

Joses and Devorah hurried from the home, but Devorah's steps soon lagged. She had given birth to her first child only a week ago. "Joses," she gasped, "I cannot. I will only slow you down. Hurry and find Mother; she needs you. Send word when you can."

"Tell Keturah and Therin," Joses called over his shoulder. "And pray, Devorah." He turned from her and broke into a trot. The early morning sunlight left her impression on his mind, hair wisped and wayward, face tight in worry, so alone in the empty village street.

Arrested at night? Detained at the home of the high priest? He wasn't sure whether to be relieved or not. Rome did not arrest him, thank God. Apparently, they saw no threat in Jesus, and they would not think twice to detain a man during Passover to keep the peace. His stomach clenched with fear. What did the high priest see? What conclusions had he come to? Was this the thing Joses and the others had dreaded all along? Perhaps Jesus would have been safer in a Roman jail.

It took nearly an hour to walk to Jerusalem from Bethany. Leaving the city gate, Joses settled into a run.

⁂

What offense was blasphemy in Roman law? By the gods, Pilate hated these people. Hated their pinched intellects, hated their rigid ways. He gripped his forehead and groaned a long inward groan. It was too early in the day for this. Too early at the break of dawn, and hours later it was still too early.

He cracked his eyes open, but the people had not gone away. He squeezed his eyes shut and cursed every deity he knew, with two extra curses for their own. It made him chuckle; would they name him a blasphemer? And how would they deal with Pilate? Ah, but he was an ignorant pagan. He did not count. There it was, then. All this man had to do was join up with the pagans. Then he could get himself out of this fix. It didn't seem likely.

Pilate had congratulated his own shrewdness in shooing the man to Herod once he discovered the man to be from Galilee. But Herod had sent him back, worse for the wear, even though he wore purple. It seemed Herod was as annoyed by the intrusion as Pilate. Perhaps he was not as uptight as Pilate thought; at least he was nothing like these other Jews. He should send him a small cask of his personal reserve from Gaulanitis. Sighing deeply, he rubbed his eyes and opened them.

Pilate studied the weary man in front of him. He tilted his head, trying to appraise him from another angle. The Jews themselves did not want this man; moments ago, they chose Barabbas. And earlier, when Pilate tried to display Roman justice, they only wanted him to give over this man without a formal trial.

Well, and what choice did he have? He had made the Jews furious too many times, what with the Temple treasury incident and the matter of the standards. Blood had spilled then, Jewish blood—and Rome would brook no more tension between the procurator and the Jewish leaders. Especially during one of their holy festivals. Jews were notoriously stubborn, as unmoving as their god. If he admired them for their fortitude, he could throttle them for their obstinacy.

The man swayed on his feet. Come to think of it, he really didn't like this man. He had tried to defend him and got no thanks in return. Not a crumb of gratitude. Pilate tilted his head to the other side; he decided he hated him simply for making him do this. Well, then. Let it be the death of a Jew to appease the Jews.

"Crucify him."

꙳

"Where have they taken him? Does anybody know?"

They dragged him here; they dragged him there. Whose report could Joses believe? "He is at the home of the high priest!" "No, he is at Herod's palace!" "The Antonia Fortress, I heard it from a soldier!" Near frantic with fear, he pushed through the streets thick with bodies. Back to the Antonia Fortress. It seemed he was always one step behind.

How could he find Mother in this mess? The Temple compound sprawled on his right, the Fortress lay ahead, and a milling mass of people were in between. And what could Joses do when he got there? How could he speak for his brother?

What events were on the move?

Jesus, arrested? Jesus, dragged before the likes of Pontius Pilate and Herod himself? Long the brothers had feared something like this, but when it came down to it, incarceration was—preposterous! Jesus was only a carpenter! Just a talkative carpenter from Nazareth!

Jesus had slipped through the crowd at the precipice that day; surely he would do so now. Surely, if God had indeed called upon Jesus to do a great work for him, then God would again protect him, allow him again to slip through grasping hands. Surely, he would.

Joses took up his shout once more. "Where have they taken him? Jesus, from Galilee? Jesus, of Nazareth? Does anybody know? Does anybody know?"

I want to believe. But how?

Did one believe from feeling or did one believe from choice? What came first? James fit the lid onto the box and rested it in his lap. Most importantly, was this belief right? If he allowed the thoughts to go their course, he ventured toward a precipice.

Is my brother one who is—

Take the thought its course.

Is my brother . . . chosen by God to—

Take the thought its *course*, you coward.

Is my brother the Christ? James closed his eyes.

Honest. But there's more.

Is my brother the Son of God? His eyes flew open. *His actual Son?*

The thoughts took him to the edge and by thinking them, pitched him over.

"Jesus . . . did it have to be this way?"

How came others to believe in his brother? How did that belief feel? Was it easy for them? Did it change them? James regarded the cart at the bottom of the slope below. Jorah was fixing a posy of wildflowers to the rail where Nathanael could see them.

Nathanael had been changed by secondhand words. James could tell it without being told. The very air around Nathanael was different. He had long wanted to tell that story to Nathanael but just hadn't dared. James, repeating the words of Jesus? Passing along a story such as that?

He noticed the box in his lap and smoothed his hand over the bumpy ridge of inlaid lapis stones. Jesus brought change, that was sure. Were they ready for it? Was James?

"So you are a prophet. A reformer. But Jesus . . . *'Love your neighbor.'* You're serious about that? Love . . . ? And *'Love your enemy'*?" Everything would be all right if it were not for the fact that Jesus meant what he said.

Do for others what you would have them do for you. Do not judge, so that you will not be judged. Words as exhilarating as they were hopeless. Who could turn the other cheek? Who could love their enemy? Why? And then came *Do not think I have come to do away with the Law or the Prophets; I came not to abolish, but to fulfill.*

"What was not fulfilled that you came to fulfill it?"

He wanted to believe, but he was terribly, terribly afraid. Oh, God, he was afraid. He rubbed his lower lip as he watched the others break camp. He could feel his heart beat faster with what he was going to pray.

"God of Israel . . . hear me," he mumbled against his balled fist. Fear rose, and his voice dropped to a whisper. "God of my fathers, do not be angry with me, but I have a question. A very terrible question: Is it right to believe in him? Do you want me to believe? Do not be angry with me, but, please . . . I need to know."

Acknowledge the Lord in all your ways, and he will direct your steps. If he doesn't first consume you with fire for asking a question drenched in blasphemy.

You are miserable because you have not decided. He did not need the voice of a Zealot to tell him what he already knew. He dropped his head and scrubbed the back of his neck. He had not seen Jesus since that day nearly two years ago. He had last looked upon him from the dust of the ground, at Jesus borne away by an angry crowd.

He had to decide; he knew it at his core. But it was a decision too great for him. Perhaps some could decide in one gallant stroke, for the nay or for the yea. He could envy it, but it was not James. He had to creep toward belief, toward the yea or nay; get hard ground beneath him as he crept. And suddenly, he knew how he would do it. His head came up slowly.

He would start as Father had told him long ago. *James, how does one pave a long pathway? One cobblestone at a time.*

There it was, the safety he needed. The first cobblestone of this pathway to Jesus was to look into his eyes. Two years since he had last looked into those eyes. Yes . . . yes! Let James look now and see what he might. Let the look be the beginning. Let the look decide whether he took the next cobblestone.

He found he could take a deep breath and, with it, found that his misery had lessened for the first time in years. It lessened by one cobblestone. Clutching the box to his chest, he rose from the side of the road and made for the breaking camp.

❧

"I saw where they took him, young fella. Outside the city, north wall."

"Outside the city? Why?"

The man shrugged. "Because they will not crucify him inside. They grabbed some poor rustic to carry his—say, young fella, are you all right?"

❧

The sun approached its noon mark. They would soon be upon Bethany, and their journey would come to an end. If Jesus was not at the home of Devorah, or of his friends Mary and Martha, then he was in Jerusalem, teaching at the Temple. Despite the crowds, they should not have a problem finding him if they asked around. Nathanael would make it to see him; he had to. James glanced at the wilted posy tied to the rail. And soon James would look into a pair of eyes very like his own.

If the others had noticed the new hope James felt, to his relief they did not mention it. It was too new, too fragile.

"Bethany!" Simon called over his shoulder.

"Bethany," James heard Judas breathe.

Jorah, ever in front of the cart, spun to reveal her sunburned, joyful face. "Can you believe it?" She hurried to the cart and lifted the flap. No matter that Nathanael was sleeping. "Nathanael! It is Bethany!"

He roused enough to blink in the sudden shaft of sunlight, and he cracked a smile at Jorah, but he drifted off a moment later. His face was flushed, and white ringed his lips.

Jorah smiled tenderly upon him, as if things were the way they should be, and let the flap fall back into place. A joyous lift in her step, she hurried to walk with Simon.

"I think you should be a doctor," James said to Jude. "Trade your tools for herbs. I cannot believe he has made it this far." But Jude did not answer.

They came closer to the city gate, and when it was still a distance away, Simon peered under his hand against the burn of the sun. "James, look. There, by the gate. That's not . . . is that . . . ?"

James followed his gaze. It could not be . . . "Keturah?"

Keturah, waiting for them? Waiting, perhaps, for him? Who else was with her? The closer they came, the more they saw. Was it . . . Tobias? But why was Tobias sitting in the dust? And why did Keturah wail? And why did the sky grow dark?

"What is happening?" Jorah turned about, gazing with fear at the sky. The sun shone brilliantly; at least it had at his last breath . . . and now the sky grew dark, for the sun stopped shining. Without a cloud in the sky, it simply stopped.

Fearful cries came from all around, from within the city, from the traveling party. The sun was a gray disc. Darkness pervaded, bringing with it a chill. The world was cloaked in shadow.

Simon had halted, and with Jorah, Judas, and Joab, he whirled about, gazing at the sky. James alone, sick with dread, kept his measured trudge to Keturah.

In the dimness he could see that her lovely lavender tunic bore the marks of one who had fallen on the ground. Her face was drawn in despair, and the wail she could not stop did not lessen or increase at the sight of James. Strangely, she did not seem to notice the sky. Her eyes were on him alone.

Tobias, Joses' gentle father-in-law, a man of propriety and fastidiousness, sat in a disheveled heap on the ground, covered in dust, his clothing rent down the middle. His wail was a sound more aching than Keturah's.

James stopped a few paces from her. Her face was striped in dirt and tears, and she pressed her hands over her mouth, covering the wail but not stopping it. She gazed into his eyes, large brown eyes tormented for him and for another.

He could barely speak for the press on his heart. "Jesus . . ." And she nodded.

A fearful ache splintered wide a crevasse, dropping James to his knees. He wrapped his arms about himself and pressed his forehead to the ground.

꩜

Joses sat alone in the darkened world. Apart from him sat some from Galilee. Most of the crowd had gone now; some had left beating their breasts. For nearly an hour, Joses had screamed himself into the dust. He tasted it now. His mouth was cracked and dry; his ravaged throat was filled with it.

Upon the neighboring hill, upon one of three crosses, was a simple carpenter from Nazareth. He had not slipped away this time.

Mother huddled in a group not far from the foot of the cross, though Joses could not go to her. He could not, he could not be where his brother hung in pain. Neither could he be away. Upon this God-cursed hill, at a God-cursed distance, he sat.

How could he tell his brothers? Oh God, oh God, oh God . . . how could he tell them? How could he tell Jorah? How could he tell his little Hepsi?

Dry weeping came again, and he pressed his face to the ground to swallow more dust with his lament.

21

Is it how you want to remember him? Tobias had called out. The words had halted James' steps to Jerusalem.

From a back room, he heard the small cry of Devorah's new baby and the rustle of Devorah's tending. It was still night. Unless the others lay awake on their beds, only James and Devorah and the baby were awake.

There would be no more cobblestones.

He rolled to face the wall. At his feet he could see Judas. Simon was on the other side of the workroom. Nathanael had been taken to the home of the physician in Bethany, and Jorah would not leave him. Joab had disappeared. He could not remember the last time he saw the lad. He had taken the lamb with him. Such a small thing to notice.

He noticed other things. The way Joses would not let his children go when he came in from Jerusalem. The way Devorah held her baby close, the way Matthias tended Devorah.

Mother was not among those returning from Jerusalem. Joses told of the last heart-tearing thing Jesus had said regarding the family. From the very cross on which he died, he commended their own mother to the hands of a disciple. Joses had to watch, broken and helpless, as Mother was led away by strangers. He had followed behind until he knew where they took her, to the home of one called John Mark.

A fearful quiet had descended upon the village, as surreal as the three-hour darkness from the sun. Animals were still; the wind had stopped. For hours, everyone in the village stayed by the city gates, silently awaiting word from Jerusalem. Travelers dragging their steps began to straggle in. Nobody went to their homes until Sabbath duty demanded they leave to light the candles and cruses.

The quiet followed the family into the home of Devorah and Matthias, a quiet broken only by whispering or when one was suddenly seized with weeping, an act as capricious as the wind. It seized James last night when he helped Matthias fill the Sabbath cruses with oil, and it seized him once when Devorah had unexpectedly placed her babe in his arms. He could only hold the little boy a moment before he had to hand him back and stumble out of the home into the evening.

There were no Sabbath prayers at its beginning, when the sun had set. And nobody could go to be with Mother—Jerusalem was too far away. From Bethany it was nearly twice the distance allowed for a Sabbath day's journey. He could not go to Mother or . . . Jesus until tomorrow. There would be spices to gather. A burial cloth to purchase.

Devorah had the baby, and Joses had his wife and children. James wanted the box. He searched through the cart after they delivered Nathanael to the doctor. He traced their steps back. It was gone. Perhaps the lamb wasn't the only thing Joab had disappeared with.

"Are you awake?" Judas murmured.

"I'm not sure I slept," James said.

"Me neither."

James pushed himself to a sitting position, settling against the wall. After a moment, Judas did the same.

The last time they had been in Devorah's home together was last Passover. Not much had changed in Matthias' workroom. James studied the tools on the shelf above the two benches until tears blurred them from his sight.

"What happens now?" Judas asked dully.

"We go back to Nazareth," Simon answered from the other side of the room, his back to them.

A tap came at the door. James whisked his arm over his face, and he and Judas exchanged looks. Simon twisted to look. Jude got up to answer it.

Joses stood in the doorway. The sight of him at the door brought the cursed capriciousness. James hung his head and allowed the tears to drip. Joses came in and closed the door softly behind him, then went to where Simon sat against the opposite wall. He settled beside him, drawing up his knees.

Presently Judas murmured with a sad half smile, "Just like back home."

And so it was. The brothers in the workroom, together to

take the news of the land. The brothers together for another family crisis. It was what James needed more than the box, what made him cry when he saw Joses.

He wiped his nose and said, "Good to see you, Joses."

Joses nodded. By the look of his face, he had not slept either. It was slightly swollen and more exhausted than James ever remembered. The reddish tinge of his beard and his hair made his face white.

"How are Ben and Hepsi?" Simon softly asked.

"I haven't told them. Not yet. Hepsi keeps asking why I'm so sad." He pressed his lips and looked down.

Joses was there. The only brother to . . .

James asked what he dreaded most. "How is Mother?"

Tears now seeped from Joses' eyes, and he didn't bother to wipe them away. "You would have to ask John that. She stays in his home."

"Who is John?" Simon asked dully.

"Not one of us," Joses whispered. At length, he wiped his face and said, "What happened to the apprentice?"

As Jude quietly told the story, images of meeting Joses at the gate yesterday when he returned from Jerusalem flickered in James' mind. He had walked with another, whose arm was tight about him, supporting. James didn't know who it was, only that the kindness of it made James weep afresh. At the sight of his brothers waiting at the gate, Joses had stopped short, then dropped his head and wept as well. They ran to him.

"Who was the fellow you came in with last night?" James asked when Jude had finished.

Joses looked at James. "What do you mean?"

"The man who walked with you from Jerusalem."

Joses glanced first at Simon, then at Judas. "I came alone."

James blinked. But . . . of course. It must have been awful for him. What had Joses endured? He had not spoken of it. "You came to Bethany with a man who had an arm around you," James said quietly. "It's all right, Joses. It doesn't matter."

But Joses was not the only one looking at James. Simon fixed him with a strange gaze, and Jude was looking at him too.

"Joses came alone, James," Simon said.

"He came alone," Judas said quietly.

James stared. He was sure . . . He gave a rueful chuckle. "I could say I had too much sun yesterday, but . . ."

"We need to see how Nathanael is," Judas murmured. "And Jorah."

Jorah. How was Jorah taking it? She was at the home of the Bethany physician.

"Nathanael will not survive." It came from Simon in a rough whisper. "We need to be with Jorah."

"Did you speak with the doctor?" Joses asked.

But the capriciousness struck again, this time with Simon. His fists were white on his knees, and he began to tremble. Muscles twitched in his face as he worked furiously to stay controlled. His words fumbled first, then came in a low, teeth-bared growl. "I want—to know—about those scars of his," he managed. He rubbed his face hard and gave a growling cough into his hands. "Tell me, James."

"From his mother," James said bleakly. "They were from his mother." Simon's face tightened. He nodded and rubbed his hand over his fist.

The tefillin. "Simon . . ." James began.

341

"Shut up, James," he said.

"It meant so much to him."

"Shut up!" A curse followed, and Simon dug at his eyes with the heel of his hand.

"It was because of the Temple, you know," Joses murmured. Like everyone else, his eyes were stained red. He stared distantly as he spoke. "A few days ago he—overturned the money changers' tables in the Temple compound. 'Stop making my Father's house a robber's den. My Father's house is a house of—'" His voice caught.

"Defiant to the end," Judas murmured.

"Prayer," Joses whispered, lips trembling. "'My Father's house is a house of prayer.'"

"'My Father's house,'" James mumbled. He frowned. Why did those words sound familiar?

"I remember too, James," Joses said. He put his head back against the wall, letting tears stream down his face. James squinted at Joses. It was there but so vague.

Joses sniffed and wiped his nose. "Don't you remember? Judas and Simon were too little. We were in—"

"The caravan," James suddenly said.

"Yes. We left for home. And suddenly Mother and Father realized Jesus wasn't with us."

"Couldn't find him anywhere," James supplied wonderingly as the memory trickled back. "They were frantic."

"Remember where we found him?"

"Back in Jerusalem, at the Temple." He gave a hard chuckle. "Talking with the scribes and the leaders."

Joses had a strange look. "Do you remember what he said to Mother and Father?" He pressed his lips together. "He said,

'Why were you looking for me? Didn't you know I had to be in . . . my Father's house?'"

Quiet crept through the workroom. The weeping would come again; it would take one or more of them soon. For now, the sons of Joseph were together in quiet.

❧

She was the doctor's wife, and her name was Abishag. Abi, her husband called her. She was soft-spoken and kind, and busied herself in the little alcove of a kitchen, peeking in on Jorah now and then. Outside the pain, Jorah noticed Abi wiping her own eyes as she went about her work.

Abi wore a two-piece head covering. Fine white linen swirled snugly about her head and neck, concealing all but the oval of a droopy, aging face. The white linen was capped by heavy green cloth that fell away behind her back. Jorah had not seen a head covering like it. And she was not sure she had ever met anyone uglier. Great yellowed teeth jutted from Abi's mouth, teeth like a horse's. Sometimes she pulled her lip down to conceal them, but the lip would ride back up. She had a faint silver mustache and silver hairs on her chin.

The weeping came again, wringing from her another ounce of misery, and Jorah cried into her sodden, wadded head covering.

Abi came at the sound. She sat beside Jorah on the guest bed, patting her back and wiping her own eyes.

"There now, child," she murmured. "My heart just—" She squeaked and covered her face with a cloth. She blew hard into it. Jorah jumped at the sound.

Horribly, the loud noise made Jorah giggle. Abi pulled the

cloth from her face, and her wet eyes crinkled with an instant smile. "It's nice to hear someone laugh at that again. I scared my own children with my blowing. A shofar blast, they called it."

"Thank you for . . . the food . . . the bed . . ."

"A pleasure to me, child."

Jorah twisted the damp cloth in her lap. "May I see him? He needs a familiar face."

"The doctor is puzzling out if there is more he can do. He does not give up, not while there is breath. So far, the lad has breath." Abi dabbed at her nose with her cloth. "There is a saying, child . . . 'While I breathe, I hope.' It's the doctor's own creed."

"Nathanael's hope died yesterday."

Her own words were thin in her ears. Weeping did not accompany them—a strange thing because it was the first time she had spoken aloud about the death of Jesus. Her face felt thick and heavy, as she did on the inside.

Presently Jorah asked, "Do you know of Lazarus?"

Abi pulled her lip over the teeth and nodded. "The doctor tended him in his illness."

"Did Jesus really . . . ?"

"Ask anyone in Bethany. Ask Lazarus. The doctor was there when he died." The teeth came out as she smiled the crinkly smile, her eyes sparkling. "And four days later, I was there when he lived again."

Jorah searched those eyes. "Then Abi, tell me why . . . why does he call a man from his grave . . . why did he do those things . . ." Her throat constricted, making her voice small. "And he made people happy . . . and then he—"

The weeping came, and Abi's arms came around her.

"They all leave, Abi," Jorah cried. "They all leave me."

"Sweet child," Abi murmured, rocking back and forth with Jorah. Abi took her crying cloth and pressed it to her face. She blew mightily into it, then wept along with Jorah.

22

In the afternoon of the third day, strange reports began to trickle into Bethany from Jerusalem.

Men gathered in groups at the city gate, discussing the news, inquiring of those entering the city from the Jerusalem road. Three rumors were repeated most often from various travelers at various times in the day. Some left for Jerusalem to see if the things were so, but came back bewildered, repeating the same three rumors:

Jesus has risen from the dead.

His body was stolen by his disciples at night.

The veil of the Temple was torn in two, top to bottom.

These three reports were equally declared as true, equally

decried as false. Other reports came in, things that seemed shameful to put on the lips: reports that other tombs had opened besides that of Jesus. Reports of Lazarus-like incidents; appearances of those known dead, walking from their tombs into Jerusalem. Reports of fantastic things that happened when Jesus the Nazarene died upon the cross.

Rumors flourished, but of them all, the three were most talked about.

The brothers gathered in the workroom to discuss these things, this time with Matthias. They were tired of trying to conceal their identities at the city gate. Too many deluged them with questions. Too many showed them sympathy or contempt.

James began it, looking angrily at the others. "Haven't we gone through enough?"

"Apparently not," Jude said, jaw working. "I cannot perceive of anything more vicious—"

"Cruel," Simon stated, his face blank.

"Spiteful," Joses whispered.

"—than rumors such as these. I wish Mother were here with us. It makes me ill to think she hears these things too."

"What if . . . it is true?"

The brothers looked as one upon Matthias, seated on a stool near the doorway. Matthias was darker than any of the brothers, both of hair and of complexion. His beard was square and thick for one so young, nearly ten years younger than James. He should have looked away at the gazes full upon him, but he did not. Matthias was from Bethany, after all. Home of Lazarus.

"What if *what* is true?" Simon snapped. "Which one, Matthias? That he has risen from the dead, or that his disciples stole the body to make it seem so? Or how about the one with the veil? Do you really believe that, Matthias? Torn top to bottom? Do you know how thick that veil is? It would take God himself to do something like that."

"Lazarus is my friend."

Chills stole up and down James' arms. What bothered James more? What Matthias said or the way he said it? That simple confidence.

"We have been through enough," Simon stated. "I say we find Mother and leave for Nazareth as fast as we can. Escape it all. We are fools to stay."

"It is still High Holy Week," Joses murmured. By his tone he knew it didn't matter.

"Best time to go." Simon shrugged widely. "We can avoid the crowds and all the nasty things that come with them." His arms came down. "I can just hear what they will say now."

"What if it is true?" Matthias insisted. "What if your brother has risen from the dead? How can you ignore the possibility? I say we go to Jeru—"

"It is over!" Simon bellowed. "For three years we all tried in our own way to put up with it. To accommodate him. But—"

"No, we didn't," James said quietly. "We failed him."

"Don't you dare come to that conclusion for me," Simon said.

James rested his head against the wall as he gazed at the beams above. "I could have been with him. I could have walked by his side like those twelve friends of his. Jesus and me, like it used to be. Maybe I was meant to be one of those twelve."

"Where is that kind of talk going to get you?" Joses demanded.

"Stop it, James," Judas said wearily. "There was nothing you could have done. Nothing any of us could have done. Joses was right all along . . . it was bigger than us. But it's over now. Even his followers are dispersed. We have to try and put it behind us."

"Maybe you can do that," James whispered. *No, please, no weeping now. Not now.*

"We all have to, James," Joses said. "We all do."

James looked at Joses. "And tell me how we do that, brother. He was innocent. He did not deserve a death like that." He had not felt the gut pain in so long, but there it was, searing out his insides. He dug his fingers at it. "He did not deserve that kind of—"

"Don't you think I know that?" Joses suddenly shouted. Angry tears sprang to his eyes. "Don't you—James, they shoved a crown of thorns onto his head! They had a sign—it said 'King of the Jews'—nailed above him!"

James wanted to crawl from the words.

"I saw his back," Joses choked. "It was so striped—so covered with lashes you couldn't see—"

But a groan strangled from James' throat, and he wrapped his arms over his head. And a growl came from Simon, like a warning.

"I was there! To see your own brother—it was bad enough—but even worse was—even worse . . ."

The door slammed. Joses was gone.

"He was good. He was good. It just doesn't make sense," James whispered. "Not a death like that."

If he dared, he would kill himself—why be a part of a world that crucified people like Jesus? And if he dared, he would go to

Simon, self-sufficient Simon, who fell to his side and lay claw-
ing the floor, helplessly shrieking his grief. And if he dared, he
would go to Judas, who rocked back and forth saying over and
over, "Clouds without water, trees without fruit."

Matthias rose from his stool and went to the door. "I cannot believe it is over," he said quietly, perhaps not expecting
to be heard. "Lazarus lives." He put his hand on the door. "He
lives." He slipped from the workroom, following Joses.

※

Joses strode quickly from Matthias' home and broke into a run.
Even worse was knowing what he couldn't bear to tell the other
brothers, because they had had enough. Even worse was the
report he had learned while in Jerusalem, that his brother had
been sold out to the priests by one of his own disciples. By the
one Joses had seen—and ignored—in the Temple compound.

Judas Ish-Kerioth. Ish-Kerioth. Ish-Kerioth.

Even worse was knowing he could have prevented his
brother's crucifixion.

※

Matthias could not keep up. His sandals pounded to a halt, and
he braced his hands against his knees, breathing hard. Joses still
ran, toward the outskirts of the city, toward Bethphage. Matthias
straightened, watching Joses run. He had his hands over his ears,
but he could still hear that unearthly wail. He watched until Joses
disappeared down the road before starting back.

He had to find out for himself. It could not be over. Lazarus
was his friend.

❧

The villagers had given direction; this had to be the place. But Joab stood before the doctor's door and could not knock.

He clutched a cloth-wrapped bundle and sent glances at people who passed, wondering if they were curious about what he held. A treasure like none other, if they only knew. If they knew, he would be attacked and robbed.

But nobody seemed to notice him. The news from Jerusalem had everyone in Bethany talking this morning. It was precisely that news that brought Joab to this doorstep.

The Teacher had risen! Joab looked in wonder at the cloth-wrapped bundle. He had risen, and so here was Nathanael's hope. He only had to get this silver box to him, and he would not die. Joab had watched and listened; he was there when the brothers discovered the box disguised in wood. He was there when they spoke of it, and he had learned of its awesome significance. It was almost as if it had remained cloaked until this space in time, this very moment when someone would need it the most.

Surely the box had powers. The man whose gift it had been had risen from the dead! After three years of healing others, performing miracle after miracle, confounding the smart people and affronting the important, he crowned his achievements with the most magnificent of all.

Joab believed it. He believed it because he had been there for some of Jesus' talks when he and Avi—

Joab squeezed his eyes shut, shook his head. No, no, he would not think on Avi. He had to save Nathanael. He had to do it for this family. He had to, for Jorah. Jorah loved Nathanael; it was plain to see in her anxious ministrations over the past several days. Joab would give her back her Nathanael, and then he would go home to Hebron. To his father and his mother, to his brother and his little sister, Marya. He would go back to the dye works and never leave again.

"Can I help you, lad?"

Joab jumped. An elderly woman stood in the doorway. He glanced at her face, saw great yellowed teeth, and looked down at the bundle. "Please . . . I have come to see Nathanael."

"Are you his family?"

"No. I have something for him."

"Nathanael is very ill. I'm afraid he—" The woman's teeth disappeared as she pulled her lip over them. "Child, not even the doctor believes he will live."

"Then I must see him now!" Alarmed, Joab quickly unwrapped the box, heedless of any passing eyes. "This belonged to Jesus. . . . Maybe it has powers; maybe it can help him!"

Her eyes were kind and full of pity. There was doubt too, but she nodded, and stepped aside. "But you must be quiet, lad. Jorah rests now, for the first time in a long time."

She took him through a passageway to a room in the back. She opened the door and stepped aside for Joab to pass. There upon a bed in the room lay Nathanael.

He was wearing the tefillin Simon had made for him. The hand wound with it lay on his stomach. The other hand rested on the leather packet.

A weary old man rose beside him. He glanced at Joab, then looked past him to the woman. The woman murmured something, and the old man came away from the bed.

Hurriedly, Joab unwrapped the box.

"Nathanael," he whispered. He held the box close to the

waxen white face. He would have thought him dead already, but for the lips that twitched. There had to be time for a miracle! Frantically, Joab worked the lid off the box, and with the lid he scooped air out of the box toward the still form. "Nathanael, breathe this; it will help you." He held the box up and blew air from it onto Nathanael's face.

"Son," the old man said behind him.

"This will help him! Please, Nathanael, wake up! Please . . ."

"He is dying."

"He can't!"

Nathanael's eyes dragged open. He saw Joab, and he tried to speak. Joab dropped close to his lips.

"You are the one," the lips whispered. "You have to tell her."

The eyelids were greasy and lavender-hued, the face white save for the bruises. And Joab knew, as he gazed upon the peace there, that the boy would die. His hands holding the box dropped to the bed, and he realized he still held it. In fury, he threw it from him and slumped into the chair beside the bed. A tearing began in his middle.

"Tell her, no stones. Caesarea."

Joab stayed where he had slumped until he realized that Nathanael wasn't talking about Jorah at all. He leaned close to Nathanael. "Who? What are you talking about?"

"My mother. Go for me. Tell her what Jesus said." The eyelids eased shut. The lips still twitched.

Joab gazed at them, then looked in desperation at the old man and his wife. "I don't understand! What does he speak of?"

The woman looked at her husband. "Jorah told me his mother is a prostitute. Surely he speaks of that day in the Temple."

"No stones," Nathanael whispered, thin and incredulous.

Tears spilled down Joab's cheeks. How different things would have been if Nathanael had been his friend instead of Avi.

The old man put his arm around Joab and gently led him from the bed. "Come, lad. I will tell you of what he speaks."

He led the boy from the room. Abishag pressed her head covering to her tears and blew as quietly as she could into it. She noticed the silver box and its lid on the floor. She picked them up and gazed sadly on them a moment. Then she fitted the lid onto the box, took the cloth and wrapped it and, cradling the box, settled into the chair beside the bed.

❧

His fingers tightened convulsively on the leather packet strapped to the back of his hand.

Mother, such impossible words. I wish I could tell you them myself, just to see your face.

"Rivkah!" his grandmother shrieked. "You are nothing but a whore! My grandson will not live in such an unholy atmosphere. I will have the priests come take him away."

"The priests? Ho, send Zakkai. He knows the way to my home."

Where are your accusers, Mother? Is there no one to condemn you?

"You disgust me. Filthy whore."

"Come back when you're not drunk."

It isn't so hard to believe, when you know someone like Annika. You would like her, Mother. She likes you already.

Slowly, the fingers clenched about the leather packet began to ease.

No stones . . . no accusers. Not for you. Not for me.

Nathanael smiled. He had known it all along. God was wearing his tefillin, and in his tefillin were these words: I shall love Nathanael, and Rivkah, and James . . . with all my heart . . . with all my soul . . . with all my strength.

It only took a little imagination, and a fellow who wouldn't throw stones.

Mother? I'm so sorry.

"Hear, O Israel . . ."

His fingers slipped from the packet.

I love you, Mother. I love you I love you I

❧

"Jorah."

Her name came through her sleep-thickened ears, but she was so, so tired. If she slept, she could not cry. If she slept, it wasn't real. *Please, let me sleep.*

"It will be hard for you. But I am with you. I am with you! Do not be afraid."

She stirred, wanting to wake, fearing it.

"I am with you always . . ."

The gentle shaking continued. She moaned softly.

"Jorah?"

Abi. It was Abi. Jorah dragged open her eyes. "Abi?"

"Child . . . sweet child." A sound like a muted shofar blast. "The doctor did what he could, bless him. He tried his best. . . ."

"No." *No!*

"He died with the *Shema* on his lips, bless him. He died a good Jew. His mother will be proud, sweet child. Carry her the news. Tell her. He died a good Jew."

23

THE SUN WAS CLOSE to the horizon. Golden light gave the world a brief golden cast. Joses ambled back to Bethany, kicking stones here and there, marveling that he could look upon a hillside bedecked in colors like a celebration and see it beautiful.

"It is too big for me, Lord God," he murmured, and sent a stone skittering to the side of the road. *He was your man. At least I thought he was. I thought I believed.*

The seedling died in the desert the moment his brother did.

Joses raised bleak eyes to Bethany ahead. *And what will you do now, with one who could have prevented it? Punish me, if you will, for allowing the death of your prophet, because the world has not seen such a man.*

He thought he had known grief when Father died. This grief was different. It was not right. Father's death was reasonable, if sorrowful. Father was old. He was ready. But this . . . he could tear out his hair for the rage and the pain. For the helplessness. The injustice.

A sound like a small squeak caught his ear. He looked to see a grubby little shepherd boy, not much bigger than Ben, watching Joses as he passed. The child was wide-eyed. Joses looked away. Even little ones recognized a brother of Jesus. What the family had already endured was nothing compared to what they would endure.

❦

The little boy watched them slowly amble down the road for Bethany. The shorter one looked at him with such sadness in his face. But the other one . . . he gave him such a nice smile.

❦

It wasn't supposed to be this way. It was the first conscious thought James put together when the roaring in his ears ceased.

The woman before him honked into a wadded cloth, murmured something James could not understand, and left. He stood in the doorway, hand on the door. He did not move for he had no place to go.

"James? What is it?" Judas was behind him.

"Nathanael is dead." There was a long silence. Then, "I will go tell Simon."

It was all wrong. Everything. Nothing was the way it should

have been. Nathanael was not supposed to die. He was to live, marry Jorah. He was to—

—And what of the other? What of the one who calmed a storm? Who threw no stones?

Boulder after boulder of unreasonable grief. James laughed out loud. Unreasonable! The perfect word. He slammed the door and turned into the workroom. Utterly unreasonable. He walked about; then he came to lean against a wall. He looked at the beams in the ceiling of the workroom.

"They say you have risen," he said to the beams. He lifted his arms and let them fall. "Congratulations. I don't believe it. You hear me?" Rage bloomed, and he punched his fist at the ceiling. "I don't believe it! And I don't care! You couldn't stay long enough to heal Nathanael? I believed that much. You couldn't stay long enough for me to look into your eyes? It was all I wanted! All I needed, and I would have believed in you to the end!"

New rumors had come earlier in the day. That Jesus had appeared to his friend Mary Magdalene, and some of the other women among his followers. To a fellow named Cleopas, and even to some of his disciples.

"If you are alive, then hear me, Son of God," he spat. "You appear to others, but not your own family? You care more about others than . . . but of course! 'Who are my brothers . . . ?'"

Unreasonable. Such a perfect word. He sagged down the wall to the floor and laughed himself to tears.

❧

Simon sat on the back porch of Devorah's home. Was there nothing but madness to hold the family together? Jude had given him the news and walked away with those strange murmurs on his breath. *Autumn trees without fruit. Doubly dead, uprooted. I can see it plain as my hand.* Then he heard laughter within the home, heard it diminish to ragged weeping.

Madness and sorrow, both without measure. Were these the things to hold a family together? Simon rubbed his hands together, looking into the back portico of the home behind Devorah's. Potted plants, a few chairs, and a table set with fruit.

So the scrappy apprentice was gone. And Joses with his new madness, that he could have prevented the death of Jesus. An hour ago he had stumbled in from wherever he had gone, blurting that it was his fault all along, that he had seen Judas Ish-Kerioth trade his inheritance for pottage. Joses seemed dully surprised when the brothers did not rise as one to crucify Joses himself. Did a plot matter now? Joses wasn't thinking right, but who could make him see it? Jesus was gone. Nathanael was gone. What did it all matter?

Scarred ones know. Trust the one with the scars.

The words lifted as a wave through him, separate from his own thoughts. Simon stilled his hands. Then madness took him too. No one immune. No one left to keep things together. Joses with his guilt, Jude with his babblings, James—but he had changed early on—and Jorah, infected with this new hatred, and now bereft of the one person who could make her happy. Oddly, all Simon wanted to do was pay another visit to a man named Kardus. Perhaps because the madness had left him.

Simon gazed at the potted plants on the porch. "What is

that like, Kardus? To have the madness leave? What is it like to have a smooth sea inside?"

He would like to sit quietly with this man Kardus, sip some good wine, and sit on that seashore. Talk about things. Talk with someone sane. The potted plants blurred before him, and he began to rub his hands again.

24

JORAH WISHED HE COULD have been buried on the ridge, in the shade of Father's olive tree.

Abi had helped prepare his body, wrapping the napkin about his beautiful face and freshly washed hair, wrapping the linen bands about his arms and legs. Jorah should have wrapped the bands about the tefillin, burying them with him, but she could not bear it. She needed something to take away with her, something that had meant as much to him as the tefillin.

He had not taken them off since Simon had given them to him days, eons ago. Impressions from the straps left ridges in his skin. She had traced her fingers through the ridges on his arm, to the ridges on his hand, to the square left by the leather packet. Impossible words, he had called them.

It wasn't until she heard a quick intake of breath from Abi that she looked to see Nathanael's legs. Scars, like a ladder, from midthigh to his hip. It was only a glance. Abi moved quickly to band the scars with the linen.

Nathanael's funeral bier was carried aloft by the four brothers and not followed by a gaggle of mourners. Simon would not allow it. A few women had assumed their services would be needed when they learned of the death of the young man at the doctor's house, but Simon drove them away. *We will mourn,* he had told them. *We are the ones who knew him.* Jorah followed the bier, Keturah by her side. Abi and her husband came last. Eight people made up the funeral procession for Nathanael ben Rivkah of Caesarea Maritima.

In the common graveyard outside of Bethany, they lowered Nathanael's white-shrouded body into the trench dug into the earth.

She loved him the day he made James laugh.

The faces of the brothers were as stone, as hard as the ones they piled upon the mound. Simon intoned prayers.

She loved him the day he dunked James in the dye pot.

Jorah placed a posy of wildflowers on the rabble of stones. The posy came apart when she did, so she tucked the flowers back together, setting a stone on the stems, and stood back, hands clasped.

She loved him the day an olive tree amazed him.

The flowers fluttered in the warm breeze, and Abi put an arm about her to lead her away. Joab lived, who could have prevented it. Jesus died, who could have prevented it. Life was nothing less than profane.

❧

The next morning, they left for Galilee.

Joses would return later to Nazareth with Abigail and their children, along with Tobias and Sarah, Therin and Keturah. He would find Mother, whom they had not yet seen, in Jerusalem and bring her back to Nazareth.

How James had wanted to go to her . . . but he felt much the same as Joses, bereft and betrayed, and that at the very end. "Woman, behold your son. Son, behold your mother." Did Jesus not trust his own family to care for her? Or was it that—and James felt the shards of guilt—Jesus did not see any of the brothers from his tormented heights, and so did his best for her? Yes, he loved his mother at the end. If his own foolishness had put him on that cross, if his own foolishness had broken his mother's heart, at least he tried to make sure, with what breath remained, that she was cared for. It was a small and bitter comfort.

James, Simon, Judas, and Jorah all wanted to leave as soon as possible.

Gathered at Bethany's foregate to say good-bye were Joses and Abigail, Devorah and Matthias, and Keturah. Simon fussed with the donkey harness while James made room in the cart for the provisions Devorah and the doctor's wife brought. Devorah had given them a sack of unleavened bread, the woman named Abi a sack of unleavened cakes. James had already rolled up the bedrolls, which had been spread in the cart. He had thrown away his own . . . it was stained with Nathanael's blood. When he had pushed the other bedrolls into a corner, he found something strange. Tucked in the corner was a little pile of coins, the coins that had been in the money box.

James stashed the sacks of food, tucking and securing them more than he needed to. It was hard to say good-bye to Joses. He hardly remembered speaking to Devorah since being in Bethany, but there his sister stood, her face so beautiful in her sorrow. He glanced at Keturah, who stood apart in her lavender tunic, her face pale and still.

Matthias stood with his arm about Devorah. The fact that he maintained that calm of his was reason enough for them to leave. Truly, there was no reason to stay. It would be pure relief to be away from the prying eyes, from the whispers. From the constant stream who offered meaningless words, from those who continually demonstrated great flourishes of wailing and grief for Jesus of Nazareth, people James did not know, people he did not care about.

Keturah came to stand beside him. "Simon says you are going through Samaria."

James pretended to check the cinches on the canvas. He nodded as he fussed with a knot.

She stood in silence, then said softly, "Be careful, James. Godspeed." She turned to leave. James raised his head.

"Keturah."

She stopped and looked over her shoulder.

"It seems we have an opening in the shop. We could use a—" But his breath caught. The wave of sorrow could have dropped him where he stood.

She smiled sadly. The breeze caught her head covering, and she pulled it down to look at him. "I happen to know someone who may be available. She is particularly good with detail work."

"Perhaps she learned from the best." Wave after wave.

"That she did, James." Her lips pressed together for a moment, and those beautiful eyes glittered with tears. So many things to make a woman beautiful . . . why did grief have to be one? Her gaze flickered to the road ahead of them. "Keep an eye on those hillsides." She turned and walked away.

Joses came beside him, gazing down the road. "I will see you in a few days. Godspeed."

James nodded. Now was not the time to tell him that nobody thought for an instant he was in any way responsible for Jesus' death. The events were like a great Roman machine, an inexorable march toward an inevitable conclusion. All prophets seemed to come to this. Even the ones with good news.

"Find Mother," James murmured. "Take care of her."

"I will."

Simon clicked his tongue, the cart lurched forward, and the brothers and the sister began the journey back to Nazareth. The small group at Bethany's gate watched them leave. Two couples with arms about each other and a girl who stood apart from the rest, in a lavender tunic that fluttered in the breeze. They stayed until the traveling party could no longer be seen on the road; then they turned, one by one, into the city.

25

THE CLOSER THEY CAME to Shechem, the more the strange thoughts came. They were wild-eyed thoughts, giddy and foolish thoughts, but had he not a right to a little foolishness? Simon did not care to see the inside of their workroom ever again. His chances to become a scribe had long since vanished, but the thought of a carving knife . . . the thought of his bench sent invisible fingers to his throat.

Why not explore the possibilities? Why not see what was out there? Normally he kept such reckless ideas in tight rein. This time he sent them on a gallop.

The crazy odd notion to visit Kardus . . . well, and why not? Did not Simon have a right to a time apart from it all? He did not even know what Kardus did to earn his living. It would be interesting to find out. He lived in a mostly pagan territory, with Jewish pockets here and there, and that was a comfort— but Simon was ready for a change of landscape. He ducked his head to hide a smile. Pagan territory, a change of landscape?

When they came upon Shechem, upon its outskirts, the thoughts agitated him even more. This road led to Nazareth. What was he doing going back to Nazareth? He could not go back. He could not.

"What ails you, Simon?" Judas asked, with more than small irritation. He walked beside him, eyes ever on the hillsides. He carried a length of grimy burlap he had picked up, snapping it at things on the road.

Judas had noticed? Well, it wouldn't be James who would. "I don't know." Simon kept his eyes averted.

Jude snapped the burlap at a gecko on a rock. The gecko skittered away. "He brings change."

Simon ignored that and, keeping his voice low, said, "What do you think about Jorah?"

Jorah and James trailed not far behind the cart. They walked together, but in silence. Simon had not heard them speak all day, not since leaving Bethany. Nor had James eaten anything. They had stopped twice for refreshment, and James did not have a crumb. Simon shrugged. Not that he fretted about it. James could take care of himself.

But Jorah . . . How he longed for her to skip up to him with a palmful of rocks. How he wished she would fix a posy in the donkey's bridle, giggling as she did so. He glanced over his shoulder at her. It wasn't only sorrow that kept Jorah silent. Her face was as dark as the cloud wrapped around her. And it bothered him that she wore Nathanael's tefillin.

He first noticed it when he glanced at her as she was adjusting her head covering. Her tunic sleeve slipped to her elbow, exposing the straps wound about her arm. It was a dark shock. Women did not wear the tefillin. There was probably a law against it, written or oral. Worse, it seemed wrong to see them there. What was in that act? A defiance. A rebellion. Against whom, Simon did not know.

He could see on her face the despair he felt. But he felt something more, something so tenuous and vague it was almost not there.

Jude glanced over his shoulder. "Give her time," he murmured. "We will all need it."

They walked for a while, until Simon said, "He *brought* change."

"What?"

"You said he *brings* change. He is gone, Judas. He *brought* change. For us, anyway."

"Yes . . . of course. That is what I meant."

"And I am not going back to Nazareth." Simon stopped the cart. Jude walked a few steps more, then stopped. He kept his back to Simon. Then he dropped the piece of burlap and put his hands on his hips, gazing somewhere ahead.

"What am I to do with that, Simon?"

James and Jorah must have figured this for the stopping place. Jorah went to the side of the road, selecting a boulder to settle upon. James went off to visit the brush. Well, it was nearly time to make camp anyway. Simon leaned against the cart and pulled off a sandal. He turned it over and went to work on an embedded pebble. "Do whatever you want with it. But I can't go back. I can't breathe for the thought."

"Of all people . . ."

"I know. But I'm not going back."

Jude turned, and his face was cold and blank— viciously neutral. Shaking his head, he stalked off for the brush, muttering, "You're all mad. The lot of you. At least I still have my wits."

Simon watched him go. Clouds without water? Trees without fruit? "That's what you think!" he shouted after him.

Jude half-turned, only to wave dismissively and keep stalking.

Simon led the donkey to the side of the road and began to unharness it. He unhooked the cart pole on one side, went around to unhook the other, and stopped, pole in hand. He felt giddiness, as though he stood on the edge of a promontory, gazing at a great lethal depth. Not going back to Nazareth? Was he Simon? What was he thinking? He had with him his writing tools, his prayer shawl, and his tefillin. A change of clothing and a bedroll. That was all. No money. Certainly none of the sense he was born with.

"I'm not going back," he whispered in wonder. He lifted his head and looked to the purple hill crests in the northeast, to the province of Decapolis.

What would Kardus think when he showed up on his doorstep again? What would he think to learn the one who had driven off the demons was dead? Was that why Simon needed to go? To tell him? It's what he would tell himself for now.

❧

Judas sought to prove his disgust with Simon by not helping to unload the supplies. That was his reason for being gone an hour now. James did not have a reason.

Twilight came fast. Jorah began to pace the length of the campsite, hands on her hips, looking to the hills flanking the road. "Where are they? What are they thinking to take a walk at this time? In this place?"

Simon avoided her eyes. He knew why Jude had not returned but could not tell her. Not yet. "Maybe they needed some time alone."

"In Samaria?"

"It isn't bad here," Simon assured her, glancing up the road. "Not in Shechem."

"Shechem," Jorah said bitterly. "The place of promise." She dropped down next to Simon. She pulled off her sandals and began to clean out the sand from between her toes. He deliberately kept his eyes off the tefillin.

Simon adjusted the metal pan set on the tripod above the campfire. The pan held only bread for the warming; there was dried fish in their supplies, but no one was eating much lately. He reached into the pan and turned the pieces of bread over, then settled back on his heels, his gaze straying once again to the northeast. *Jorah, I'm not going back. I'm off to see a man who had touched something so strong it drove away a legion of demons. Maybe I want to see if the miracle held. See if the death of Jesus did not erase all the good he did while he lived.*

"You're always saying I'm the coward." James stood on the other side of the campfire, Jude right behind him. "Just who is the coward, Simon?"

Jorah lowered her sandal. "Where have you been?" she demanded.

Simon poked the bread about in the pan. "So Jude told you."

Darkness from twilight cascaded down James' face while fire-light lit it from below. The effect was not pleasant, not with that pinched snarl in the thin face. "You of all people," he sneered.

"Funny, that's what Jude said." Simon took a cloth and wrapped it around the pan handle. He removed the pan and set it on the ground, then rose to look at James across the campfire.

"What are you talking about?" Jorah said uncertainly.

"I am going to Decapolis," Simon said without taking his eyes from James.

"You're what?"

Simon thought he had no more weeping left. He had cried himself dry, soul and spirit, cried himself hollow for his gentle brother and that cocky apprentice, for his mother and his brothers, for his sisters and for himself. Cried until he thought it was enough, but looking at James, new grief came.

Where was the old James he knew? He began to fade the day Jesus left. Who was this standing before him? James, the old James, had contentment of life, had a sense of humor and a wonderful laugh. Simon loved to hear it, that old laugh.

This pale, thin man with hatred on his face was not the brother he grew up with. James might as well be dead, right along with Jesus.

"I am sorry, James," Simon said sadly. "Sorry that we were not strong enough for it, none of us. He had to be somebody's brother."

Jude folded his arms. His face matched that of James. There would be no understanding from either of them, and Simon did not expect it. Did not deserve it. "When are you leaving?" Jude asked.

"You mean it?" Jorah gasped, coming beside Simon.

He could leave in the morning. They were just past the road that had broken north for Beth Shean. But he didn't want them to travel the Samaritan route without him. He owed them at least that. "I'll stay with you until we reach Kfar Otnai. You'll be fine after that. Then I'll take the east road to Beth Shean."

James said he was a coward. Perhaps it was so. There were many reasons he was going to Decapolis; there was only one reason he could not return to Nazareth. It was why Jude and James glowered at him; they were in sick dread of it too.

"But why, Simon?" Jorah cried, grasping his tunic. He pulled her in with both arms and held her tight. Her cries were muffled against his chest. Had he any weeping left, he would cry with her.

He rested his cheek against her head. "Because I cannot walk into that workroom, knowing all hope of his return is lost."

26

JAMES WAS ALREADY as a hollowed-out bowl, thin as it could get without complete ruin, yet the adze chipped again.

He had not said good-bye to Simon but watched him go. He had left with a small sack over one shoulder, bedroll over the other. The lord of the tack mallet had one sandal flapping and didn't seem to notice. He had a waterskin dangling at his side and two loaves of bread in his tunic pocket. Jude had forced him to take a dinar and several copper prutas.

James sat with his back against the olive tree. Someone had been here, a child most likely, maybe one of Eli's grandchildren; a small pile of pebbles lay nearby. The white stones ringed about the tree were all in order. He looked up into the branches, thick with slender green-gray leaves. It still bore fruit, this most ancient of trees, the oldest olive tree around. Joseph had once taken an expert in husbandry to this ridge to show him the tree. The man had been delighted, and confirmed what Joseph had known, that it was at least a thousand years old. The man had gone to bring others to see the tree. They had taken away cuttings from it. It had greatly pleased Joseph.

Come harvesttime they would clean it of the fruit and bring the olives to the press in the village. They would filter the oil, draining it through sieve after sieve. They would fill crocks and amphoras, sell some of it, store most of it. They would cure some of the harvest in brine. It had been so year after year since Joseph came to Nazareth, over thirty years ago.

It was a week now since the party of five to Jerusalem had returned a party of three. James wanted to tell Simon it wasn't so bad, that first day back in Nazareth—the first day back in the workroom. Perhaps the dread of it was finished on the road home. Unlocking the workroom door, pushing it open. The kiss on the mezuzah.

The corner bench was doubly empty now. Nathanael had left a few tools out, and James felt dull pain as he watched Jude slowly put them away. Once when Jorah was busy with laundry in the back, and Jude was at market fetching items for her, James was alone in the workroom. He paused at his workbench and set down his nail jar, then looked over his shoulder to take in the shop. He went to the center of the room and stood beneath the awning. He lifted his chin—listening. Birds from outside. The muted slop of the laundry tub in the back. A distant shout of a child, one of Eli's grandchildren. He did not hear what he listened for, and what that was he did not know.

He wasn't the only one. He'd seen Jude pause at his hunk of white stone, caught him glancing over his shoulder.

"Feels different in here," Jude had said quietly. "You feel that?"

James had nodded, glancing too, but the conversation went no further.

It wasn't the absence of Jesus and Nathanael. It wasn't the absence of Simon. It was a different sort of emptiness. A very large emptiness. It made Judas work the stone roller outside, and it made James come daily to the ridge. It was restlessness.

He drew his knees up and rested his wrists on them. A week ago he could barely leave the workroom. Now he couldn't stay. He wondered how Simon was, if he—

Consider it all JOY!

His heart stopped, then started again. He sat up and with eyes huge in fear, looked to the left and right, expecting to see the indigo-clad madman from the East. He looked behind him. Where did that come from? Was it a shout? Did he hear it; did he imagine it? There was no one around, but he could feel the echo. His skin still stood out an inch! God of Israel, was he going mad? He didn't mind dabbling in madness if only it didn't make his heart seize.

Once his breathing settled down, he rested against the tree again, warily scanning the places he had already looked. He had not thought on that crazy notion for a long while. It sounded like what it was, an empty new philosophy, this time not born in Greece but in the East. Consider it all joy. Surely a bizarre new philosophy, because you had to bend God-given logic for it.

James could not consider a trial joy unless he could see

something on the other side of it. Something worth the trial. The ball-in-a-cage puzzle when he was seven—how many times did the frustration of that project bring him to furious tears? But the joy when he presented it to Joseph. Or what about a mother giving birth? Consider those trials joy, sure, because there was something on the other side. Something worth it. He thought of one of his father's favorite psalms: "We went through fire and through water, yet you have brought us out to a place of abundance."

Pain isn't such a bad thing, Son, Joseph had told him long ago, *if it takes you where you want to go.* Well. There it was, the reason misery could eat him whole, because this pain didn't go anywhere. It never had, for three long years. Pain with nothing on the other side. Why consider this joy? Why not take a hammer and pound his toes for no good reason? Where was the God-given logic?

He got up from the tree. He went and stood on the crest of the ridge and looked to where the hill tumbled down to the rocky expanse below. His gaze followed the bottom of the ravine to the hills opposite him, followed the line of those hills south toward Megiddo. Looked beyond Megiddo to Samaria. Looked past Samaria to Jerusalem, where they crucified his brother.

"Nathanael is the only one who had it right," he said to the ever-silent God.

It only makes sense, James. Love the Lord your God? With all your heart? That, James, is much to ask.

"Much to ask, Nathanael?" James whispered. "It's impossible."

You were the only one honest enough to say it. He once

said he didn't come to abolish but fulfill. I asked myself, Nathanael, what was not fulfilled that he came to fulfill it? I wish I knew the answer to that. I wish I knew what he was thinking. I wonder if it's wadded up with the *Shema*. I wonder if, by saying what he said, that . . .

He knew it was impossible too.

James tilted his head to the side, gazing toward Jerusalem. Love the Lord your God with all your heart, with all your soul, with all your might? Why do you ask such hard things?

Do you love God, Nathanael?

"I do not know him well enough to love him."

We're just little humans. Is it fair for you to ask humans such a thing? Nathanael was the only one I knew who had the guts to bare that wide. I never thought about how big the *Shema* was. Well, you know what? I think I learned a little about honesty from Nathanael. I think I'm ready to say that I'm not sure I ever loved you. Really *loved*. Jesus I loved. But you? I don't even know you.

Do you want to know something? It's hard to be a Jew in this world. Hard on the outside and harder on the inside.

James lay down on the ridge on his side. He laid his head on his arm and his Jerusalem gaze drifted to the hazy blue sky.

Is this the way it's supposed to be?

I don't know why you made me.

Look at me. If I am made in your image, what a poor Ruler of the universe you must be. Made in your image; that's as hard as the *Shema*. Jews in your image. Gentiles in your image.

If I believed that, it would change everything.

It would make you my Father. And it would make you their Father.

Stop making my Father's house a house of merchandise.

Didn't you know I had to be in my Father's house?

My Father . . .

They say you have risen. If I believed that, it would change everything.

A tear rolled to the edge of his nose and dripped off.

It all comes down to belief. Belief is a hard thing, God. I stand up in the surf only to get slammed down again. I pray and get a portion of hell as my answer. There's a pattern in it all, Joses said. I can't see it, God. I can't see why he came. Belief is too hard for me. Faith is too hard. I will go mad trying to figure it out.

Why does it seem that Nathanael died knowing something so good? What have I missed? I grew up in it all; I grew up with everything centered about you. I had good parents. I went faithfully to synagogue. He was the son of a whore. He was abused by his own mother. It should have poisoned him. But he died in peace.

What did Nathanael believe?

You know what? There's only one thing I believe. One thing I know: I know who I was when he was here. And I liked that person better.

"Jesus . . . ," James whispered.

"James."

Slowly, James lifted his head.

27

"I THINK HE WENT to the ridge. I don't know."

"How long has he been gone?" Jude asked.

"I don't *know*." Jorah slid the stick into the wet tunic and twisted it until a stream of water drained into the laundry tub. She untwisted it, pulled out the stick, and dropped the damp tunic on the others. Then she picked up the heavy basket of wet laundry and went to the clothesline strung in the back of the courtyard.

"This isn't going to last," she said loudly.

Jude dropped to the couch and put his feet up on the small oval table. He reached for the bowl of dried fruits and nuts on the table and reclined with the bowl on his stomach. He picked through it; apparently, he wasn't going to ask anytime soon what she meant.

"Not for me, it isn't," Jorah declared. She draped a tunic on the line, then held it aside to grab a couple of towels. She held one up and grimaced. Why couldn't she get them as white as Mother did? She flung the towels over the line, sneaking a peek at Jude. He was peeling a dried fig. He was the only one she knew who did that. He would also peel an orange so clean of the white pith that it looked indecent.

"What isn't going to last?" Jude finally asked in a not-very-interested tone. The stupid fig interested him more. He pulled off the leathery peel in tiny strips, making a little pile on his stomach next to the bowl. He would surely put them on the oval table when he was done, and she would be the one to clean up the sticky mess.

She'd had a week to work it to eloquent perfection. It was good enough to record on papyrus. A rabbi would weep. She only had to know when to say it. Well, this was jolly well when.

"Do you think I'm going to cook and clean for you boys the rest of my life? I am sorry to say it is not so. Do you think I will clean up fig peeling—" she threw that in, pure inspiration—"and haul water and hem tunics and feed goats and collect eggs and grind wheat and spin wool and—" she grabbed a breath—"weed the garden and preserve food and do it all again the next day, all for you boys, for the rest of my life? I am sorry to say it is not so. Get married and let your wives do that."

"You want to leave too?" Jude put his head back and dropped the peeled fig in his mouth.

She opened her mouth and closed it. She studied him a moment. "*You* want to leave?"

He finished eating the fig and rummaged in the bowl for another. "I don't want to stay. I'm not going to."

Jorah blinked. "Me neither," she said softly. She looked at the dark, wet head covering in her hand. She held it out from her and let it drop into the laundry basket, took a deep breath, held it, and exhaled slowly. Right now, this moment, was the best she had felt in a long, long time.

She ducked past a hanging tunic and went to sit next to Jude, tucking her legs beneath her. He was busy peeling. She leaned to look into the bowl and selected a portion of dried pear. Then she shifted so she could watch Jude while she ate.

He seemed to find it amusing and began to flick glances at her while he stripped his fig. Finally he rested his hands in his lap and looked her full in the face. He had a half smile, which soon faded. After all, when was the last time they had looked into each other's eyes? He resumed peeling. "You're a tough woman, Jorah."

"Maybe not tough enough. I want to leave, after all."

"I don't think staying has anything to do with being tough. I think we all have different roads to take." He looked at her again. "Where is your road?"

"Caesarea Maritima."

His eyebrows came up. "Caesarea?"

She nodded and fell to examining what was left of her pear. "He was from Caesarea. I want to find his mother. Abishag said to tell her he died a decent Jew. And maybe I should bring her his tefillin; I haven't decided that yet. But, Jude, those aren't the only reasons. I want to see if Theron the mosaicist still lives near Cousin Thomas. I'd like to know if he thinks I have talent." She shrugged. "You never know. I really may have talent for it, Jude. I might."

"You might. I think you should find out."

Jorah looked up. "You really think so?"

"I'll take you there myself. You can stay with Cousin Thomas."

"Oh, Jude! That would be—" She threw herself in a hug at him. It toppled the bowl and made Jude protest and laugh.

"Now look what you've done." He pulled his feet from the table and leaned to pick up the fruit.

She joined him, and as she dusted off fruits and nuts and tossed them into the bowl, she said, "When? When will you take me? How about after Sabbath? Maybe a few days after Sabbath. I can make sure you're taken care of before I leave. I can talk with Annika, and we can hire someone from the village to come a few days a week and do laundry and make bread—"

"I don't think that will be necessary," Jude said. He wrinkled his nose as he picked up the naked fig. It had tumbled to the ground and collected a coat of dust.

"What do you mean?"

"I don't think there will be anyone here." He set the bowl on the table.

Jorah studied this brother. The sudden pang for him made her put aside the excitement of Caesarea. She sat back on her heels. "Where will you go? Will you be okay?"

"I'll be fine, Jorah. I don't know about James, but I'm going back to Jerusalem."

"Why?"

He took a deep breath, sighed, and gave a small rueful grin. "I don't know." His gaze went to the curtain flap at the small-yard. "I just know it's time to leave. Jerusalem seems the best place for now. It seems like a place for answers. I have many questions, Jorah. I get the feeling I never should have left. I want to talk with Matthias. I want to find some of those disciples. I want to ask them things, the way Joses wanted to do a long time ago."

The thump of the workroom door sounded beyond the curtain flap. They expected James to come through the passage, but instead heard various noises from the workroom. Jorah and Judas exchanged a glance, then got up to go to the workroom.

James had a rough sack, and he was filling it with strange things.

Judas and Jorah stood by the curtain flap and watched. He snatched an item from his shelf, examined it, and added it to the sack. Then he dashed to the corner bench, took the vase off the shelf that Jorah had made for Jesus, and put it in. He went to Simon's bench, and his gaze flitted all over it. He selected the olive bowl, the last project Simon completed, and dropped it in. He went to Jude's bench and looked it over well. Then he took a medium-sized mallet, Jude's favorite, and put it in the sack.

"James!" Jude said. "What are you doing with that?"

"Come on, Jude, you won't be using it anymore." James went to Joses' bench and studied it thoughtfully.

"That's my favorite tool," Jude protested. He came along-side James to stare at him and his sack. "What are you doing?"

"I know it's your favorite. That's why I want it." James

frowned as he studied the things on Joses' shelf. He selected the ball-in-a-cage puzzle Joses had made when he was a child.

"James! Put that back."

James went to Father's bench, and here his shoulders came down. "The box," he muttered. "That's what I would have taken. The perfect thing. I hope Joab knows what he's doing. I know he took it." He tapped his fingers on his lips, then pushed aside some junk to reveal Father's nail jar. He emptied it onto the bench and added the jar to the sack. He was leaving the bench but stopped to grab one of the nails and put it in the sack too.

"What are you doing?" Judas demanded.

Jorah leaned against the doorway. "What happened, James?"

He was at his own bench now, picking things up to look them over and setting them down again. At first he did not seem to hear her. He was in the middle of examining the wooden box Jesus had made for him when he froze and set it down. "I can't tell you because you won't believe me. All I can say is everything is different."

He refused to look at them. Instead, after a moment's pause, he roused himself and immediately began to rummage in his drawer. He came up with a dirty scrap of leather, which he shook out and wrapped around the box, then he put the box in the sack.

"You saw him, didn't you?" Judas said.

It took a moment; then her breath stopped. It came again in a gasp.

Jude went to James. "Look at me," he said. "I want to see your eyes when you say it."

James looked at him and simply said, "I saw him."

Jude backed away, turned to his bench, and grabbed the edge to steady himself. He dropped heavily onto his stool. Jorah's legs could hold her no longer, and she sank to the ground. James slowly took hold of his own stool, slowly sat down.

"He's alive," James whispered. "It changes everything."

※

How to tell them? It was useless. Words were sawdust.

How could he tell them that everything everything everything was changed? Everything! Not an inch of his soul untouched; how could he make words for that? How could he say what he felt? It was so utterly hopeless he decided not to say anything at all. They would ask about it one day, probably they would, but on the pathway home he had decided if he even tried to tell it would . . . Well, Jesus the crucified appeared to James—what more did he have to tell them?

Maybe an hour had passed since he had returned from the ridge. Jorah still sat at the smallyard entry, arms about her knees. Judas sat on his stool, hunched at his bench, idling with a nail.

They were out of his hands. James wasn't afraid for them anymore; he would not worry for them. God would take care of them. He would pray for them. They were on their own, to muddle their way to him as he had done. And how had he done it? And what had he done to earn himself an appearance? "Nothing," he marveled beneath his breath. "Nothing."

"Do you think he will appear to the rest of us?" Jorah presently asked in a very small voice.

"I am certain of it," James replied.

"What is it like to believe in him?" Jude asked, turning the nail in his fingers. His voice was dim and cool.

James lifted his head and watched the summer awning gently rise and fall in the breeze. He picked up a scrap of wood and gripped it hard. He looked out the door to the ordinary day. "It is familiar." Then he said, "Like the sky. Like the earth. It is hard ground beneath my feet. And it is . . . relief."

"You're not afraid anymore," Jorah said in surprise. She rose from the wall and went to examine James. She looked wonderingly from eye to eye. "You're not afraid. You weren't afraid when he was here. None of us were."

Judas sat straight on his stool and looked out the doorway. He was a stark outline against the brightness of the day. His head tilted, and as he looked out he murmured, "I always said to myself, I liked me better when Jesus was here."

James smiled slowly. "You too?"

"That's what I said to myself," Jorah put in. "Sort of."

"You think you're going to talk about it someday?" Jude asked, still looking out the door.

"Probably not."

Jude nodded. "Then I won't ask." He turned to look at James. "Well? Jerusalem?"

James regarded his brother, this son of Joseph. He was the one who looked most like Mary. Thin face, hollows in the cheeks, dark puffy curves under the eyes. James found himself smiling.

"What?" Judas asked.

"What we've been through together," James said in wonder. "What we've been through. I'm glad it was you, Jude." He looked at his youngest sister. "I'm glad it was you, Jorah."

"It's not over, is it?" Jude replied.

"No, it is not over. Remember Father's verse? He brought us through fire and water, out to a wide place. I will spend the rest of my life learning of this place." Then he said, "Yes, Jude. Jerusalem."

❦

Simon would have to calm their alarm first, when they saw him return without Jorah and James and Judas. Then he would have to explain why he had come all the way back to Jerusalem. What would he tell them?

Maybe Matthias wouldn't be surprised. For that alone he would avoid him. Devorah? He wasn't sure. And what would Joses say? Maybe he could avoid them all, skip Bethany altogether. He wasn't going to Bethany, oh, no. He knew exactly, precisely where he was going.

At least he wouldn't have to tell Jude and James. That was one solid relief in this convoluted journey. *You never went to Decapolis?* they'd accuse when he returned home. And he would say, *No. Because I wasn't half an hour on the road to Beth Shean, just about to the Kishon River, and I knew that I had to go to Jerusalem. Knew it was Jerusalem all along.* And they would reply, *You knew? That's it?* And Simon would answer, *Yes. Because I am mad mad mad.*

"Ho, that's not all, brothers," he muttered beneath his breath, keeping quiet lest those passing him on the Roman road should hear. "You want to know just how mad I am? I'm not only going to Jerusalem, but I know where in Jerusalem I am going. I'm going to the south part of the city, to the Essene

Quarter, not far from the Essene Gate. And there I will find an upper room, a place where Jesus held Passover with his friends. And what will happen then? Your guess is as good as mine and probably better. Because, after all, I am mad. Me, of all people."

Then Simon laughed, and those passing did hear. But Simon did not care. He might be mad, but he was never more certain of himself. Certain and crazy. That made him laugh harder. At least he wouldn't soon have to explain himself to James and Jude.

28

It was springtime in Galilee.

Vibrant color rang in the fields, a shofar blast of poppy red, heather purple, daisy yellow and white. The color dazzled and heartened. The backdrop of green made the flowers lovelier, and their fragrances filled the warm breeze.

The last of Joseph's tribe in Nazareth would leave in the morning. James had gone to Annika to tell her they were going first to Caesarea Maritima, and then Jerusalem. Perhaps never to return. After she spent ten minutes in arm-raised consternation over the whole thing, she baked them a storm of honeycakes.

Annika and Jorah sat at mending in the courtyard. "What has happened to James?" Annika muttered as she bit off thread from a tunic. "Yesterday he said to me, just as happy as a child, 'Mulaki is still at his old corner! And did you know he got married?' And I said, 'James ben Joseph of Nazareth in Galilee, what do you mean he's still there? He never left!'" She shook out the tunic and leaned to see through the doorway to the workroom. She had pulled aside the curtain and hooked it on a nail because she didn't want to miss any activity. "This is the old James. The one I liked. Who absconded with the sorry selfish one?"

"Jesus appeared to him," Jorah replied matter-of-factly.

"Ah." Annika nodded. Well, and Annika had prayed for James, hadn't she?

The pebbled blackness was gone. The walking shroud had disappeared. He still had a foul mouth. Not a minute ago, he'd loosed a wicked word when he dropped a carved box on the floor. Annika had hollered at him, and he had yelled back, "It's all Joab's fault! I wouldn't have had to use my own box if he hadn't taken ours! Look at this—it has a nick!"

But there was no rancor in it, save the vile word, and, truth to tell, Annika didn't think it terribly wicked of him. She'd said worse and double for things less.

Annika smiled and murmured beneath her breath, "It's good to have you back, James of Nazareth."

She liked what he had told her yesterday. There was a great deal of hope in it. He had sat at the old oak table in her kitchen, as he had done so many times before. They talked over plates of raisin cakes and cups of watered wine.

I thought all I ever wanted was to be normal again. I thought that in being normal I would find myself happy again. But Annika . . . that's settling for a world less. Happiness isn't joy, and joy isn't what I thought it would be.

And what is that, boy?

James had gone quiet. He gazed out the window to the commonyard, then he said, *A wide place. You can breathe there; you can put your weight down and it won't give. And I think joy is very like belief itself, and I think we won't allow ourselves joy because we are mean. But it's there, and it's worth it. Right on the other side of pain.* At that James had looked her straight in the eye, and Annika would remember his words until she died. *I can consider it joy because he's there, Annika. On the other side of it all.*

"If I ever get my hands on that Joab . . ."

"Oh, enough with the whining," Annika scolded and leaned to peer at him. But apparently James had already forgotten Joab. She watched him set the box on his bench. Then he went to the doorway and folded his arms and leaned against it. He stood there long, gazing outside. While his eyes stayed on the view, his hand went to the mezuzah, and he put his palm flat against it. Then he turned to look at the mezuzah, really look at it. Annika held her breath. What an expression on that face! She watched in pure pleasure until he turned into the workroom; then she hastily pulled back from view.

Annika smiled, and with a great, happy sigh took a towel from the mending basket. "My, my," she said. "Good to have you back, boy."

Jerusalem, AD 57

James, a bond-servant of God and of the Lord Jesus
Christ, to the twelve tribes who are dispersed abroad:
Greetings. Consider it all joy, my brethren, when you
encounter various trials, knowing that the testing of
your faith produces endurance. And let endurance
have its perfect result, so that you may be perfect and
complete, lacking in nothing. But if any of you—

Simon lifted his hand. "Hold up." He dipped his pen and
touched the excess to a scrap of felt. "Lacking . . . in . . . nothing." He scratched the last letter on the scroll. "Go on."

"But if any of you—"

"You know, others may be perfectly content not to know
what Jesus said to you in Galilee that day. I am curious, James,
and it doesn't make me a sinner."

James had his back to Simon. His brother could not see the
slow grin. James went to the window and placed his hands on
the sill. He looked on the commonyard and saw a little boy
at play, creating a city with rocks and cast-off pieces of wood.

"There are some who doubt it happened," Simon added.

"I don't care." Then he said, "Paul believes me."

"Sure. You both have some brotherhood of the appearances going. Why Jesus didn't appear to me . . ."

James shrugged. "He liked me better. Always did."

Simon laughed out loud. "Sure, if it makes you feel better. I think he just felt sorry for you, as he did Thomas. The rest of us could believe without an appearance."

James couldn't help laughing with him. He put his hands behind his back and turned to stroll back to Simon. "Where were we?"

"'If any of you . . .'"

"Lacks in wisdom," James said very pointedly, "let him ask of God."

"Oh, very good," Simon muttered. "Charming." He dipped his pen, touched the excess to the felt, and put the pen to the scroll again.

Author's Note

Then he appeared to James . . .
I CORINTHIANS 15:7 (ESV)

"That there was a meeting of James and the risen Christ is certain.
What passed at that sacred and intimate moment we shall never know.
But we do know . . . James who had been the hostile and unsympathetic
opponent of Jesus became His servant for life, and His martyr in death."
WILLIAM BARCLAY, *The Letters of James and Peter*

Research is to writing what a hinge is to a door. The story of James turns on John 7:5: "Not even his brothers believed in him" (ESV). It turns on 1 Corinthians 15:7, where we learn that Jesus appeared to James after his resurrection. It turns on Acts 1:13–14, where we learn James was with the believers in Jerusalem before Pentecost. The epistle of James is certainly a hinge, and in some fascinating historical documents, I found other hinges as well.

The early Jewish historian Flavius Josephus speaks of the martyrdom of James in his *Antiquities of the Jews*. Eusebius, a Greek Christian writer (circa 260–339), draws his account of James from an earlier writer, Hegesippus, a Jewish Christian historian who belonged to the first generation after the apostles. Jerome, Latin Bible translator and scholar (circa

347–419), refers in his writings to a fragment of an apocryphal Gospel of the Hebrews, which provides another account of Jesus' appearance to James after the Resurrection.

From the sources outside canonized Scripture, I pick and choose what I actually believe about James. For instance, I would like to believe Hegesippus, that James' knees were reputed to be as leathery as a camel's, from his earnest habitual prayer upon them. The idea of James refusing to eat until he saw Jesus risen from the dead, as Jerome quotes the apocryphal Gospel of the Hebrews, is the dramatic sort of thing writers love. Eusebius even says that James was so esteemed for his righteousness, by Jew and Gentile alike, that the sack of Jerusalem in 70 ad was payback for the martyrdom of James the Righteous. (This may have been news to Vespasian and Titus. If the Romans had no qualms about crucifying Jesus, it is doubtful they would have torn their garments over his younger brother—let alone level an entire city.)

These historical documents contain fascinating hinges, but we cannot be certain what is true. Even in the event of James' martyrdom, we have options: Hegesippus says he was thrown from the parapet of the Temple, then stoned because the fall didn't kill him, then clubbed because the stoning didn't kill him. Josephus doesn't mention the Temple at all, nor the clubbing; only that James was delivered along with others to be stoned on a charge of breaking the Law.

The hinges in the Bible hold the most fascination for me. It was the life of James, not his death; his unbelief, then his belief; what he said and what he didn't say that gets my attention. I wonder why he never once mentioned his common blood with Jesus? Instead of beginning his famous epistle with "James, a blood brother of the Lord Jesus Christ, so listen up . . . ," he opened with "James, a bond-servant of God and of the Lord Jesus Christ." He went from blood brother to bond-servant, and for me it means the story of James is not about James at all.

The hinges I found in books reminded me of the shells and stones I found in Israel.

I tend toward sentimentality, and arrival in Israel for contextual research was only the beginning of a sticky, humid, nonstop epiphany. As we walked out of the Tel Aviv airport, I breathed to my husband, "Jack, Jesus walked here." When I got out of the car in Nazareth I said, "Jack, Jack . . . Jesus walked here." When we walked along the beach of the Sea of Galilee, Jack snapped the coolest picture of a trail of my footprints on the shore. I picked up shells and stones and crooned, "Jack . . . Jeeee-sus walked here!"

The headiness had me fit to walk on water. I was about to attempt it when Jack spoke.

For the whole trip, he had remained silent while listening to my impassioned ruminations. While I bawled and sprawled and wailed over a stone Jesus may have kicked with his sandal toe, Jack maintained an indifference that irritated me. It was on the shore of Galilee when Jack had had enough.

"Tracy." He put his hand on his chest and said, "Jesus walked here."

It's neat to think the stone I brought home was kicked by Jesus. And maybe the fact that James had blood in common with Jesus awed a few people he hung around with; James himself had enough indifference not to record it. Stones in Israel, hinges in history books, even common blood—all quite interesting.

Rich Mullins said, "Where are the nails that pierced his hands? Well, the nails have turned to rust, but behold the Man."

What if James had knees like a camel, and what if people thought he might walk on water too, and what if we put Josephus and Eusebius in a ring and let them fight it out while we placed our bets? I fancy James himself wouldn't care what the historians said about him. If we asked him about his knees or what was up in 1 Corinthians 15:7 or what exactly happened at his death, I fancy he'd only shrug and say something like my husband did that day in Galilee, just one thing:

Jesus walked here.

Tracy Groot

Discussion Questions

1. If you are not familiar with the epistle (letter) of James in the Bible, take a few minutes to read it. What themes from the epistle has the author woven into this novel about James? Do you like the way they are incorporated? Why or why not?

2. James struggles to accept that his brother Jesus is truly acting in the will of God. Have you ever faced a similar challenge with someone you love? What is the best way to approach such a situation? How does James deal with it?

3. Many people wanted Jesus to be a different kind of deliverer than he turned out to be. In what ways do people still try to overlay God's plans with their own motives and goals? How have you seen this in the lives of people you know?

4. Joseph, who has died before the novel begins, continues to have great influence in the lives of his children. How

have your parents or grandparents impacted your life in ways that will continue—or have continued—even after their deaths? How can you have this kind of influence over younger members of your family or circle of friends?

5. What did you think of Annika? Have you ever known someone like her? What are some of the important roles such people fill in our lives?

6. Various characters in the novel experience a specific calling from God: *Seek James.* Did this seem realistic to you? What are some of the ways God might call or direct a person today? How have you experienced his direction?

7. How does Nathanael's opinion of religious people change as he gets to know James and his family? What are some of the differences between an outward display of religion and true faith? Can the two coexist?

8. Nathanael reflects that "it was not Mother's fault she was the way she was. Nathanael was very sure she would be . . . different today . . . if her own mother had been like Mary. Or Annika. . . . A pity, that one could not choose one's own grandparents." Do you agree that our choices are largely determined by our upbringing? How does personal responsibility come into play? Do we have more control over our lives today than Nathanael's mother would have had in her time and place?

9. Nathanael says, "It is much to ask," referring to the command "You shall love the Lord your God with all

your heart, with all your soul, with all your might."
Why was James shocked by Nathanael's reaction? What
was it about Nathanael's perspective that prompted his
question? What are some beliefs or assumptions that
we take for granted, which might strike the uninitiated
more forcefully?

10. Later Nathanael says, "It makes you wonder if [God]
    loves us the way we are supposed to love him. . . . Does
    he have a mezuzah in his doorway in heaven? . . . Does
    he wear things on his arms and forehead? . . . Does he
    love us?" How would you answer Nathanael's question?
    (If you need help, read some of these passages from the
    Bible: Isaiah 43:1-4, 49:15-16, 54:10; Lamentations
    3:22-24; Jeremiah 31:3.)

11. Why does James tell Nathanael the story of Jesus and the
    woman caught in the act of adultery? What effect does it
    have on Nathanael?

12. What does it mean to James when he discovers the box
    inlaid with lapis lazuli? Has God ever used something
    like this to reveal truth to you—something that was
    there all along, but the significance of which you never
    saw before?

About the Author

Tracy Groot is the author of three Christy Award–winning novels—*Madman*, *Flame of Resistance*, and *The Sentinels of Andersonville*—along with *The Brother's Keeper*, *Stones of My Accusers*, and most recently *The Maggie Bright*.

She loves books, movies, knitting, travel, exceptional coffee, dark-chocolate sea foam, and licorice allsorts. She lives with her husband, Jack, in a Michigan home where stacks of books must be navigated to get anywhere, and if she yet lives at the reading of these words, she is likely at work on her next historical novel.

For more information about Tracy and her books, visit www.tracygroot.com.

1

JORAH WATCHED as Annika marked the height of the child with the flat of her hand and scored the limestone wall with her thumbnail. The child stood back and watched the addition of his newest notch.

The occasion was a solemn one, Jorah could tell, a mysterious bargain struck between the old woman and the little street scamp. After making the mark, Annika pursed her lips and, with a mistrustful look at the boy, bent to examine the distance between the last notch and the fresh one. The mistrust turned to surprise, and her fists went to her hips. She regarded the child with suspicious interest.

"Well, Jotham. What have you to account for nearly two finger-spans of growth? Are you wearing sandals?"

"No, Annika," the child said, lifting a foot for examination. "I have been eating the loaves."

One eyebrow came up. "Every day?"

"Every day." He nodded, dark eyes large in his thin face.

She glared at him a moment more, then the eyebrow came down. "Good boy."

His face broke into a sunny smile, and he turned to skip to the tall cupboard in the kitchen. He waited until Annika got there, and she reached to take down a wooden box. Jorah could not see what she gave Jotham, but the boy received it with a smile, then scurried through the kitchen and out the door.

Annika watched him go, smiling fondly. "Little rogue."

Seated at the table, Jorah looked out the window to watch him dash away. "Little ungrateful wretch. I didn't hear a thank-you."

Annika replaced the box. "One thing at a time." She turned to the shelves and took down the cups to set them on the table. She waved a few fruit flies from the pitcher of watered wine and set it next to the cups, then she set out a loaf of spiced honeycake and fetched a few plates.

Gazing out the window, chin on her fist, Jorah murmured, "It's hard to think of him as a boy, but he was, you know. A little boy like that."

Annika hesitated only a second as she sliced the bread. "Which him would you be speaking of?"

"You know."

"I do. Try and say his name now and again. Else it would be as if he never was."

Pain surged. As if Nathanael never was? But he was. And never would be again.

Jorah made her lips small to keep them from quivering. Annika was busy with the serving, she would not notice when Jorah pretended to adjust her head covering to wipe away tears.

Three weeks since they had buried Nathanael at Bethany. Three weeks of endless tears, and they did not appear to be slowing. There was too much to grieve over. The loss of the man she would marry. The loss of her old life. The loss of . . . but she could not think about Jesus. She lost him long ago, the day he left their home.

Annika was speaking. ". . . family from Sepphoris still interested in your place?" She shook her head and gave a heavy sigh as she slid a slice of honeycake from the knife to a plate. "I never could have imagined such a thing: no tribe of Joseph left in Nazareth. My steps may stop at the well, but my heart will ever wander past it. Up that old hill to that old home."

"They are interested. But Jude and James do not want to sell until they talk to Simon about it, and he's off on some crazy lark to Decapolis. They want to talk with Joses and Mother too, but that's not the reason they're going to Jerusalem." No, it was the same old story. People leaving her for God. Jorah never seemed to figure in.

"So," Annika said as she slid onto the bench across from Jorah. "Caesarea Maritima for you."

"Someone has to tell her."

They fell silent. Jorah's glance kept straying to the uncut portion of Annika's honeycake. What was it about that loaf . . .

Annika was right. Soon all of the children of Joseph would be gone from the home forever. In just a few hours, Jorah and James and Judas were leaving, she for Caesarea Maritima, they for Jerusalem. The home would be an empty shell. As she was without Nathanael.

Why would a loaf of bread . . .

She remembered. This time she could not conceal the tears.

"Child," Annika said softly, reaching to grasp Jorah's hand.

"He brought them bread," Jorah gasped, and bit her lip. Sorrow wrapped around her like an old black garment.

Nathanael had brought them bread, one of Annika's loaves. He went back to ask the strangers to join their party on the road to Jerusalem, so they would feel safer traveling in a larger company. For bread, they gave him blood, his own. He died days later of the wounds.

Jorah sagged and rested her forehead on the table. Grief upon grief. Nathanael and Jesus, dead within days of each other, both murdered. One was said to have risen again. Well, Jorah never saw him. The other lay beneath a pile of stones in a common grave outside Bethany. No rumors of resurrection there.

Her face became humid with her breath on the table. "I would kill Joab if I could," she breathed into the old oak. "I would kill him, Annika, God help me I would."

"I would lend a hand."

Jorah looked up, scowling. She drew her sleeve across her face. "You would lend a hand," she sneered.

Annika smiled sadly, cheeks pushing skin into a multitude of soft wrinkles. "You and me both, Jorah. We'll be the terrors from Nazareth. Instruments of God's vengeance. What do you say?" She balled her fist and held up her arm to show she still had some muscle.

Jorah couldn't even smile.

Did everyone change as much as Annika had in the past month? News of Jesus, and news of Nathanael . . . Annika had gained ten years with all the news from Jerusalem. That made her old indeed.

"You would not kill a fly if it bit you twice." She hated the sound of her own voice. All the crying made her speak through her nose.

Annika snatched her fist from the air. "You would not either," she retorted. "Judas tells me that boy was not responsible for Nathanael's death. He said that Joab tried to save him—that he killed the one who attacked Nathanael. Stop making him responsible for your pain. That's cowardice, Jorah. You are not a coward."

"Joab could have prevented it!" Jorah spat.

"Jorah, Jorah," Annika said, voice low. "Sorrow is enough to bear."

"He was going to marry me, Annika."

The old woman nodded heavily. "I know, child. I know he loved you."

Did Nathanael talk about her? Jorah scrubbed her eyes, then poked at the honeycake on her plate. "You knew he loved me?"

"He was addled over you."

"I didn't—know if he loved me as—" She swallowed the words and scowled at her plate. She didn't want to cry; she was tired of sounding ugly.

Honeycake. The way her mind worked these days, sluggish as an overfed ox. Annika told her a soul hobbled in grief moved slowly for a time, like a wounded animal. She felt doubly dosed with pokeweed.

She touched the cake on her plate. Touched the wine cup and watched a fruit fly imbibe on the rim. These days she would do crazy things, like see a flower sprig in the midst of a crying spell. She'd take and hold it close to her face and see satin sparkles, pattern, and color. She'd take an orange peel and squeeze oily spray on her hand, and marvel at the fragrance. She'd examine a pinch of sand. So many colors. How could someone say, "It is the color of sand," when sand was a rainbow up close? Marveling at orange peel and sand did more than speaking with a rabbi.

She picked up a slice of honeycake. "I used to make them exactly as you told me, and mine would always turn out dry,"

Jorah murmured. "You probably told me wrong on purpose, else lose your reputation for the best."

But Annika was in her own thoughts. "Even Judas leaves me," she grumbled unhappily, "and he is my least favorite. What is Nazareth without a single member of the Joseph clan?" She hesitated. "Jorah. I know what James believes of Jesus. How does Jude feel about . . . the rumors?"

Moist and delicious. Or it would be, if its flavor hadn't fled at the mention of her oldest brother. Jesus! *Oh, God . . .* But no—no. Jorah had piled that way with boulders. She set the bread down and brought her palm close to inspect a few crumbs. "Why don't you ask Jude?"

"Fair enough. One thing at a time." Whatever she meant by it, Annika left it. "How long will you stay in Caesarea?"

"As long as it takes me to find her."

"You are sure your father's cousin still lives there?"

"Yes. Simon and Joses visited Thomas on the trip to sell the benches. He lives across the commonyard from a famous mosaicist. I should like to visit his workroom. I have a talent for mosaics, you know." She brushed the crumbs from her palm to her plate.

"Child?"

Jorah looked up.

Annika looked at her long. "You do a good thing. A hard thing. To tell a mother her son is dead . . . I am proud of you, Jorah ben Joseph."

Jorah hoped her smile did not look fake. Annika would not be proud if she knew the real reason she was going to see the woman.

"Oh. I nearly forgot." Annika got up and went to her

bedroom in the back of the house. When she returned she was folding a long cloth, a narrow linen tablecloth. "I made this for Rivkah. Please take it to her for me."

Rivkah? But of course. Nathanael's mother. It was hard to think of her with a name. She who gave him birth . . . she who gave him scars.

"Annika." Jorah hesitated. "Did you know of Nathanael's scars?"

Surprise, then wariness came into Annika's face. "What scars?" she said sharply.

"When Abi and I wrapped Nathanael's body for burial, we found—" She squeezed her eyes shut. Orange peel fragrance. Flower petals. "There were—scars on his thigh. Old ones. From childhood." She clenched her teeth. Grains of sand. A mosaic. "Nathanael told James his mother did it. To let the evil out."

When Jorah looked at Annika, she found she had aged again. She was looking out the window, chin in her hand, tears brimming. "Six different shades of ugly, all of us," she murmured, and a tear dropped away. "He wanted to tell me. He tried to tell me, but couldn't bring himself to do it. It would have shamed her more than him." She sniffed. "Poor thing."

Through her own tears, Jorah suddenly smiled. "He would have never let anyone call him a poor thing."

"I wasn't talking about Nathanael." Annika wearily pressed her fingers against her eyes.

The smile dropped. "Why is *she* a poor thing?"

"She hated herself, not Nathanael." Annika wiped her nose with a fold of her tunic. "Oh, Jorah, what we are capable of. God have mercy on us."

Jorah could only stare, then look away. Annika could say what she wanted, but she had seen the scars with her own eyes. God would not have mercy on that. Never that.

He's dead now, Jorah would tell Nathanael's mother. She knew exactly what tone she would use. She had rehearsed it several times, whispering to a fingerprint of sand. *I know what you did. I've seen the scars. And now your son is dead. You never deserved him, and now he's dead.*

It was the only thing to give true comfort. The only thing to help her breathe. At the times when the grief would consume her, when she would suffocate and go mad, she would think on these words and allow them to calm her.

She owed it to Nathanael if only to raise a voice against an old, horrific deed. If only to not allow it to go unnoticed. It was God's justice, after all. God knew what Rivkah had done, and he would expose it through Jorah. It was Jorah's mitzvah, her responsibility to Nathanael's memory.

Calmness came, like wine warming her blood, and she actually smiled at Annika.

Annika smiled back, if uncertainly.

Yes, Jorah would go and tell a woman that her son was dead. *Let those words score that heart as she had scored Nathanael's leg. Let her take those words to her grave, as Nathanael took the scars to his.*

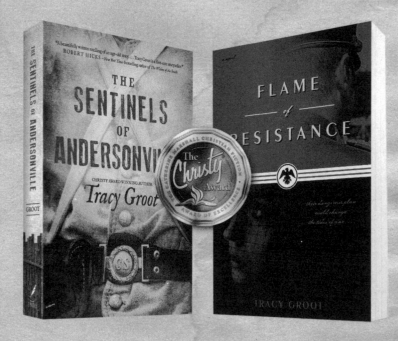

TYNDALE HOUSE PUBLISHERS IS CRAZY4FICTION!

Fiction that entertains and inspires

Get to know us! Become a member of the Crazy4Fiction community. Whether you read our blog, like us on Facebook, follow us on Twitter, or receive our e-newsletter, you're sure to get the latest news on the best in Christian fiction. You might even win something along the way!

JOIN IN THE FUN TODAY.

 www.crazy4fiction.com

 Crazy4Fiction

 @Crazy4Fiction